OTHER NOVELS BY KD McQUAIN

NYV: PUNK

AMYM: The Mamluk Who Defied Death

NYV: Goth

By
KD McQuain

This novel is dedicated to all of my friends. Thank you for always being there. Many of our adventures together have inspired this story, though names may have been changed to protect the guilty. I am grateful to have you all in my life.

First Printing, 2018

ISBN-13: 978-0-578-43422-3
ISBN-10: 0-578-43422-9
Black Marque Press
A division of Skully Enterprises
3325 Vickers Switch Rd
Christiansburg, VA 24073
www.SkullyEnterprises.com

Library of Congress Cataloging-in-Publication Data

McQuain, KD (Kevin Daniel) 1969-
NYV: GOTH / by K.D. McQuain — 1st ed.
New York Vampire: Volume 2
First edition: October 2018
Christiansburg, VA
Black Marque Press
p. cm

Cover spread Design, layout and Illustration by
Devilfish Ink -Graphic Arts & Printing, Philadelphia. www.devilfishink.com
Cover Photography by Mark Rodgers

Being friends with a vampire can be hazardous to your health. That's what Christian's tribe of New York City street punks has been finding out the hard way. Ever since his transformation, the people who get close to him have been dropping like flies at the hands of the fiend that infected him. His girlfriend Cara was dead and his roommate Rachel lay grievously wounded as he headed towards an uncertain and perilous future. Now he must quickly learn to defend himself if he is going to face The Chord and find a place in vampire society. Fortunately, he has his sword-wielding mentor Amym and a beautiful Gothic exotic dancer named Joyce, to help guide him.

[1. Vampires—Fiction. 2. Supernatural—Fiction. 3. Gothic—Fiction. 4. Punk—Fiction. 5. New York (city)—Fiction.] I. McQuain, K.D. II. Title.

Table of Contents

PROLOGUE

Anjou, May 1432

The boy followed along behind his guide, the imposingly large servant of the Lord of Château de Champtocé, Étienne Corrillaut, known to the common people as Poitou. Having never been in such a large and beautiful place, he looked down at his shabby clothing, they were fine for a village boy, but he wished he didn't feel as out of place as he knew he must look among these fine surroundings. The servant stopped in front of a heavy wooden door and knocked with firm raps of his beefy knuckles on the thick planks.

"Come!" called a commanding voice from the other side of the door.

The man pushed it open and ushered the boy inside. "This is the boy you asked for Lord Barón. Boy, this is Gilles de Montmorency-Laval, Maréchal de François, Barón de Retz, Sire d'Ingrande et de Champtocé and your new master."

"Thank you, Poitou," replied a man in a fine doublet who sat in a chair with intricately carved arms, drinking bright red wine from a crystal goblet. He was seated before the largest fireplace the boy had ever seen, large enough to roast an entire cow. "Don't just stand there, boy. Come let me have a look at you."

The boy shuffled across the carpet with hesitant steps, his hands nervously clutching at the fabric of his pants. When he finally came to stand before one of the heroes of Siege of Orléans, the man who everyone believed was the wealthiest in the country, he wiped the sweat from his palms and stood as still as he could with his eyes fixed on a spot on the floor a few feet in front of him. The man rose to his feet and walked a slow circle around the boy.

"You have done well, Poitou. He is a fine looking boy, but I cannot have a dirty lad dressed in rags deliver my correspondence."

Finally, he came to a stop, looking into the boy's downcast face. "What is your name child?" He asked gently.

"Galip, my Lord. Galip Jeudon," the boy mumbled quietly.

The Barón looked the boy over critically. "And how old are you?"

"I don't know, my Lord."

"I would hazard to guess... twelve years, perhaps." He paused, contemplating. "Very well. My man will see that you are cleaned and dressed as befits a page in my employ, then we will see to it that you are properly fed."

"This way, boy," ordered the huge man who held open the door.

Galip was led along the château's dimly lit passages and down a narrow spiral staircase to the kitchens. In the middle of the room sat half an oak barrel filled with steaming water and a three-legged stool with a rough cake of lye soap. "Get undressed and wash yourself," Poitou commanded. Once Galip had removed his clothing and lowered himself cautiously into the warm water, Poitou scooped up the threadbare rags and left the room.

Galip pulled his knees up tight to his chest and did his best to lower himself as far down as he could into the barrel. He didn't much mind the lack of room, what the cask lacked in diameter it made up for in depth. Besides, being able to soak in a tub of hot water was an uncommon luxury for a furrier's apprentice. He closed his eyes, relaxed into the water, and breathed in the heavily wine-scented steam.

He was so relaxed that he'd nearly fallen asleep when the barrel was suddenly overturned and he was dumped out onto the cold stones of the kitchen floor. "Dry yourself and put these on. The Lord Barón is waiting," Poitou said, tossing a bundle of cloth at him. Galip hurried to comply, vigorously scrubbing his skin dry with the course towel that was left for him. He dressed as quickly as he could, repressing his astonishment as he forced his fingers to manipulate the buttons on the finest clothing he had ever worn.

Poitou kept a brisk pace as he traveled the château's stairways and corridors, with Galip struggling to keep up behind him and they soon arrived at a well-lit room in the upper level of the castle. A banquette table ran the entire length of the room, with enough chairs to seat twenty to a side. Sitting at the head of the table, the Lord ate from a plate of fine porcelain, facing a massive fireplace in which a small mound of cloth smoldered and smoked atop the blazing fire. Upon closer inspection, Galip discovered that what was burning were his clothes. They were little more than rags compared to what he now wore, but watching the flames consume them added to his feeling of dread that he would have nothing if he were to be turned out. He imagined himself walking back to his family home without a stitch to cover his same.

Over the fireplace hung the Lord of the Manor's standard, a shield bearing a sable cross emblazoned upon a field of gold. The king had bequeathed upon him the right to decorate his coat of arms with a royal semée border of azure with golden fleur-de-lys for his valiant conduct during the renewal of the Hundred Years War.

"The Lord, Gilles de Montmorency-Laval, Maréchal de François, Barón de Retz, Sire d'Ingrande et de Champtocé, Lord of Brittany and Anjou," announced the servant. "My Lord, here is the boy you asked for."

"Very good, Poitou," The Barón said, indicating with his delicate silver fork that the boy should take the seat that had been prepared several places down the table. "Sit," he instructed through a full mouth.

Before today, Galip would never have dreamed of sitting at such a grand table, even if he was alone in the château. Now he was commanded to set his unworthy backside on one of the silk covered chairs. He stood unmoving with his mouth agape until Poitou prodded him from behind and sent him stumbling forward. "Yes, my Lord. Thank you, my Lord," he stammered as he slid the chair loudly out from the table.

"I assume you are hungry." It wasn't a question or an invitation, so Galip sat quietly as a plate was deposited on the table in front of him by a terrified-looking scullion who practically ran from the room and closed the door behind her. When Galip made no move toward his utensils, the Lord said, "You should try the Partridge, it's quite good."

"Thank you, my Lord," the boy replied, tentatively lifting the fork that lay on the table and began picking at the bird lying on his plate.

"I understand you are apprenticed to the furrier Guillaume Hilairet," The Barón said between bites.

"Yes, my Lord," the boy replied, fidgeting uncomfortably in his new clothing.

"Is your suit ill-fitting?" The Barón asked casually.

"No my Lord, I'm certain it is only that I am unaccustomed to such fine things. It is truly the most splendid garment I have ever worn," the boy replied with a nervous smile.

"Are you certain that is all that troubles you? Well… out with it boy."

"Well my Lord, I hesitate to say so, but it is terribly warm."

"If you are in discomfort, you may remove your doublet."

"Oh no, I couldn't possibly my Lord."

"You can. I insist." The Barón commanded. "I will remove mine as well if it will comfort your mind."

"If you are certain, my Lord."

"I wish you to be at ease. If you persist, I will have to make it a command."

After a moment's hesitation, Galip yielded. "As you wish, my Lord."

The Barón watched with mounting anticipation as the boy struggled to remove the heavy brocade doublet, staring fixedly as it pulled his shirt up to reveal the soft white skin of his belly. When he was finally free, Poitou was there waiting to take charge of the costly garments.

"There, that's much better. Don't you agree?"

"Truly, my Lord."

"Now please, eat. Poitou!" he called to his manservant. "Get the boy a drink."

The hulking servant filled his glass with a warm cocktail of dark wine, sugar, cinnamon, cardamoms, and grains of paradise called hippocras. Galip took a small sip, the heady aroma and decadently sweet taste were wondrous to a boy used to drinking nothing but water or an occasional glass of watery wine. He quickly finished the entire glass, yet as soon is it was emptied, Poitou was at his elbow to refill it. Their food long since eaten and cleared away, Galip sat basking in a warm, happy glow of intoxication. He laughed companionably at what seemed the appropriate points as the Lord

Barón recounted tales of his glorious battles in service to The Dauphin..

"Do you know why you have been brought here, my boy?" The Barón asked.

"Yes, Lord. I am to be your Page. I was told I would be delivering messages and running errands from the château to Machecoul."

"Would that position make you happy? Would it… please your parents?"

"Oh yes, my Lord. Very much so," Galip nodded eagerly.

"Then, I am sorry to inform you, that is not your purpose here." He paused to enjoy the look of confusion and disappointment on the boy's face before he continued. "No, you have been brought here for my pleasure." A loud sound echoed through the room, causing Galip to jump in his seat. He turned to look for the source of the noise and discovered Poitou bolting the door shut. A short braquemard sword with a thick double-edged blade now hung ominously from the man's thick leather belt.

"This has been a most enjoyable evening thus far, but now we have come to the pinnacle of the evening's amusements," the Barón said as he gestured his servant into action. A heavy rope was lowered from a hook in the ceiling to land heavily in a coiled heap on the table. Galip lept to his feet in surprise, nearly tipping over his chair. Instinctively, he reached behind him to catch it before it fell, when Poitou's meaty fist collided with the side of his head. A blinding white light flashed across his field of vision followed, by darkness as his body toppled limply to the floor.

After some time, Galip's eyes began to flutter open. At first, he couldn't make sense of what he was seeing. The room was upside down and seemed to be spinning slowly around him. His head throbbed and the side of his face ached from the blow. When he tried to raise his hand to check his injury, he discovered that his arms were restrained behind his back. Sudden terror brought his mind into sharp focus, and he instantly became very aware of his situation.

The rope that had been lowered from the ceiling was tied around his ankles and he had been hoisted up to dangle with his head a foot above the floor. The table at which he had enjoyed the

5

Slowly the Barón's breathing returned to normal and he released his steadying grip on the boy's thigh. He crossed back to the table and finished his drink in a single gulp. Then, setting the glass back down, he picked up the small carving knife he had used at dinner and returned to where Galip dangled.

At first the boy believed that the Barón intended to cut him down as he had promised, but instead, he began spinning the boy in a circle, increasing in speed until the boy could not focus on what was happening around him.

"Please, I'm going to be sick," the boy implored.

Galip felt a sudden heat in his legs followed by a stinging pain. He craned his neck to see what was happening above him, and through the disorientation of being spun, he saw the Barón use the blade of his knife to inscribe a shallow spiral into his pale skin. The boy tried to kick out but the rope held him firmly, and all he managed to do was buck and jolt himself, causing his bonds to press more deeply into his flesh. The Barón struggled to hold the boy still, his hands slipping in the blood that was seeping down the length of his body, leaving them both covered in sticky red smears.

Finally, he cut the rope and let the boy fall with a hard thud. Immediately he pounced on the boy, pinning him to the floor, his weight pressing the boy's blood slicked legs into the wood, his arms wrenched painfully between his body and the floor beneath him.

"PLEASE, MY LORD! PLEASE!" The boy shrieked in pain and terror, but his distress only seemed to excite him further.

"Shhhhh. Calm yourself, my child," he said, placing his bloody fingers against the boy's lips. "I told you this was all just a game, and soon it will all come to an end."

"I just want to see my parents again." The boy wept.

"And you will, my lad," The Barón assured him. "In the hereafter."

The Barón began to side himself back and forth along the boy's blood slick thighs, squeezing them between his own. Gradually he felt the boy begin to become aroused; his small member began to rise and slide between the cheeks of his backside, the sensation greatly increasing his own excitement. He turned around and began to stroke himself against the boy's belly, the rhythm of his movements leaving a dark red streak where his cock rubbed against the pale skin.

Galip clamped his eyes and lips shut as tightly as he could and turned his face away, not wanting to see what was being done to him and ashamed of his bodies involuntary reaction. However, a sudden sharp pain in his abdomen followed by a popping sound caused his eyes and mouth to open wide with shock. He looked down at the source of the pain and saw that the Barón was using the knife to slowly cut his way up the center of his belly from his navel to his ribs. The shock of what he was seeing vanished under the excruciating pain and Galip began to scream.

The Lord Barón clamped his left hand firmly over the boy's mouth to quiet his screaming while he reached into his abdominal cavity and began extracting his intestines with his right. The Barón piled the fleshy coils on his lap and let them drape down around his waist, wriggling with pleasure at their slippery warmth.

Watching the fear, pain and desperation play across the boy's face added another facet to his delight. He rocked back and forth, thrusting forward, stabbing himself into the glistening red links, increasing his frenetic pace until he was nearing his climax.

"Now Poitou! Do it now," the Barón screamed.

His hulking manservant quickly crossed the room and swung down with his short sword, severing the boys head from his shoulders with a single stroke. The Barron snatched up the disembodied head and gazed into the boy's eyes, watching the life fade as he shuddered with release.

When the last spasms of both pleasure and death had finally subsided, the Barón stood up and collected his glass from the nearby table while Poitou hoisted the body back into the air. He placed a wide brass basin with a hole in the center atop a large decanter beneath the dangling body to catch the blood. The Barón extended his arm and placed the glass in the red flow until it was half filled, then brought the thick, warm elixir to his lips and drank deeply. He felt drained, both physically and psychically, but he knew that the blood would soon revive and invigorate him.

He returned to his chair and waited as Poitou dressed and sectioned the carcass, depositing the viscera into the fire and adding an armload of wood to bring the blaze to a roar. He skewered the haunches and hung them from the iron firedogs to roast, turning them occasionally as he continued dissecting the boy for disposal.

When the meat had cooked and the offal had been reduced to ash, the Barón and his loyal servant sat down at the table, across from the vacant-eyed head of the former furrier's apprentice which stared at them from atop a silver serving platter. The two skewered slabs of meat with their silver forks and sopped up the juices with thick slices of coarse bread.

Chapter 1

Chris lay back into the enveloping embrace of the black leather upholstery of the town car, his eyes skimming unseeingly over the cityscape as they rode north along the FDR Drive. The bright orange sun was just beginning to peek out from between the buildings across the river, but its warmth did not touch him as the events of the previous few hours replayed in his mind on an endless loop.

The night had started off as well as he could have imagined. He had gone to the Ritz for the biggest show of the year with Joyce, a stunningly beautiful Gothic stripper. Most of the woman who danced at Billy's Topless couldn't even remotely be called Exotic but Joyce certainly was. The fact that he later discovered she was also vampire only slightly diminished the experience. What really turned the night to shit was when he got back to his crappy Alphabet City apartment to find that another vampire had come and crucified his roommate Rachel with kitchen utensils in the middle of the living room.

He had only recently begun realizing that he might have romantic feelings for Rachel, but having her unborn baby cut from her belly pretty much put an end to that. Then the ancient psychopath turned his attention to his ultimate goal: Killing him.

Chris had no real idea why he was the subject of the vampire's murderous intent, he was just relieved that Amym, his mentor and benefactor, had turned up in the nick of time. Though not as old and powerful, Amym was also a vampire, and one with exceptional combat abilities. The two of them had been able to fight off their attacker, Gilles, and Amym assured Chris that Rachel would live, although the unborn baby likely would not. The baby wasn't Chris', but rather the byproduct of a misguided romance with a Spanish Harlem coke dealer, but the crushing weight of everything that happened had left Chris in his current, near-catatonic, state of depression.

Chris sat in the back of the black town car staring vacantly out the window as the car crossed the George Washington Bridge into New Jersey. The glittering expanse of the Hudson River and the dull gray concrete of the city gave way to lush greenery as they veered onto the Palisades Parkway. He had no idea where they were going and didn't really care. All he cared about was that, once again, he was running away from everything he knew. It had only been a few months since he had left his rural East Texas home and his eccentrically religious mother to make his way to New York. It was on that journey that the course of his life had been irrevocably altered. A sea of green passed by unseen as he reflected on the events that had conspired to bring him to this place.

A lot had happened to him in the past few months, more than he had ever imagined when he left home after his fifteenth birthday. While waiting for a late night bus in Joplin, Missouri, Chris had been attacked and nearly killed by what he thought was a naked and filthy homeless man in the bus station restroom. The bum turned out to be a vampire looking for its next meal, and it was only the suspicious nature of the gun-wheedling ticket clerk that had saved his life, though not before he had been infected by the creature's blood, changing him into a vampire also. That had been his first encounter with Gilles, the vampire who had plagued his nightmares ever since, and that was ultimately the reason Amym was now taking him out of the city.

He had ended up in New York City, living on the streets with a tribe of punk kids who had become like a family to him. Through them he had met his first love, Cara, only to kill her in a drug-induced bloodlust. *If Gilles had just finished the job back on that floor bathroom back in Joplin, none of this would have happened*, he thought. *Gilles would never have come to New York and Cara would still be alive.*

His thoughts returned to Rachel. He had been at the strip club to watch his neighbor Monika dance when he'd met Rachel trying to get a job at the club to support herself during her pregnancy. His vampire mentor, Amym, who now sat in the front passenger seat next to Steve, the enigmatic driver, had provided Chris with a run-down apartment, and Rachel had been staying there with him until the Gilles had returned to finish him off.

Chris wasn't sure if she had survived the attack; her wounds were severe, and even with his heightened senses, Chris hadn't been able to hear the baby's heartbeat. Amym had tried to be reassuring, but Chris was still guilt-ridden and worried for her. He thought that if he had just died, then Rachel and her baby would be alright.

He imagined going back to that day and retroactively giving his life to protect Cara and Rachel and all the others who had been hurt along the way. It was a romantic fantasy of imagined adolescent gallantry, but of course it didn't amount to anything and Chris began to feel disgusted with his self-indulgent delusions of adolescent heroism.

The tree-lined parkway opened up to the wide expanse of the New York Throughway and the car sped along the nearly empty northbound lanes. For just a moment Chris was relieved that they weren't heading south with the throng of morning commuters trying to get into the city to start their workday. Then depression set in again and he rested his temple against the tinted glass of the car window, watching the industrial landscape of Rockland County scroll past.

His guilty feelings were compounded by the fact that Joyce, who he had a huge crush on for the past few months and had been having the most intense erotic dreams about, was sitting in the seat right next to him. He was vaguely aware that Joyce and Amym were talking, although he couldn't really tell if they were talking to each other or to him. He really didn't care what they were saying and closed his eyes to block them out. He listened to the thumping rhythm of the tires rolling over the seams in the cement roadway, eventually succumbing to the soothing monotony of the sound and falling into an exhausted sleep.

He lay quivering, cowering in the darkness, doing everything he could to suppress the screams of agony that threatened to give him away to the hunters who still scoured the streets above. His flesh, scorched black as coal, still sputtered and hissed with the agonizing embers that burned beneath his skin. The pain was relentless but he knew that it would pass eventually. He knew he would have to rest there, in the filthy basement of the Lower East

Side tenement where he had sought refuge from the sun, until nightfall. Then he could return to his cell to begin the healing process. It was by no means the height of luxury he was accustomed to: It was a squalid hole deep beneath the city, forgotten by time, but it was safe and dark. If only it wasn't so far away.

Chris awoke with a start. He could still feel the burning of his flesh and his throat was sore from holding back the screams. "Good, you're awake," came Amym's voice from outside the open car door. "We have to change vehicles."

He didn't ask any questions; he simply stretched and climbed out of the back seat to stand blinking in the bright sunlight. They were parked outside a large one-car garage on a wooded lot along a winding two-lane road.

"Are you alright?" Amym asked, placing his hand gently on Chris' shoulder. "Joyce said you were having another dream."

"Yeah, I'm okay I guess. It's nothing I can't handle."

"Would you mind telling me what the subject of the dream was? It could be important."

"It wasn't anything crucial. I was in a basement and I was burning. I mean, he was burning. He was in a lot of pain and he's scared. That's all. I don't think he's used to being hurt like that."

"No, I would imagine not. Did you get a sense of where this basement might be located?"

"Not really. I don't think it was all that far from my place, but I'm not really sure."

Amym climbed into the front seat of the car, pulled a phone in a black leather bag from beneath the passenger seat, and started dialing. It wouldn't have been hard for Chris to eavesdrop on the conversation, but just then the garage door began to roll up and the front grill of a shiny black Chevy Blazer came into view. The engine roared to life and the SUV rolled slowly out into the leaf-mottled sunshine. Joyce was in the driver's seat and Chris' breath caught in his throat as she smiled at him and gave him a wink. Chris was still amazed that, as beautiful and exotic as she was, with her jet-black hair streaked at the temples with purple, her eyes decorated with heavy Egyptian style makeup, and a line of Rhinestones glittering beside her artfully manicured eyebrow, she could actually like him.

The SUV came to a stop once it had cleared the garage and the door began to lower as did the passenger window. "You need a ride?" Joyce asked him with a smile. "Climb in."

Chris hesitated. "Um... front or back?"

"Up here with me," she replied patting the seat next to her. "I have the AC on high, these black cars can really bake in the sun," she said as he stepped onto sidebar and climbed in. The thought of the black leather heating up in the sun brought his dream back and suddenly he was watching the skin on his arm crumble and fall away like bits of burnt paper to reveal smoking orange embers.

"Hey? Are you okay?" Joyce asked with genuine concern, laying her hand on his arm.

Chris took his seat and closed the door. "Yeah, sorry. Just remembering something."

"I know this is difficult, and I'm so sorry for what happened to your friend, but we are here for you," she said reassuringly.

Curiosity finally winning out over his depression, Chris asked, "Where are we going anyway?"

"A place where you'll be safe while we sort all this out. It's about another hour or so, then we'll have lunch and figure out our next step. Good, here comes Amym."

Chris turned to watch Amym close the passenger door of the town car, still carrying the bag phone with him, and start walking toward the Blazer as Steve made a three-point turn, pulled the car back on to the road, and drove away.

They drove for nearly an hour, past the houses and small towns that lined Route 28 until they reached Big Indian. Turning onto Oliveria Road, they followed the winding path of the Eusopus Creek for several miles farther until Joyce pulled the SUV into the driveway of a well-maintained cottage, partially hidden from the road by tight clumps of trees. She drove across the lawn and around to the back of the house where a heavy chain blocked the entrance to a dirt road that cut into the dense forest of trees. Amym hopped out of the back seat, unlocked the rusted padlock, and moved the chain aside to let the SUV pass. Then, he relocked it with a forlorn look at the mud caked on his Italian leather shoes and walked back to the waiting vehicle. When he was settled back into his seat, they continued along the path until the gate was lost from view behind them.

"So um... this is a little creepy," Chris stated, trying to make light of his growing apprehension.

"This is Sundown Wild; our destination is not much further," Amym replied as Joyce cautiously maneuvered the vehicle over the road that was little more than a pair of neglected ruts with an occasional boulder or sapling sticking up from the mud. They continued for what felt to Chris' spine like hours as the car bounced and jostled over potholes and rocks. The car bucked its way down the secluded road through the woods until they crested a hill. The valley opened below them into a small well-manicured meadow, a stream bisected the clearing separating two identical looking two-story rustic-looking lodges.

Turning to look at Amym in the back seat, Chris asked, "What is this place?" showing the first signs of interest since they had left the city after fighting off the creature Gilles.

"Many years ago it was one of the small Jewish resorts that dotted the Catskills. When their popularity waned, it was purchased by The Chord to be used as a refuge where those of the Lesser Blessed may recuperate, heal, train, and hone their abilities. Or, in your case: Learn." Amym said referring to those who hadn't been born vampires but had been infected by them either by accident as Chris had or intentionally like Amym.

"What am I supposed to learn, how to be a better vampire?" Chris asked turning around to face his mentor.

"As a matter of fact, yes. We have been given a few short months to teach you everything you will need to not only survive, but to prosper and become useful in our society."

"What if I don't want to be a productive member of vampire society?" Chris asked petulantly.

Amym became very serious and looked directly at Chris. There was no anger in his look only a calm sense of determination. "Then you will be eliminated. The Chord will not allow inferior of useless creations to exist." Chris turned back towards the front to think about that as the car continued its descent into the valley.

"Welcome to Haven," Joyce announced, putting the SUV in park and shutting off the engine.

Chris was suddenly filled with questions: What is the Chord, the men in black tactical uniforms that swarmed the apartment after they had fought off Gilles? How was he supposed to be useful to them? Who and what were the Lesser Blessed? There we so many things he wanted to know but couldn't find it in himself to begin asking the questions. So, he just kept quiet and took in his new surroundings.

Chris watched as fat bumblebees seemed to float on impossibly small wings in the flower beds that lined the covered wooden wraparound porch as Amym led him up the steps to a brightly painted red front door. The railing was made from tree branches stripped of their bark, sanded and stained a deep brown to match the natural edged wooden siding of the building.

The door opened as they approached and a slim man who looked to be in his early fifties, with short cropped salt and pepper hair and stiffly pressed khaki uniform stepped out onto the porch. "Welcome back, sir. Everything is waiting as requested."

He stood aside and allowed the trio to enter before closing the door behind them.

"Good, and the specialists I requested?"

"The first will arrive tonight. The others will require somewhat more travel time, but all will be here before the end of the week."

"That will be fine. Thank you, Everton."

"Of course, sir. Refreshments are waiting and a meal will be prepared shortly." He indicated that they follow him across the large central hall to where a table waited with a silver tray of triangular sandwiches with the crusts cut off and a tall glass pitcher of pink liquid on a matching tray, glistening with condensation. He poured out three glasses, then excused himself and exited through a swinging door along the back wall.

Chris' stomach was still rolling from the drive and wasn't up to eating anything, but the heat and humidity were oppressive even under the breeze of the fan mounted high in the ceiling above. He picked up a glass and took a hesitant drink. He didn't know what he had expected would be served at a vampire training compound, but it certainly wasn't lemonade. As he sipped, he looked around and took in his surroundings.

The main hall was a forty-foot square space open to the vaulted ceiling, supported by enormous wooden beams. A balcony that wrapped around three sides of the parameter looking down into the room, was lined with closed doors; the railing was a smaller version of the one on the outside porch. Mounted animal heads looked on with glassy eyes from their wooden plaques on the walls; they seemed to be reproaching him as if he was personally responsible for their current predicament.

Amym set his cup down on the table and turned to Joyce. "I have some business to attend to. Would you show Chris to his room? I imagine you must be exhausted after your ordeal."

"Yeah, I guess so," Chris admitted.

"I thought as much. Go and get some rest. Lunch will be ready soon, and then we can discuss your future."

Joyce took him by the hand and led him up the wide staircase to the balcony. He was watching Amym go back out the front door when Joyce stopped and opened a door for him. "I'm right next door if you need anything, and Amym will be in the corner room," she said, indicating the doors. "There's a library just below his room if you want something to read." She paused for a moment to consider her next words. "I know how hard this all can be to take in, so..."

"How could you? How could you possibly know how hard it is?" His voice full of petulance.

"Because I've been through it too. I wasn't born like this, you know; only the ones who change us are. The rest of us start off as normal people, with lives and families. Then one night, all that disappears: They come into our lives, changing us, destroying everything we care about. And if we're lucky, we get the opportunity to work for them, forever. So yeah, I get it." She wiped the corner of her eye with a knuckle and retreated into her room, closing the door behind her with a loud click.

He had regretted his words even while they were pouring. He hadn't meant to say anything that would upset her, and if he had only thought about it before opening his stupid mouth... It made perfect sense that she would have experienced something like what he was

17

going through. He just needed to fully express his self-pity before he could accept any sort of understanding or commiseration from someone else. He also realized that his interest in Joyce had increased, if that was possible, since he had learned that she had been infected just like him.

He stood in his darkened room feeling awful, the new guilt adding another layer to all the other things he felt guilty for. He searched the wall next to the door, feeling blindly for the light switch, he ran his hand over the wall in large sweeping gestures but found nothing. He was about to open the door to allow more light in but realized that he really didn't need it. He was conditioned by his previous life to feel the need for light to see in the dark, but he could see quite easily without it.

He looked around the room to begin to familiarize himself. There were heavy curtains over the window on the far wall letting in the barest hint of pale gray light, a twin bed took up the majority of the small space, an end table was squeezed in next to it with a utilitarian looking lamp, and a three drawer dresser rounded out the furniture. Another door, which he assumed was a closet, dominated the adjacent wall. He hadn't seen a bathroom but he didn't need to go so he decided that he could wait to look for it later.

He unlaced his boots and pulled them off, then laid back on the bed. The springs creaked under his weight but the mattress was firm and comfortable. The comforter, decorated with black bears and pine trees, smelled freshly laundered. The concert the night before, the after-hours club with Joyce, the fight with Gilles, and the drive to the country retreat had left Chris completely exhausted so he closed his eyes hoping for the welcoming embrace of sleep. Images of Rachel hanging in the living room doorway by her wrists, covered in blood, her abdomen slit open and her organs tumbling out onto the rough wooden floor, tormented him. There had been so much blood; just thinking about it made him feel queasy and his mouth filled with saliva. He was sure there was no way Rachel could have survived the brutality of the attack, no matter what Amym said.

He wanted to cry even more, and he certainly had a lot to cry about but was afraid that if he started he might never be able to stop. Instead, he tried to pull himself together. He began to pull his Docs back on but decided to try to avoid disturbing anyone while exploring, and set them back down next to his bed. He walked down the stairs as silently as he could and continued to the main floor and out onto the porch. Chris stood and looked out over the valley. Aside from the two lodge buildings, there was no sign that human life even existed outside the compound.

He became aware of a presence behind him by a subtle clearing of the throat and turned to discover Everton standing patiently in the doorway. "Lunch is served in the kitchen," Everton announced, but made no move to go back inside.

"Thank you, but I'm not really hungry," Chris said.

"As you wish," Everton said. "Even so, it would be wise to come and get acquainted with Lavinia, and to become familiar with the layout of the estate." He turned sideways and held his arm out, inviting Chris to precede him back through the doorway.

"There are six bedrooms upstairs with three full baths. Only three are currently occupied by Joyce, Master Amym and yourself. Here on the main floor is the common room," he said following Chris back into the lodge and gesturing to indicate the large open central hall with rustic-looking couches, recliners and an assortment of tables and lamps arranged around the massive river rock fireplace.

"Through the French doors is the library, which I would urge you to become familiar with as it is quite well stocked."

He led Chris across the room to a pair of swinging doors with round porthole windows. He pushed open the right door and held it for Chris. "Lavinia, you have a guest," he announced.

The kitchen was a large commercial-style space with room for a number of cooks to work simultaneously. The stainless steel counters and white tile walls gleamed, and not a single copper-bottomed pan was out of place. Even the spices in their glass jars had their labels aligned. A round table with six white spindled chairs occupied the right quarter of the room where a single place setting lay neatly arranged.

A woman came out from behind the counter removing her black apron to reveal a spotless white uniform. She was a large woman, tall, with broad shoulders, a round face with red cheeks and an ample bosom that strained the buttons of her jacket. "You must be Christian," she said in a thick accent that Chris couldn't quite place, and pressed a glass of cold red liquid into his hand. "I have heard a lot about you. You must be hungry, yes? I'll prepare a plate for you."

"Thank you, but I'm not feeling up to eating right now."

"I understand. You have had a trying day. Not to worry, drink, drink. It will refresh you after your travels, and I promise you, dinner will be spectacular."

"Lavinia is a wonderful chef," Everton stated, making a show of whispering conspiratorially.

"And you will come to see me in the mornings for breakfast and we will have our talks, yes?"

"Our talks?" Chris asked, confused.

"Yes," Everton interjected. "Lavinia, in addition to being a wonder in the kitchen, speaks more languages than you could count."

"I am very pleased to be able to help you become conversant in many different languages." She said smiling and Chris took a tentative sip of his drink.

It was thick like tomato juice, but also had a hint of ginger and honey, leaving a spicy tingle on his tongue. "Mmmm! This is really good."

"There will be a pitcher in the refrigerator at all times, along with many good things to eat. You may help yourself to whatever you like throughout the day, but be sure to leave room for dinner, okay?"

"Sure, thank you," Chris said.

"You would like more?" Lavinia asked. He hadn't been aware that he was so thirsty, but looking down, he discovered that his glass was nearly empty.

"No," Chris answered. "I mean, it's really good, but one glass is fine for now." He tipped the glass up high, swallowing the rest in one big gulp, and let the last drops fall onto his tongue. He then handed the emptied glass back to Lavinia. "Thanks."

"I'm so glad you liked it," she said with a wink as Everton guided Chris out of the kitchen.

"At breakfast, you will have language lessons here with Lavinia. Then t'ai-chi on the lawn. After lunch, you will have your afternoon training in the dojo, located in the other building. You will begin with basic hand-to-hand combat skills and work your way up to more advanced martial arts training. Then you will eat dinner, and after your meal, Master Amym will guide you through mental defense exercises, if his schedule permits. The dojo will be available to you in the evening, to continue your training or you can use the sauna or Jacuzzi. You will also have full access to the library. There is a wide variety of books on any subject you could wish for, and if there is something you can't find, just ask and we'll get it for you. By the time you leave here, I expect you will have read them all."

"That sounds like a lot." Chris felt like he was physically deflating under the weight of the work ahead of him. "I won't even have time to sleep."

"Yes, it is a lot," Everton agreed. "Your education has been seriously neglected from what I understand. That will be quickly remedied, and you will find that you don't need nearly as much sleep as you think." He led Chris to the bottom of the stairs. "I suggest you settle in. Your training begins with breakfast at five in the morning. If you are late, you will have less time to eat, and I guarantee you will need the energy."

Chris lay on his bed, unable to sleep. Too much had happened in too short a time, and he was finding it impossible to sort through his feelings. There was sadness and guilt over what had happened to Cara and Rachel, and anger at Gilles for changing his life and hurting his friends. There was even excitement at the prospect of all the things he might be able to learn here at Haven. He hesitated to admit it even to himself, but there was also some excitement about being there with Joyce.

Chris had discovered her hoard of toiletries and beauty products when he had visited the bathroom down the hall. The small bottles and jars filled the air with the exotic smells of soaps and perfumes, like an apothecary of the sensual. Just the knowledge that she was in the next room, maybe already asleep or getting ready for bed – was enough to make his heart start to beat faster.

21

A subtle movement in the corner of his eye caught Chris' attention. He looked up to see Joyce standing in the open doorway of his room, holding a cardboard box. He sat up with a start, as if he had been discovered doing something naughty.

"How are you doing?" she asked with a slight smile curling the corner of her mouth.

"Okay, I guess. I just can't stop thinking about... everything, I guess. I don't know," he trailed off, not sure what he was saying or what he should say.

"Sure, it's normal to be upset and angry, even scared, after everything that's happened," she said, setting the box on the floor and sitting on the bed next to him. "I'd be worried about you if you weren't."

"It's all my fault. If he had just killed me back in Joplin, none of this would have happened. I've been thinking that maybe I'm meant to be alone. I mean, all the girls I like seem to end up dead, my friends... I guess I'm just destined to be by myself for the rest of my life. However long that'll be. It's the only way to keep people safe." *Well, maybe not all the girls*, said the voice in his head. Joyce was sitting so close to him on the bed that their knees brushed against each other whenever either of them moved. Chris' mind was brought back to the dreams he had been having of Joyce.

"Well, I'm still here," she said smiling.

"Maybe it would be safer for everyone if I stuck to girls who were like me. You know, vampire girls," he suggested. "It's either that or become some sort of priest."

"Well, those are options, but I don't think you have to resort to anything so drastic," she said, laughing slightly at his obvious attempt at flirtation. "With a little time and patience, you will be more than capable of controlling your urge to feed, even under extreme conditions. And once you complete your training, you will be better able to defend yourself against those who would threaten you. So I don't think you need to devote yourself to a life of celibacy just yet."

Chris' mood fell, and he remembered what they had been talking about. "I tried to protect Rachel, I really did. He was just so much stronger and faster than me. And then he cut her... and there was so much blood." Joyce moved closer to put her arm around him and pulled him toward her. He rested his cheek on her shoulder, and the tears that he had been holding in finally broke loose, falling onto the faded black fabric of her shirt, leaving dark spots on the front of her shirt.

"I know. Amym and I both know you did everything you could. He even told me that he might not have been able to fight off the vampire if you haven't been there to help."

"If it hadn't been for me, nothing would have happened to her at all. If she hadn't met me..."

"If she hadn't met you, who knows where she would have ended up. I was there, remember," she reminded him.

Rachel had left home when her mother discovered that she was pregnant by her coke dealer boyfriend and wouldn't get rid of the baby. She had tried to get a job working at the strip club where Joyce had been dancing but quickly decided that it wasn't for her. However, the owner wouldn't let her leave the club without paying him his cut. It seemed so long ago, but when Chris thought back, he clearly remembered Joyce stepping in and offering to cover it for her. Rachel had moved in with him into the rundown Alphabet City apartment on Avenue C and 9th Street that Amym had lent him.

It had been a strictly platonic relationship, but it had been her presence that had transformed the apartment from a bug-ridden flophouse where he crashed with his street punk friends, into a place where Chris felt like he actually lived. When the creature that changed Chris into a vampire tried to kill her in that apartment to get at him, it had been Amym's fighting skills that had saved them both.

"You were there for her when she needed someone. You were a good friend to her, don't lose sight of that," Joyce said seriously.

"Okay," he mumbled into her shirt.

"And try not to worry about her too much right now. From what I understand, she's making good progress and will hopefully make a full recovery before too long." Her hand was stroking his back in a comforting way, but the physical contact and her scent were beginning to make his pulse race.

Chris was starting to imagine that maybe some of the things he had been dreaming about might come true when Joyce abruptly moved back away from him. "Hey! I brought something for you."

She reached down and collected the box from the floor and passed it over to Chris.

"What's all this?" Chris asked, pulling open the cardboard flaps and peering into the box.

Inside was a red and black Sony w800 Walkman with a pair of large over the ear Cowboy headphones and a number of plastic containers molded to look like books. He flipped through the cases: Spanish, Chinese, Italian. He picked one up to examine it, the cover had Berlitz German written in large letters. When he popped open the case, he discovered seven white cassette tapes.

"These are language tapes. Listen to them before you go to sleep. You'll be surprised how fast you pick things up," she advised.

She laid her hand on his thigh, looked into his eyes, and gave his leg a squeeze. "It's going to be alright, you'll see."

"You sure about that?" Chris asked skeptically, closing the case and returning it to the box that was tactfully perched in his lap.

Joyce smiled. "Just remember that you're not alone in this. You have friends who are here for you. So don't hesitate to ask for help when you need it, okay?" she asked reassuringly without actually answering his question.

"Okay," he said as she stood up and started out of the room.

Joyce stopped at the door and turned back. "You should start thinking about going to bed soon. It's going to be a grueling day tomorrow, and you'll want to be well rested." When she closed the door behind her with a soft click, Chris let out a long breath through his pursed lips.

He took out the Walkman, and after untangling the cord, fit the headphones over his ears. He reached into the box and blindly pulled out the first case his fingers closed on Portuguese. He put tape one in the deck and pressed play.

There was an audible click as the Walkman's motor reversed direction to play side A, and after twenty seconds of waiting, an enthusiastic voice came on. *Portuguese is the national language of both Portugal and Brazil. In the former, it is spoken by the entire population of 10 million people, including those in the Azores and on the island of Madeira. In Brazil, it is spoken by virtually everyone, save the country's few hundred thousand Indians. As*

Brazil's population continues to soar, so does the number of speakers of Portuguese.

As the instructor repeated conversational phrases, alternating between English and Portuguese, and Chris' eyes began to slowly close from exhaustion.

Chapter 2

It took everything Chris had to pull himself out of bed. His eyelids felt like they were lead weights, and everything was sore. His heels felt like he was walking on nails as he descended the stairs to the empty common room, but he trudged himself into the kitchen and dropped into a seat at the table.

"Bom dia. How did you sleep?" Lavinia asked from behind him.

"Bem, obrigado," Chris responded without thinking.

"Good. I hope you're hungry," She called.

"I am," he said, realizing that he really was very hungry. He had decided to skip eating throughout the previous day and had only had one glass of juice. Now his stomach was starting to feel painfully empty.

Setting a glass of deep red liquid on the table in front of him, Lavinia announced, "Homemade Blood Orange juice." Then, she hurried back into the kitchen and called out, "Breakfast will be ready in a moment."

Loud hissing and gurgling sounds filled the room for a few moments, then a matching glass of steaming brown liquid with a thick layer of white foam and a plate of toast was deposited on the table with a clank. "Galão, and torrada with butter," Lavinia announced with finality.

"This juice is really good," he called out after taking a sip from the blood orange.

"Good, it will give you energy," she said, placing a large heavy plate on the table in front of him and pushing his chair in closer. "And this will give you stamina." She pointed out each item on the plate. "Fried eggs, black pudding, made with pigs blood, codfish cakes and beans, and rice. Enjoy!"

"Thank you."

"You need to meet your instructor outside at 6:30," she said. "So, you'd better eat quickly."

Chris gobbled as much of the delicious food as he could, keeping his eyes on the wall clock. Everything was wonderful, but

Chris was surprised by how much he liked the sausage. He was tempted to ask for more, but there wasn't enough time. He dropped his fork onto the plate with a loud clatter and headed outside calling out, "It was all delicious, thank you!"

He hurried out into the dew-dampened grass, expecting to find his instructor waiting for him, but the front lawn was empty. "Follow the path," suggested a feminine voice from the porch behind him.

Chris turned to find Joyce, sitting on the porch swing, a steaming cup cradled in her hands, with her over-sized Swans nightshirt hanging loosely off her shoulder. "Oh, hey."

"Hey yourself," she said with a mysterious smile. "You're doing really well with your language studies."

"I listened to a tape last night, but I fell asleep. Why?" he asked, confused.

"Well, you seem to have learned enough, but you'd better get going or you'll be late."

"Yeah, right," Chris stammered. "Okay, see ya." He said and started jogging down the fieldstone path that led around to the back of the lodge.

The stone path wound around the property and transitioned to dirt as it passed beyond the tree line. He continued along the trail until he came to a small clearing. A thin fog was settling onto the ground, coating everything with shimmering drops of due. A lone figure stood motionless in a martial arts pose as if he had been paused in the middle of a move. Chris couldn't see his face clearly as he was backlit by the rising sun streaming through the trees. After a moment of standing there awkwardly, Chris cleared his throat.

"You move like an ox. I could hear you coming the moment you entered the woods," the man said without moving anything but his lips. "And you're late."

"Yeah, sorry. I didn't know where I had to go."

"Your excuses may seem important to you, but they mean nothing to me. Your lateness is a mark of disrespect, and it wastes my time."

"Yes, sir. It won't happen again," Chris assured him and received an unconvinced sounding grunt in return.

"My name is Shihan Hisao. When you speak to me, you will address me as Sensei."

"Yes, Sensei."

"Over the next few days, we will develop your strength, agility, mental acuity, and basic combat skills," he said finally moving from his pose and coming to stand rigidly in the center of the clearing. He gestured that Chris should come and stand in front of him.

"T'ai chi ch'uan training involves taolu, which will teach you solo hand and weapons routines and forms. Neigong, breathing and meditation exercises. Qigong, movement and awareness exercises. And sanshou, self-defense techniques," he explained. "Hand to hand training begins tomorrow, but today, you will practice meditation and the Yang forms."

"Yes, Sensei."

They worked on breathing techniques and the precise execution of the forms until lunch when, exhausted and sweaty, Shihan Hisao released him. "Learn to read your body, listen to it, understand and control the pain and fatigue. Go and meditate on the forms, visualize them in your mind until you can see them in any order, in any combination. Tomorrow we will meet in the dojo."

"Yes, Sensei. I'll be on time," Chris assured him breathlessly.

"There is a good selection of martial arts movies in the video library. I would recommend that you start watching them. Pay close attention to Tomisaburo Wakayama, Sho Kosugi, and Dan Inosanto, though there are many talented martial artists in those films," Shihan Hisao suggested as they walked along the trail. When the path opened up onto the lodge grounds, Shihan Hisao gave him a curt bow that was little more than a slight nod, then headed towards the front of the main building. Chris thought about following and getting something to eat, but his aching muscles protested, and he decided instead to visit the dojo and check out the Jacuzzi.

Chris crossed the practice room, then proceeded to the spa. The walls and floor were covered in white tiles with bamboo mats on the floor to prevent slipping. The center of the room was occupied by the large wood sided Jacuzzi tub; the water was warm but the jets were off. The left end of the room held two black padded massage tables draped with thick white towels, and a doorway

28

leading to a group shower. On the right side, a single door was centered in a wooden wall spanning the width of the room.

While searching for the controls for the tub, Chris noticed a faint orange light coming through the small window in the door. Thinking it was a maintenance room where he could turn on the jets, he pulled open the door and was immediately hit in the face with a wave of blistering heat.

"Keep the door closed please, you're letting out the heat," someone said and Chris quickly shut the door behind him. In the corner of the room, hidden from the view of the window, sat Joyce. She reclined on the upper level of wooden benches, lit by the dim glow of a forty-watt bulb reflecting off the wooden walls, bathing her in soft yellow light. Her sweat dampened hair was plastered to her face, and she had only a towel wrapped loosely around her giving Chris a view up the entire length of her shapely white legs.

"Oh, hi," Chris said, fumbling for something nonchalant to say. "What are you doing? And why's it so hot in here?"

"It's a sauna. It's supposed to be hot," she replied. "It's wonderful for sore muscles."

"Oh," he said, feeling stupid.

Joyce closed her eyes and leaned back against the wooden wall. "Why don't you go take off those sweaty clothes and come relax for a while?"

He stood there, stunned motionless, unable to say anything. Being naked with Joyce, alone in this dimly lit little room, was like one of his dreams. The ones that made him blush when he thought about them. Who knew what might happen. "Are you just going to stand there?" she asked. "There are towels and cubbies in the shower room where you can leave your clothes."

"Oh, okay," Chris stammered before hurrying off to the showers.

He quickly took off all his clothes, shoving them into the empty cubby next to the one that contained Joyce's pile of black cloth and lace. He wrapped a towel as securely around his waist as he could and raced back to the sauna.

While he had been gone, Joyce had repositioned herself on the bench. She lay on her back, which had caused the corner of her towel to fall to the side, revealing even more of her thigh and hip.

Chris stood in the center of the small room, unsure of what to do next. "Throw some water on the rocks and have a seat," she said and shut her eyes, concealing the purple glow that was beginning to form beneath her eyelids.

He looked around, trying to figure out what she wanted him to do. *The rocks* he understood, there was a metal grate on the wall next to the door that held a pile of black volcanic looking stones, but the water he wasn't entirely sure about. "Near the floor, there's a spout with a metal cup. Just pour a cup full on the rocks to release the heat," Joyce supplied.

Chris did as he was asked and was hit in the face with a blast of steam. "Mmmmmm, that's better," she purred. "The heat will soothe all your aches away. It opens the pores and helps you get rid of any toxins that might be lurking inside you. Dies, inks, lead, mercury, arsenic, other poisons, and impurities can be expelled with a little concentration."

"The heat does all that?" Chris asked with amazement as he climbed to the second tier of benches opposite where she lay.

"The heat just helps with focus," she explained. "You're already thinking about the sweat beading on your skin, so you just have to concentrate a little harder and push the impurities out."

They remained silent for a while, letting the heat penetrate deep into his tired muscles. He was achingly aware of both their states of undress and a voice in his head suddenly said, *go ahead and take a peek, it won't do any harm*. He argued with the voice, worrying about what she would think if she opened her eyes and found him staring. *She worked in a strip club*, the voice said, *she's used to men looking at her, and it's not like she doesn't know you're here*. It was a halfhearted argument at best, and one he had no intention of winning.

He raised his eyes, taking in every curve as he slowly caressed her body with his gaze. Tendrils of purple snaked from her temples, behind her ears, down the length of her white neck, and between her breasts. As he watched, beads of sweat rose to the surface of her skin laced with tiny swirls of color like wispy clouds of purple smoke. They gathered together and set off to follow the same path, like a map that leads to hidden treasures, only to disappear beyond the border of white terrycloth.

"I'm going to have to re-dye my hair soon," she said without opening her eyes, making Chris wonder if she had been reading his mind.

"Why don't you just use your powers to change your hair color?" he stammered awkwardly.

"I'm fickle," she replied. "I like to change too often and it's not that easy to alter your image of yourself and be able to maintain it long enough to effect a lasting change."

After a few minutes, Joyce interrupted the silence. "How did your first session go?" she asked.

"It was okay, I guess. He had me doing a lot of stuff, and I didn't seem to be doing anything right."

"Yeah, Shihan Hisao can be pretty hard on people, especially when he's first getting to know you. It'll get better and a lot faster than you imagine."

"I hope so. He wants me to watch a martial arts movie."

"Sure, you'll be amazed how much you can pick up watching those movies. You should watch Mad Monkey Kung Fu, it's one of my favorite Shaw Brothers films."

"You watch Kung Fu movies?" Chris asked, genuinely surprised.

"Channel 11, Fist of Fury Theater every Sunday afternoon. Helps me wake up after my Saturday night shift. I love the bad English dubbing."

Every time he learned something new about her, she seemed to get even cooler. He thought back to the time he had seen her dance at Billy's Topless: It was as if the rest of the club had completely disappeared and all he could focus on was her. She was far more attractive than the rest of the dancers combined, not all marked up with needle tracks and bruises, and she was also a much better dancer. Though he had to admit, his neighbor Monika, who was the one he had originally gone there to see, was pretty good too.

"What do they have planned for you later?" she asked him.

"I'm supposed to talk to Amym, but I haven't seen him. Should I just go to his room?"

"If he's here, you'll find him in his office."

Chris looked confused. "He has an office here?"

"Yeah, it's upstairs. Right abouuuuuuut there," she said, pointing to a point high on the far wall. Her arm movement made her towel start to slip, but to Chris' chagrin, she caught it almost instantly. *Maybe vampire reflexes aren't always such a good thing*, he thought with chagrin.

After dinner, Chris headed back to the dojo. The lights in the practice room were off, but there were lights on the second floor, so he hesitantly began climbing the stairs. He was standing on the balcony looking around, trying to picture where the saunas were in relation to where he was. His eyes scanned the area in an effort to figure out the angle that Joyce had been pointing to, and then noticed rice paper doors that led to Amym's office. Suddenly, he heard Amym's voice from the room at the end, "Down here Christian. Please come in."

Chris went to the last door and cautiously slid it open. Inside he found a warm room, the light dimmed and yellowed by rice paper shades, with a rattan mat that covered the center of the bamboo floor. Amym sat in a dark-red, leather-upholstered chair, and indicated that Chris should take a seat in the matching sofa opposite him.

"How has your first day been?" he asked.

"It's been okay. A little weird at first, I mean, when I woke up I could speak Portuguese. I only listened to part of one tape before I fell asleep, but the rest of the day was pretty good."

"Very good, I'm relieved to hear it. You will find that you can pick up languages quite easily; I'm sure your mind was still absorbing the information even after you fell asleep." *That sounds terrific, I will definitely try it again and see what happens*, he thought. Maybe he could learn everything while he was asleep. He'd have to try putting a book under his pillow.

"As a matter of fact, you will be able to learn just about anything you open yourself to. I'm sure Shihan Hisao will give you plenty to work on in order to protect your body, and I will do all I can to ensure you are able to defend your mind."

"Okay," Chris said, not sure exactly what that meant but it gave Chris a lot to think about.

He wondered what sort of superpowers he would have: He could certainly imagine the benefits of being super strong, super fast, or being able to bend people's will. Of course, living forever didn't sound too bad either. He wasn't so sure about the whole turning into a bat thing, but he could sort of see the upside of that too.

He stopped in the kitchen and got a tall glass of juice from the fridge, then headed to the library. *Everton certainly hadn't been joking about it being extensive*, he thought looking around the room. There were shelves lining every bit of wall space from floor to ceiling, wrapping around the door and windows. There were two invitingly soft-looking, brown leather wingback chairs with a small round table between them holding a reading lamp. The shelves were labeled with their subjects: History, philosophy, religion, science, and fiction. Many of the books were in languages that Chris wasn't familiar with, which was a little concerning because Everton had said he was expected to read all them. He looked with deepening apprehension at the endless spines all neatly lined up.

He decided to start with something entertaining, so he headed for the Fantasy shelf. He flipped absently through the row of paperbacks until a particularly lurid cover caught his attention: *Mercenaries of Gor* by John Norman. It depicted scantily clad women in chains standing atop scaffolding, surrounded by soldiers dressed like Roman Legionaries. At the top of the book, it said it was the 21st in the series, but the cover was too lurid for him to pass up.

He lay in his bed reading about the virtues of female slavery in a male-dominated fantasy world until the hero, Tarl, was arrested, his fate uncertain. Hints of betrayal helped prime the story for its continuation in the next book. Christ thought about heading back to the library to look for book 22 but figured it was getting too late to start another story. A quick glance at the bedside clock shocked him. He had assumed that he'd been so engrossed in the story that he hadn't noticed how much time had passed, but the clock showed that it had been less than an hour that he had been reading.

Chris couldn't remember ever reading a five-hundred-page book that quickly. At that rate, there was still enough time to find and probably read the next book before it got too late, but he remembered being late to practice that morning and promising that it wouldn't happen again. He grudgingly decided to put on another language tape instead and see if he had as much luck as he had the night before. He chose French as it was part of his family heritage, put in tape one, and lay back on the bed to listen.

When he opened his eyes, he found Joyce laying on her side next to him, her head resting on one arm while her other hand traced patterns on his chest with her black lacquered fingernails. Thin chains from a delicate bracelet stretched across the back of her hand to connect to a ring on her middle finger. "I'm sorry if I'm interrupting," she whispered. "I thought you could use some company after such a hard day."

Chris rolled over to face her and the headphones were pulled back off of his head by their wires. The futon mattress was hard under him. She was dressed in nothing but few layers of tantalizingly sheer, bright purple and blue colored scarves draped in strategic locations. The orange glow of the streetlights gave her pale skin a slight saffron hue, and dawned on him that he was no longer in his room at the lodge, but rather back at his Avenue C apartment.

This must be a dream, he thought. And if it was a dream, then he could do whatever he wanted without feeling embarrassed or nervous. He reached out and put his hand on her thigh, running it slowly up and under the scarves to her hip. "You are bothering me, but in a good way," he said, groaning inwardly at the corniness of the line, but this was his dream right. She gave a slight laugh and looked at him wantonly from under her heavy black lashes, lifting her leg slightly to brush against the front of his pants. He leaned in to kiss her, and she rolled onto her back inviting him to follow. She wrapped her arm around his back, her fingertips stroking the back of his neck.

His growing arousal was making his pants uncomfortably tight, so he decided that he didn't want them on anymore. And as if by magic, they were gone and his bare leg was enveloped in the smooth warmth of her thighs. He took her hand, holding it firmly to the mattress above her head, and snaked his arm beneath her neck.

Joyce slid her thigh up along his and curled her calf around his back. She moaned into his mouth as his stiff cock pressed against her cleft.

He reached around, gripped the round orb of her ass, and pulled her more firmly against him, feeling his shaft slide slowly, inch by inch, into her molten core. She arched upwards, pressing her breasts against his chest, her nipples straining stiffly against the sheer material that covered them. He pushed himself deeper into her, feeling himself enveloped within her heat. His lips brushed softly over her cheek and down her neck to the hard ridge of her clavicle. Her fingers squeezed tightly against his and she moaned softly with pleasure.

Out of the corner of his eye, Chris noticed movement from the bedroom door. He lifted his head and turned to see Rachel standing in the open doorway. Her outstretched arms gripped the door frame at head level, her body draped in layered veils of reds and purples. Her small mouth turned up at the corners into a tight bow as she smiled down at him.

"I hope you don't mind, I invited Rachel to join us if that's okay?" Joyce asked, lifting herself up and laying soft kisses on his chest.

"What a wonderful surprise." Chris thought it was a terrific idea, and reached out in invitation for her to come into the bed with them.

Rachel dropped her arms to her side and took a step toward the raised captains bed. Her movements were jerky and stiff, and Chris noticed that her veils clung damply to her body, accentuating every curve. She took another halting step and Chris began to smell the meaty, metallic scent of blood. She reached up between her breasts and unclasped the golden chain that held the veils in place, letting them fall to the floor. Chris let his gaze slowly slide over Rachel's body, her full breasts stood out proudly, her nipples looked very dark in the dim light against her pale skin.

As his gaze descended further, Chris became confused by what he was seeing. He had thought that when she dropped her veils, she would be fully exposed, but the lower half of her body was obscured by thick coils of rope that glistened wetly as they wound around her waist and hips. The coils cascaded over her legs and wound around her feet like snakes. She took another step closer and the odor increased. Rachel leaned forward, placing one hand on the mattress, and suddenly Chris knew.

The rope that entangled her legs tumbled from the gaping cavity of Rachel's abdomen where Gilles had cut her open, killing the baby that grew inside her womb. Chris recoiled in horror, pulling away from Joyce to escape to the far side of the bed. His legs became tangled in the discarded sheets and veils and he began to panic. He kicked out, becoming desperate in his attempt to get away from the rebuke of Rachel's corpse.

He sat up in bed, breathing hard, a trickle of sweat rolling slowly down his cheek. He looked around the room for Rachel's specter, which fortunately was nowhere in sight. He was just starting to relax in the knowledge that it was all just a dream and how he was now awake in his bed at the lodge when he saw Joyce open his bedroom door.

She stood in his open doorway with her legs bare, stretching upward like a two-lane highway of alabaster femininity to disappear beneath the oversized Swans t-shirt she slept in, faded from black to a light gray from many washings. Her black hair hung in wild curls past her shoulders, her face framed with purple. Even without makeup, she was stunningly exotic; her thick eyelashes surrounded her lavender eyes with a thick black outline, and her lips were naturally a dark red, like a Red Delicious apple.

"Are you ok? I thought I heard you call out," she asked with concern.

Chris scooted back on his bed, bunching the blanket in his lap to conceal his fading erection. "Yeah, just a nightmare," he said, flushing with embarrassment.

Joyce crossed the room to sit on the edge of the bed. "Do you want to talk about it?" she offered.

"NO! I mean... No," he stammered.

"Sometimes it can help to talk these things through," she prompted.

"It's okay, I'm awake now, but thanks anyway."

"Okay, if you're sure..." she said getting back up. "But remember: I'm just next door if you need anything, okay?" She walked back across the room and started closing the door. "Sleep well," she said and shut it with a soft click of the latch.

Chris leaned back against the headboard and let out a deep sigh. He needed some time to process, and he certainly didn't want to share any part of it with Joyce. Not that she wouldn't be understanding, he was sure that she would, but it would be mortifying to have to tell her about the sex dreams he'd been having about her. He reached down into the box of language tapes and swapped tape one for tape two in the walkman. Hitting play, Chris hoped that the monotone drone of the instructor would be enough to prevent another dream.

She stopped to lean against the twenty-foot tall cyclone fence to catch her breath. She had run all the way from Chrystie Street across town to the William F. Passannante Ballfield at Houston and Sixth. Her heart was pounding hard in her chest, which she still found confusing.

She couldn't believe she had come so close to being caught by the group of men who had been hanging around in the dark, but the park really wasn't a particularly good place for a young girl to creep around in the early hours of the morning, even one like her. She couldn't help but imagine what they would have done to her if they had actually caught her, and it would have scared her half to death if she hadn't been already been a walking corpse. Still, she figured gang rape was gang rape, and even dead, she could feel physical sensation and still had all of her human emotions and fears intact. If she didn't know better, she would have thought she was still alive.

She was covered in grim from head to toe, and all that was left of her clothing was a tattered t-shirt and a badly abused pair of jeans that were quickly becoming baggy and hanging loosely on her as her body slowly wasted away. Add to all that the fact that her once creamy white skin was now filthy and covered with rat bites, and her dirty disheveled hair looked like they had been nesting in it, which they probably had been. Her appearance should have been enough to scare away any rational person, but she supposed a group of guys who had been drinking Wild Irish Rose in the park until almost four in the morning while they waited to unload the last of their smack, weren't the most rational bunch.

She entered the asphalt-covered lot and crossed to the back fence behind the basketball hoop. She took a quick look around to make sure that the windows of the neighboring apartment building were still dark and that there was no one on the sidewalks that would notice her suspicious activity. Satisfied, she began to climb. People would soon be waking up and getting ready for work. She was well aware of the fact that the sun would soon be coming up and she was cutting it extremely close.

She had never been much of an athlete: Never played sports in school, preferring a cigarette and a cute boy to strenuous activity. She had finally given up both going to school and smoking, though it had taken dying to finally get her to kick the habit. She had also been forced to give up boys to accommodate her new so-called lifestyle. It mattered to her, but there wasn't anything she could do about it. Besides, what cute boy would be interested in her now.

Climbing was hard for her; not having much upper body strength to begin with, she had been watching her body deteriorate over the past few months until her skin hung loosely on her bones. The metal bit into her fingers, and the toes of her sneakers didn't fit into the diamond-shaped holes enough to give her much support as she struggled to climb higher. She had thought the undead would be super strong, but that hadn't worked out in her favor either. At least she wasn't a mindless, shambling corpse, so her existence could have been marginally worse. Though, the idea of being mindless did have its appeal sometimes.

There was a jingling sound as she hauled herself through a hole that had been cut in the fence about fifteen feet above the ground, and began climbing back down the other side. When she reached the bottom she had to reach across a three-foot gap and grab a hold of the gray painted bars of the fire escape attached to the building that abutted the park. She climbed down the rickety ladder and dropped down into a narrow, basement-level alley that ran between the buildings about ten feet below the playground.

She turned the corner and stopped at her usual morning dumpster. She hadn't found anything to eat all night, and Caffé Dante always threw out the most delicious sweets. She noticed a half-eaten piece of cheesecake that beckoned her with its decadent cream cheese filling and gram cracker crust but perched like a maraschino cherry on top of a Sunday sprinkled with damp coffee grounds, sat a whole mini éclair. She wondered if some wonderful café employee had left it there specifically for her to find, and silently blessed him or her while she relished the scrumptious morsel. She stood savoring the delicious sweetness, the chocolate icing was starting to sweat in the morning heat, but the cream filling was still cool.

A loud clang echoed unexpectedly down the alley. She jumped nervously and turned to look, relieved to find that it was still deserted but a quick glance at the lightening sky warned her that it was time to get moving again. She needed to get back to the lair before her master returned from his nightly hunting sortie. She had learned from excruciating experience what would happen to her if she wasn't there waiting for him, though it wasn't unusual for him to arrive in the last moments before dawn.

Stuffing the last of the pastry into her mouth, she jogged down the alley and around the next bend. Three cement steps led down to a black steel basement door, which fortunately was always left unlocked. She could only imagine if her master arrived to find her sitting on the steps waiting for him to break it open. She pushed the door open slowly to mitigate the creaking of rusty hinges and peeked around the edge, making sure the room was empty before stepping inside.

The boiler room was dark and creepy, and smelled of mold and damp and spilled heating oil. The summer had been brutally hot, but at least it was cooler underground she thought. The only light was from a single bare bulb, hanging over the large stinky oil tank, bathing the room in a yellowish light and concealing the corners of the room in deep shadows. She closed the door behind her and quietly crossed the space to a small access door near the floor behind the furnace. The padlock that had once secured it had been twisted off and the metal was so mangled that it would never come off the broken hasp. Her master must have done it when he first found the lair, she assumed.

A dark narrow shaft descended another thirty feet below the earth to an unused mechanical room off the IND subway line at the bottom. The master's lair could only be accessed by a rattling, pitted metal ladder that shook precariously on the rusty anchors that were supposed to be securing it to the wall of the shaft. She didn't have a lot of confidence in the reliability of the ladder, and never dilly-dallied on her way down even if she wasn't sure what horror she would find at the bottom.

The chamber's only doorway had been sealed with cinder blocks and a green metal locker had been thrown over on its side in front of it to serve as the master's bed during the daylight hours. She sighed with relief to discover the room still vacant and took her place amid the soiled rags that littered the floor to await his impending return. It was pretty disgusting but she figured it was better than being buried in a coffin, but only a tiny bit better.

The appearance of her master floating silently down the shaft without seeming to use the ladder always startled her, and she quickly lowered her eyes in supplication. She silently warned herself to never again raise her eyes to him while he was awake, but once the sun was up and he was lying on his locker like a corpse, she could do whatever she wanted. And when she had first been brought here, with her throat and abdomen torn out, she had spent a lot of time studying him while he slept.

Her master had looked like a homeless man when he had come to her at the scene of her death. He had told her how she had died, murdered in a fit of passion, and who had killed her. He said that he could use his powers to keep her animated so long as she served him and obeyed his evil whims. He hadn't used those exact words of course, but that's what had happened. He had asked her if she wanted him to allow her to die or if she wanted to continue as his servant. She hadn't wanted to die; there were still so many things she wanted to do, though it didn't appear likely that she would ever get the chance to do them now.

She had thought he would just want to fuck, it's what most men seemed to want from her, so she reluctantly agreed, even though the thought of screwing some old homeless guy was totally disgusting. But what he had actually wanted from her turned out to be so much worse.

He never told her his name, just ordered her to call him master. At first, she refused. She was a strong, independent young woman, and wouldn't play along with his chauvinistic fantasies of patriarchal dominance, even if she was dead. But after he started walking away, leaving her to lay in a puddle of her own coagulated blood, she decided that calling him master was a small price to pay to stay alive, or animate, or whatever you call what she was. After he had bound the worst of her injuries in strips of shredded sheets to prevent her dripping all over, he easily picked her up, tossed her over his shoulder, and carried her down into his lair.

During those early days, while her injuries closed and the damage to her body was repaired, she had been so grateful to still be conscious that she would have submitted to almost anything. But as time went on, his demands became more extreme, and his punishments for disobedience increasingly severe. At the same time, his appearance began to improve in part because she was forced to bring him money every evening, which he used to buy new clothes, colognes, and jewelry. It didn't matter to him what she had to do to get it, how she had to debase herself in front of those condescending suburban douchebags on their way to and from their oh-so-important and lucrative jobs in the financial district.

She had checked the newspapers for days after her murder, hoping that there would be something – anything – that would indicate that someone was looking for her or investigating what had happened to her. Yet day after day, she found nothing. Her master had told her that she was "unloved" and "unmissed" by her friends and family. She knew that most of her friends wouldn't be too concerned when she stopped coming around; it wasn't unusual for people on the scene to just disappear for a while without telling anyone, especially during the summer when everyone seemed to be traveling. But, surely her mom would have noticed that she hadn't been back to their apartment in a while to collect the rest of her things and raise some sort of alarm.

"It is gratifying, as usual, to see my little pet waiting patiently for my return," he said in a tired, raspy voice. This was his regular greeting for her when he arrived back at the lair each morning. However, it was his next words that would determine how the rest of her day would go.

If he said, "The hunting was not good tonight. The weather is keeping all the little darlings indoors," then she could be in for a difficult few hours.

But, something was different: The tiny room was beginning to fill with the overpowering stench of burnt meat, and the silence of the room was interrupted by a faint crackling sound. She looked up to see orange glowing embers pop and hiss deep within the cracked recesses of charred bark that was his flesh. She quickly averted her eyes, keeping them downcast as she'd been taught through his many harsh and thorough lessons. Her hopes for the evening sank into her nearly empty stomach as he took a seat on the edge of the locker. "Come pet," he commanded in a strained voice, causing her to scurry on her knees across the litter-strewn floor to kneel at his feet.

She took her position on the floor between his spread knees, with her back to him, and braced herself for what she knew was coming. He placed one uncharacteristically warm hand on the side of her head, wrenching it roughly to the side by her hair, exposing her neck. He used the other hand to pull her shirt and bra strap out of his way. The pain, when it came, was excruciating as always. Her master didn't simply bite her to get to her blood: He liked to chew on her neck and shoulder, grinding her flesh between his sharp teeth, mashing it into a blood-soaked pulp before drinking from her mangled arteries. Even more than the shock of agony, she was amazed at how the torturous pain quickly subsided the more he chewed, and how her torn skin knit itself back together showing no sign of the trauma she had endured mere minutes after he had finished.

It was one of the side effects of the power that kept her animated her master had explained: It let her dead body heal quickly when he fed from her, but without his attentions, any injury would linger and fester until the next time he needed her. It was the pattern of her new existence, as reliable as the sun that he avoided so determinedly. He would hurt her, then heal her over and over again whenever it suited him.

The other side effect was equally disturbing. As the pain subsided, she was overtaken with a warm, tingling sensation that spread out from her neck until it seemed to engulf her entire being in an aura of ecstasy that kept her hovering on the edge of orgasmic

42

release long after her master had finished with her. Even if it hadn't been for the restorative power he had over her, this intoxicatingly erotic sensation was so addictive that it might have been enough to keep her coming back anyway.

When he had sated his thirst, he wiped his blood-smeared mouth with a crunchy bit of stained fabric that passed as a handkerchief and lay back on his makeshift cot. The metal walls of the locker made a loud bang as his weight distorted the steel sheeting beneath him. "I will require you to obtain more money, much more, in the coming weeks. It is time for you to move my lair to somewhere with more... *panache*. You will also need to care for a child I shall be acquiring soon."

"But I'm doing the best I can," she said with more than a hint of desperation. She turned her head around suddenly to face him and said, "It's all I can do just to get those greedy yuppie fuckers to fork over a little change." Her protests stopped suddenly when she saw the condition her master was in. His skin was burnt black and small trails of smoke wafted into the chamber's stale air from tiny orange glowing specks, like coals that popped and flared from within the recesses of his scorched flesh. She knelt with her mouth hanging open, transfixed by what she was seeing. Without thinking, she asked, "What happened to you?"

The back of his hand smashed viciously into the side of her cheek, sending her flying across the room to lay sprawled on the filthy floor. "Mornings do not agree with my constitution," he growled. When she could begin to think again, she realized all the mistakes she had just made: She had looked at him, she had talked back, she had made excuses for her failure, she had questioned him and made note of his weakness. She knew that the only reason she was 'alive' was because he still needed her, and she wanted to stay alive in, whatever manner was available to her.

Where there is life there is hope she kept telling herself. "I'm sorry master, I forgot my place," she said with her head bowed.

"I do not care how you obtain the money I need, just get it. Must I remind you that you continue to exist only so long as I find you useful? When you cease to be useful, or your presence becomes disagreeable to me, I will cease to allow you to continue being," he warned.

He brushed away the thin coating of ash from his sleeve with his wickedly sharp fingernails. It was a futile effort as the light dusting of cinders was replaced by large flakes of black char. "Now, you *WILL* get me the money I require, you *WILL* find me a place to reside that suits my needs and my station, and you *WILL* care for the boy child when I bring him. Do you understand all that, *esclava*?"

"Yes, master," she responded contritely, more out of habit and conditioning than any genuine acquiescence to his demands.

"Good. You know I don't enjoy disciplining my pet," he said reproachfully.

In fact, she knew the exact opposite to be true. He was a sadist who thoroughly and completely enjoyed inflicting torment, and if she didn't need him to go on functioning, she would have done... something, she thought. She hadn't the faintest idea what she could do to get away from him. But even if she could get away, where could she go? Who could she turn to now that all the people who were supposed to love her had betrayed or abandoned her?

"But you must learn to keep your place. The sun has risen, and it is time for me to rest and recuperate. Tomorrow evening you will have better tidings for me upon waking." He lay back on his metal bed and was still as stone in minutes.

She waited. They were so far underground that she had no idea if the sun was really up yet or if he was just setting another trap so he could punish her again. It had happened enough times in the first weeks that she knew better than to move an inch until she was absolutely sure he was down for the day. Only then could she curl up on her bed of rags and get a few short hours of sleep before going back out on the street.

But today was different: He had revealed that his condition was due to exposure to the coming morning. That fit with what she knew about vampires, leaving her to ponder the possibilities. She had seen a movie in April with Tim Curry and Tom Cruise where they used a series of mirrors to bring the sunlight into a dark cave. She wondered if something like that could work here. If she could burn him up while he slept...

She imagined mirrors reflecting the sunlight from the park, down the alley, into the boiler room, down the shaft, and onto his bed. It would be complicated but worth the effort when she imagined him burning up, unable to escape the lair through the blazing shaft of sunlight. *But where would that leave me*, she thought. She needed him to remain animated, and as bad as things were, and they certainly were bad, she wasn't yet ready to throw in the towel and pull her own grave closed over her.

Instead, she poked at her swollen cheek with the nail of her dirty index finger, feeling the puffiness subside and the bruising fade between one probing poke and the next. All the bites and bruises would be healed, and her skin would be clear and free of all blemishes when she woke. It wouldn't last long; the rats would once again come in the dark to begin nibbling on her putrefying flesh. The sores and welts would return soon and she would slowly deteriorate until the next time her master needed to feed.

As she succumbed to exhaustion, she wondered what else she could do to look even more pathetic, more in need than she already did, what she could do to make those rich bastards downtown part with more of the cash her master needed. She had no idea how she would accomplish all the things her master had demanded, but she knew she had no choice but to try.

Chapter 3

In the morning, Chris had breakfast with Lavinia and practiced what he had absorbed from the tapes the night before. She tried to trip him up by switching between languages in the middle of sentences, alternating from French to Portuguese, back to English, then shifting into French again. By the time he had finished his meal, he had no idea what language he was speaking, but he seemed to be becoming much more fluent with each.

He arrived in the meadow with a few minutes to spare, but Shihan Hisao was already there waiting for him. Chris crossed the damp grass to stand before his instructor. "Good morning, Sensei," he said cheerfully bowing his head, but only received a stern grunt in response.

"The forms we went over yesterday, show me," he said with a gruff authority.

Chris went through the forms, receiving instructions and correction for any small imperfection. *Keep your arm straighter, keep the angle higher.* Once he had done them all to his Sensei 's satisfaction, he was left alone to complete one hundred repetitions.

He went through the motions, keeping his movements as close to perfect as he could. His muscles strained to keep his limbs steady and still while he went through the exercises in slow motion the way he had been shown. He became aware of motion behind him and thought that maybe Shihan Hisao was still there watching him. But as he pivoted on the ball of his foot, he saw that a deer had entered the glade and was happily eating the dew-soaked grass without any concern for what Chris was doing. It lifted its head to watch him curiously as it chewed, then bent back down to continue grazing, its ears turning in all directions listening for any sign of danger. Eventually, the doe took several unhurried steps and left Chris once again alone in the clearing.

At first, the sequence took several minutes, and he had to concentrate on every slow and deliberate movement. But as the motions became ingrained in his muscle memory, his speed and fluidity began to improve dramatically. It became a challenge to see how fast he could go without degrading the quality of his forms, and by the time he had completed all one hundred repetitions, he would have appeared as nothing more than a blur to any normal observer.

When Chris had completed his exercises, it was still mid-morning and rather than go back to the lodge and wait, he decided to go and explore the woods. Sundown Wild seemed to him like an appropriate name for the deeply shadowed wilderness. He started by following the deer track out of the clearing, moving quickly between the trees, imagining himself a native hunter silently tracking his prey. He had no idea how far he had gone, but after a while, he could hear voices in the distance ahead and slowed his pace to approach cautiously.

Sunlight filtered through the canopy of leaves to shine brightly on a large pool of blue-green water surrounded by moss-covered shelves of flat, gray stone. Set in the wilderness of the Catskill Forest Preserve, the Blue Hole is a deep, natural feature formed by sand and gravel swirling in an ancient whirlpool, carving a depression in the rocky streambed of the Rondout Creek.

Below, in the water, two figures splashed and laughed, sending ripples across the surface of the pool while a third person lay on the sun-warmed rock. She was twenty at most, her long straight auburn hair had been braided into thin strands that extended from her temples. She had removed her shirt and bunched it up under her head as a pillow, her flowing purple and white paisley skirt hiked up around her thighs. Her skin shown like gold as she lay topless in the sunshine.

Chris walked out of the trees and onto the flat surface of a boulder protruding out over the water. "Hey man, good to see ya," called the guy in the water, causing the girl he swam with to turn and look up at him also. Chris looked down at them; the guy seemed to be in his early twenties, with long, sun-bleached blond hair in dreadlocks, and a scraggly blond goatee. The girl, somewhat younger, had straight, wet hair that looked black as it spread out around her shoulders and floated out across the water.

He took a good look at their faces but didn't think he had ever seen them before. "Sorry, but I don't think we've met," he said.

"Naw, it's all righteous man. There are no strangers, man, just people you haven't met yet. This is Skye." The girl treading water next to him gave Chris a small wave. "I'm Kimber, and up there is Zara."

"Hi," said the topless girl without looking up from her rocky perch on the opposite side of the pool.

"I'm Chris," he said, waiving awkwardly to them all.

"Good to see you, friend Chris," said Kimber.

"Hey, Kim, why don't we invite Chris to swim with us?" Skye asked.

"Yeah, that'd be cool. Why don't you get out of those city clothes and come swimming with us?"

"Well..." he hedged. "I need to get back before long so I don't know."

"Come on Chris, live a little," Skye called. "The water's perfect. Don't you want to come swim with me?" She looked up at him, her wet lashes fluttering in the light glittering off the rippling surface of the water.

Why not? Chris thought. He had nothing he needed to get back for until dinner, and the day was beginning to heat up, even in the woods. Decision made, Chris quickly stripped down to his underwear feeling very self-conscious about being watched by Skye and Kimber. When he looked over, Zara hadn't seemed to take any notice of him since saying hi, which didn't bother him since he kept glancing up to check her out when he thought the others weren't looking.

He searched for a good way to climb down to the water but there didn't seem to be a path on his side. "Just jump!" called Kimber. "The water's really deep."

Chris swallowed hard, then remembered that he wasn't an ordinary person: He was a vampire and had nothing to be afraid of by jumping into a pool of water. At least, that's what he thought before he jumped. The shock of the cold mountain runoff that filled the pool made it feel as if his entire body was trying to contract in on itself. Tiny white bubbles rose past him in the light-green water as he swam back to the surface. "God, that's cold!" he shouted.

"Yeah, it takes a few minutes to get used to," Kim laughed.

"Why didn't you warn me?" Chris demanded.

"Because you wouldn't have jumped in. Also, makes your dick tuck up like a scared turtle, but don't worry, the girls get it.

Their cool chicks," Kimber said, giving Skye a wink. "And it makes their nips hard as rocks," He whispered conspiratorially, which earned him a face full of water from Skye.

"So, where are you from, Chris?" she asked.

"I'm from Texas but I've been living in New York for a while," he told her.

"What brings you out here?" Kim asked.

"I'm staying near here with some friends."

"That's cool," Kim said. "We've been traveling together a while, checking out the scene in different places, you know. We've been staying at this cool hotel in Mount Tremper called La Duchesse Anne. That's where we got turned on to this place. Isn't it amazing?"

"Sure is," Chris said. "But it's still fucking cold."

"Hey, after this, you wanna come back with us? We'll pack a bowl and we can make some coffee pot pizza," Skye offered.

"What's coffee pot pizza?" Chris asked.

"Oh man! So dig it: This place is nice and all, but there's like nothing in walking distance, you know. No grocery stores, no restaurants, not even a gas station. So, before we got back from Woodstock last night, we picked up some English muffins, some spaghetti sauce, and a can of Parmesan. We've been making these little pizzas in the coffee pot. It's the only thing that we can use to heat them up, you know. But their actually pretty good, especially when you're really baked," Kim explained, laughing as they all climbed out of the water and lay on the rocks to get warm.

Zara sat up, resting on one elbow and shading her eyes with her other hand to look over at Chris. Her chest was flushed from the sun and a light sheen of sweat glistened on her breasts. She lifted her knee to turn further towards him, and Chris couldn't help looking at her legs extending from the folds of her skirt. Her creamy white thigh stood out in smooth contrast against the prickly looking hairs on her shin. "So Chris, you wanna hang with us or not?" she asked in a very direct manner.

"Um... yeah, I'd love to, but I've got to meet up with my friends. Maybe I could hook up with you guys later on?" he asked plaintively, trying to keep his eyes on her face and not stare at Zara's pert breasts.

"Yeah, I guess that'd be cool. We're gonna be heading back to Woodstock to hang on the Green later. Come hang if you want," Kimber offered.

Chris headed back to the lodge and spent the rest of the afternoon reading. There was so much he didn't understand about how this new existence of his worked, and he hoped to find some answers buried in the miles of shelves. He pulled out books on folklore, myths and the supernatural, and by the time dinner was ready, he had read through several of them. There were some interesting ideas about vampires being able to fly or turn into bats or fog, which Chris thought could be useful. One book even said that vampires couldn't cross moving water, which he knew wasn't true. Manhattan was an island and it seemed to be crawling with them. There was another idea that he thought sounded like fun, and he decided to do a little experiment.

Before heading to Amym's office in the dojo, Chris stuffed a handful of dried beans from the kitchen into his pocket. He had read that in Europe, people had spread various seeds or sand on the ground around the graves of those they thought might have been the victims of vampire attacks. It was believed that those who had been infected suffered from an Obsessive Compulsive Disorder called Arithmomania and that the scattering of small objects would keep them busy counting until the sun came up and destroyed them.

As soon as he entered Amym's office, Chris pulled out his beans and tossed them into the center of the room hoping to catch him off guard. There was a blur of motions, and suddenly, Amym was standing in front of him. "I believe you dropped these," he said, holding the desiccated pintos in his open hand.

"Sorry, I was just testing some folklore," Chris admitted with embarrassment.

Amym put his hand on Chris' shoulder. "I know what you were doing. I suppose it didn't occur to you that you would also have been affected if the myth had proven correct?"

"No, I guess I didn't think of that," he mumbled, crestfallen.

"And who did you imagine would pick them all up?"

"You're right. I didn't think it through very well."

"No, you didn't." He guided Chris into the room and closed the screen behind them. Chris took his seat on the couch and prepared to be chastised. "But, no harm done. You could offer them back to Lavinia, but I doubt she'll want them now." Amym sat down in the chair facing Chris. "So, tell me what you have gleaned from your research."

Chris went through the list of abilities and weaknesses he had compiled from the books he had read. Not just the ones from the library, but the vampire pulp he had been reading before. He remembered the copy of Anne Rice's book Rachel had bought him from a street vendor after he told her what he suspected about himself. *If she had just listened, maybe she would have gone home and been okay*, he thought.

"There are certain traits that all Lesser Blessed have. Our bodies are enhanced by the infection: We can repair damage rapidly, our muscles are stronger, our bones are harder, and our nervous system responds much faster. These traits can make us seem invulnerable, but we are not. We have heightened physical senses, like hearing vision and olfactory. Our heightened neuro-responses give us heightened intelligence, which allows us to learn faster and remember longer. It sometimes seems as if we can never forget anything, no matter how we might wish to," Amym said with a note of sadness creeping into his voice.

"We can live a very long time, though I suspect we are not immortal. We don't age unless we choose to, and we don't weaken unless we stop feeding."

"Feeding? You mean like, drinking blood right?" Chris asked, seeing as this was the first time the subject had come up.

"Yes," Amym answered matter-of-factly. "Human blood is the source of our strengths. If you stop feeding, eventually your abilities would fade, and you would become, for all intents and purposes, a normal human."

"You mean, I could just walk away from this and be a regular kid? How long does it take to be normal again? I mean, the only blood I've had was from Cara." He remembered the last time he saw her: Laying in a pool of her own blood on her bed in Fetus squat, her throat torn out by his teeth in a frenzy of drug-fueled lust.

Amym could see the sadness coming over Chris and reached out to put his hand on the boy's knee. "I do not believe her death is your fault. I'm not sure if it was simply the hallucinogenic you had taken, which I sincerely doubt, or if it was the creature who transformed you influencing your mind. Or, perhaps it wasn't you at all."

"Who else could it have been? I was the only one there."

"Were you? How are we to know? It might as easily have been Gilles coming to destroy you, and Cara was simply in the way. Perhaps he was interrupted by squatters making noises in the building and left before he was finished." He let that idea sink in before continuing. "Besides, it is not strictly true that hers was the only blood you have had," Amym suggested. "When you were hospitalized, you received several pints of transfused blood. That is why you healed so quickly from your attack. I have also made sure you received some small amount at each of our encounters."

Chris remembered the glass of tomato juice he drank at Amym's apartment after Cara died, and how much better he felt after drinking it. He had attributed it to coming down from his high, but maybe there was more to it. He thought about meeting Amym at the Aztec Lounge, an Alphabet City dive bar where Amym held court, and something about the way he interacted with the waitress struck him. "At the bar, you took blood from the waitress, right?"

"Very good. I used my thumbnail to open her finger and let a few drops of her blood fall into your glass."

"But, she didn't even notice," Chris protested.

"It's a simple trick really," Amym explained. "With practice, you can hold a persons attention to the exclusion of all else with nothing but eye contact. They will hear nothing but your voice, see nothing but you. It can be very useful. Not only can blood help us heal ourselves, we can also repair minor injuries to others just as easily. Our saliva is a strong anesthetic and acts as an anticoagulant while we feed, but promotes rapid healing afterward. Melissa was completely unaware of the injury to her finger, which had fully healed by the time she returned to the counter"

"Is Lavinia giving me blood here?" Chris asked.

"This is a haven for Lesser Blessed, a place where we come to recuperate and learn. There is blood in everything we eat and drink," Amym said patiently.

Chris became queasy; his stomach beginning to rumble, but the more he thought about it, the more he realized that it wasn't nausea. It was hunger. "With each passing day you are growing stronger, your abilities are developing and becoming more pronounced. In addition to the strengths we all receive, each of us is also graced with what we call a blessing or gift. Some might be granted telepathy, persuasion, or astral projection. I, for example, can predict the future. Not the whole future... just my own immediate future. That, along with my speed and strength, allow me to be a better fighter. I can see what moves my opponent will make moments before he makes them. I see what all the various outcomes would be so I can be prepared to counter whatever comes. We have yet to discover what your abilities may be, but when they become apparent, Joyce and I will help you develop them as well."

Chris thought for a moment. "You said we don't age unless we want to, but you don't think we're immortal, which means that you're not sure. So, that could mean that I might be a teenager forever, right?"

"When I said *unless we want to*, I was being quite literal. All Lesser Blessed can alter our appearance to one degree or another, but some can fully transform themselves. Though, that may take centuries to perfect. Your own appearance has certainly begun to change in the months we have known each other. You are noticeably taller, more filled out, your hair has become longer and darker. For all intents and purposes, you appear to have aged several years. Your eyes have also begun showing their hue, though I have never seen one of us with multi-colored eyes before."

"What does that mean?" Chris inquired.

"When our blessings are manifested, they are reflected in the color that shows in our eyes when we exercise those abilities. You may have noticed that mine are a dark orange when I fight, which is because I am using my blessing to predict my opponent's next moves."

"Right, I saw that when we fought Gilles. And Joyce's turn purple sometimes, so what does that mean?"

"It is not for me to tell you another's blessing, but you are unique in my experience. I have seen your eyes change to show every color of the rainbow. Perhaps your blessing is not yet settled. Only time will tell."

Amym had given Chris a lot to process, and he wanted some space to think things through. He needed to be away from all-things vampire for a while. Besides, there was the possibility of meeting up with Skye and Zara if he could just figure out how to get to Woodstock.

If he followed the deer trail, he would end up at the swimming hole, though that might not be the right direction. Everton, Lavinia, and Shihan Hisao all arrived the same way he had, down the dirt drive. If he went that way, he thought he might be able to get a ride when he got to the road.

He took off at a jog and quickly arrived at the locked chain blocking the drive. There were lights on in the cottage, and Chris was tempted to sneak up to see who it was, but he didn't want to get caught. He figured it was Everton and Lavinia anyway because they weren't staying at the lodge, but never seemed to be very far away. He cut through the woods and met up with the road about a quarter of a mile away.

Before long, he could hear the loud sound of a car approaching from behind, it's engine straining like an overworked moped, and when he turned around and saw headlights, Chris started waiving. A canary yellow, 1975 AMC Gremlin pulled over, and the driver reached across the passenger seat to crank down the window. "Everything Okay?" he asked.

"Yeah, I'm trying to get to Woodstock. Am I even going the right way?" Chris asked.

"Well, you're heading in the right direction, but it's a long way off. I'm headed that way if you want a lift," the man offered.

He wasn't sure about accepting a ride from a complete stranger. After all, the last guy who'd given him a ride had turned out to be a pervert, but walking off into the night looking for a town

54

he'd never been to that was a long way off, whatever that meant, didn't seem like a great option either. "That'd be great, thanks," Chris said. The man unlatched the door and pushed it open for him from the inside.

Chris climbed in, settled himself in the perforated black vinyl passenger seat, and reached for the door handle to pull it closed. To his surprise, there was no handle. In its place was a rectangular hole in the yellow metal with a piece of wire coat hanger sticking out. "Just pull it from the window," the guy said. Chris was still searching for his seatbelt when the man forcefully rammed the shifter into gear, revved up the engine, and bullied the protesting vehicle into action.

The ride seemed very long, and after they each attempted to start some small talk with 'Are you from around here?' and 'What's happening in Woodstock?', they fell into an awkward silence. The driver, who introduced himself as Brian, slowed the car down and turned onto a small back road and headed into the darkness, brushing Chris's leg uncomfortably with the back of his hand each time he changed gears.

Chris started to psych himself up, he was becoming convinced that the guy was taking him out into the middle of nowhere to molest and kill him, and dump his body in the woods. He played the forms Shihan Hisao had taught him in his mind. Chris was pretty sure he could take the guy once he got out of the car, but the lack of a door handle made him think that this had been a setup from the start. He thought about pulling the wire loop and seeing if the door opened. If it did, he could just dive out the door and roll off the road. Chances were good that he wouldn't be spotted once he was past the tree line, but getting free of the seatbelt without alerting the guy could prove challenging.

He had to restrain his hand from reaching out to pull the wire and was just about to go for it anyway when he saw lights begin to appear further down the road. At first, only the lights of one isolated house broke the darkness, but soon there were more and more appearing along the side of the road. Eventually, the way was lined with ramshackle old Victorian farmhouses. Soon they crossed the little bridge over Tannery Brook and entered the town of Woodstock. Chris could feel the tension melt off him as the deserted street began showing signs of life, and when the car pulled up to the curb at a large traffic island in the center of town, Chris got out of the car with a grateful sigh of relief.

The island was centered around a flagpole ringed with stone benches. A small lawn to the right was crowded with young people. They stood talking in groups, sat on the grass listening to a guy in a tan suede vest play an acoustic guitar, and did tricks with their skateboards along the edge of the curb. Chris scanned the various groups looking for the bathers from earlier in the day, especially the bare-chested, but aloof Zara, but he couldn't spot any familiar faces among the crowd.

Chris was feeling completely out of place amidst this group of second-generation flower children in his black military clothes and Dr. Martin boots. Suddenly, he noticed a small clump of kids standing outside a pizza parlor across the street. There was a boy with a shaved head wearing a Vietnam era jungle jacket with an anarchy "A" in bright white paint on the back. Next to him was a shorter kid with a wide mohawk hanging limply over to one side, wearing a black leather motorcycle jacket and holding a skateboard at his side, a backpack nestled on the ground between his feet. Chris was just starting to plan his approach; he didn't want to look like some sort of New Jack poser by just walking up and saying 'will you cool kids be my friends?' Then the kid in the leather jacket turned and Chris got a glimpse of his face.

He immediately called out "Adam" and started crossing the street The boy turned towards him, recognition dawning on his face.

"What's up, Chris? What are you doing here?"

"I'm staying with some friends. I was supposed to meet a girl here but she doesn't seem to be around. What are you up to?" Chris asked.

"Just hanging out. My parents have a place here and I come up with them some weekends. This is Geoff," he said, introducing the boy in the army coat.

"Hey, man. How's it going?" Geoff said absently as he continued scanning the crowd. Suddenly, his face seemed to brighten as he found what he'd been looking for. "Hang on a sec," he said and took off, weaving his way through the throng.

"So, we were about to head over to the Artist Cemetery to hang out if you wanna come with," Adam offered.

Chris looked around at the people on the Green, but there was still no sign of Zara, Skye or Kim. The thought of hanging out with Adam sounded a lot better than just trying to hitch back to the lodge. "Okay, yeah. That sounds cool."

"Just gotta wait for Geoff to get back, then we'll head out," Adam said.

It was only a few moments before Geoff came jogging back across the street. "All set. Let's go," he said.

Adam hoisted his bag, which made the familiar dull clinking sound of forty-ounce beer bottle jostling around as he settled it onto his shoulder. He dropped his deck on the sidewalk, and the trio started walking and rolling down the short alley known as Old Forge Road.

"Hey, wait up!" Called a voice from behind. The group stopped and turned: Two girls, their teased out hair and long flowing skirts back-lit by the street lights on the Green were hurrying after them. "You guys going to the Artist Cemetery?" the taller of the two asked rhetorically. "Can we come?"

"Sure," Geoff said.

Adam made the introductions. "This is Jen and Shaina," he said, indicating the shorter girl.

"Hey, I'm Chris."

"Cool," Jen said offhandedly as they started walking again. "We were trying to score some smoke but didn't have any luck."

"No sweat, I got some from Ridge Runner," Geoff stated.

"Who's that?" Chris asked.

"He's this old hippy who lives in the woods. He comes out of the mountains with a trash bag of weed sometimes. It's cheaper than the crap you get from other dealers, plus it's natural," Geoff explained as the group cut through a yard and turned left onto Mountainview Avenue. They walked passed a gravel lot with three-foot diameter cement pipes piled up in a triangular stack. Chris figured they were going to be used as sewage pipes, but until then they seemed like a private place to hang out.

When they passed under a streetlight, Chris got his first look at the two Girls. Jen was taller, with teased out brown hair and a dyed black swath covering her face down to her nose. She wore a black t-shirt that had faded to a light gray under a black cardigan and a full-length black skirt. Shaina was only around five foot two, slightly overweight, with short hair dyed a dark orange that haloed her head like a birds nest. Her eyes were surrounded with heavy eyeliner and mascara that was leaving black flakes across her pale cheeks. Her clothing was nearly the mirror image of Jen's, and it was painfully obvious that she lived her life in the other girl's shadow.

They hopped a drainage ditch and started up the neatly manicured hill of the cemetery. When they reached the top, they picked an inviting looking spot and sat down. Chris found a headstone that read "Scully" and leaned back against the cool, gray granite. Adam opened his bag, cracked a forty, and passed it around while Geoff removed a sandwich baggie from the deep recesses of his jacket pocket, and began to pack a small pipe.

"You guys don't think it's creepy hanging out in a cemetery?" Chris asked when the bottle made it's way around to him.

"I think it's peaceful," Jen said. "It's pretty quiet at night. Only a few people come up here to hang out or fool around." She looked furtively at Geoff from under her veil of hair.

"I think if I was buried here, I'd rather listen to people have a good time. Maybe even watch them screw once in a while. Better than just lying there and rotting, you know?" offered Adam.

"Yeah, I guess so. I hadn't really thought about what it would be like if you were trapped with your body forever. I mean, no heaven, no hell: Just darkness and dirt for all time."

"Don't forget worms eating your eyeballs?" Geoff said and tossed a handful of grass at Shaina, peppering her clothes with green blades.

"Ewww gross!" she shrieked in surprise.

She stood in the shadows on the corner of Eighteenth Street and Tenth Avenue, against the brick wall of a dilapidated industrial building. Her arms wrapped tightly around her body. Not from cold;

the night was oppressively hot, but from embarrassment. Her scalp itched terribly from the cheap black wig she'd gotten from a run-down shop near Third that catered to hookers and tranies.

She had traded her usual filthy garments for some poorly fitting lingerie stolen from a sidewalk bin on Fourteenth Street. The black satin and lace stood out against her white skin to produce what she hoped would be an alluring effect. She had grabbed what she thought would fit her okay, something that she would have been popping out of when she was alive, but now hung loosely off her shrunken form like some grotesque, pornographic scarecrow.

Cars drove past slowly, but most continued on once the drivers got a better look at the wares on offer illuminated by the saffron glow of streetlamps or the brief but stark glare of headlights. Fortunately for her, this part of the block was darkened by the abandoned High Line Viaduct, the elevated West Side spur of the Central Railroad overhead. She hadn't been waiting long; just enough to attract the attention of the other working women. Soon their pimps would come to find out who she was, and she had to pick a target before things got even more dangerous for her.

There were certainly better neighborhoods she could be working, but there she stood a much higher likelihood of being arrested and left to rot in a cell. Here, she was unique among the large black woman and the ethnic spectrum of transvestites who normally serviced the area. A virtual United Colors of Sex-Workers. Besides, the contrast between her white skin and black lingerie made her look like a china doll, hard to miss even in the flash of passing headlights.

A brand new, dark blue BMW 635csi pulled over. The driver extended his arm out the window and called her over to the car. She slowly peeled herself off the wall and strutted awkwardly across the sidewalk. She wasn't used to wearing high heels, and she was more than a little unsteady as she did her poor imitation of the languid stroll used by the women working the streets. Her heels clicked on the pavement, echoing loudly between the buildings. She rested her forearms on the door, leaned towards the open window, and asked, "You looking for a good time?"

"I'm looking for something special," the man replied.

"Well *Special* is my middle name, honey," she joked, eyeing his expensive suit and watch.

"And what's your first name, Nothin?" the man asked while looking her over and chuckling to himself at his own cleverness.

There was a time, not that long ago, when that remark would have gotten him a broken nose. But now, she decided to let the insult slide. *He'd get his soon enough anyway*, she thought. "What are you looking to spend?" she asked as she peered inside the car looking for anything that would identify the jerk as a threat.

"I was thinking... twenty," he offered.

Cheap son of a bitch, she thought, hoping her elbows dented the metal. "I could party with you for twenty, but I don't know how special you expect it to be."

"Why don't you get in and we'll talk it over."

She walked around the car, slipped into the passenger seat, and closed the door behind her. "You have a place we can go?" He asked.

"We'll have a good time, baby. Don't you worry," she said imitating the women on the corner. "Take a right at the corner. There's a parking lot next to the pier." He followed her directions and pulled into a vacant spot facing the river. He left the car running but shut off the lights to keep from drawing too much attention, even though the whole neighborhood was virtually deserted at night. He unbuckled his belt and began working his pants down over his hips.

"Hang on a second, honey. We have business to finish first," she stalled.

"We agreed on twenty."

"Sure we did, but I haven't seen it yet." She said looking nervously out the window, wondering what was taking so long.

He fished in his pocket until he got a hold of his wallet, pulled out a twenty-dollar bill, and slapped it down hard on the black leather dashboard. "There," he said with more than a little irritation in his voice. "Are we good now? I don't have all night."

She picked up the bill and tucked it into her shoe. She couldn't believe this was actually happening; she had never considered herself a 'Good Girl', she ran with a rough crowd when she was alive and she had been with her share of boys, but this was certainly a new low. She leaned over him, bracing her weight on the

60

center armrest as he reclined his seat all the way back. She reached out and took hold of him, stroking his limp little dick with growing apprehension.

"Hey," the man started, "I'm not paying for a hand job. Get in there and start using that slutty mouth of yours." He reached up and grabbed her by the back of her neck, pushing her head down towards him.

Suddenly, the driver's side door was pulled open with the tortured scream of tearing metal as the hinges gave way. It flew across the parking lot, sending orange sparks shooting out in its wake. "What the fuck!" the man shouted in surprise, sitting up abruptly and pushing the girl out of the way. Hands reached in through the hole in the side of the car, grabbed the man by the arm, and pulled him from the vehicle, wrenching his shoulder painfully from its socket.

"Aaaggghhh!" the man screamed in pain. "What the fuck?"

He was slammed face down onto the hood of the car as if he weighed nothing, leaving a man-sized impression in the metal. The hair at the back of his head was seized in an iron grip, and he was pulled backward with a knee pressing painfully into the base of his spine. His arms flailed uselessly behind him, trying to get a grip on his attacker until he felt a sharp pain run across his neck. He looked through the windshield and saw the prostitute quickly look away and cover her eyes with her hands. As much as she disliked guys like this, she didn't want to watch what was happening.

Heat spread down his chest, then he was spun around and pushed back onto the warm steel. He clutched at his throat, trying to staunch the flow of blood. He had seen enough death to know his time was almost up. He thought about all the mistakes he had made in his life: The wife that left him, taking his kids with her when she found out that he'd been fucking around with one of his work contacts, fucking STDs, the offer to go into business with a friend that he hadn't pursued, the boat he never had the money to buy, and the comfortable life he had provided for his family that never felt like enough.

His shirt was torn open and a hand with long, sharp nails plunged into his chest, shattering his sternum as he watched in horror. He felt the icy fingers close around his heart and begin to pull. His arteries gave way with loud pops and the pulsing organ was extracted with a sickening sucking sound. The man looked up into the face if his assailant for the first time; there was no anger, no hatred, no emotion of any kind on the face of his murderer. There was no joy or satisfaction in the kill, only concentration on the job at hand. The fiend brought the heart to his lips with a blood-smeared hand and sucked the quivering chambers dry in a single large gulp. As his vision faded from blood loss, he watched the man tilt his head back, and let the final drops fall onto his outstretched tongue.

The girl was already busy searching the car for anything valuable. The center console produced an assortment of cassette tapes – Glenn Frey's Smuggler's Blues, Asia's 1982 self-titled debut and the Miami Vice soundtrack – as well as a Motorola Bravo pager and a few Triboro Bridge and Tunnel tokens. She dumped everything into her bag to sell later and turned her attention to the glove box. She popped it open and froze when she found a black Smith & Wesson Model 10 snubnose .38 Special revolver resting on a stack of unpaid parking tickets. Its wooden grip was wrapped in a ball of electrical tape with the sticky side out. Acting on impulse, she snatched it up before her master could see it and stuffed it way down in her bag, under her clothes.

After finding nothing else of value, she climbed out of the car and shouldered her way past her master to get to the bloody body. "Took you long enough," she said. Not long ago that sort of impertinence would have earned her a beating severe enough to leave her incapacitated for days, but as her efforts had improved her master's living conditions, he had afforded her a certain amount of leeway. She also suspected that, at some level, he liked her asserting herself, within limits.

She pulled off the short black wig and stuffed it into the top of her bag, covering her meager haul. "I thought I was going to have to go through with it and actually blow this guy."

"Perhaps next time, I'll wait until you have finished," he told her with a wicked grin that said that was exactly what he intended to do.

She opened the dead guy's coat and noticed the tan leather of a holster peek out from under his arm. She deliberately ignored it and dove into his pockets. One produced a small stack of bills in a brass clip and a handful of coins. She gave the money clip to her master and dumped the change in her bag. His back pocket bulged with a thick wallet. She struggled to remove it and quickly flipped through its contents. She could use the credit cards to make a few purchases before the body was discovered and an investigation started, then she could sell them on the street and let someone else deal with the heat. However, when she flipped the wallet open, she discovered verification of the nagging suspicion that had been building in her mind. The gold and blue badge of a Transit Authority detective.

"Shhhhhit, you killed a cop!"

Chapter 4

It was nearly sunrise when Chris got back to the lodge. It had turned out to be a pretty good night, despite the girls' absence. Adam said he and Geoff were going to the community center later that morning to play soccer with Darryl, the bassist from the hardcore band Bad Brains, and invited Chris to meet them there. He said he would try, but he knew he wouldn't be able to get away from his training until that night, if at all.

When he came around the front of the building, he found Everton tending the flower beds. He looked up from his work and indicated with a shake of his head that Chris should go inside. He crossed the great room and almost collided with Lavinia on her way out of the kitchen.

"To proinó eínai páno sto trapézi (Breakfast is on the table)," she said.

"Efcharistó," Chris replied, automatically transitioning to Greek.

She held the door and followed him back inside where he found Joyce at the table facing him across a cooling plate of chicken Souvlaki with Tzatziki, pita, and a spinach, mushroom and feta omelet. Chris plopped down in the empty chair and took a bite.

"You are about to get a scolding," Lavinia cautioned, giving him a wary look as she poured him a glass of red-tinted juice.

"Good to know," he mumbled through his food.

Joyce leaned back in her seat, her arms crossed, and asked, "Did you have fun?"

"I did actually," he replied, shoveling for omelet into his mouth.

"I'm so glad to hear it," she said sarcastically. "I was up all night worrying about you."

Chris partially swallowed his mouthful of food and choked out, "Why?"

"Why!? Oh, I don't know, maybe because I'm your friend and I care about you. Because there's a True Born out there who wants to end you. Because... I don't know why else right now. That should be enough for you to let me know what you're up to." She took a moment to compose herself. "You're safe here, that's why we came. If we don't know where you are, we can't protect you."

"Yeah, I guess so," he said feeling guilty. "I just went to Woodstock to hang out with some friends."

Shocked by his carelessness, Joyce exclaimed, "You told your friends you were here!? Why? How? There are no phones in Haven."

"No, I just went there and there they were. It was nothing planned or anything," he said a little defensively.

Joyce got up from the table and walked to the door. "We'll talk about it later. I need to get some sleep, and you have practice in five minutes, so you'd better hurry."

He crammed in a few more mouthfuls, then ran back outside and down the path to the clearing. Shihan Hisao was there waiting for him with two wooden poles pushed into the soil to form an X behind him. "I'm sorry if I'm late, Sensei," he said, catching his breath.

"Even if you are on time, you are still later then me," he indicated that Chris should come stand in front of him. "Today, we will put what you have learned into practice." He gave Chris a slight bow and threw a punch at Chris' face.

Chris, who had still been rising from his own deeper bow, hadn't been prepared for the attack. He moved to the side but not fast enough to avoid getting clipped in the cheek. He recovered quickly but was deluged with punches and kicks; he managed to block a few, but the majority had easily found their target.

"Your reflexes are too slow. You have the ability to move faster, to think faster. Let your body take control of your defense and use your mind to plan your attacks." He crouched into a fighting stance. "Again," he ordered.

Bruises came and went as the morning progressed, and by the time he was allowed to take a break, Chris was blocking nearly as many as he wasn't. He lay back in the grass to catch his breath, watching the clouds slowly drift over the trees, when a rattan pole suddenly landed on his chest.

"This is a bo, the staff used in Bojutsu for its strength and flexibility. Once you are competent, you can substitute almost anything for a staff; a broomstick or mop handle can be most effective. I will demonstrate and you will follow."

Shihan Hisao led Chris though a lengthy series of thrusting, swinging, striking and blocking techniques, then watched closely as he repeated the patterns on his own. After a number of repetitions, he grunted in satisfaction and left Chris to continue practicing on his own until lunch.

Chris closed the door as quietly as he could, then tiptoed off the porch into the front lawn. Once he reached the grass, he moved quickly into the shelter of the surrounding trees. If he followed the driveway he would probably have to hitchhike again, but if he went west through the forest, he could save several miles and get back to Woodstock sooner. He took off at a jog, picking up speed as his confidence increased. He imagined himself moving between the tree trunks and dodging the low hanging branches like a ghost, leaving no trace except the faintest hint of a breeze to stir the leaves.

When he reached town, the streets were quiet. He walked past the police station, town hall and a small house with tie-dyed curtains and posters of Jimmy Hendrix and Bob Marley on the porch. He crossed the little bridge over Tannery Brook and rounded the bend to the village center. He stopped to look around but the Green was empty. Gone were the clusters of hippies playing guitar and the old timers regaling the teenagers playing hacky sack with tales of their glory days. Even the pizza place was dark.

Chris stood in the empty street weighing his options: He could go to the cemetery on the chance that there were people he knew hanging out there, or he could just head back to the lodge and call it a wasted trip. He didn't want to go to the cemetery alone; he clearly remembered having to approach groups of strange kids when he first got to New York. The nervousness and apprehension of those days were still palpable, and Chris had no interest in being in that situation again.

Just then the door of the Corner Cupboard across the street opened with the tinkling of a bell, and Geoff came out with a paper bag cradled in his arms.

"Hey man! Wait up." Chris called as he jogged to the opposite side of the empty road to intercept him.

"Holy crap. You scared the shit out of me. I thought you were the cops."

"No, just me."

"Come on. Let's get out of here before they do show up."

"Why? What's going on?"

"I don't want to get caught buying beer... again. My mom would lose her shit. Hey, too bad you didn't make it to the community center earlier. You missed a good time."

"Yeah, sorry I couldn't make it to play soccer with your guys."

"It wasn't a real game or anything, just kicking the ball around. But it was way cool hanging out with Derryl. He signed my shirt!" Geoff said, pointing to a scribble of black marker on his plain white t-shirt. "Now all I have to do is draw a Bad Brains cover around it. I'll probably do Banned in D.C."

"That's cool," Chris said casually. "So, uh... where are you headed?"

"A few of us are hanging out behind the Lake," he answered. "I just went on a beer run because I know a guy."

Chris imagined them hanging out on a small sandy beach, or lounging on the rocks around a swimming hole. However, when they arrived, he found only a large white shingled barn-style house half a block down the hill from the Green. The former restaurant had been converted into the Joyous Lake in 1971 and had been one of the hottest clubs outside the city throughout the seventies. It was a required stop for bands touring the East Coast and had hosted acts like The Band, Muddy Waters, and Bonnie Raitt.

Chris could see people sitting on benches in the dark as they climbed the steps to the wooden rear deck of the nightclub. There were some he knew from the previous night, Adam Jen and Shaina were there as well as some he hadn't met, but introductions were quickly made as Geoff began passing out the forties from his bag.

After an hour of drinking, smoking, telling stories, and some not always, good-natured teasing, people began to drift off in different directions. That's when Adam invited the stragglers back to his parent's house to crash. He led the group out of town, passed the country club where Geoff stopped to kick out the headlights of a few luxury cars parked on the grass for some event.

"That's not cool, man. Those people worked hard to get those cars," Adam complained.

"No they didn't," Geoff insisted. "They make other people work hard without paying them a fair wage, just so these fuckers can horde their money to buy these pretentious status symbols. A fucking broken headlight won't even inconvenience them very much. I should be setting them on fire! That would show them," he said as Adam walked ahead with the girls and left Chris behind. Geoff stood on the bumper of the nearest car and pulled with both hands until the Mercedes ornament popped of the hood. "Now I just gotta find a chain to wear it on," he gloated to Chris.

"What's his deal?" Chris asked Geoff as they balanced on the top of a stone wall that prevented the stream running along the road, separating it from the golf course.

"His parents are members of the country club. He likes to pretend they aren't as rich as they are, but they're freakin' *loaded*. I guess he thinks he has to hide it to fit in but I don't see anyone else around here with a weekend house. Do you?"

They turned up a narrow dead-end road. The house was dark, and Chris shushed the giggling chatter of the girls as Adam was unlocking the door. "It's cool, my folks have gone back to the city."

"And they left you here by yourself?" Jen asked. "For how long?"

"I don't know… a couple of days probably. It's no big deal. Come on in," he said, holding the door open while everyone shuffled inside. "My room's up here."

They tromped up the stairs to his small attic room over the garage. There were no windows, but the steeply sloped ceiling was painted flat black, which made it seem much bigger than it actually was. "I just got this new movie," he offered, picking up a VHS tape off a pile next to his 32" TV.

"What is it?"

68

"Hey Good Lookin'. It's a Ralph Bakshi movie about Brooklyn gangs in the 50s." He pushed the tape in and turned the TV on. While the opening sequence of a talking garbage can began playing, he opened the hatch to the roof crawl space and pulled his eighteen-inch glass bong and a sandwich baggie from their hiding place nestled in the insulation.

"Won't your parents notice the smell when they get back?" Chris asked as the pipe was passed around to him. A trail of pungent smoke rolled from its open chamber to drift through the still air.

Adam passed him the warm lighter. "Naw," he said, struggling to talk without exhaling. "They think it's incense."

Chris took a hit and passed the apparatus to Jen, who was lounging between Geoff's legs, her arms resting on his bent knees and her head laying back against his chest. She handed it backward to him and idly stroked his shin as she watched an animated greaser in a Zoot Suit, stereotypically named Vinnie, standing on top of a stolen car. He was giving a motivational speech to encourage the Stompers to rumble with the Black Chaplins.

Soon, Chris was struggling to keep his eyes open. His eyelids fluttered and red-headed Crazy Shapiro was diving into a pile of hamburgers in the back seat and surfacing with Eva's pink panties in his mouth.

'Here I am right in the middle of it - defiant youth in action!'

Nantes, October 1440

Soft footsteps made a subtle scraping sound as they approached down the darkened stone corridor. A man wearing the familiar brown robes of the Franciscan order stopped outside the bars and stood silently as he watched the prisoner who sat motionlessly in the darkest corner of the cell. His once fine garments, now soiled and torn, were barely visible in the gloom.

"Begone, monk. I have no need of your ministrations," came a raspy voice.

The young man placed a nervous hand on the cold metal bars. "I can help you," he whispered. "I can keep you from the flames."

The prisoner shifted his position, his interest aroused. "Pray tell. How might you accomplish such an unlikely feat?" He asked.

"A bargain has been stuck with the Bishop," the monk said eagerly.

"I have been accused and shall be condemned on the testimony of peasants and traitors. So, why should he make such a bargain?"

"Because you will show contrition for your crimes," the monk said. "You will beg the forgiveness of the church, even reciting the De Profundis before your execution. In return, you will be strangled, and your body taken down before it can be reduced by flame."

Slowly the man climbed to his feet. "So, I would be saved from the flames, though I would still be dead. How does that help me?"

"Would you truly be dead, lord? I had supposed that perhaps you were beyond such concerns," he said, a note of doubt creeping into his enthusiasm.

"Do you suppose a man might experience the embrace of the executioner's garrote, and yet live?" he asked incredulously.

"Not a man, no. But you?" He let the implication hang in the stale air like the stench of unwashed bodies and soiled straw that permeated the dungeon.

"So, I am to be snatched away from the clutches of death, even in the midst of my own execution, just like the Judean Nasarani you all profess to worship." He crossed the small room. Though they were of nearly identical height, he seemed to tower over the robed man. "And what do you expect to gain by facilitating this miracle?"

The monk took a small step back from the bars and whispered, "Life everlasting." He paused, waiting for a response. When it seemed like none would be forthcoming, he added, "But in this world, not the next. If you survive the execution, I want you to make me as you are."

"My astrologist once told me that I was destined to become a monk in some abbey," he said with a smirk. "I did not believe him."

Chapter 5

Chris was pulled from sleep by the heavy bass chords of the Neanderthals - Era of Discord blasting from across the room. Slowly he opened his eyes and propped himself up on his elbows. Adam was sitting cross-legged next to the cassette player, his bong nestled in his lap. "Wake and bake?" he asked, smoke rolling from his mouth to hang like a halo around his head.

"Sure," Chris answered as the glass pipe was passed over to him. He flicked the wheel of the lighter and took a hit. The pipe bubbled and gurgled like a science experiment feeding the water-cooled smoke up into Chris' waiting lungs.

"Let's go get something to eat," Adam suggested, and the two of them went down to the kitchen. They came back a few minutes later carrying a jar of peanut butter, a sleeve of saltines, and a bowl of frozen grapes. When they opened the door to the bedroom, Geoff and Jen were busy making out under a blanket, and Shaina was pretending to still be asleep.

Adam pulled a grape from the bunch and threw it at the writhing pair, aiming for the shadowy opening in the blanket. "Hey! That's cold," yelled Jen. The boys laughed and took turns tossing grapes into the hole, cheering whenever they got a squeal out of Jen. Eventually, Geoff popped his head out of their cocoon and demanded that they knock it off so he could finish, but he did stop to eat a grape off Jen's chest before pulling the blanket back over their heads.

"Let's leave them alone for a while," Chris insisted.

"When you're done, we'll be out by the pool," Adam called over his shoulder. Shaina quickly scurried out of her bedding to join them as they headed back downstairs so that she didn't have to listen to their sex noises by herself. She felt like enough of a third wheel as it was without adding that humiliation.

Soon, the pair opened the sliding glass door, squinting in the bright mid-morning sun. They stepped down onto the back patio where the others were sitting on plastic deck chairs around the in-ground pool. Geoff had put his jeans on, but nothing else. Jen was fully dressed and had even teased her hair out to cover her eyes. The grapes were gone but Geoff stuffed a peanut butter cracker into his mouth.

"That didn't take you long at all," Adam teased.

"Too Drunk To Fuck?" Shaina offered, using the Dead Kennedys song to poke fun at him.

Geoff stomped over to her, "Shut the Fuck up." he said, and tipped her chair over, dumping her shrieking into the pool.

"That was messed up," Chris said as he and Jen rushed to help pull the struggling girl out of the water.

"You're such an asshole," Shaina said, sitting on the edge of the pool, water streaming from her dark clothes.

"Whatever, Snausages. It was just a joke, so fuck you if you can't take it," Geoff snapped defensively.

"Well, it wasn't funny," Jen said, coming to kneel by her drenched friend. "Why do you always have to be such a jerk?"

"You must be hot in all that black. You wanna go for a swim too?" he threatened.

Jen ignored him and helped Shaina to her feet. "Come on, let's get you dried off," she said before leading Shaina inside, both giving Geoff murderous stares as they passed.

"What was all that about?" Adam asked once the girls were gone.

Geoff chuckled. "Well... I'm not looking for a girlfriend, so now I'm just the jerk that she hooks up with sometimes. All the benefits, none of the headaches," he said smugly, stuffing another cracker into his mouth.

Jen came back out a few minutes later. "Shaina's in the bathroom and her clothes are in the dryer," she told Adam.

"No problem," Adam said.

Geoff grabbed Jen around the waist and pulled her struggling halfheartedly into his lap. "Take it easy! Don't break my parent's chair, *okay!?*" Adam warned the pair.

"Hey, why'd you call her Snausages anyway?" Chris asked.

"Oh man, that's a good one," Geoff said, getting ready to dive into his story.

"No! It's completely fucked up," Jen corrected leaning back against Geoff's bare chest, her arm raised up and resting on the back of the chair behind his head.

"Okay, so last year there was this huge party. Everyone was there. Anyway, Shaina gets wasted and passes out in some guys bed."

"She didn't mean to get drunk," Jen said, coming to her friend's defense. "She just didn't know how strong the punch was. I heard they went down to Pennsylvania to get Everclear so nobody could taste it."

"Anyway," Geoff continued ignoring her. "So, there she is, passed out, and a couple of Cheese Whiz get this idea."

"What are Cheese Whiz?" Chris asked, trying to follow along.

"They're the top jocks, you know, the football team, Lacrosse, soccer – whatever. The Big Cheese, Cheese, Cheese Whiz..." Geoff explained, but Chris just looked at him blankly.

"A bunch of fucking douchebags," Jen muttered.

"Okay, I gotcha."

"You know, the cheese in a can? Looks like bathroom caulk? You really need to watch more TV."

"We're gonna have a TV party tonight," Adam sang softly.

"Nah, Let's get sushi... and not pay!" Geoff quipped back. "Anyway... So, they go to the kitchen and come back and – now, I've heard this story a couple of different ways. Either they fucked her with a hot dog, or they filler her up with cocktail wieners. In that version, she had to go to the hospital to have them removed."

Chris could believe that someone would do that; he had heard stories about similar assaults on scene girls ever since he got to New York, but still. "That's so messed up!" he exclaimed. He could feel anger starting to build within him on her behalf; he began to feel hot, his jaw started to ache, and his mouth filled with saliva.

"She didn't have to go to the hospital," Jen corrected, "And those assholes should have been arrested."

"They probably would have been, but no one would say who it was, and the only witness was unconscious," Geoff said, but Chris felt sure that he could convince them to give up the person without too much effort and began imagining appropriate punishments. "Besides, it's not like they raped her or anything."

"Of course they raped her!" Jen said, getting upset. "What would you call it if you passed out and a bunch of fucktards started shoving things in your ass? Would you call it rape then, or would it still be some kind of joke?"

"Alright, lighten up. I didn't mean anything by it. Shit."

Just then, the door slid open and Shaina came back out, cutting off any further conversation on the subject. A large pale, blue bath towel was wrapped around her leaving her chest, arms and legs shining white in the sun. She threw herself into a chair as far from the pool and everyone else as she could, and tugged the towel down into her lap to cover her damp underwear. "What are you guys talking about?" She asked.

"Nothing!" they all tripped over each other to say.

"Hey, I was just messing around. Sorry if I took it too far. Okay?" Geoff offered.

"Sure, whatever." She crossed her arms tightly over her chest defensively.

Chris had been fighting his growing apprehension the whole morning, but he couldn't put it off any longer. He had been out all night and missed his morning practice, which would cause him no end of misery he was sure. Not to mention, he knew he had disappointed Amym. "Hey, guys, I really need to get going," he announced apologetically getting up from his deck chair.

"Okay," Adam said without much concern.

"It's been real, and it's been fun, but it ain't been real fun," Geoff quipped.

Chris slid the door open and went back into the kitchen, walking through the living room to the front door. He stopped on the front step trying to get his bearings and figure out what direction he needed to go to get back to the lodge when he noticed the black SUV idling in the gravel drive. Cautiously, he started walking towards the open window of the driver's door. Amym's driver, Steve, sat in his black leather seat, studiously reading a paperback copy of Margaret Atwood's Handmaid's Tale.

"How did you know where I was?" Chris asked.

"It's my job to know everything I need to know, and not to know what I don't," the man said without looking up from his book. "Hop in, I'll give you a ride back."

When the car came to a stop in front of the lodge, Chris pulled the door handle and climbed out of the passenger side back seat. As he came around the back, an open-hand slap hit his face, sending him sprawling on his back in the sun-warmed grass. "Where the hell have you been?" demanded Joyce angrily.

"Out with friends," Chris said defensively. "What's it to you?"

"I told you it wasn't safe..." she said with exasperation.

Chris climbed to his feet, anger and resentment building. "You're not my mother, and you're not my girlfriend, so you can't just tell me what I can and can't do," he said defiantly.

"Amym and I have put ourselves on the line for you, to try to make you into something that the Chord might find useful enough to allow to keep living. If you fail, we fail, and we'll all pay the price for it." She paused to take in the angry, sulking boy glaring daggers at her. "I get it that you feel like your trapped here, you are understandably upset by everything that's happened and want to assert your independence. I really do understand that, but just remember that this isn't just about you anymore."

Chris looked sheepishly down at his boots feeling ashamed. "Hey, I'm sorry, okay? I do realize what you and Amym are risking to try to help me, and I do appreciate it. Really. And about that girlfriend thing..."

"Don't worry about it," Joyce said, hoping to cut him off before he got into an area that would be harder to navigate.

Chris pressed on, glancing up at her from beneath his lowered lashes. "No, I was just thinking..."

"Okay, stop there," she cut in forcefully. "Look, I like you Chris, I do. And we're going to be spending a lot of time together over the next few weeks, and we will get to know each other very well. So, let's leave it at that for now and concentrate on all the things we both need to accomplish in a very short amount of time, and not complicate it with a lot of other stuff that's not going to help either of us right now. Okay?"

"Yeah, sure," he mumbled, feeling even more embarrassed.

She took a step over to him, put her arm around his shoulder, and started leading him away from the lodge. "You know you missed your morning lesson with Shihan Hisao, right?"

"Yeah, I know."

"He wasn't happy about it," she cautioned.

"Well... I don't think he likes me anyway," Chris muttered.

"It doesn't matter if he likes you. He is a professional and deserves your respect."

"I guess so."

"He's waiting for you now. I just wanted to talk to you first." She climbed the steps to the dojo, opened the door, and stepped aside to let Chris enter before following him in and closing the door behind her.

Shihan Hisao stood in the center of the room, eyes closed, as unmoving as a statue. Chris had the impression that he may have been standing there like that all morning while waiting for him to arrive and wondered if he was awake or asleep. "I'm sorry I missed our lesson, Sensei," he said softly. "It was childish and disrespectful to you, and it won't happen again," he promised again.

"Did you practice your forms?" he asked quietly without opening his eyes.

"Yes, Sensei," Chris said.

"Show me."

Chris went through the routine slowly, concentrating on each move to make sure they were as flawless as he could. He saw Joyce move to the far side of the room, standing quietly with her back against the wall to watch him. As he passed in front if his instructor, Chris noticed that his eyes were still closed, and started to wonder why he bothered trying so hard to keep his form right if the man wasn't even going to watch. He finished standing directly in front of his instructor's inscrutable face.

Slowly his teacher opened his eyes, looking directly at him for the first time since he arrived. "Continue doing your morning practices, then come here for your daily lessons." From beneath his robes, he produced a double-edged tactical fighting knife.

"From this point on, your training will become more difficult. But, when we are finished, you will have become one of the People of the Knife," he said. "You will learn to defend against an attack by an armed opponent, as well as how to mount an effective counter-attack."

"Do I get a knife too?" Chris asked excitedly.

"When you are attacked, it will likely be by surprise, therefore you must first learn to defend yourself. Assume first position," he instructed.

Chris took his place on the mat and readied himself for instruction. Instead, his teacher attacked him with such sudden ferocity that Chris had a hard time following the movement of the knife. Light flashed off the blade as he raised his arm to block a reversed backhanded slash. The impact of his teacher's wrist on his forearm was jarring, but not as much as the pain of the knife tip puncturing the brachioradialis muscle and slicing around the circumference of his arm.

He stood in shock; he had been expecting a lesson, not a real attack. He tried to lift his arm to examine the wound but he couldn't bend his elbow. Just as this realization struck him, his teacher followed up with a slash aimed at his abdomen. It was only Chris' heightened reflexes that allowed him to hop backward quick enough to avoid being disemboweled. He was about to congratulate himself when he received a roundhouse kick to the side of his head that sent him staggering back.

The rest of the lesson was a blur of pain, ending with Chris on his back, bleeding into the tatami mat. "Add what you have learned here today to your morning practice and return here at nine tomorrow," Shihan Hisao instructed. He dropped the bloodied knife on the floor with a thud and left without another word.

Within seconds, Joyce was there helping him sit up. "Here, drink," she said and held a glass to his lips. He took a small sip, then began to swallow it down as quickly as she poured it into his mouth. The humiliation of his defeat was compounded by her presence, but even so, he was grateful that she was there. He could feel his strength starting to return as the first gulp reached his stomach. When the glass was empty, he lay propped against Joyce's lap.

"I thought he was going to kill me," Chris panted.

"He took it easy on you," she replied dismissively.

"He cut the shit out of me!" Chris protested.

"Yeah, but you can still walk on your own, or will be able to soon. It could have been a lot worse. I'd get used to it if I were you because it's likely to stay this way from now on," she cautioned.

"Terrific." He could feel his body healing, but his pride would take a while longer to recover. "What was in the glass?" He asked.

"Blood," she said.

"I figured that, what else?"

"Straight, Just straight, unadulterated human blood. As fresh as we can get it up here," she said. "It's the quickest way to recover."

She helped him to his feet and supported him as they made their way to the lodge. "Sorry about getting blood on your clothes."

"Why do you think I wear so much black?"

"I thought it was just because you look awesome in it," he replied with a mischievous smile.

Joyce laughed. "Yeah, okay. Down tiger." She pushed open the kitchen door and deposited Chris into one of the chairs. She went to the stove, ladled out a bowl from a steaming pot and placed it on the table in front of him.

"What is it?" he asked, looking into the cloudy brown liquid.

"Czernina. It's a soup from Poland, made with blood, fruit, vinegar, and honey. It's good for you, eat up."

As soon as he was seated, Joyce left him to fend for himself. It took an hour and three more bowls of the sweet and sour soup before Chris felt recovered enough to venture from the kitchen. Joyce had cleaned his blood from the knife and left it on the table next to his bowl. When he had finished clearing his dishes and wiping up the red smears from his place at the table, he picked the blade up and went outside.

His sensei had shown him, with no uncertainty, how much he still had to learn, and he was determined to make a much better showing at tomorrow's lesson if for no other reason than to avoid the pain of multiple stab wounds. He couldn't imagine how much worse it would be if they started working with swords. *Could vampires regrow limbs?* he wondered, but quickly decided it was best not to find out.

He walked down the path to the clearing in the woods and went through his practice forms. Only this time, he incorporated the knife moves his sensei had demonstrated earlier, imagining his attacks and how his invisible opponent would try to counter them. He jumped and rolled, letting loose kicks and slashes that left his enemies lying in bloody imaginary heaps on the ground around him.

The next time he faced Shihan Hisao, he wouldn't be the one in pain, he told himself as he absently swatted at a fly that had been buzzing around his ear. Rather than shooing it away, this just seemed to piss it off, causing it to become much more aggressive in its attempt to get to Chris' ear. He jumped back and took a swipe at it with the knife. It was close, but the fly managed to avoid being sliced in half by less than an inch.

Chris took this as a challenge and repeated his routine, increasing speed until he finally eliminated his winged opponent. He was just beginning to congratulate himself when he heard the buzzing of wings. At first, he thought that maybe he had missed the fly, but when he listened closer, the buzz became the drone of dozens of flies diligently searching the clearing for decay to feast upon.

He spent the next few minutes slicing the wings off every insect he could find, imagining that he was in a battle for his life – the last line of defense against an army of winged invaders. Gradually, his enthusiasm changed to anger as the flies took on the specter of the creature who had attacked him and permanently altered the course of his life, the devil who had tried to destroy everyone Chris had grown to care about: Cara, Rachel, and her unborn baby. Tears were streaming freely from his eyes by the time the last fly fell.

He stood with his head down, trying to get his emotions back under control, when he heard a slow, deliberate patter of applause from behind him echo sarcastically across the glen like a hushed crowd at a golf tournament.

"Nicely done. I'm sure you'll make a very fine exterminator, the terror of all that buzzzzezz," Everton said with deadpan sarcasm. "Now, if you are about finished, Amym would like to see you in the dojo."

The anger and depression he had been feeling became irritation at having his privacy intruded upon and mocked. "Fine!" Chris snapped as he stomped off down the trail. He was glad that Everton was walking slowly and, as the distance between them increased, he was able to wipe his eyes without feeling as if he were being scrutinized and judged. When Chris cleared the trees he headed directly for the dojo and was happy to notice that Everton split off towards the lodge.

The inside was pitch black; the lights were off and the shutters were closed, plunging the practice space into complete darkness. He reached out for the light switch, which he thought should be on the wall by the door. "Leave them off," came a disembodied voice from the darkness.

"What's going on?" Chris asked starting to get a little nervous.

"If you are determined not to stay where we can protect you, then we will have to step up your training so that you can protect yourself," said the voice of his mentor.

"I'm sorry about sneaking out again. I already had it out with Joyce, and I know what you are doing for me."

Amym continued as if Chris hadn't spoken. "You need to learn not to rely on any one sense too heavily. Prepare to defend yourself."

"Come on! It's already been a really bad day... do we have to do this now? How about if we..." His complaint was cut off by a fist smashing into the side if his head. Bright spots flashed in front of him as he staggered trying to keep his feet. "Shit, that hurt!" Chris exclaimed.

"In addition to the wavelengths in the visual spectrum, we have the ability to perceive infrared radiation. You also have your hearing, senses of smell, and touch – all of which are vastly superior to what you once knew when you were human. You need to accept that and learn to make use of them. What can you hear?"

Chris listened closely and thought he could hear a slight rustling sound accompanied by a subtle shift in the air just before a foot buried itself in his stomach, sending him flying backward to land hard. He rubbed the side of his head where it had made contact with the floor. "Open yourself to fully inhabit your body. Eliminate outside distractions and push past what you thought were your limits. They no longer apply to you."

Chris sat up, closed his eyes, and focused on the space around him. There was a sound, like the fluttering of bird wings in the far distance. He turned all his attention towards the sound. The closer he listened the more he could discern it was footsteps, bare feet on the Tatami mats, toes digging in to quiet each step. Chris started to smile, he was really doing it, he could actually hear Amym moving around the dojo.

"The opportunity to defeat the enemy is provided by the enemy himself. Attack him where he is unprepared, appear where you are not expected." Suddenly, Chris was grabbed by the front of his shirt and lifted off the ground, then a hand slapped him hard across the face.

"Being aware of your surroundings includes knowing when you are about to be attacked and where the attack will originate. Try again."

Once again, Chris focused on the sounds in the room. He could hear the wood under the mat creek somewhere to his right. He strained to hear footsteps as he had before but there was none of the telltale rustling, only another creek of the subfloor. *You are not capable of this*, came a voice in his head. *You have no chance of survival without your friends.*

He tried to block out his doubt and listen to the space around him. He heard the wood creak as it shifted a little, closer than it had before. Instinctively, he dropped to the floor just in time to feel the wind from Amym's kick sail over his head. *You will not be so lucky again, once your friends are all dead.*

"Better. Now open your eyes. What do you see?" Amym asked.

Chris turned his head from side to side but the shutters were very effective at blocking out even the suggestion of light. "I can't see anything, just black," he said.

"Black is not an absolute. Look for the nuances, the subtle differences in the darkness. Put it together with what you hear, what you feel, what you smell. Use all your senses to map out your surroundings in your mind."

The more Chris thought about it, the more he thought that maybe he could detect deeper and lighter shades of darkness. He turned his head in the direction of a slight rustling sound in time to see a vaguely oval-shaped patch of a slightly lighter shade of black, rushing straight towards his face. He blocked the blow just as his sensei had taught him, and kicked his leg out to sweep his opponent off his feet. To his dismay, Chris found nothing but empty space. As he came back to a ready stance, a foot slammed into his back between his shoulder blades. He landed face-first on the mat but rolled away before his opponent could stomp on his stomach, and hopped back onto his feet.

"Do not swallow bait offered by the enemy. Were you able to see me?"

"I could see something, I guess it was you."

"Good. With practice, you will be able to see and feel the heat coming off your advisory, feel the changes in the air when they move, predict what they will do by a shift of their weight or a muscle twitching beneath the skin."

No, this is all for nothing, the voice taunted within his head. *You cannot escape your fate.*

Amym did something on the far end of the room and the shutters began to open, letting in the afternoon light. Chris looked down and covered his eye to block the sudden brightness and noticed the dried blood from his earlier practice staining the mats. It brought back the image of Rachel's blood pooling on the green painted floorboards of the Avenue C tenement they had shared only a few weeks earlier.

Your friends will suffer and die because of you, and there is nothing you can do to prevent it.

"Are you okay?" Amym asked coming over and laying a supportive hand on Chris' shoulder.

"What's the point of all this? I'll never be strong enough to face that monster on my own, all that will happen is that the people close to me will keep getting killed. Maybe I should just go and face him now and get it over with."

"Come up to my office," Amym said gently and led him up the stairs.

When they were seated and Chris had a cup of blood-laced tea, Amym leaned forward in his seat, "So what's going on? I understand your depression and your guilt, those will lessen with time, but it seems to me there is more here."

"It's nothing. Just... the more time I spend learning how to defend myself, the more of a waste of time it seems, you know? I just don't see the point."

"Do you want to live?" Amym asked.

"Yeah, sure I do, but..."

"No! Do you really want to live? Because you don't seem to realize how vulnerable you are right now. If you do, you will have to rid yourself of all negative influences, both internal and external."

Chris thought about that for a moment. "What do you mean external influences? You mean... like... my friends?"

"You are bonded with the creature that changed you, you have a psychic link. When the Gift is bestowed upon someone deliberately, that link can be an effective means of control. However, in a situation such as yours, where the Gift was passed accidentally, that link could be an annoying distraction. A liability."

"So, he could control me? Could he take over my body and make me do things?"

"I have never heard of one being able to completely take over someone's body, but I suppose it's not an impossibility. What the link does is it allows the maker to subvert the will of the Lesser Blessed to a greater or lesser degree, depending on the maker's desire and the strength of his progeny. You will feel the pressure of their will steering you towards their ends. You may hear their voice in your head telling you what they want. You might even have visions of them."

"I have been having dreams. Some are awful...." Chris hedged, not wanting to tell Amym about the more explicit dreams he'd been having recently.

"It's likely that you have been under psychic attack, though probably not a deliberate one. You need to take this seriously: If he can get into your thoughts, then he could get you to give him your location and seek out those you care about. He could simply force you to lower your defenses and kill you outright, or he could break your will entirely and make you his slave."

"What can I do about it? My abilities are pathetic, he could tear through me like nothing."

"Not long ago, you were unaware that you had any abilities. Give it time... they will improve with practice like any other skill. As for what you can do? First, you must be aware of how these attacks can manifest. You may hear voices in your head, you may have recurring or frequent nightmares, you could have visions or hallucinations, experience feelings of irrational fear, anger or sorrow. You might have the feeling of being watched when no one is there or feel their touch on your skin. These are all signs that your maker is influencing you."

"Yeah, I've had most of those."

"The techniques for defense are simple, so simple they sometimes seem ridiculous, but they are difficult to implement. The first thing you need to do is be fully present in the moment. That means don't think too much about what has happened in the past and what you think will happen in the future. Don't worry about what is happening somewhere else outside your influence and don't let those things affect the present. Fear leaves you open, so address the things you are frightened of, accept them as your feelings, change what you can and accept the fact that you can't change them all. You can use deep breathing exercises to help combat fear and anxiety," Amym explained.

"Secondly, include time for meditation in your daily routine. Practice visualization techniques, like making a wall of fire, water, earth or air as your shield against the aggressor. Picturing something you have actually seen in your mind – a bonfire or a waterfall can make your shield even more effective. You can also picture something like a bubble, or an additional layer of skin surrounding your body, then imagine it becoming hard, impermeable, so that nothing your adversary tries will penetrate it."

    "Don't worry, I'm pretty good at this," he said reassuringly. "Come here in the evenings after dinner, and I'll help you practice."

Chapter 6

Ile de Biesse, October 25, 1440

A soft rain was falling in the early morning hours. Leaves blew across the pastures until they littered the roads like a carpet spread over the sticky mud. The day had not yet dawned, but already a crowd of local townspeople had begun to gather in the streets of Nantes outside the ducal palace where the trial was being conducted. Not a soul in the area wanted to miss the final confessions and condemnations.

The prisoner was led into the chamber before an angry throng which had gathered to see that justice was finally done. He was pushed down roughly into the plain, wooden chair that occupied the center of the room. A long table stood on a dais at the far side of the room, and the face of the Bishop looked down sternly while the rest of the collected clergy were occupied shuffling papers and exchanging whispers between one another.

A Deacon stepped forward from the end of the table. "Gilles de Montmorency-Laval, having heard the charges presented against you, having been read the testimonies of the witnesses and the accounts of those who conspired with you to commit your heinous crimes, have you anything to say?"

This was what he had been preparing for: The performance that would determine the course of his existence. He clasped his hands together in his lap, rose to his feet, and slowly lifted his eyes to the table. His gaze looking beseechingly along the panel of priests until he stopped at the disdainful face of the Bishop.

"It is very true, my lords, that I have done many terrible things," he began.

"What things, my son? You must unburden yourself by making a full account of your crimes. Only then will your soul find peace," the Bishop said.

"It is true that I am a sinner, and of all sinners, perhaps the most detestable, having sinned with my body and soul in many, many occurrences." Gilles could feel the weight of twelve hundred

86

years of church doctrine pressing down on him. He was surprised to find that a part of him actually did want to unburden himself and did want to return to the good grace of the one holy Catholic and Apostolic Church. It was simply the influence of long years of living within the Church's influence and nothing based upon reality, but it disturbed him that he should be even remotely swayed by their superstitions.

"But the truth is also that I have never lacked in my duty toward religion: Hearing many Masses, Vespers and Prayers, fasting at the holy times of Lent and at Feast Day vigils, confessing and deploring the said sins that Nature has made me commit, and receiving very devoutly the blood of Our Lord at least once a year."

"And what of heretical writings?" asked the Bishop.

"Yes, many such blasphemous books had I among my possession," admitted Gilles.

"Many of the volumes that were uncovered are known to the church, yet some few are as yet unknown. Like this curious volume," he said, reaching to receive a leather-bound codex from one of the deacons.

"That is an evil book, your holiness," Gilles cautioned.

"Undoubtedly, but we cannot decipher its meaning," the Bishop said as he casually turned page after page of indecipherable symbols. "What is contained within these foul pages?"

"In truth, I do not know, your holiness – nor does any man alive. It was written by the hand of the Devil himself in the language of the Fallen. I pray that you burn it along with all the others for the sake of the immortal souls of all that might encounter it."

"Yes, perhaps, but now the moment has come to render account to God."

Gilles took a deep breath before beginning. "I have ravished children from their mothers. These children... I have killed them or had them killed, either by slitting their throats with a dagger or knife, or by separating the head from the body with an ax, or by breaking the skull with a stick or hammer, or by splitting their chest, or by opening their belly. Sometimes, by attaching them with a cord to an iron hook, other times by burning them..."

The accused seemed to be working himself into an agitated state, so the Bishop interrupted his litany of tortures and murderous techniques. "How many children?" he asked sternly.

"The count would be long, and I recall less their names than their heads before and after death. In truth, the demon tormented me often, and I confess to having invoked him many times. But, before doing it, I heard Mass and confessed myself so that the devil could not bite into my soul," Gilles insisted.

"How many children?" demanded his inquisitor.

Gilles bit down hard onto his tongue, the sharp pain making his eye start to water. He hoped it gave the impression of genuine contrition he was trying to portray. He lowered his head, eyes downcast, and let the tears trickle along his cheeks. "Around one hundred and twenty each year," he admitted through his tears.

After a moment the Bishop rose to his feet and descended the dais to stand in front of Gilles. He placed the weeping man's head onto his shoulder. "Cry," he said, genuinely moved. "Cry so that your tears can cleanse the churning charnel house of your soul."

"I, who was the instrument of my own downfall, may I be, by my repentance, the instrument of my salvation."

Gilles allowed himself a few more moments before straightening up. "My lords," he said to the assembled clergy, then turned to address the audience. "And you, good people who are in this place, hear my last confession and interest yourselves in the salvation of my poor soul as a reward for my admissions. I have merited an exemplary punishment both by men and by God, whose punishment I accept with patience as the expiation of my sins and preparation for eternal life."

When the sentence of Cord and Fire was finally pronounced, Gilles again asked to speak. "I, detestable sinner that I am, thank God for having had me condemned according to my merits. My sins are so grievous as to warrant no reprieve, and I heartily agree that my life should be forfeit in penance for my crimes. I ask only to be executed at the same time as my misguided accomplices so as to be afforded the opportunity to exhort them and show them the example of dying well."

"Your request shall be accorded, My Lord, and, because of your contrition, I again accord you that, the execution over, your body shall be removed from the fire before it starts to burn, and shall be carried into the church of your choice."

When there were sounds of descent from the gallery, Gilles rose and faced the audience. "Good people who are here present to see what will be my end. I remind you that I am your Christian brother. Therefore, pray for me. I entreat the fathers and mothers of the children that I have killed to please forgive me and pray God for me in memory of the Passion of Our Lord. Do not be more inflexible toward me than God! When my soul leaves my body, I desire that, with my money, there be founded at Machecoul, Tiffauges and other places, Masses and Anniversaries in memory of certain mistreated children. For which I feel a bitter displeasure."

"May my Lord Saint Michael receive you and present you to God," the Bishop said, laying a comforting hand on the shoulder of the condemned.

Chris lay on his bed, his eyes closed, headphones covering his ears, listening to his pre-recorded instructor repeat conversational phrases in German. The air in the room suddenly began to swirl and change directions, enhanced with a fragrance that he recognized instantly. He opened his eyes and found Joyce closing the door behind her. She was wearing an oversize t-shirt, her coal black hair hanging in wavy curls halfway down her black, her alabaster legs vanishing beneath the faded, black cotton. She turned around and crossed to his bed. The mattress shifted, and she sat down on the edge. Chris scooted over to give her space, feeling a little self-conscious about his lack of clothing being next to her with her lack of clothing.

"Deutsch lernen?" she asked as he took the headphones off. "Do you need any help with your lessons? I'm quite fluent, and I thought that after such a difficult day, you could use some company," she said smiling down at him. " I hope you don't mind."

"No! Why would I mind?" he stammered.

She turned towards him, one leg laying flat in the bed, her bare foot tucked behind her other knee. Chris' heart began to beat faster at the way the muscles of her dancer's legs bunched. He followed the curves of flawless white skin up her leg until he caught a glimpse of her black panties nestled into the soft waves of her inner thighs. "I thought you would probably enjoy a full body massage, and then next time you can return the favor," she said, waving a bottle of oil in the air.

"'Um... okay. Sure," he said, pulling his attention back from her tantalizing depths.

"Now you just lay back and relax. This will make those tired muscles feel much better." She swung her leg over to straddle him, her knees making deep indentations into the bedding, her feet hooked above his knees.

She squeezed out the oil into her palm, then tossed the bottle away. She warmed it up by rubbing it between her hands before applying it to his chest, working it in with her strong fingers. The hem of her faded Bauhaus - Bela Lugosi's Dead t-shirt was pinned between them, being stretched and pulled far down between the mounds of her breasts. She leaned forward, bracing herself with her hands on his chest. A necklace of shiny black beads on a silver chain swayed hypnotically like a pendulum as she slid forward and back, grinding her pelvis against his.

"Do you like this?" she asked, reaching up to roll the beads between her glistening fingers. "You should keep it with you. It will protect you. It would be a good idea for you to keep them on you at all times."

She sat upright and lifted the necklaces over her head, took him by the wrist, and raised his hand. Gently she wound the delicate string of beads around his wrist, resting the back of his hand against her chest to close the clasp, then lay his hand on her thigh as she continued grinding him into incoherence.

Chris lifted his other hand to the opposite leg, and when she didn't protest, he slowly began sliding them up the length of her muscular thighs. Her skin was warm and smooth, and he could feel the muscles flex under her silky skin. He began to notice himself swelling uncomfortably with arousal.

His hands traveled further until they found the taut fabric of her shirt. He slid his fingertips beneath the folds and pulled her shirt out from between them, exposing a wedge of black cloth. The front of her panties had a pair of bright, white fangs with BITE ME written in dripping red letters.

She reached down between them, her hand sliding easily beneath the elastic of his shorts. Her fingers felt cold as she wrapped them around the base of his cock, freeing him from his uncomfortably twisted positioning. Her fingertips stroked the length of his shaft, sending a shudder through him when her fingernails scraped lightly across the crown.

She lowered herself back down, nestling him into her warm cleft, and resumed rocking back and forth. Chris wrapped his hands around her hips, his fingers tightening, pressing into the soft flesh as she brought him closer and closer to release. Her dark hair hung down around her obscuring her face, hiding her expression. But through the black strands, he could see the flash of her lavender eyes and her sharp, brilliantly white teeth against her cabernet-colored lips.

Soon, he was torn between feelings of pleasure and pain as the friction increased; the soft fabric of her panties began to rub uncomfortable against the sensitive underside of his shaft. He reached around behind her, gripping her ass, pulling her firmly against him as he finally let go and collapsed on to the bed beneath her.

Chris sat up, panting. He was alone in his room; his sheets tangled around his legs, headphones lying forgotten on the mattress next to him. His cock was achingly hard from the dream. He reached up to wipe the sleep from his eyes and heard the clatter of beads. He held out his right hand and there, wrapped around his wrist, was Joyce's necklace. *So it couldn't have been a dream*, he thought. *At least not entirely.* But what was real and what was just in his head, he couldn't quite decide.

He got out of bed and pulled on a pair of black fatigue shorts, then headed towards the library. He paused in front of Joyce's room, tempted to knock, but he couldn't quite seem to raise his hand to do it. He thought about his hand knocking on the door, her opening it in her nightshirt. Would she be wearing the same one she wore in his dream, he wondered. Would she be happy to see him, or would she be pissed off that he had woken her up? As a more experienced vampire, did she still sleep? Did she only sleep during the day? Would he eventually become completely nocturnal? *Maybe I could find a book on it,* he thought as he continued along the balcony.

When he entered the library, he found Amym sitting in one of the wingback chairs reading a book with a cracked leather binding. "Good evening, Christian," he said, closing the book and laying it on the end table. "I hear you are making good progress with your hand to hand training. I'm sorry that I scheduled our lesson right after your fist edged weapon session. If I had known, I might have postponed, though I trust you were fully recovered."

Chris flopped down into the other chair. "Yeah, I was okay. I thought it would be more fun and less... stabby," he said.

"Shihan Hisao can be a hard master. How have your language studies been going?" He asked. But before Chris could answer, he said, "That is an interesting bauble you are wearing," indicating the necklaces wound around Chris' wrist.

Chris blushed. "Well... I had this dream, and when I woke up, there it was. I think maybe Joyce gave it to me."

"That would make sense. That is black tourmaline, a gemstone from Sri Lanka used for protection. Now that I think about it, perhaps she would be better suited to work with you on your mental defenses after all. Joyce is a master of psychic influence." He gave Chris a mischievous smile.

"That's a little bit scary."

"Then perhaps you should be a little bit *wary*," Amym joked, chuckling at his rhyme.

Chris sat silently, picking at his nails. "Um..." he finally began. "If someone is in your dreams... do you just see what they want you to see?"

"Your dreams are still your own. Your mind can determine what happens if you are aware that it's a dream and have the desire to control it. The intruder can influence it, change the setting, set the situation, but you would be able to control your own actions and even determine the outcome. With practice, of course."

"Would they be able to see what I see?" Chris asked with growing apprehension.

Amym took a moment to study Chris' face before answering. "If someone has invaded your dreams, then they are sharing the experience with you. They will be in control of the scenario, bending it to their own ends unless you wrest away control and alter the direction, either consciously or subconsciously."

"Oh, okay. Thanks."

"Did you have something specific you were concerned about?"

"No! Nothing specific. I was just wondering," Chris said quickly, hoping to end that line of discussion before anything too embarrassing came out. It was going to be hard enough facing Joyce now that he knew more about how this whole thing worked. Maybe she hadn't been in his dreams at all. Maybe they were just normal dreams that she didn't know anything about, he hoped.

Chris looked down at his hands, fidgeting with the beads, painfully aware that Amym was just sitting there watching him. The silence seemed to stretch on and on, and Chris wished he would just pick his book up and go back to reading. However, he just kept looking at him with a bemused expression on his face. "These creatures... the vampires... what are they?" He finally asked. "Where did they come from?"

Amym took a deep breath. "Their story is one you are likely familiar with, although the Judeo-Christian account is extremely one-dimensional. After the expulsion from Paradise, God sent the Watchers to oversee humanity. They were not supposed to interfere with human development, but they couldn't help playing God themselves. They bred a new race among the population and introduced concepts that had not previously been dreamt of before. Their offspring were the Nephilim, enormous creatures with insatiable and indiscriminate appetites," Amym explained.

Now that they were in familiar territory and Chris felt confident that his extreme religious upbringing gave him the knowledge he needed to participate in the conversation without feeling like an idiot. "I know all about them," he said. "God sent the flood to wipe them out."

"The flood was caused by a combination of heavy rains and an untimely earthquake that weakened the earth where Khasab now sits, on the outskirts of Dubai. A natural dam collapsed, allowing the Arabian Sea to rush into the valley of Ur, drowning the Nephilim and most of the human population beneath what is now the Persian Gulf. Some might say it was a simple natural occurrence, others would see the direct hand of God setting things to rights," Amym continued.

"God destroyed the Nephilim and set the rainbow in the sky as a symbol of his vow to never again inflict such destruction upon the earth. Then, Noah and his family rebuilt the human race," Chris said, though his feeling of self-assuredness was starting to fade.

"A very sweet and simple fable," Amym said, an indulgent smile crossing his face. "But the truth is often messier than the retelling. There was no Noah. The Semites first heard the flood story during their captivity in Babylon and incorporated it into their own mythology. The original story told of a man named Atram-Hasis, who survived the flood in a round coracle boat made of reeds called a ma-gur, used to transport livestock from one bank of the river to the other. Whether his survival was by chance or divine interference, no one will ever know. But, however you view these events, the story did not end there. A single Nephilim survived and spawned the vampire race and the watchers were 'bound in the valleys of the Earth until the day of judgment.' At least, according to some of the oldest human writings. But, the important thing is that the Watchers were not destroyed. The vampires believe that they sleep until the day that they can be awakened to resume the war for supremacy in the Far-World."

Chris thought for a moment before finally saying, "I don't understand. What is the Far-World?"

"The Far World has been called by many names, but for ease of explaining it, we'll use the word *heaven*."

"Vampires want to take over heaven!? How do you know all these things?" Chris asked with both astonishment and doubt plainly visible on his face. He had never had any cause to question his mother's teachings that the bible was the literal word of God, written down without error by his faithful emissaries on Earth and dutifully imparted to the masses so that all might find their way to

God's grace. What Amym was telling him was shocking, but if there was nothing substantial to back up his claims, Chris felt that he could dismiss them and remain confident in his beliefs.

"There is a book, known as the Gibborilium, kept by the True Born and passed down through the generations. Each vampire copies his from that of his sire, and each adds the important events that occur during his lifetime to it. Therefore, no two copies are quite the same. I have never seen a complete copy, but from the fragments I have collected from those creatures I have been called upon to dispatch, the most ancient stories appear to be identical. At least, from what I could decipher."

"Why couldn't you read them? I thought we could learn languages."

"We can," Amym assured. "Any *human* language. But, the oldest passages are written in something else. To me, it looks like columns of constellations, but I have been able to identify a few characters that I believe represent names."

"Can I see these pieces?" Chris asked.

"I would happily share them with you, but when I kill an ancient, I am required to collect these texts and return them to the Chord. I assume it is to ensure their destruction but there is a possibility that they are collecting and collating a central history of their race. However, I can do the next best thing." He took a sheet of paper and pencil from the writing desk and began scribbling furiously. With his enhanced memory, Amym could easily reproduce exact replicas of the texts. When he was finished, he handed the completed document to Chris.

On the page were column after column of diagrams that did resemble constellations without the familiar human and animal shapes connecting the dots. Chris pondered the patterns, running his eyes up and down the columns. There were symbols that seemed to repeat but he wasn't sure if they were letters or some sort of pictograms, or maybe something else entirely.

"A portion of this alphabet, containing only 22 symbols, was discovered and made public in occult writings of the sixteenth century. It was called Angelic script, or the Celestial Alphabet, which seems as appropriate a name as any other, so it has stuck."

Chris lay the page on the polished wooden table, studying line after line of tightly spaced, handwritten symbols packed onto the sheet. "It looks like a simple replacement cipher. Each symbol represents a number, and the number corresponds to a letter, right? I read about them in that codes and ciphers book. I just can't figure out which language."

"All of them, if you know the key. But, there's more to it than that. The symbols don't correspond to numbers. No, I believe they represent sounds. And the constellations may have meanings in numerology. I'm not sure what else. The difficulty is that there are more sounds represented than the human voice is capable of."

Chris looked at him uncomprehending. "The modern English alphabet has twenty-six letters, but it once had twelve more that have been replaced over time by combinations of other letters, like Yogh which is now GH, or Eng now ING," Amym explained. "Other languages have more or less letters. For example, German has 30 letters, Persian has 32, Irish only 20, and Chinese may have as many as 60,000 characters representing different concepts rather than distinct sounds.

"Ant idea what it says?"

"There is a divergence in the vampire community," Amym said. "Most are content to maintain the status quo, to maintain their highly influential, yet nearly invisible presence in a human-dominated world. A few would like to dominate and subjugate all of humanity. To be the undisputed masters of this reality. There is, however, a growing number that believe they can return to the Far-World by fulfilling an ancient prophecy and waking the Sleepers."

"How do they plan to take over? I mean, God would stop them. He is God after all," Chris suggested.

"This text, I believe, is the key to understanding. Decoding it would explain why they are so secretive about it, and why they will protect its mysteries with their immortal lives."

Chapter 7

After breakfast, Christ walked across the dew-dampened grass to the dojo. It had been a long summer and the early morning fall air had a definite chill to it. He opened the door and stepped inside, expecting to find his teacher waiting for him in the center of the room for the start of their lesson. What he found was Sensei Hisao, Amym, Joyce, and a man he had never seen before standing around a folding table covered with black, hard-sided cases of varying sizes.

Chris stopped a few feet away out of respect for their conversation, despite the ease with which he could overhear every word they said. His eyes wandered the room in a self-conscious way of trying to appear not to be eavesdropping. After a few moments, Amym waived for him to join them.

"Chris, this is Michèle Blanchard. He is one of a very few who can be considered the best weapons maker in the world."

The man extended a calloused hand. "Hello, Chris," he said, pronouncing it as *aloe* in his thick French accent. "It is a pleasure to meet you."

Chris thought about replying in French as he shook the man's hand across the stack of cases, but decided that it might come across as rude or presumptive. "Nice to meet you also." He replied instead.

"Michèle has brought new toys," Amym said with a hint of child-like excitement.

"Are were ready then?" the man asked.

"Yes, please proceed, Maître Blanchard," Amym replied eagerly.

The weapons smith took the two smaller cases off the top of the pile and set them aside. He opened the longest one and turned it to face Amym. Inside, nestled into custom cut foam padding covered with black satin, lay a sword. "It is loosely based on a Yatagan, but shorter, like a Katana. Designed for close quarters combat. I assumed you wouldn't be using it from horseback."

"No, that is unlikely," Amym said with some humor, anticipation, and something akin to lust clearly visible on his face.

Michèle lifted the sword from the case and slowly removed the black, leather sheath. "The blade is made from a thousand layers of forge welded Damascus steel." He rested the blade across his forearm and extended the hilt to Amym, who carefully studied the acid enhanced patterning in the metal after accepting the weapon. "The grip and scabbard are calfskin with silver fittings. I have given it an Egyptian motif in deference to your background."

Amym stepped back from the table, bouncing the blade in the air a few times before beginning his practice forms. After a less than a minute, he returned to the table, slid the blade back into the scabbard, and lay it back into the depression in its case. "It is a masterpiece. I am humbled to accept such a fine weapon," Amym said with a bow.

"It is only piece of steel. Pretty, but only as fine as the one that wields it. May you ever be victorious while it is in your hand." He slid the case to the side and moved the next largest case to the front. He opened it to reveal a black and silver over/under shotgun in a black leather sheath, a coil of belts wound around it. The Smith picked it up, slid it from the sheath, and handed it to Amym. The silver barrels shortened to the point that only two inches protruded beyond the end of the shells, and intricately engraved filigree decorated their truncated lengths. The stock had been removed and an ebony ball handle grip inlaid with an elegant floral pattern of mother of pearl and silver wire installed in its place.

"I started with an Ithaca 12 gauge shotgun and shortened it as much as possible. The kick would break the wrist of a normal man, but I imagine you will be able to handle it," he chuckled slightly. "The engravings and filigree on the grip were designed based on the photos you sent of your flintlock, and all the metal parts have been polished and chromed to prevent corrosion."

"The craftsmanship is extraordinary. I'm honored," Amym marveled while running his hand across the exquisite detailing.

"It took two months to engrave and I had to bring the engraver out of retirement, so I wouldn't count on him being available if you ever want another done. Training a competent could take twenty years, so I'm glad you pay well," he joked.

"This is true, but the shock of a high price tag does not outlive the memory of poor quality. I will treasure these for many,

many years, but you might want to get started on plan B just in case," Amym said and motioned for Chris to come closer. "And now, I also have something for you. Sensei Hisao, if you would do the honors."

When Sensei Hisao stepped up to the table, the Smith picked up the smallest case and handed it to him. Chris' teacher held the case in his hands and regarded him seriously for several long moments. "Christian, at first I doubted that you had the discipline to achieve any level of mastery. Now I am happy to say that you have indeed proven me wrong. You have worked hard over the last few months and you should be proud of your progress... as I am." He released the clasps and opened the lid.

Chris looked inside the open case, nestled in its bed of shiny black fabric was a black handled, fourteen-inch khukuri knife in an unadorned black leather sheath. His face looked completely crestfallen. Joyce and the surrounding men began trying to suppress their smiles, but she did give him a reassuring wink. Michèle extended his hand. "If you would, please."

"Of course, thank you so much," Chris said trying to be polite, despite his disappointment. When he took the knife from the case, he discovered that the other side of the handle was white.

"One side is Ceylon ebony from southern India, the other is bleached White Oak from Connecticut. The rivets are surgical steel: They will not tarnish. And while normally I would say they would never break, I know the sort of punishment they may be subjected to." Chris slowly drew the sheath away from the blade. As soon as the metal was exposed, he could see that it was made of the same marbled steel as Amym's sword. His pulse began to quicken as another half inch was revealed, showing that the blade was also engraved.

He pulled the sheath away and looked in wonder at the design carved into the metal of the inwardly curving blade. The side with the ebony handle depicted highly stylized fire and smoke, while the oak handled side was decorated with rolling clouds. "I had asked that it be designed to represent the dual nature of man in the Nepalese style, which is where this type of blade originated," Sensei Hisao said.

"The scabbard can be worn either across your lower back or between your shoulder blades, with the handle up or down as you prefer."

"It's incredible. I don't know what to say. Thank you," Chris stammered.

"You have earned it with your dedication and hard work. I know you will use it with skill and discretion," he said, beaming with as much pride as his stoic face would allow. Joyce put her arm around Chris' shoulder and squeezed in next to him to get a look.

Amym turned to the smith. "Thank you, Michèle, your timing was impeccable," he said, shaking the smith's hand. Then, turning to where Joyce stood congratulating Chris and admiring the intricacies of his new weapon, he said: "It is time for you two to pack your things, we have been recalled to the city."

"What's going on?" Joyce asked, her expression of pride and pleasure immediately evaporated and she was now all business.

"I'm not sure, but I expect that the Chord feels they have given Chris long enough to prepare and now wish to examine him themselves. We must all endeavor to make the best impression possible."

The car came to a stop in front of an embossed, aluminum-paneled office building on Fifth Avenue, between 52nd and 53rd Streets. Chris' nerves had been getting worse and worse throughout the drive down to the city from Haven. Steve got out of the car and stood beside the passenger door, waiting for Amym's signal to open it for them.

"Before we go in," Amym began. "I need to impress upon you the gravity of this situation. The Lesser Blessed are only tolerated so long as we serve a purpose. I have proposed an idea for their consideration, but I haven't received a response. Do not do anything that might be considered irreverent or disrespectful." He stressed and paused long enough to emphasize the importance of what he was saying. He needed to make sure Chris was taking this seriously. "All our lives depend on it."

As Amym turned and headed in the direction of the entrance, Joyce linked her arm with Chris' and tilted her head towards his. "Everything you want is on the other side of fear. The challenge is letting go of it," she whispered in his ear.

The three of them crossed the white marble lobby. An illuminated ceiling sculpture, made up of gently curving metal panels titled "Landscape of the Cloud" by the Japanese sculptor Isamu Noguchi, gave the feeling of walking among the clouds. A guard stepped out from behind the information desk and met them at the bank of chromed elevator doors. He nodded politely to Amym, pulled out a ring of keys on a retractable chain attached to his belt, and started flipping through the keys. Chris thought that the entire situation bore an uncanny resemblance to Saint Peter struggling to unlock the pearly gates.

When the guard finally located the correct key, he inserted it into an unmarked keyhole on the panel next to the elevator door and turned it until both the up and down buttons lit. When the doors opened, Chris followed Amym and Joyce into the compartment. All the numbered buttons were lit up as if some kid had run his hands across them all. The doors closed behind him, and he waited for the floor to lurch as the elevator started to move, but nothing happened.

They stood waiting for what seemed like an eternity. Chris was beginning to wonder if they were stuck and should call someone to let them out when the doors opened again. He expected to step back into the lobby, but during the few minutes they had been inside, the whole building seemed to have changed.

Rather than the harsh, white marble and bright lighting of the building's entrance, they exited into a perfectly ordinary-looking office lobby. Chris wasn't sure what he had been expecting; maybe something grander, more opulent, with lots of gold, or more ominous with everything painted black and lots of fire, Instead, the completely normal, human-looking receptionist behind a standard wooden desk, pressed a few buttons on a numeric keypad and the elevator doors slid quietly closed behind them. When Chris turned his head at the sound, he noticed that there were no buttons to call for it to return. He didn't even know what floor he was on. Chris was unsure if they had they gone up or down, or been transported into another dimension entirely. It was impossible to say. A few short months ago, things had seemed so normal. Now, it seemed anything at all could happen.

The receptionist stood up and walked around her desk to one of several pairs of double doors that lined the room. She pushed the doors open and stepped aside. "Gentlemen and lady, please make yourselves comfortable in the conference room until you are called. Can I get anyone anything while you wait?" she asked.

"Thank you, no," Amym answered for the group as they each chose a spot around the oval conference table and sat in the plush, black leather, high-back executive chairs.

Chris noticed that when the receptionist closed the doors, they had no handles or latches on the inside, only large expanses of polished wood. He wondered if they would even be able to break through them if they needed to, or if they were reinforced somehow. *Maybe the whole place is vampire proofed*, he thought.

After what felt like forever, the doors finally opened and a tall man with perfectly combed black hair and an expensive suit entered. He closed the door behind him and said, "Amym, it's good to see you again."

Amym stood up and bowed his head to the man. "And you also, Bashshar."

"It has been too long. I will admit that I have missed your presence since I have been away."

"Did you find what you were looking for?" Amym inquired.

"No, not yet, but the search continues," he said with a sigh. "I have presented your proposal to the Chord and it seems as though it may be a possibility, but the other members would like some clarification. If you would please accompany me, we'll see if we can't accommodate you on this matter."

As he led Amym towards the door, it opened automatically, allowing them to pass out of the room, then closed again behind them. "What do you think that was about?" Chris asked.

"You, of course," Joyce replied and busied herself with twirling one of her purple streaks of hair around the index finger in a nervous tick that Chris had never suspected she had.

Chris sat quietly, wondering what, if anything, the future held for him. When the door reopened, a young Spanish man in a white lab coat entered carrying a small, metal tray covered with a white cloth. "Hey," the man said jovially. "Are you Christian? I'm Raymond. I just need to take a small sample for our records."

"A sample of what?" Chris asked nervously.

The man pulled off the cover, and laying on the tray was a syringe and two empty glass tubes. "Blood, of course. It's sort of our specialty around here," he said with a wink that was intended to be reassuring.

"What do you do with it, drink it?"

"Did you want to do shots?" He held up one of the tubes and wiggled it back and forth. "These don't even hold a mouthful. With these, we can determine the lineage of your sire and test the strength of your bloodline." He inserted the vile into the syringe, laid it back onto the tray, and picked up a length of latex tubing. "Do you have a preference?"

"Of what?"

"Right or left arm?"

"Oh, left, I guess," Chris said and held out his bare arm.

The man wrapped the tubing tightly around his bicep. "When we're finished I'll bring you in for your evaluation."

Even though he had spent the previous few months being beaten and sliced up with a wide variety of weapon, Chris didn't want to watch the needle puncture his skin. Instead, he turned his head to look at Joyce, who gave him a reassuring smile just as the point was pushed into his arm. "There we are," the tech said. Chris looked down to see a spout of dark red blood begin to fill the vile. After a few seconds, the full tube was swapped out and the second vial inserted in its place. When the syringe was removed, the tech pressed his thumb over the puncture for a few seconds. Upon removing his finger, Chris expected there to be a small wound or at least a red spot, but his arm was already fully healed.

The tech stood up and organized his tray. "All set?" he asked Chris.

"Not really."

Joyce came around the table and gave him a hug. "You'll be fine," she said reassuringly.

"You're not coming with me?" Chris asked with surprise.

She shrugged her shoulders and replied, "I wasn't called."

A distressed look flashed across his face. "But... you'll be here when I come back though, right?"

"I hope so," she said somberly. "Now go. You don't want to keep them waiting."

Chris followed the tech out of the conference room and across the lobby to another set of heavy wooden double doors. They stood there waiting for several seconds before the doors were opened from the inside. The room beyond was dark, and the tech stepped to the side to allow Chris to enter. He expected the man to follow him in but the doors closed between them. A few steps in front of him, Amym stood in the center of the room, facing a curved table where thirteen men and women, of various ages, all wearing expensive black clothing and jewelry, sat under individual mini spotlights set high in the darkness above.

Amym turned to look at him, gave him a small smile, and indicated that he should come and stand next to him. "This is the boy in question?" a man in a black silk shirt with a silver crew cut asked.

"It is, my lord," Amym answered.

"And it is your true belief that he is suited to the task you propose?"

"It is, but I would ask to be allowed to assist him, at least in the beginning, my lord," Amym requested.

"That is not possible. We have other matters that require your attention. You will be given instructions shortly, I assume you are prepared to travel?"

"As the Chord wills," Amym replied with an immediate bow of his head.

"I would allow you to send the other one – the girl, if you wish."

"That would be of great benefit. Thank you, my lord Consul."

The man looked around the table at the other mostly bored-looking members. "Are we in accord then? How say you?"

Several members gave their responses, not all of them positive, but a few remained silent. "How says the Consul from the Inland Empire?"

After a moments silence, a young woman with long, blond hair and a low-cut, black dress leaned forward from the shadows and placed her white arms on the dark wooden table. "I have my doubts about this plan. It has the potential of exposing us, with little benefit that I can see. Therefore, my vote is no."

"And how says the Sea of Grass?"

"The Sea of Grass votes no," said a large man with a gravelly voice and a thick Asian accent.

A middle-aged man in a black pinstriped business suit quickly said, "The Storm King Empire votes yes!" This earned him a nasty look from the Sea of Grass representative.

"The vote is balanced with six in favor and six opposed. How says The Mountain Empire?"

Bashshar stood up and looked around the table. "I have listened to this proposal and I find merit in it, otherwise I would not have brought it before the Chord. Therefore, my vote is yes."

Chris was escorted from the chamber and back to the conference room where Joyce was pacing back and forth. When she saw Chris, she ran over and wrapped her arms around his neck and squeezed him tightly. He folded her in his arms and held her until she started pulling away. "So, I guess it went okay," she said, trying to sound casual.

"They voted yes, but I'm not exactly sure what they were voting on. You were worried about me?"

"You? Why would I worry about you?" she asked as she surreptitiously wiped a tear from the corner of her eye. "Anyway, Amym told me what he had proposed, but things could have changed in the meantime."

The door opened again and Bashshar stepped into the room flanked by another man in a black on black suit. The man stopped and waited just outside the door. "Nothing is certain in life," he began, "but for now, we have an assignment for you. Please come with us... both of you."

"Shouldn't we wait for Amym?" Chris asked.

"He has been given another assignment and will not be joining us," Bashshar said with finality as he led them across the lobby to the open elevator doors, which opened automatically at their approach. When they were all inside, the man in the suit pressed a sequence of buttons on the panel, lighting up a random-looking series of numbers that Chris guessed was some sort of combination. The elevator lurched and started to rise. The digital floor display remained dark, so he had no idea how far up they were going. They stood in an awkward silence; Chris did his best not to spend too much time looking at the others and focused his gaze on the reflection of their feet in the lower part of the polished metal doors until the elevator came smoothly to a stop.

When the doors opened again, they found themselves in a high-ceilinged, luxury apartment. Floor to ceiling windows were covered with a tinted film, casting the clean white decor of the room in a slightly purple hue. They stepped into the white marble tiled foyer. "This is one of our guest suites. Please make yourselves comfortable here while preparations are made," Bashshar said before leading the group into the living room.

In the corner, a nude woman knelt with her head bowed. Her straight brown hair hung down past her shoulders, obscuring her face. At a subtle gesture of Bashshar's hand, she rose to her feet and came closer, waiting slightly apart from the group. Bashshar took a step back, giving them an unobstructed view. "Please, help yourselves," he said as the woman pulled her hair away and bent her neck to the side.

Chris was stunned that he would offer up this woman to be fed upon as if she were a tray of hors-d'oeuvre at a cocktail party. As repulsed as he was by the situation, he couldn't keep his eyes off the woman. Her pulse beat rapidly beneath the taut skin of her neck. Her dark nipples stood out stiffly from her small breasts and her chest rose and fell with her deep breathing, whether from fear or excitement, Chris couldn't be sure.

"What? You're not hungry? Well, no matter, it will keep," he waived the woman away dismissively as if he were shooing an annoying waiter.

While Bashshar sat down in the corner of a pristine, white sectional couch, Chris and Joyce took chairs on the opposite side of the glass coffee table where a cut crystal vase filled with purple columbines had been placed.

"What a lovely touch," Joyce said as she settled into her seat.

Bashshar smiled at her, "They match your eyes, my dear."

Chris' eyes were continuously drawn to the woman who, having been dismissed, had returned silently to her kneeling position in the corner, presumably to wait until once again summoned to provide her blood for their consumption. "You said we have an assignment. What are we supposed to do?" Joyce asked to draw him away from his brooding thoughts and back into the discussion at hand.

"For the past few thousand years, the Brethren have kept a low profile. More recently we hid in the dark places: The GoGo clubs, Beatnik coffee shops, and transvestite bars. Really, anywhere that attracted a more disreputable element and where the dregs would not be missed once the sun came up. But now, with radio, televised news programs, telephones, and now computers and pagers, it is becoming nearly impossible to stay in the shadows," he explained.

"Many of us would like to take a different path, and some would prefer to exercise a much more dominant roll in global affairs. When it was discovered that you had been given the Gift, Amym brought an idea to us. Rather than maintaining our futile attempts to remain hidden, we would offer the world a distraction… You. You will be our diversion, keeping the imagination of the world focused on the outward trappings instead of the underlying truth.

"You will recruit a group of adolescent humans who will look and act as if they were the vampires of popular fiction. You will be provided with everything you need to maintain the illusion of being a supernatural superstar, drawing as much attention to yourself as possible. Our logistician here will see to it," he said, indicating the black, suited man standing behind them. He leaned forward, resting his elbows on his knees, and looked Chris in the eye. "Do not fail us in this task." He turned to Joyce. "Either of you. The consequences would be… regrettable."

He stood up and straightened his clothes. "Now, I will leave you to it. The three of you have a lot of planning to do," he said and started heading across the foyer to the elevator. The doors opened as he approached and Amym stepped purposefully into the apartment.

"I thought you would already be on your way," Bashshar said, surprised to see Amym there.

"Yes, master," Amym said, dipping his head in supplication. "I was given permission to say my goodbyes in the event that the situation unfolds poorly."

Chris' excitement at seeing Amym was quickly turning to fear as thoughts of being left unprotected started to creep into him. "How long will you be gone? How can I get in touch with you if I need you?" he asked, stepping forward to interject into their conversation.

Amym laid his hand gently on Chris' shoulder. "You can't. You know nearly as much about my assignment as I do. Ours is not to reason why, ours is but to do or die. Don't worry, you are a perfectly capable young man and as well prepared as you could be. Promus will see to it that you have what you need and Joyce will be with you. Never underestimate her abilities. I'll be back as soon as I am able." He turned to towards Joyce and nodded, his face a mask of stoicism.

"Your belongings have already been brought up," Bashshar stated as he and Amym stepped onto the elevator. "You should have everything you need, but should there be something you require, simply press 0013 on the phone." He pointed to a white phone mounted to the wall in the hallway in front of them. "Make yourself at home."

The chrome doors slid closed, leaving Chris standing alone in the foyer. A familiar feeling of isolation and apprehension pressed down on Chris like a weight.

"Alright then. You will need to be high profile in a specific sub-cultural sort of way. We will need to find some way to increase your visibility. I'll have to think about that." He turned thoughtful, "Can you sing or play an instrument?"

"No," Chris admitted.

"That's too bad," Promus replied absently. "We could get you lessons."

"What about a dance club?" Joyce interjected suddenly.

"A dance club? What do you mean?"

Joyce had been giving this a lot of thought since Amym first told her about his idea to make Chris a vampire distraction for the public. "If we could secure a good location, we could throw our own club nights. We would choose the music and design the atmosphere to suit. We would control the crowd, control the alcohol, and set Chris up as a beautiful vampire lord overseeing his court. His own Nocturnal Empire," she explained enthusiastically.

No one said anything as Promus thought over the suggestion. Finally, he began to nod. "Yes, that might work very well. But, I don't like the idea of only having a weekly or monthly event in an existing club. It should be something completely new, and something completely within our control," he said.

"Setting up a whole new club could be very expensive. Not to mention, finding a good location. Will the Chord allow that level of investment?" she asked.

"Leave that to me," Promus said with a smile. "I believe I have the perfect place in mind as long as I can get approval to use it in such a public way. In the meantime, we need to do something about you two. You need to be the new vampire power couple – king and queen of all things nocturnal."

"Right, but I don't think the whole 'European Prince of Darkness' is the right way to go with Chris' persona. It seems too cliché to be believable. What if we stuck to Chris' background? A Texas theme," she suggested.

"Ohhh, a dark cowboy motif, a haunted gunslinger. I like it. I'll need to find an expert in vintage western wear. We need wardrobe, an acting coach, a language coach... I'm thinking something vaguely European without being specific. Just a little cosmopolitan flavor," Promus said, speaking to himself as he made a list of the things he needed to arrange. "And what about you, dear? A cross between Miss Kitty from Gunsmoke and Morticia Adams?" he suggested, baiting her.

"I'll take care of my own wardrobe, thanks all the same," Joyce replied dryly.

"As you wish. I'll have the designers sent up as soon as the arraignments are approved and we can discuss your ideas with them," he said coolly, his enthusiasm dampened somewhat by her unwillingness to play along. "I will still request the acting and dialect coaches. I don't want you to sound like Clint Eastwood, but you could still use a little more of a western twang for effect," He told Chris. After a moment of silence, he let out a big sigh as if he had been doing something strenuous. "Okay, that's enough for the time being. Get settled in and I'll start making arraignments." He walked to the elevator, which opened for him as he approached. "Ta-ta for now," he called as the door closed.

"So, what do we do now?" Chris asked.

"We wait. We have been given our task and preparations will start being made to help facilitate it, but for now, we're stuck here." She looked around the apartment. "Not bad as far as cages go. It could be a lot worse."

"Do you know when Amym will come back?" he asked hopefully.

"No, but I wouldn't expect him in the near future. The Chord has their plans for us all." Chris looked depressed. "Look, I like Amym, I do. He has helped me more than I would ever care to admit. But, I never lose sight of who he is, what his position is within The Chord. This is a competitive society and everyone is trying to maintain their position or even advance in importance if possible."

"What do you mean?"

"The Lesser Blessed are only allowed to continue so long as they serve a purpose. Flourish or perish. Even then, we are only allowed a lifespan of five hundred years. Not too shabby, but none of us ever die of old age," Joyce explained,

Chris gave that some time to sink in but he kept being distracted the presence of the naked woman still kneeling in the corner. "What do we do with her?" he asked quietly, indicating the woman with a subtle, sideways nod of his head in her direction.

"She'll wait there until one or both of us feed from her, then she'll go back to wherever the Chord keeps their donors."

"It doesn't creep you out? Her just kneeling there like that?"

"Not really. Long ago it might have, but there are things you get used to if you want to continue in this life."

"Is she a slave?" Chris asked.

"Not in the way you are thinking," she admitted. "Our saliva has certain traits: It can heal minor wounds and acts as an anesthetic to ease the pain of feeding. It can also produce an overwhelming feeling of euphoria that can be as addictive as heroin. So, even though she is a volunteer, it's not by any means a selfless act."

"Why is she naked?"

"It's a sign of submission. The Brethren insist on it. It is also for convenience so they don't have to waste time unwrapping their food, there are more places on the body to get blood than just the neck. But really, I think they just like it. It makes them feel powerful, that's also why all the donors are relatively young and attractive. Although, if you were to ask them – which I wouldn't recommend – they would probably tell you it's for their ability to replenish."

"Won't she just tell them what we say?"

"You mean… like a spy?" Joyce asked with a huge gasp, sounding utterly shocked by the notion. "You need to understand this: There are no secrets here. Everything we do or say while we're here is being monitored. Even your thoughts and feelings could be scrutinized when you are in their presence. It may feel like a violation of your privacy, but think of it as a continuation of your training. If you can protect yourself here, you'll be able to out there also."

She put her hand gently on his shoulder until he nodded. "Now... let's go pick our bedrooms," she said as she quickly turned and ran off laughing to check out the rest of the apartment. "I get the biggest one," she called out as she disappeared down the hall.

She heard the hatch open and close at the top of the ladder, and took several deep breaths to steady her nerves. The sound of her master descending the tunnel to the lair was louder than usual and when he came to rest on the rubble-strewn floor, there was a brief scuffling in the darkness.

"Light the candle, Pet," her master ordered, and she hurried to obey.

She fumbled for the spot on the battered metal desk where the candle and matches were kept, struck a match, and held it to the wick. It lit easily in the still air and quickly filled the dingy space with its warm yellow glow. She sat back on her heels, her eyes lowered in supplication until she heard the dull thud of something soft hitting the ground nearby. Glancing up, she saw the body of a child curled into the fetal position at her master's feet.

"This is Boy. He will be residing here. You will feed him, you will care for him. If he dies, you will pay for it, so I recommend that you put your best effort into keeping him alive."

Her first thought was to be angry that she had this extra burden; more responsibility meant more opportunity to be punished being forced on her. Then grudgingly, she thought about the boy lying on the floor. She wanted to ask where he had come from but knew better than to question her master too much. She watched the unmoving form on the floor until she saw his body swell with the intake of breath, sinking her heart into the pit of her stomach. It's not that she wanted the boy dead, but even that would be better than the hell that would be his life there.

Her master dabbed at dark stains on his new clothing, clothing that she had debased herself to get the money to buy. "His parents were exceedingly reluctant to give him up," he said, stuffing his handkerchief back into his coat pocket.

"You killed them?!" she asked before she could think of how foolish she was being.

"Naturally," the master said with an amused chuckle before lying down on his steel cot in preparation for the coming day. "Though, he doesn't know it. And you will keep your mouth shut about it. It's a curious name though – Boy - but he has it written on his belt buckle. I believe I like it."

She waited a long time to be sure that her master had fallen asleep, then crawled over to the still form. He was a young, dark-skinned boy with kinky hair. Probably black but maybe Puerto Rican or Dominican, it was hard to tell without turning him over. He was no more than ten or eleven, and small for his age, making him seem even more vulnerable.

She placed her hand gently on his shoulder. "Hey, are you awake? What's your name?" she asked. When there was no response, she continued. "Don't want to talk? I don't blame you. I'm sorry about your parents," she said sympathetically. "It's pretty messed up isn't it?"

She sat down next to him and leaned back against the wall. "He sleeps during the day, so if you do want to talk, that's the best time. I wish I could tell you that everything will be alright, but it won't, and I'm not going to lie to you. We're both in a pretty bad situation," she said while trying not to think about the awful things she was sure the master had in store for him. "But, I'll do what I can for you, okay?" The boy shifted, laid his head in her lap, and began to weep softly. After a few seconds, so did she, for the first time since her death.

"I'm back, and I've brought goodies!" a jovial voice announced from the foyer. Chris had been sitting on the white couch watching TV to pass the endless hours, and besides food deliveries of both the take out and human varieties, this was the first time they had had visitors since they had been shut up in the apartment. He switched off the episode of Ryan's Hope that he was only half watching and got up as Promus came into the living room, followed by a whole crew of people carrying an assortment of boxes, bags, and cases.

Promus turned to a large man carrying a cardboard box. "Just put that down over there out of the way," he said, pointing towards the living room. "Christian, those are for you to learn all you can about vampires in popular culture. They will help give you an idea of what your target audience expects. Knowing your market is key to successful sales."

Chris pulled open the flaps and found stacks of books, VHS tapes, and Laser Disks. "What did you get?" Joyce asked excitedly looking over his shoulder. He started pulling out handfuls of books: Vampire Junction, I Vampire, The Vampire Lestat and Fever Dream. He didn't know any of them, but he did recognize Anne Rice as the author of a book that Rachel has bought for him earlier in the summer from a Second Avenue street vendor. Chris didn't want to think about her so he quickly switched to the movies: Fright Night, Once Bitten. "Ohhh, that's a great one. We can watch that tonight," Joyce suggested, snatching out a Laser Disk copy of Vamp. "Grace Jones is gorgeous… and creepy. You'll love it."

"Geniuses, this is Christian and Joyce. Christian, Joyce, these are the geniuses who will be transforming you into the dark stars you will become." Joyce was taken back into her bedroom by two women who shut the door securely behind them. Probably going to do something very girly, Chris thought as images of a lingerie-clad pillow fight popped unbidden into his head.

Promus led him back to the couch and introduced his crew who were taking positions around the room. "This is Francine. She is a fashion superstar and will be your designer." Chris shook hands with a middle-aged woman with dark blond hair shot through with strands of gray and horn-rimmed glasses. "Next, we have Carl. Hailing from Denver, he's one of the best boot makers in the country." A large, bald man with a ruddy complexion, a warm smile, and a firm handshake leaned in to say howdy.

"Over here we have Manny. He's an expert hat maker out of Austin. That's your neck of the woods, isn't it?" Promus asked, not waiting for a response before introducing the last member of their group. "And Jesse, from Albuquerque, is one of the finest native silversmiths anywhere."

When Chris finished shaking everyone's hands, they all took their seats around the coffee table. "When I got the call about this project, I really got inspired," Francine said while laying a small, black leather portfolio on the glass tabletop. "I worked up a few design ideas and would love to get everyone's input." She opened the zipper and pulled out a stack of colored pencil renderings.

They passed the drawings around while she described the black western shirts, leather pants, and long black coats. Everyone but Chris seemed to have something to say about the fabric, textures, colors, and accessories that would best compliment the outfit.

Francine had him stand up with his arms out to the side so she could take measurements of his chest, arms, waist, neck, and inseam. Then, it was Manny's turn to check the size of his head. "Are you going to keep your hair this length?"

"He really needs longer hair, don't you think? How do you feel about a goatee... or maybe a soul patch?" Francine asked while Carl had him step into a shiny, silver contraption to measure his feet.

Soon, they were eagerly talking among themselves, completely oblivious to Chris' presence. His head was swimming from the barrage of words they were throwing around: Snakeskin, suede, alligator, filigree, stars, frock, Turquoise, embroidery, double-breasted, heal guards, mariachi. It was all becoming too much.

Chris slipped away while they were busy discussing where to get the best devil horns for a hatband, and ducked into the bathroom. He turned on the cold water and gulped it down from his cupped hands, then splashed his face. When he looked up, the face that looked back at him, studying him curiously, was unrecognizable to him as his own. There was in his reflection, the half-forgotten image of the person he had been, overlaid on top of someone new. As if he had aged several years in the past few months.

He touched his face, tracing the hard line of his jaw with his fingertips. He couldn't remember if it had always been so square. He knew he had lost all the child-like softness through months of training, but he was looking much more like a man than the boy he remembered being.

A gentle knock brought him out of his thoughts and back to the situation at hand. "Chris? Are you okay in there?" Joyce asked through the door.

He unlocked it and opened the door. "Yeah," he said. "I guess all the attention was getting to be too much for me. I just needed a minute to get myself together."

"You just need to realize that those people are here to make you look and feel as good as you possibly can. They will make you into the image of what other people want to be. That, and a generous dose of charisma and attitude will attract people to you like flies to shit, which is the goal after all. So, just go with the flow and let them do what they do best."

"Okay," he said smiling. Chris could tell Joyce had been enjoying herself and wished he felt the same. Maybe if they had been including him in the decisions, it would have been more fun, he thought. "Hey, do I look different to you?!"

"What do you mean?"

"Just... like... do I seem older or anything?"

"Of course you do. You have been through a lot – more than anyone of your chronological age should. You have matured beyond your years. Not to mention, your rock hard muscles," she said with a wink.

Chris started to blush. "But, it seems like more than that to me."

"It seems like you're changing faster and more dramatically than time, age and exercise would account for?"

"Yeah, I guess."

"It seems that way to me too, but I know something you don't: Vampires, and even Lesser Blessed to some degree, have the ability to alter their appearance. It's not easy and it can take a lot of time, but it can be done. I just never even suspected that one as newly changed as you could do it. Even if you could, it would be subtle and slow, over several months at least."

"You told me a little about it, but how does it work?" he asked.

"Everyone has an image of themselves in their mind, a picture of themselves that they can visualize when they imagine themselves in a situation. Most of the time that image matches their reflection in the mirror, but if you can change your mental picture of yourself and hold it firmly in your mind, over time you can change your physical appearance to match. So, when they tell you that you can be anyone you want, you really can, but only if you are disciplined enough. And, it takes forever."

"How long? I mean, I've only been a vampire for like... six months. Is that enough time?"

"I doubt it. The older True Born can do it in a few days maybe, or a few weeks. I'm not sure exactly. They don't tell us about those sort of things."

"Can you do it?"

"Sweetie, this doesn't happen overnight. It's taken me a long time to look this gorgeous," she said, striking a pose for his appreciation: Hands on her hips and her jaw raised in a look of haughty superiority.

Chapter 8

Weeks passed and there were many more fittings where they both tried on their teams work. Joyce's always seemed to include exclamations of happiness and excitement, but Chris figured she cared about clothes a lot more than he did. There were also regular deliveries of music, books, and movies. Chris suspected that Joyce had a lot to do with the music selection since she was having regular meetings with Promus to make plans for the club. They discussed sound system designers, who the DJ ought to be and set designers to give the club the perfect atmosphere. That was probably when she gave him her wish list of Compact Disks. The latest delivery was a veritable who's who of recent Gothic Rock: Siouxsie & The Banshees, Bauhaus, Christian Death, The Marianist Sisters, Clan Of Xymox, Ministry and Swans.

Chris spent his time reading and listening to the music of bands he had never heard of before. The somber music and all-white furnishings pushed him into a lethargy of deep introspection that began to border on depression until the day that Joyce announced that she would be giving him dance lessons. "You need to be a Goth icon. You can't be slam dancing in the pit like a punk kid anymore," she said. He wasn't a big fan of dancing, even though it didn't seem all that different from practicing his forms, except that he got to have his hands on Joyce a lot of the time. That, in itself, was enough to make Chris forget his reluctance and dedicate himself to hours upon hours of intensive practice.

Chris was so engrossed with his Waltz lesson – Joyce's hand in his, his arm around her waist, her body pressed firmly against his, moving in perfect synchronization around the apartment – that he didn't notice that Promus had come into the apartment until he started clapping. It was really starting to bother him that they had no expectation of privacy at all, that they could be watched, eavesdropped or intruded upon at any time.

"I have good news, Liebchens. Today, you get to go to your new home. Isn't that fabulous? Don't worry about packing anything,

I have already arraigned for it to be boxed up and delivered. So, chop chop," he said, clapping his hands. "We have a lot to do."

He took them down to the lobby; it felt like forever since the day Amym had led them in past the security desk. His eyes scanned the area as he crossed the lobby, hoping that maybe Amym would be waiting just around the next corner, leaning against the white marble walls in his black silk, an amused smile on his face, his mere presence assuring that everything would be all right. They exited through the revolving doors and climbed into the waiting limousine, but there was still no sign of him.

The car drove them downtown to Fourteenth Street, then turned west. Chris stared out the window at all the places that had been so familiar to him just a few months earlier. Everything looked the same, but he felt more like a tourist, visiting the city for the very first time. As they approached the Hudson River, they took another left on to Washington Street, crossed Thirteenth, and pulled over to the curb in front of the closed gate of a meatpacking plant. It was a doorway that Chris was very familiar with.

The Meatpacking District of New York sat on the site of the Sappokanican Indian village, which translated to the 'carrying place.' Supposedly, due to it being the center of trade between the Indians and the original Dutch settlers, the name was applied to the whole region of the island later called Greenwich Village. Prior to the War of 1812, the U.S. Army hastily built a secondary fort on the site. Named for the hero of Fort Stanwix, Colonial army General Peter Gansevoort, grandfather of author Herman Melville, the fort was built of Newark red sandstone and the exterior was whitewashed, resulting in the nickname White Fort.

In 1849 the Army abandoned the fort and its total demolition was completed in 1851. The old building materials were dumped to fill the small bay and create the freight yards. Eventually, the yards became the Gansevoort Farmer's Market, an open-air space for the buying and selling of regional produce. Bustling with horse-drawn carts piled high with goods for sale, the market quickly becoming unmanageably overcrowded, and the city began making plans to construct a covered market in its place.

The Gansevoort Market officially opened in 1884 on the enormous paved open-air block between Gansevoort and Little West

12th streets. The market survived until 1949 when the old Gansevoort produce market was demolished and the city built the Gansevoort Market Meat Center on the site because meat had, by then, replaced produce as the bulwark of the neighborhood.

Promus produced a set of keys and opened the steel door leading into the building. It seemed like a lifetime had passed since he had been to the loft apartment above the slaughterhouse, but when they climbed the stairs to the third floor and opened the door, he was stunned at how much it had changed. Walls had been moved, the bedroom where he had first glimpsed a trio of beautify women waiting for Amym was gone, and the whole front of the building was now dedicated to the dining and living rooms. Where there had once been only a small, galley kitchen, an enormous open chef's kitchen now faced the bank of windows across the dining room table.

A massive shelving unit covering one wall of the living space held a stack of expensive looking electronics, as well as an assortment of antique, leather-bound volumes of classic literature, CDs, records, VHS tapes, and Laser Disks. A three-sided sectional couch faced a rear projection television that was large enough to charge admission.

They followed Promus down a hallway to where the practice room had been. "Through here is the dormitory where your coven will stay. Do you like that? I had a difficult time deciding what to call a community of Vampires. It's such a novel concept. Anyway, they have everything they need: Showers, restrooms, a makeup station, clothes, beds – all the comforts of home."

"You're right, that will certainly be something new and different," Joyce agreed.

"What do you mean?" Chris asked.

"Vampires are territorial hunters, predators. They don't typically live in groups," she explained.

"But, there were thirteen vampires in the Chord, and all the Lesser Blessed that work for them. There seem to be an awful lot them lurking around the city," he pointed out.

"New York City has enough population to support the Chord for a brief time, and only a few Vampires actually reside here. Most only gather when there is business to be attended to," Promus interjected.

"Like, what happens to me?"

"Your situation is just a side note. That's why you were given time at Haven to prepare. There are larger issues being dealt with than the fate of one Lesser Blessed. You two will be in here." He used a second key to open a steel fire door and ushered them inside.

Chris and Joyce stepped into what he would imagine a luxury bedroom suite in an updated medieval castle would look like. An enormously heavy canopy bed dominated the room, massive dark wooden pilasters were carved with entwined nude nymphs, its king size mattress was overhung with thick burgundy velvet drapes, held open with gold rope tiebacks attached to thick iron rings. Matching iron candelabras held tapered candles scented with Sandalwood and Jasmine.

I'm going to be sharing a room with Joyce! Chris thought excitedly. More than that, he would be sharing a bed, and this was for real and not just one of his dreams. It was all he could do not to laugh out loud at his good luck, and he had to fight to keep the stupid grin off his face.

Promus pointed to a wooden door with a large glass window. "In there is your closet and bathroom."

"That's what I was waiting for!" Joyce practically squeaked endearingly with a girlish excitement and rushed forward towards the closet door.

"Well, you will have to wait a little bit longer. We have something else to see first."

"Excuse me, where did you move Amym's room?" Chris asked.

"If he is reassigned to New York, other accommodations will be made for him," Promus announced pointedly. "Now, if we can continue?"

He led them back out into the hall, unlocked a heavy wooden door that was stained a dark brown to match the rest of the décor and pushed it open. Behind it lay a dingy looking staircase lit by a single bare incandescent bulb. Its battered, brick walls showed signs of recent plaster removal, and the cement steps were still covered with a thin layer of dust.

They began following him down, and the door closed solidly behind them. Chris noticed that it was actually another steel fire door with a wood veneer on the loft side to make it less conspicuous. Down and down they went. Chris estimated that they were at least three stories below street level when the stairs finally stepped out into the end of an arched, brick tunnel.

In the early days of industrialization, barges had been used to ferry cattle across the Hudson River from holding pens in New Jersey. Large herds of cows were then driven through the streets of Manhattan. Increased demand for beef had caused cow-jams that blocked the streets and train lines of the Meatpacking District, which was filled with slaughterhouses, hide stretchers, bone-boilers, and lard renderers. So many traffic and freight train accidents occurred that Tenth Avenue became known as Death Avenue, and the railroads were eventually forced to hire men known as the West Side Cowboys to ride their horses waving flags in front of the trains to keep the tracks clear.

In the 1870s, the original ten-foot wide by eight-foot-high, oak-lined tunnel had been built to safely convey the cattle from piers, under the street and tracks, to the meat industries multi-story stockyards. The days of the West Side Cowboys were now long past but their legacy lived on at Boots and Saddle, the Christopher Street bar where shirtless studs in black leather chaps slung cheap beer for appreciative crowds of gay men.

Promus led them down the gently sloping tunnel and into what had been the underground cattle pens. The facility had been closed up after the invention of refrigerated train cars in 1880, which allowed already processed meat to be transported into the city on a daily basis. What remained of the site had long since been forgotten, except for some vague rumors among utility workers.

"What do you think?" he asked them, turning with his arms out to his sides to indicate the dimly lit cavern. "I think The Shambles would make an excellent space for our purposes."

"It's absolutely gorgeous," Joyce said, walking to the center of the room and twirling around under the twenty-foot high vaulted brick ceiling. "The bar should go along that wall, and the DJ booth should be raised up over there so he can see the whole room. But how will people get in? They can't very well come through our loft."

"I have had engineers all through it. We can extend the front stairs of the building down so that they would come out over there, behind that wall." He pointed to a section of brick at the far end of the room away from where they had entered. "We can tap into the water and sewer lines so restrooms can go there. The back tunnel and stairs will be for your use only."

"Oooo, we can get some velvet ropes and a bouncer to guard the tunnel and make it seem even more exclusive," Joyce offered.

"I like it. Do you think the guards should be armed?"

"Gilded uniforms and halberds might be a little much for a New York dance club. It's not the Vatican after all, but I get what you're saying. Maybe just a couple of big muscle types in tight, black t-shirts would be enough."

"If you say so," Promus said, sounding a little put off by her lack of appreciation for Fifteenth-century pageantry. "We have secured a reliable and discrete contractor. I'll send him around to see you in the next week or so. I'll leave the day to day details to your discretion, but consult me if there are any large financial decisions that need to be made."

She turned to Chris. "We really need to tour the other clubs in the city to make sure that ours is the best. Maybe even put some of your new dancing skills to the test." Chris swallowed hard. Dancing in public wasn't at the top of his list of things to do. "What have we got to wear?" Joyce asked Promus with a smile.

The closets were filled with new clothes. Chris stood looking blankly at racks of black cloth, unsure of where to even begin. On a shelf was a row of boots: pairs of Custom cowboy boots with stars, skulls, and crosses decorating the leather, fourteen hole Doc Martens, and ankle-high soft, leather boots with pointed toes and Cuban heels. A glass-topped display case held a variety of jewelry and accessories, and on a high shelf, a row of white Styrofoam heads gazed vacantly down at him from under their handmade western hats.

"Here, let me help you," Joyce offered. She flipped through the hangers and pulled out a linen shirt, a leather vest, and leather pants with subtle flames stitched into the outside of the legs. "I'll let you find your own underwear and socks," she said, draping the outfit over his arm, then turning back to make her own selection.

He went out to the bedroom to get dressed. The cloths felt strange; the leather was heavy and confining but looking in the mirror, he had to admit it was a good look. He selected a pair of black alligator boots with silver toe-caps and heel-guards. A new black leather belt with the Texas buckle that Mrs. Brooks had given him for his birthday before he left home made him pause with sentimentality and he began to wonder how his mother was doing now that she was alone.

"You have the shirt buttoned up too high," Joyce said from behind, startling him as he threaded the belt through his pant loops. He clasped the belt while she undid the top two buttons, then stepped back to take in the overall effect.

She stood wearing a black and purple corset that matched the streaks in her teased-out hair and pushed her milk-white breasts up and out in front of her. Her already slim waist was synched into an impossibly small circle. A long, ruffled, black skirt hung nearly to the floor, and she wore black lace, wrist-length gloves.

"You look incredible," Chris stammered.

"You clean up pretty good yourself," She said with a smile. "But, you really need to learn to accessorize."

She opened the case, took out a sterling silver bracelet made from a heavy linked chain, and clasped it around his right wrist opposite the string of black beads he hadn't taken off since the day he woke up wearing them. "Now all you need is a hat, coat, and your khukuri."

"Do I really need to carry that big knife?" he asked. "It's heavy, and I'm really good at hand to hand."

"I know you are, but never go out without your weapon," she warned. "It won't do you any good if you don't have it on you."

"What about you? I don't see anything deadly strapped to you."

"I'll have you know, I am a very dangerous woman. Thank you very much. And this," she twirled around to let him admire her outfit, "is a virtual armory."

Grudgingly, he belted the knife across his lower back and covered it with a long black oilskin Duster. He put on a narrow, black leather cowboy hat with bright red horns protruding from the front of the hatband and Joyce finished off his outfit with a pair of Ray Ban Aviator sunglasses. She moved in closer, her body gently brushing against his, her hands moving to his hips. She raised her eyes to his and checked her lipstick in their mirrored surface.

"Okay, I think we're good. Shall we?" she asked cheerfully, taking his arm and walking him out of the apartment.

They made the rounds of all the hottest clubs in the city: 1018, Area, Danceteria, LimeLight, Palladium, Paradise Garage, Tunnel, and The Saint. They made notes of who had the best lighting, sound, DJ, and overall atmosphere. Joyce seemed to know everyone at every club and was contentious about introducing Chris as her *companion*. They made sure to dance at least once at every club after working the crowd so that they were sure everyone would be watching. At first, Chris was petrified about the scrutiny, but after the second club, it became just another routine.

Their performances were met with looks of admiration and appreciation as the other patrons cleared the dance floor to make room for them and they always left before the applause died down and the spectators returned to the dance floor. They exited The World on east 2nd Street and walked the three blocks to their last stop, dashing across Houston even though there was hardly any traffic at that hour.

225 E Houston Street, on the corner of Essex, had originally been built to house the Provident Loan Society, a non-profit organization born in response to the financial panic of 1893. They flourished by providing short-term pawn loans at a lower rate than traditional loan sharks.

The fifty-foot square, Houston Street branch was built in the Classical Revival-style in 1912 with yellow Roman brick and a marble base. At the top of the building, a copper cornice topped a simple terra cotta capital that still showed a hint of the signage on both façades, clearly reading THE PROVIDENT LOAN SOCIETY OF NEW YORK.

The bank operated the branch for decades, but divested in 1966. Shortly thereafter, the building was purchased by the abstract expressionist artist Jasper Johns, and served as both his residence and studio space through much of the '70s. Its current incarnation was one of the city's only gothic nightclubs: Chaos.

As they approached the club, the doorman got up off his stool where he had been collecting the five-dollar cover charge for Albion Night and unlatched the velvet ropes that surrounded the entrance to admit them. Joyce laid her hand on his shoulder and smiled her thanks as they walked past the short line of people waiting on the sidewalk to enter.

Chris followed her inside the former bank lobby. The windows had been painted black to block out the streetlights outside and large speakers hung from the ceiling by thick chains. She led him deeper into the club, holding onto his hand and waiving to people she either knew or recognized among the crowd along the way. They descended the wide stairs down to a lounge built into the bank's vault and made their way to the bar. They ordered their drinks, and just as the bartender was setting them down on the worn surface, Chris was stunned immobile. There, standing right in front of him, was Lucifer.

Chris hadn't seen him since the night they had fought at Positively 8th street Pizza, but he was unmistakable in his black leather vest and long, platinum blond hair. The muscles on his intimidatingly huge arms flexed as he scrubbed out the dirty glasses behind the bar. When Chris was new to the city, he had been defending one of his friends from Rocky Horror against Lucifer's taunts when the hulking biker had decided to drown him in the pizzeria's toilet. Chris had only been saved when the porcelain bowl broke beneath them and he smashed Lucifer in the head with a heavy piece of ceramic, knocking the roid-freak unconscious.

Chris quickly turned his back to the bar and busied himself with sipping his drink and scanning the crowd from behind his glasses, hoping not to be recognized. The last thing he wanted was for them to get into another fight, even though he was pretty sure he could take him now. They were trying to attract attention, but he

125

didn't think that brawling in a dance club was exactly what Joyce had in mind.

Sensing his discomfort, Joyce turned to Chris and asked, "Hey, are you okay?"

"Yeah, I just had some beef with the guy behind the bar a while back, and I didn't want him to recognize me and start trouble," he admitted.

"The blond muscle head?" she asked. "I don't think he'll be any problem." She leaned forward over the bar, the bodice of her corset offering up the pale mounds of her breasts for easy viewing, and called out, "Hey, Fabio!" It only took a moment for her to get Lucifer's attention.

He made his way over. "What can I do for you?" he asked with a sleazy leer on his smug face.

She lowered her head and looked up at him from under her heavy lashes. "For me? Sorry big guy, you don't do anything for me," she stated. "But, I think you have some unfinished business with my friend."

Chris turned around to look at him, lowering his sunglasses. "You," Lucifer said when he finally recognized Chris. "I was looking for you half the summer."

"Well, I'm here now," Chris said with resignation.

"You look different. Anyway... I just wanted to talk to you about what went down at Pos. I was having a bad night and I guess I was being kind of an asshole. I don't blame you for sticking up for your ummm, friend. So, as far as I'm concerned, everything's squashed, okay?"

Chris wasn't sure how to respond. He had spent the better part of the summer looking over his shoulder in fear of being jumped after their fight, which he now knew he only won because of his enhanced vampire strength. Lucifer was a bully who had been picking on one of Chris' friends, a tranny boy named Ainsley, who later ended up being brutally murdered. But he was no longer the scared kid he was back then, and was about to get into it again with the homophobic asshole when Joyce cut him off.

"Do you like working here?" she asked.

"Yeah, I guess it's alright. I'm going to school, so working nights is impotent."

"Where are you studying?"

"I'm in the Dental Hygiene Program at the NYU College of Dentistry."

"That's fascinating. So you want to be a Dental Hygienist, not work in nightclubs?"

"What I really want to create my own line of cosmetic implants, which is why I'm specializing in Implant Dentistry. Why all the questions?"

"Christian and I are opening a new club in the West Village soon and we may be looking to hire some extra help. Why don't you write down your number and I'll have our manager call you," she said, sliding a cocktail napkin across the bar towards him.

"If you wanted my number, you just had to ask," he said, flashing her his best Richard Gere look from American Gigolo. She gave him a placating smile in return and handed the napkin over to Chris.

"Why do you want that guy at the club?" Chris asked once they were back outside.

Joyce stopped and looked at him. "Are you jealous? You are, aren't you?" she asked, a smile tugging at the corners of her mouth.

"I'm not. It's just... that guy's a jerk," he said defensively.

"I'm absolutely sure he is, but I get the feeling he might be useful. Are you hungry? We could stop and pick up a hobo."

"I really hope you're joking. But yeah, I could eat," he said uncommittedly. "What are you thinking about?"

"Katz' Deli is right here," she said indicating the large white florescent sign the protruded over the sidewalk one block west.

"How about Chinese?" Chris offered. "But, where can we go that's open this late?"

"There's only one place, but it's awesome," Joyce said excitedly, grabbing his arm. "And lucky for us, it's not that far. Do you want to walk it or take a cab?"

Chapter 9

Chris and Joyce walked west on Houston and turned left on Chrystie Street heading south along the darkened expanse of Roosevelt Park, named not for President Franklin Delano Roosevelt, but for his mother Sara. The shadowy figures of dealers, junkies, and the homeless moved eerily in the darkness. The light from the occasional streetlights struggled to penetrate the thick, leafy canopy of the trees.

They walked the full seven-block length of the park to Canal Street. Dealers started to approach them every few steps but thought twice about soliciting the ominous looking Goth couple wearing sunglasses in the dark and faded back into the shadows. If they weren't there to cop dope, they probably had a death wish.

At the end of the park, the couple turned right on Canal Street, then left a few blocks later onto Mott Street. They passed a row of shuttered, street-level shops selling a wide variety of Chinese souvenirs. Piles of reeking black plastic bags full of restaurant trash were stacked on the curb awaiting the early morning pickup.

Under a brightly lit fluorescent sign reading WO HOP 17 RESTAURANT, a metal railing, worn smooth by uncounted years of patrons hands, led the way down a bright-red tiled staircase into the building's basement. The only twenty-four-hour Chinese restaurant in New York, Wo Hop had been run by the same family since it opened in 1938. It served old-fashioned Americanized Cantonese comfort food that hadn't changed since World War II.

Chris had to duck to avoid hitting his head on the sign as he followed Joyce down the steps into the brightly lit, rectangular room. Mirror-covered columns stretched from the green and white checkered linoleum floor to the acoustic tiles in the drop ceiling and the walls were lined with a mosaic of headshots of up-and-coming actors from the last twenty years.

"Nǐ hǎo" Joyce called in greeting as the glass door swung closed behind them.

"Huānyíng. Zuò zài nàlǐ," a middle-aged waiter replied, pointing at one of the vacant light-green formica tables scattered around the dining room.

Chris pulled out one of the worn wooden chairs for Joyce, then took a seat opposite her. The waiter spread out napkins and utensils on the table, then handed them each a menu.

"So, what's good here?" Chris asked.

"Everything... and nothing," she said. "This is one of those antiquated places that still serves the post-war American idea of what Chinese food should be. They haven't embraced the idea of serving *authentic* Asian cuisine."

Joyce ordered the fried dumplings, which she said were the best in the city, and steamed pork buns while they decided on what else they wanted. Chris looked over the familiar dishes listed on the menu: Chop suey, chow mein, moo goo gai pan. Familiar dishes, yet all with exotic-seeming names.

The sound of feet coming down the steps, followed by the door opening, drew Chris' attention to the entrance where a group of young Chinese men filed menacingly in. The restaurant staff stopped what they were doing to take notice of their arrival, then just as quickly, lowered their heads and diligently returned to their tasks. The group took seats in the two back booths under a wall of mirrors and waited for service. From where they were seated, the men had a clear view of the entire dining room and kept an eye on the front door. However, their attention seemed to be focused on Chris and Joyce.

Chris could see them looking over and talking among themselves, obviously discussing them, and he could sense Joyce becoming more and more tense under their scrutiny. "What's going on?" he asked her in a hushed voice.

"Nothing," she said with a forced smile. "I'm sure everything is fine."

But when Chris looked again, one of the men was sliding out of the booth and heading towards their table. He seemed young, in his mid to late teens. He had long, silky black hair in the back, cut short and spiked up in the front like a New Wave Chinese mullet. He wore dark sunglasses and a white leather motorcycle jacket with a black and white bandanna tied loosely around the ankle of his boot.

When he reached the table, he pulled out a chair, stepped over the seat, and straddled the back, facing Chris.

"You got a lot of nerve coming in here," he said, looking at Chris. "Did you think that just by changing your look I wouldn't recognize you?"

Chris looked back at him; he seemed familiar, but he couldn't place from where. "I'm sorry, I don't think I know you." The other gang members were watching the exchange expectantly, and Chris could see Joyce's eyes beginning to glow with a subtle purple light.

"Dude, don't look so worried. You don't remember me?" he pulled his glasses away from his eyes.

"Holy Shit! Chung? How have you been, man?" Chris exclaimed excitedly. "Joyce, this is my friend Chung."

"Hey," he said casually. "So, you went Goth, huh? I almost didn't recognize you."

"Yeah, same here. Last time I was you, you had a twelve-inch Mohawk. You went with the whole Chinatown gang thing?" Chris asked.

"Please! It was fourteen inches, and I kinda had to. You remember that party at my place after my dad died?"

Chung's father had cut his leg in a fall and, instead of going to see a western doctor, relied solely on traditional Chinese remedies and soon developed a fever and an infection. Not long after, his foot began to turn black, then ended up becoming gangrenous. He eventually agreed to allow amputation, but by then it was too late to save his life.

After the funeral, Chung's friends threw him a party at his apartment, and several hours of drinking later, decided to fix the awkward layout of the unit. The music on TJ's ghetto blaster was cranked up to cover the sound of boots, and Chung's small hammer, knocking down the living room wall. White kitchen trash bags full of plaster chunks and broken lath were quietly taken downstairs and dropped on the sidewalk in front of the neighboring building anytime someone went on a beer run.

Chung explained that the next day, after all of his friends had gone back to their lives, his landlord had evicted him from his apartment at 3rd and B because of the damage they had done. With nowhere else to turn, Chung had joined up with Chinatown's notorious Ghost Shadows gang to avoid being homeless.

"Wǒmen zǒu ba. We have business to take care of," his friends called out to him as they exited the dining room through a pair of swinging gray doors with a diamond shaped windows, into the kitchen.

"Hey, I gotta go. It's good to see you, man. I work in Paradise Park during the day, or come by Tech Billiards some night so we can catch up," Chung offered before hurrying off to catch up with the others.

Once Chung had disappeared, Chris leaned across the table towards Joyce. "Are you okay? What was all that about?" He asked.

"Nothing. I just have a thing about Chinese gangs."

"Yeah, I got that, but I thought you were going to lose it there for a minute."

"I have my reasons," she said under her breath.

"Anything you want to talk about?"

"Not really."

They finished their meal in relative silence. Joyce didn't seem interested in talking and Chris didn't want to press her. She had been right about the food, and as four o'clock approached, more people began streaming in to feast on the large potions once the clubs and bars let out. Chris grabbed a fortune cookie off the table and followed Joyce to the counter to pay their bill, tearing open the cellophane wrapper as they climbed back up the steps to Mott street.

"What does it say?" she asked.

Chris held up the slip of paper and read "Learn Chinese pig."

"The other side jackass."

"Oh," Chris said feigning a dawning understanding and turned the paper over. "You will be hungry again in one hour."

"You know, those aren't even Chinese," she said cracking open her own cookie. "They're Japanese. They didn't start becoming popular in Chinese restaurants until the Japanese internment during World War Two."

They walked along in silence for several minutes before she spoke again. "My parents were from Poland," Joyce began quietly as they continued walking back to the loft, her head lowered, staring solemnly at the pavement passing beneath her pointy black boots.

"Mother was a stage actress and father was a laborer. When World War One broke out, they fled their home, came to America and eventually made their way to Hollywood. Mother went to work in the movie business: She was beautiful, with a dark exotic look that was very popular at that time." It still was Chris thought as he fixatedly watched her painted lips while she spoke.

"Father got a job selling cars, which were becoming increasingly affordable thanks to assembly line production and increasingly popular as more people became recreational drivers, taking day or weekend trips all across the state. Eventually, they were able to buy a little house in the hills behind the HOLLYWOODLAND development sign.

"Mother took a break from acting when she got pregnant in 1922 and stayed home to raise me. When she finally decided to go back to work, she found that she was no longer in demand. Other actresses had popped up to take her place since producers believed her thick, Polish accent wasn't suited to working in talkies."

"What are talkies?" Chris asked.

"Movies weren't like they are now, they were black and white and didn't have sound," she explained. "Those advances came later. Anyway, the cars continued to sell even after the stock market crashed in 1929, though not nearly as well as they had before, and money was starting to get pretty tight. Mother went to work in hair and makeup, keeping all the young starlets camera ready. I know that it was hard for her to watch other women achieve the career success that she had aspired to. She knew that the only thing that stood in her way was her inability to completely shed all traces of her homeland. She put on a happy face at home, but father and I always knew how heartbroken she was."

"Anyway, with both of them working, we all rode out the depression without truly feeling it the way that so many people did, but the global financial crisis and international politics still weighed heavily on us. Everyone was on edge, and when Germany invaded Poland in 1939, my father was one of the people most outspoken in advocating for the US' entry into the war."

"I finished high school and then started going to secretarial school so that I'd have an easier time getting a job, but when the army created the Women's Army Corp in 1943, I decided to join up. I was posted to Hawaii where I could put my new typing skills to work for the war effort."

"When the Japanese attacked Pearl Harbor, I wanted to do my part so I volunteered to help out in the hospitals by just talking or playing cards with the wounded soldiers. Most of the time, a smile and a kind word would go miles as far as helping the G.I.s feel better. That's where I met Louis."

"He had been badly burned on the legs in a gasoline fire after the battleship USS Nevada was hit by dive-bombers during the second wave of the attack. Soon, I found myself spending all my free time with him. I would push his wheelchair around and as he recovered, we would go for walks and eventually dancing."

"Dancing on a Hawaiian beach at sunset was one of the most breathtaking experiences of my life, so when Louis got down on one knee and asked me to marry him, I said yes without a second thought."

"Pretty soon he got his medical discharge and went back to California and eventually I returned home to join him. We were married in a small ceremony at my parents' home surrounded by family, friends, and a few fellow service men and women we knew. We couldn't afford a honeymoon, and couldn't think of anywhere we would have wanted to go anyway. The two of us had already fallen in love in one of the most beautiful places on earth, anywhere else would be a disappointment after that."

They kept on in silence for several minutes. Joyce seemed lost in her memories, reliving in the good times before she felt up to continuing. "After the war, there were a lot of social changes going on. Women, who had been recruited to do the jobs that men had typically done during the war, began to quietly rebel when they were told that they needed to go back home and start families. Blacks, who had just started serving in the military alongside their white counterparts, began taking a stronger stand against racial injustices."

"We moved to San Francisco, where Louis managed a small jazz club in the Fillmore district. Louis' club was about listening to great black musicians and starting to break down racial divides," she said with some obvious pride. "All the greats of the time played there: Charlie Parker, Count Basie, Ben Webster, and Earl Hines." Chris had no idea who those people were, but he assumed they were musicians of some kind.

"It seems unbelievable now that it was once socially unacceptable for white kids to even listen to colored artists. Without those pioneers, pop stars like Prince and Michael Jackson wouldn't exist today. Artists started playing Bebop, which wasn't intended to be danced to. You were supposed to listen and contemplate it as an art form. Beboppers introduced faster tempos and improvisational, experimental instrumentals, developing what people now call *modern jazz*. It was a very exciting time for music and we were in the perfect place to experience it."

"During the war, there was a huge need for workers in the East Bay shipyards, building large freighters to bring supplies to the front. And, while the army did admit some blacks in support positions, there was no large-scale utilization of black troops. So, the absence of the white men in the area left a huge vacancy in the labor pool to be filled by women and blacks.

"The Bay Area had seen a six-hundred percent increase in black population during the last years of the war, and jazz was hot in what was starting to be called the Harlem of the West. It was the beginning of the Beat Generation, but the stereotypical black barrettes and sunglasses hadn't caught on yet. G.I.s were starting motorcycle clubs and riding up and down the coast making as much noise as they could. They were mostly pretty good guys, they'd just had enough of taking orders. Instead of going to work or school, or using their G.I. bill money to buy houses and settle down, they would build the loudest bikes they could and live their lives on the fringes of society."

Joyce broke off her account. The pre-dawn was just beginning to lighten the sky as they walked slowly along Washington Street, past the UPS depot and the new Saint John's Park Freight Terminal at pier 40. It was named for the nearby Saint John's Park, which had now become the eastbound exit of the

Holland Tunnel and had been the terminus of the New York Central Railroad's abandoned High Line that ran up Washington Street past the loft.

Joyce walked along almost robotically, still fixedly watching the sidewalk slip past. "One night, a man came in at closing time," she continued. "Louis had already sent everyone else home and I was waiting at the bar while he closed up. 'Sorry, we're closed,' he said, expecting that late arrival would simply apologize and leave. Instead, he locked the door behind him and took off his dark overcoat and Trilby hat. He turned out to be a forty-ish looking, completely bald, Chinese man named Low Yet, wearing an expensive suit who looked like an upper-level member of one of the organized crime gangs."

"Tongs had been in San Francisco since the railroad expansion of the 1800s had attracted huge numbers of Chinese immigrants to the west. We had been dealing with periodic shakedowns ever since Louis started running the bar, so neither of us were completely surprised by the visit. I think we both expected another extortion demand, so we were completely taken back when the man set his hat gently on the freshly wiped bar top and said in perfect English: 'I have no interest in your money or your establishment.'"

"'Then what can I do for you?' Louis asked, leaning against the bar between where I sat on one end and the man stood at the other."

"'There are flowers blooming in a little desert town, beautiful, young blossoms that are ready to be plucked. Hotels being built in Nevada due to the legalization of gambling, and the New York gangster Bugsy Siegel is developing the next and grandest project to date: A hotel and casino called the Flamingo. There is a huge amount of money to be made, and I want a piece.'"

"'That sounds great but what does any of that have to do with me?'" Louis asked confused."

"'Almost nothing,' the man replied, taking very slow, deliberate steps toward where Louis stood. 'But, it does have a great deal to do with her.' He looked past Louis, directly at me. I sat up on my stool, alarmed. *What could this have to do with me*, I wondered. 'I am in need of an agent – a young woman specifically – to gather information that I can use to cut these blossoms,' he replied, 'and I have chosen you.'"

"'My wife's not going anywhere with you,' Louis said, becoming more aggressive in his effort to defend of me."

"'She will go or stay as she decides.' He looked past Louis and straight into my eyes. 'Well, my dear, will you come with me and leave your husband here?'"

"'I said she's not going anywhere!' Louis repeated more forcefully. Then, he made his last mistake. He grabbed the man by the shoulder. At first, I couldn't believe what I was seeing. The man's face contorted into a snarl of rage, and he took Louis by the front of his shirt and threw him into the air with one hand. Louis was not a hulking sort of man, but he was no lightweight either. The strength it would take to do what I was seeing was simply unbelievable... simply inhuman."

She paused and wiped her eyes, taking a moment to gather herself before she was able to continue. "Louis' back hit the ceiling with so much force that it shattered the plaster and sent a shower of small particles raining down. I closed my eyes for a moment to shield them from the white dust and reopened them just in time to see the man reach up towards Louis as he began to fall back towards the floor. Everything seemed to move in slow motion; the molts of dust settling, Louis' shirt fluttering, the pained expression on his face as he fell."

"It looked at first like the man intended to catch him, but he kept his fingers ridged. When they came into contact with Louis' chest, they slipped effortlessly through his clothing and into his belly, splitting him open as easily as a knife through water, eviscerating him. He caught him by the ribs like they were a handle and held him up on his feet as his organs spilled out onto the floor."

"I couldn't breath. I was stunned by the horror of what I was seeing. But when I did finally come to myself again and was able to move, I launched myself at the man's back. I had seen enough wounded men during my stint in the army to know that Louis was dead on his feet, but I wasn't what you would call rational at that exact moment. I felt that if I could get past this man who had come to put an end to our life together, I could hold Louis together, keep him alive until help arrived. It was delusional, and I think I knew that even as I was completely convinced I could do it. I never came anywhere close to actually trying it though."

"I clung momentarily to the man's back, trying to claw his hand away from Louis. I saw my fingernails crack and break off against his skin but seem to have no effect on him, except to further enrage him. He reached back with his free hand, grabbed me by the neck, and tossed me the full length of the bar as if I weighed nothing. I crashed head-first into the brick wall and heard the crack of my neck breaking right before I lost consciousness."

"When I came to, my chin was pressed into my chest and I could hardly breathe. I could feel my heart rate slowing but not much more. At that moment, I knew... I was about to die. Our murderer stood over me for a moment, then squatted down to look me in the face. I couldn't move my head and I couldn't look up enough to see his face. I refused to spend my last moments staring at the crotch of his pants, so I closed my eyes and concentrated on just keeping my heart beating."

"'It is a lost cause, my dear,' he said. 'Your husband is dead, and soon you will join him. It is a shame that one so young and pretty should have her light snuffed out before you have reached the full bloom of womanhood. Would you like me to help you? To save you from the nothingness that awaits you?' He was silent for a moment as if he expected me to answer him. 'I'll accept your silence as affirmation of your agreement,' he said before lifting my limp wrist to his mouth. I knew that Louis was already dead, and as much as I hated him for what he had done, if I had been able to speak at that moment... I'm ashamed to say, I might have begged him to save me."

Chris knew what was coming next. "His teeth tore easily through my skin," Joyce said. "I couldn't feel anything, but I heard the tendons in my wrist snap as his teeth cut through them and severed the arteries. I could hear the wet sounds of him sucking and clamped my eyes shut as tight as possible. I could feel my heart beat becoming weaker and weaker and bean to welcome the cool embrace of death. I had no concept of time as I lay there waiting to die. Gradually I lost all awareness of sound and sensation and was sure that I was crossing over. I wondered if I would see Louis again."

"Once I regained consciousness, I discovered that I was slung over the man's shoulder. My head bouncing limply against his dark brown overcoat as he walked. I later learned that he had sliced his hand with his thumbnail and pressed it to my wrist to bestow his Blessing."

She paused to blot a tear from the corner of her eye with a black lace handkerchief. "So, when I say that I understand what you have been going through, I really do."

Chris felt some embarrassment at the attitude he had given her in his early days at Haven. "Sorry about all that. So, what happened then?"

Joyce took a deep breath. "Well... after I changed, he kept me with him, inundating my mind with a continuous stream of instructions and commands. That is, until one day in frustration, I simply blocked him out. I had no idea what I had done or how I had done it, but I was immensely grateful for the mental silence."

"Low Yet was not happy about my new found ability and ordered me to never use it again. I didn't know how I was doing it, so I didn't know how to stop doing it. Truth be told, I don't think I would have stopped even if I did. He beat me severely, but the only other thing he could do would have been to kill me, and that was out of the question, seeing as how he needed me too much for that.

"He brought me back to Hollywood and put me in a mob brothel where I could keep tabs on city officials, movie stars and mobsters. It was hard being back home after everything that happened, to see all those familiar places and people but never being able to see my parents. Eventually, I was sent to work as a hostess at one of Siegel's parties at his Beverly Hills home where he busied himself arraigning loans from celebrities with no intention of ever paying them back. It wasn't like they could force him to pay back the money. He'd just refuse or knock them off if they got too pushy."

"In 1947, I got a job as a cocktail waitress at the newly opened Flamingo hotel in Las Vegas. Low Yet wanted me to use my enhanced hearing to get information for him that he could use to increase his leverage with the mob, who were largely in control of Las Vegas gambling. And I did give him some information that he found useful, but I also kept a lot of what I learned for my own purposes."

"In a relatively short amount of time, I was able to amass a sizable fortune - for the time - due not only to my heightened hearing, but my other mental abilities that Low Yet had failed to tell me I might develop. In the two years I was there, I learned to not only read people's thoughts but to implant my own suggestions into people's minds. For example, I could make the big winner give the nice waitress a five-thousand dollar tip on a ten dollar tab. I did everything I could think of to keep him from finding out how well I was doing, but eventually, I became careless."

"One of Low Yet's informants saw me playing cards at another hotel and told him about my big payout. He demanded that I turn my winnings over to him. He was making deals to start bringing huge amounts of heroin into the country and needed more money for startup costs. Every dollar he could get from me was one less he would have to take out of his other businesses or borrow from the Italians. He nearly tore me apart to get it when I refused."

"I was planning to kill him. I didn't know how to do it but I was sure it could be done. So, I started observing him, looking for signs of weakness. That's when Amym showed up. He had been sent to convince Low Yet to keep a lower profile. Apparently, his smuggling activities were drawing too much attention from the authorities, and the Chord was becoming annoyed."

"He must have been told to use whatever means necessary because when Low Yet refused to cooperate, Amym simply killed him. Normally, the Chord would have either had a Lesser Blessed eliminated as the prodigy of an apostate, or brought in for reassignment. But Low Yet had never sought their approval for my change in the first place so, like you, Amym was able to get me some time to learn to be more valuable."

"Did you go to Haven too?" Chris asked.

"No, I was in Nevada, so he brought me to a place called Angel's Rest in Oregon. That's where I received my training, similar to what you got before being presented to the Chord."

Chris unlocked the door to the loft and held it open for her. "Well, I'm really glad they found an assignment for you. Is that what you were doing at Billy's Topless?" he asked sheepishly, remembering the night he had gone to the low-end strip club in

Chelsea to get a peek at his neighbor Monika. She was pretty, but he hadn't been able to peel his eyes away from Joyce.

"I've had a lot of assignments over the years, and not all of them have been glamorous. Eventually, you learn to take advantage of the perks while they are available," she said with a slight smile as they stepped over the threshold into their own little haven.

Chapter 10

Pet sat on the pavement outside the Chambers Street subway station, panhandling for spare change. The sun would be going down soon and she hadn't been able to collect nearly enough money. She re-tallied after every contribution and the current total was only $21.62. Not enough to keep her from being punished, but maybe enough to avoid any broken bones. Those sometimes took days to reknit.

She watched the legs of the men and women hustling past her on their way home from work. The women in the knee-length skirts and sneakers, the men in dark slacks and shiny dress shoes. Younger ones off to the gym or meeting friends for drinks at the nearby bars, and the older ones heading home for dinner with their families. Not many noticed the filthy girl huddled against the dark-green, cast iron fence that surrounded the subway entrance, except to step around her.

She had perfected an expression of despair and learned to divorce her mind from the activity swirling around her. She stayed devoid of all conscious thought and just enjoying the warmth of the late afternoon sun shining on her face. At least until she was brought out of her trance by the dull clink of coins falling into her cup. *Another seventeen cents... twenty-one seventy-nine*, she quickly calculated before vegging out again.

The next time she looked up to check her surroundings, there were legs standing in front of her. It took her a moment to focus enough to see the denim of the man's jeans and the clean, but worn, white high-top sneakers. "Hey, are you okay?" he asked, squatting down to talk to her. It had been a while since anyone but her master had spoken to her, and he usually just spoke at her and didn't need or want a response except *yes, master*. Now, she had to actually pull her thoughts together to process what was being said to her and determine how to respond.

"Uuuuumm, yeah. I'm okay, I guess," she stammered.

"If you don't mind me saying so, you kinda look like shit," he smiled. "Smell like it, too." He was a friendly looking Hispanic man in his early thirties. He had a folding metal luggage cart with a cardboard box bungee corded to it that was lined with a black trash bag.

"Oh, aren't you sweet. Thanks so much for noticing," she responded with the saccharine sweetness of the naturally sarcastic. Just because she was dead didn't mean she liked being called out on her ratty appearance, or lack of personal hygiene.

"If you need a place to get cleaned up, there's a women's shelter not too far from here," he suggested.

"That's okay, I got a place," she said. She couldn't go to the woman's shelter because they'd ask too many questions. They'd probably take her into custody and try to return her to her mom. Then, her master would kill her, and probably her mom too. And where would that leave Boy, she thought.

He didn't believe her for a second. *Wherever it was she was sleeping, there certainly wasn't running water*, he thought. "Sure, sure. No problem. Are you hungry? I've got sandwiches," he offered with a wink.

She was always hungry. It was hard to get food when you looked like she did and all your money went to a ghoul who kept you perpetually trapped between life and death. "Yeah, I could eat. What've you got?"

The man looked happy as he pulled the box closer to peer inside. He dug around for a few seconds and popped up with a saran-wrapped sandwich in each hand. "I got Peanut butter or cheese."

"Cheese, please," she said and accepted the shiny package from his extended hand.

"How'd you come to be on the street?" He asked as he watched her unwrap her dinner. "I don't mean to pry, but there are places you can go as a juvenile. Places where you can get some real help."

"Of course you mean to pry... but it's cool. I've got someone counting on me to look out them. And... there are other reasons." It felt good to be eating food. Real food. Food that no one or nothing else had already been eating. She closed her eyes and savored the taste of two imitation cheese food slices nestled comfortably between the pillow-like pieces of processed white bread.

"Who're you looking out for? A boyfriend? Sibling?"

"Brother," she said around a mouthful. It was the closest thing to the truth that would make any sense to someone who wasn't familiar with the interpersonal relationship dynamics of sadistic bloodsucking ghouls, their undead minions, and their orphaned blood slaves.

"Okay, cool. Would you like something to bring back for him?" he offered.

"Sure, can I get one of the peanut butter sandwiches?"

"Yeah, of course. Why don't you take a few," he insisted before putting three sandwiches in a white plastic shopping bag from D'Agostino Supermarket. "And some milk for strong bones and teeth." He took out four pint-sized cardboard cartons of milk, two at a time, and placed them into the bag before tying the handles together and holding it out to her.

"Thanks." She knew the boy would be grateful for the food. The only thing he got was what scraps she could scrounge for the two of them while she was out hustling money for the master. Boy's main purposes was to serve as food, which took *that* burden literally off her shoulders. That, and to satisfy the masters even more disturbing carnal urges. She knew her master didn't care overly much what condition the boy was in, so long as she kept him alive and making blood during the day, compliant at night and didn't let him leave the lair.

She still didn't know his name. He didn't talk at all in the master's presence and really didn't say much any other time either. The master had explained to him that he was an orphan now and that his parents had been killed in a random holdup on their way home from the corner store. She knew that Boy knew the truth, but she supposed it didn't really matter if he knew what really happened or not. The effect was the same: Complete, emotional devastation.

He didn't deserve the brutal existence he was being subjected to, and she did whatever she could to make it a little easier for him. When he had first been brought into the lair she had tried to get the master to continue feeding from her, but he seemed to take particular pleasure in abusing the boy in every way imaginable. They both cried a lot at first, but it's amazing what people can get used to over time. She wondered if, when the master finally killed him, he would end up like her: A living corpse. She hoped not; anyone who endured what he did, absolutely deserved to have it come to some sort of end. Eventually.

"Look, my name's Hector and I hope I don't see you out here again. But if you see me, I'll have a sandwich for you," he told her seriously.

"Cool," she mumbled and gulped down her bite. "Thanks again."

"Yeah, no problem. Take care of yourself, okay?" He said seeming genuinely concerned for her well-being.

She stretched out on the warm sidewalk to relax and finish eating, making the oblivious commuters notice her, at least enough to step over her outstretched legs like a speed bump that might shake loose some of their change. The air was starting to cool but there was still a little over an hour of daylight left. She always tried to stay in the sun as long as possible, constantly aware of what awaited her when it went down.

"Hey, you wanna make a quick twenty bucks?" She looked up to find a young, professional-looking man in his late twenties standing over her with an expression of smug confidence on his face.

She gave him a superficial once-over: Dark suit, yellow power tie. Typical Wall Street yuppie type. A recent college grad eager to work his way up the ladder to broker one day and settle into a salary in the upper six figures. They sometimes hassled her a little, especially when they were in groups, and she wouldn't want to be an exotic dancer after they'd had a few too many. But, there were certainly worse things than them in the world.

She knew better than to ask, but evening was approaching, and the after-work crowds would be disappearing soon. She was quickly running out of time and another twenty dollars would go a long way towards keeping her in one piece for another day. With a sigh of resignation, Pet finally asked: "What exactly did you have in mind?"

Tonight, they were on a mission, and Chris couldn't help a feeling of pride as he strode down Sixth Avenue with Joyce beside him, her hand resting lightly in the crook of his arm. The heels of their boots clacked loudly on the pavement as they walked, and the people on the busy street seemed to part in front of them like wheat before a combine.

As they rounded the corner at Gray's Papaya and continued onto 8th Street, Chris watched the way people responded to Joyce: With a deference that bordered on reverence. They stepped instinctively out of her path. Her magnetism drawing shy glances from both men and women, with admiration for more than just her beauty.

He had been feeling like a stranger, like one of the tourists coming to visit on holiday, but on the corner of MacDougal, they ran into Adam and Jen outside the Häagen-Dazs. "Hey, guys!" Chris said coming up on them unnoticed.

Adam looked up and said, "Hey, Chris! What's up?"

Chris pulled a postcard-sized invitation from the pocket of his duster and handed it to his friend. "Chris and I are opening a new club next week, that'll get you in opening night," Joyce told them.

"Cool. We'll try to make it!" Jen said excitedly, snatching it from Adam's hand.

"Anyone else around?" Chris asked.

"Don't know," Adam said, talking through a mouthful of Pralines and Cream. "We just got here."

"Hey, did you hear about Geoff?" Jen asked.

"No, what?"

"Geoff got busted for burglarizing a construction site for power tools."

"No shit." It didn't really surprise Chris that Geoff got arrested. It was bound to happen eventually, he just figured it would be for fighting or vandalism, maybe possession, not burglary.

"Yeah, he was walking down the street carrying an armload of tools when the cops caught up to him. He looked at them and said *you got me.* So, needless to say, he's gonna be away for a while."

"So, are you down for the weekend?" Chris asked Jen.

Jen bit her bottom lip anxiously. "Well, I was staying at Family House for a while until I could get a ride down. Adam's been letting me stay at his place while his parents are upstate, but I'll have to find something else soon. I'm hoping to stay in the city."

Chris looked at Joyce, who gave a slight nod. "We have room for you if you want to crash with us," he offered.

Jen looked Joyce over. She knew she was no threat to the older woman: After all, she was beautiful, with perfect hair, perfect skin, perfect clothes. *If Chris is with her, why is he inviting me to stay?* she wondered.

"Sure, thanks."

"Oh, hey, I don't know if you've heard, but there's been some guy coming around the last week or so asking about you," Adam told him.

"Really? Who is it?"

"Don'no," Adam answered around his plastic spoon.

"What'd he want?" Chris wondered.

"Didn't say, but he looked like a cop: Tweed blazer, bad haircut, worn-out brown Hush Puppies. Anyway, I thought I'd give you a heads up."

"Cool, thanks for letting me know. I'll keep an eye out," he said, giving Joyce a concerned glance.

"Hey, speaking of cops, you used to live next to Dan the Chicken Man, right?" Adam asked, starting to get excited.

"Yeah. Why?"

"You're *NOT* gonna believe it! So, they were cleaning out the lockers at Port Authority. You know, when people don't come back to get their stuff for a long time, and they find one of those five-gallon paint buckets full of human bones. I don't know how they did it, but they traced the bucket back to the Chicken Man. Turns out, he killed his girlfriend, cut her up, and served her to the homeless at the Tompkins soup kitchen. I even heard someone found a finger in their bowl, but I don't believe it, 'cause someone would have told the cops right then. Anyway, when they picked him up, he had her skull tucked away in his bag, just walking around the park selling pot like nothing was up. Crazy, right?"

Chris and Joyce said their goodbyes and their hopes to see them at the opening, then continued on MacDougal Street to Washington Square Park. "Do you believe that story Adam was telling about Monika?" Chris asked.

"I don't have any reason not to. I'm sure some of the details are exaggerated, but the basics are probably true. This is a dangerous world, and people die or go missing every day. It didn't help that Daniel was completely bonkers. I told her to leave him but she was determined to get that apartment away from him. Rent Controlled apartments are hard to come by, but it wasn't worth the risks she took."

Rent control began in post-war 1920 as a way for the city to deal with the shortage of low-cost apartments that was causing an epidemic of rent strikes. These apartments could be passed down to direct relatives if they had inhabited the unit for at least two years prior to the leaseholder's death or departure. Even then, the rents only increased by four percent each time the lease was renewed.

"I can't even imagine how cheap it would be after one hundred or so years. Hmmm, maybe she was on to something after all," Joyce mused.

Chris considered her response as they made their way past the army of dealers who crowded the shadowy walkways into what he had recently considered his second home: The Washington Square arch. Her apparent coldness toward Monika bothered him, they had been friends and coworkers at Billie's after all, but he supposed that she had watched a lot of people die over the decades.

Chris couldn't begin to calculate how many hours he had spent hanging out at the edifice commemorating the centennial anniversary of George Washington's presidential inauguration over the previous summer, but he figured that beneath the arch's decorative rosettes would be a good place to look for more people to attend the opening. He wasn't surprised to find a group of around twenty Punk and Goth kids killing time sitting on the cobblestones.

As they approached, Chris scanned their faces and recognized Opus sitting with his back against the white marble. People called him that because his large nose reminded them of a comic strip penguin from the newspaper. It didn't help that he always wore English riding boots and an antique tuxedo jacket with tails either. As they got closer, Chris identified two more of his old friends, Mike Parish, and Mim, hanging out among the crowd nearby.

"Hey guys," Joyce said cheerfully.

"Hey," they said with reflexive sullenness, looking up to see who was talking to them. It wasn't unusual for tourists to come up to them asking to take pictures of the freaks to show off to their friends when they got back to Iowa. However, the people standing over them weren't overweight Midwesterners in souvenirs Cats t-shirts. They were actually a couple of stunning, well dressed, Goths.

"Joyce!" Mike exclaimed and jumped up to give her a loose hug and an air kiss on the cheek to avoid messing up either of their makeup. "Oh my *GODDD*! I haven't seen you in forever."

"You remember me?" Joyce asked with a smile.

"Of course, how could I not remember you!? You're responsible for the best night of my life." He clutched the sticker-covered, black metal lunch box that had been signed by his idol, Eric Arcane. After the Marianist Sisters show at the Ritz, they had all crammed into the back of a cab together. Just being in his presence at the after-hours club would give him bragging rights for years to come.

"Who's your gorgeous friend?" he asked, looking over at Chris without recognition.

"Good evening, Michael," Chris said, smiling at him from behind his mirrored glasses. He then looked down to where Mim and Opus sat against the base of the arch, "Miriam. John."

"Ho-ly Craaaap!" Mim exclaimed. "Chris, is that you? How've you been?"

"I'm fine," he replied, losing his cool and grinning broadly at his friends.

"You sure are! I almost didn't recognize you. Did you get taller?" Mike asked.

"Maybe. I wanted to come invite you guys to the opening of our new club." He handed each of them an invitation.

"This is your place?" Mike asked, looking impressed at the card.

"Ours, yes," Chris stipulated.

"What sort of place is it?" Opus asked skeptically.

"It's a Goth club," Joyce explained.

"Like Albion night? Cool. Is it gonna be once a month?" Mim asked.

"No, it's every night. It's a full-time Goth club: The bar will keep dusk till dawn hours, although liquor will stop being served at four. The DJ will start at midnight, so we will begin charging a cover at eleven."

"Could we get some for Melissa and Kelly, too? I bet they'd *love* to go."

Chris thought back, he could remember everything about them: What they looked like, smelled like. He remembered every word they'd ever said to each other, but for some reason, he could not remember why they had been friends. He figured that it must have been the insular tribalism of the Punk scene. The inclusiveness of being separated from the mainstream had made them feel as if anyone who looked like them or listened to the same music they did was their lifelong friend.

Now, he was part of a much smaller subculture, and the majority of its members were definitely not his friends. That realization, however, made him feel even more isolated. But maybe that was a reason to bring his old friends closer and not push them away as Joyce had advised. He smiled, showing off the tips of his canines. "Those passes are good for two, but take as many as you want. Invite whoever you want." Chris pulled a small stack of cards from the pocket of his duster and handed them over to Mike. "You should come find me at the club. I think we might have some things to talk about," Chris said seriously.

"Okay, sure. Good seeing you two."

"You also."

"See ya, Chris," Mim called as they started walking away.

When they were out of earshot, Joyce turned to him and said, "Don't get too close to your old friends. Remember, you are a Vampire Lord now, and you have an image to maintain. They need to look up to us, to see us as something to aspire to. Anything else puts both them and us in jeopardy."

"Okay, I get it. It's just... they're my friends."

"I know, and I'm not saying that they can't still be – maybe even more sometimes. You just have to remain aloof." She said snuggling up close to him and matching her steps to his. "Be friendly, but not friends. At least until there comes a time to *not* be friendly. Remember, you are the master here, and they are only along to serve you."

"Should I have laid on an accent to make myself seem more aristocratic?" Chris teased.

"You know, I thought about that, but there wasn't time for a trip to the mountains of Carpathia," she quipped and held out the edges of her black velvet coat, flapping it like a pair of wings.

They walked east, past the bronze statue of General Giuseppe Garibaldi atop its graffiti-covered stone pedestal and continued along Washington Place where, in 1911, the deadliest industrial disaster in the city's history occurred at the Triangle Shirtwaist Factory.

They passed the cube at Astor Place and started down Saint Mark's. Suddenly, a familiar fragrance wafted past Chris, causing him to turn his head toward the source of the aroma. Halfway down the block, he saw her coming out of a storefront; her hair was different, but he would have recognized her anywhere.

Chris quickly wove his way through the throng of people that jammed the sidewalk. "Rachel!" he called, catching her by the shoulder.

She turned to look up at him; her long, brown hair brushed across the back of his hand, sending a chill through him. "Who are... do I know you?" Rachel asked. For a split second there was a glimmer of recognition in her eyes, then Chris watched as it quickly faded away.

"I believe we met once," he said. "Perhaps it was in another life. I apologize for disturbing you."

Her girlfriend grabbed her by the arm and started leading her down the street. She leaned in towards her surreptitiously. "Who was that?" she whispered.

"I have no idea," Rachel replied.

"A little creepy for me, but still kinda hot. And I do like older guys." They both turned to look back over their shoulders at him, then start laughing and ran away down the block when they saw that he was still watching.

"Don't take it personally. Her memory was wiped during her recovery." Joyce explained sympathetically. "She would have no recollection of ever meeting you or anything about what happened to her."

"And the baby?" He asked, dreading the answer he knew he would receive.

"There is no baby," Joyce said sadly. "It couldn't have survived the trauma of her injuries, but if she's lucky, she may still be able to have children in the future." She gave him a moment to process. "Come on," she finally said wrapping her arm around his waist. "I'll buy you a drink."

They continued East until they reached First Avenue then turned south, walking past Third Street to the Lismar Lounge where two years later Jane's Addiction and White Zombie would each play some of their earliest shows. The front windows, overshadowed by black awnings, were painted with stylized flames and a pair of white Jolly Rodgers adorned the flat black doors that led into the eclectic East Village dive. Chris followed Joyce past the bar and took a seat near the pool table.

They hadn't talked during the walk because Joyce had let Chris have some time to think about what had just happened. It was one thing to be told that Rachel would be okay after being crucified with flatware, her unborn baby gone, and to know that she wouldn't remember what had happened to her. However, it was very different to come face to face with the fact that she no longer knew him – that their friendship was over as if it had never been. As if they had never been close.

"How are you doing with that?" Joyce finally asked, breaking the silence.

"I don't know. It feels weird... like everything that happened only happened in my mind, you know? Like... I might as well have just made the whole thing up."

"It might seem that way now, but keep in mind that she is alive, and that's something to be very happy about. She is much safer not remembering. The Chord doesn't like witnesses or loose ends."

"I guess so," he grudgingly admitted. "I just wish... I don't know... that things had been different."

A man tripped over his own feet and stumbled into their table. Joyce and Chris snatched up their drinks before they could spill. Chris reached out to steady the table as Joyce put up a hand to keep the obviously drunk man from falling on top of them. His bleary eyes cleared as he looked at her, and a wide smile bloomed on his slack face. "Hey! I know you," he slurred.

"Do you?" Joyce asked disinterestedly.

"Yeah, you're that dancer, right? Nightshade or something spooky like that. I used to watch you dance all the time. Where've you been, baby?"

"I've moved on, why don't you do the same," she suggested.

"Nawww, come on. I wanna see you dance. How about in one of these booths? I've got money," he said, reaching into his front pocket to retrieve a crumpled wad of bills and sprinkled them onto the tabletop. When she didn't look up, he changed his tactic. "Okay, then how 'bout I buy you a drink and you give me one dance up on the bar? Come on, just one dance?"

Chris started to stand up. "I think you need to leave," he said in a low growl. Joyce put her hand against his chest to keep him from getting up from his seat.

"I wasn't talking to you man," the guy said, leaning over to poke Chris in the chest with his index finger.

Chris was on his feet instantly. He grabbed the man's finger with his left hand and twisted it inward, causing him to bend forward as his arm was wrenched in its socket. Chris brought his knee up, smashing the drunk's nose. He then twisted the arm the opposite direction, pulling the man back upright, and forced him to bend backward. Then, Chris delivered an open-palm strike to his sternum.

The man flew twenty feet through the air before coming to a bone-jarring landing on the worn, beer-sodden planks. Chris took his seat as a small group gathered around to see if the man was still alive. "I could have handled that, you know," Joyce told him, clearly irritated by his show of machismo.

"I have no doubt that you could, but you shouldn't have had to," he grumbled.

Slowly, a smile crept across her face. "Did it help?"

Chris thought for a moment then smiled back, "Yeah, I guess it did."

The bartender came over, righted the table, and set another round of drinks in front of Chris. "I'm sorry, but after this, I gotta ask you to go. I gotta say: That hit was amazing."

"Thanks," Chris said and swallowed the drink in a single gulp. He extended his hand to Joyce. "Let's go."

She accepted his help up, abandoning her untouched cocktail, and let him lead her out of the bar. She smiled inwardly, recognizing that he was starting to become the more assertive, self-confident person that she needed him to be. That, she knew, would be vital if they were to be successful in the tasks yet to come.

The other patrons stepped back as they made their way towards the exit, and Chris got the feeling that it was more of a display of deference and admiration than caution.

Chris knocked on the partially open door of the small storage room that had been converted into the loft's office. "Hey, Joyce? There's a guy here to see you."

"I didn't hear the bell. Who is it?" she asked distractedly as she poured over the papers littering the desk in front of her.

"He said his name is Steve. Real rugged type. You wanna come out or you want me to let him in?"

"Yeah," she said, shuffling her papers into a neat-looking pile that she would just have to spread out again after he left. "He's the contractor overseeing construction downstairs. Go ahead and let him in."

Her high-backed executive chair creaked slightly as she reclined back, resting her elbows on the black, pleather-covered arms to wait for their visitor. Chris was followed by a large man in a dusty flannel shirt and faded jeans that were at least one size too small to be comfortable. Joyce looked him over; she had no doubt that they were worn strictly for the positive effect they had on his appearance she thought appreciatively.

"Hey Steve, how's everything going?" she asked as he stepped past Chris into the cramped room.

"I don't know what kind of pull you people have with the city, but I've never seen a liquor license come through so fast."

"It helps to have friends," she replied with a smile.

"Right. The inspector has approved the M.E.P. Structural, mechanical, electrical and sanitation are all good to go, so we're set to get started on the finish work."

"That's great news. Has the designer been in touch?"

He leaned casually against the door frame, his broad shoulders spanning the opening as well as any door could, edging Chris out of the conversation.

"You know, its the strangest thing. We got the preliminary designs months ago and sent back the changes that the engineer required, but I haven't gotten anything since then. Have you?"

"No. Aside from all these bills from the Subs, it's been pretty quiet for a construction site."

"*Sooooooo*... any idea when we might get some design help?"

"Can I help?" Chris asked from where he hovered behind Steve's massive torso. "Maybe we could just design it ourselves."

"No, I don't think so. I'll call Promus" Joyce said with a sigh of someone who was frustrated with dealing with yet another problem. "Actually, now that I think about it, that might not be such a bad idea. Okay, let's go down and look over the drawings that we have and see what needs to be done."

Steve led them down the newly-completed stairs past street level, below the building's basement, deep into the belly of the island. They had done a good job making it look as though the staircase had been there for generations, he thought. The edges and corners of the bricks were chipped and worn and deep depressions had been ground into the marble treads by countless feet. "Is all this recycled?" Joyce asked.

"Yeah. They were bulldozing a burned-out tenement building on Avenue C and 9th. We were able to salvage a lot of material for free, except for the labor, but I definitely think it was worth it to make everything match." There was an obvious pride in Steve's voice. There were several buildings that matched Steve's description in that area, but the only one that came to Chris' mind was the one that Cara had died in.

When they reached the bottom, Steve turned to Joyce, "Here's where the new construction joined up with the existing brickwork. See if you can tell which ones are the new bricks."

She studied the masonry in the harsh glow of the utility lights strung near the ceiling. The differences were subtle but plainly visible to her enhanced vision. But, to preserve his pride in his work, she said, "No, I can't tell at all." Steve smiled and continued into the cavernous space.

Chris, who hadn't gotten a good look, turned to Steve and asked sarcastically, "Aren't you going to show us?"

"Why? It doesn't matter if you can't see a difference, that's all that's really important," Steve said dismissively over his shoulder as he kept walking.

Chris was not at all happy with the dismissive tone this man was taking with him, and his jealousy and anger were beginning to get the better of him. His eyes began to shine with the multicolored hue that signaled he was subconsciously gathering his power.

Get control of yourself, admonished Joyce's voice in his head. He turned his gaze from Steve's broad back to catch her warning look. *He doesn't know about us. And don't worry, he's not my type. I'm just working him to get the job done on time.* Chris didn't know if that was supposed to make him feel better, but he turned away and took several calming breaths to get himself under control and allow his eyes to stop flaring.

When Steve walked them to the center of the room, Chris was struck by how the high-vaulted, brick ceiling gave the space a feeling of awe, as if they were standing in the nave of a cathedral. "The plumbing's set up for men's and women's restrooms over there," Steve said, bringing Chris out of his reverence and back to the utilitarian purpose of their visit.

"There needs to be space in both for plenty of sinks and makeup counters," Joyce insisted. Steve gave her a questioning look but shrugged it off, deciding that she probably knew what she was talking about based on the amount of makeup she seemed to be wearing.

"The bar should be along that long wall over there, and I think it should be really long, like… it should take up the whole length. And it should look as old as the rest of the club," Chris said, inserting himself in the discussion and maybe even beginning to get a little bit enthusiastic about participating in the process of helping to build something that could be very cool.

"There's an architectural salvage place on Second Avenue and Houston: Irreplaceable Artifacts. If anyone has what you're looking for, they will," Steve offered, looking directly at Joyce. "They'll probably have a lot of stuff that would look good in here."

"I know the place," Chris interjected. "It's right near CB's"

"Who?" Joyce asked herself as she searched her memory for the name of the owner. "Evan. I'll call him and make an appointment. I might be able to get us a discount if we put together a large order," she said, giving Chris a wink.

Chapter 11

"Are you ready for this?" Joyce asked Chris as they got dressed to go down.

"Not really," Chris admitted.

"Just try to look bored," she suggested. "If you don't know what to say to someone, just keep your face as expressionless as possible, and look away as if you've completely lost interest in them. Bring those black Lennon glasses with you just in case."

He checked himself in the mirror. He looked every inch the Gothic vampire cowboy: His hair had grown down past his shoulders and darkened until it seemed to swallow the light, his clothes were a mixture of Victorian elegance and old west functionality with a modern Punk influence. "You'll do fine," she reassured him handing over a warmed glass of blood to calm his nerves.

Chris took a sip and looked over Joyce's outfit. "And you are stunning, as always. I'm going to be kept busy fighting off your admirers all night."

A wicked smile crossed her face. "*Or*, I could just beat them all off myself, if it gets to be too much for you," she offered.

"Har-har," he said in a deadpan voice and swallowed the last of his blood. "Okay, let's do this."

"Not so fast partner. You're forgetting something." She snatched an unused eyeliner from her makeup table and headed towards him.

"Common, really? You know I hate wearing makeup, it makes me feel… well…"

"Girly? Are you worried about your masculinity?" she asked with a glance towards his groin.

"No!" Chris scoffed.

"Good. Now either get used to it or just change your appearance the way I do." She deftly applied heavy black outlines to his eyelids and blended dark eyeshadow to give him a sunken, haunted look.

"There, much more mysterious." She said giving him a last looking over. "Now we can go."

He led the way from the bedroom they had been sharing platonically – except for in Chris' imagination – for the past two months. He steeled his nerves and began the long descent down into the club.

Bouncers in black flight jackets stood on the sidewalk outside the door, seemingly impervious to the dropping temperature as they kept the public waiting less than patiently for the signal to open. Those with passes were quickly ushered inside past the milling crowd while the rest kept their hands buried in their coat pockets and stomped their feet to keep the late January chill from their toes. The walky-talky emitted a garbled squawk that no one could possibly decipher, but security determined that they had the go-ahead to open the club to the public.

"Ladies and Gentlemen!" The bouncer called out and everyone stopped talking to look at him. "Welcome to The Shambles!" He unhooked the black velvet ropes and let the crowd begin filing through the door.

The lower they went, the louder the music became. The pounding of the bass reverberated through Chris' body, causing his bones to vibrate to the rhythm. At the bottom of the stairs, a heavy wooden arched door from an old Catholic church had been installed to prevent club goers from seeing inside. He pulled it open and stepped into the brick tunnel. Joyce took his arm and they proceeded along the gentle downward sloping passage towards what had been dubbed The Pens.

The tunnel was lit with fluorescent black lights that gave their skin the appearance of a tan and their teeth a bluish glow. Alternating colored lights splashed the bricks with purple and red as they approached the red velvet rope that was stretched across the tunnel entrance, blocking it off from the rest of the club. Two large bouncers in tight-black, high neck shirts, and slacks flanked the opening, and Chris was glad to see that the man who opened the rope for them was Charlie, the six-foot-two, two hundred eighty pound doorman from the Aztec Lounge where Chris had first met Amym. He had compromised his uniform with his signature barrette and twenty-hole oxblood Doc Martens, which set him apart from the other members of the security team and added to his level of intimidation, despite the ever-present coke bottle lenses of his glasses.

Charlie escorted them across the club to the VIP area and then clipped the ropes closed behind them. Chris took his seat at the end of a large, thickly-padded, high back couch drinking powdered pink lemonade concentrate and Gin with ice cubes made of frozen tonic water. It was a little fruity, but the glass glowed blue and pink under the ultraviolet lights that were mounted beneath the frosted glass table. Joyce lounged provocatively next to him like an odalisque, watching the crowd dance. Occasionally, a man would approach the ropes, Charlie would discourage them from trying to enter, but they would lean across to try to talk to Joyce over the music. However, for the most part, she would ignore them after giving them a brief look.

Joyce propped herself up on her elbow. "Come on," she said, setting down her half-empty glass of green-glowing Absinth. "Let's give them a show." She took Chris by the hand and led him out to the center of the dance floor. The music faded out and they stood in the center of the room in total silence except for the hushed murmur of bewildered onlookers as they waited for the DJ to play their prearranged song.

When the music started, they began dancing. Their movements were so graceful and fluid that the crowd stood in stunned amazement until their performance had finished.

Their audience erupted in enthusiastic applause, then returned to dancing as the DJ transitioned seamlessly to another track. Joyce gave Chris a deep kiss, then walked to the bar, pulling the eyes of everyone in the room along with her as if she were dragging them behind her by invisible strings.

She took a spot next to an empty stool and waited for the bartender to serve her. All the staff had been well rehearsed with the owners' expectations. The DJ knew what songs they wanted him to play under certain circumstances, the bartenders knew what they drank, and security knew who the VIPs and celebrities were who could enter the lounge. Joyce could also use her mental persuasion to subtly influence the outcome that she wanted if necessary. So far, everything was going according to plan.

The seat next to her was occupied by a middle-aged man who looked decidedly out of place in his tweed coat, corduroy pants and worn, brown leather loafers. "That was really something," he commented, leaning over to yell at her over the music.

She smiled at him as if he were some small, disfigured animal, just pathetic enough to be considered cute. "Thank you."

"So... Do you drink blood?"

"Pardon me?" Joyce asked in surprise.

"I heard this was supposed to be a vampire club," he said, turning towards her and laughing nervously.

"It is," Joyce replied casually.

"So, how can you tell if someone's a vampire?" the man asked, leaning in closer and speaking to her in a flirtatious, and mildly conspiratorial way.

"That's what the mirrors are for," she whispered back to him, her warm breath on his cheek sending a shiver down his spine.

The man looked at the bar-length mirror mounted on the wall behind the liquor bottles. "What do you mean?" he asked, confused.

The bartender set a pair of glasses in front of Joyce and backed away with a smile to attend to other customers. "If you look closely and you don't see someone reflected in the mirrors, they're the vampires."

The man looked up at his own reflection in the glass, then his eyes scanned the room briefly before coming to a stop on the place next to him. He inhaled sharply in surprise as he discovered that the exotic woman he was talking to him no reflection.

"You're a..." he stammered, turning back towards her only to discover that the seat next to him was now empty. The man smiled, amused at both her joke and at himself for jumping to ridiculous conclusions. He swiveled around and his eyes skimmed over the crowd looking for her but she was already fading from view, threading her way easily into the swirling mass of black-clad dancers, a cut-crystal glass cradled in each hand.

"You have room in your coffin for two?" he asked softly, admiring the view of her receding form as a young man pushed his way through the crowd to fill her vacated spot at and leaned across the bar trying to get the bartender's attention.

The man turned back around, glancing up once just to make sure the boy next to him appeared in the glass. He chuckled softly with relief and silently chastised himself for being concerned in the first place.

Joyce moved through the dancers with a graceful fluidity back towards the VIP area. The dancers seemed to move out of her way as if compelled by nothing more than her presence. The velvet ropes parted as she approached, and she took her seat next to Chris.

"Your cop is here looking for you," she announced.

Chris instantly tensed up and looked around the club. "At the bar, you can't miss him." She playfully bumped her shoulder into his, "Don't worry, I don't sense any hostility from him, but I didn't probe too deeply. The image he has in his mind doesn't even remotely resemble you anymore, so I can't imagine he'd be able to recognize you now."

Joyce began scanning the minds of the people in the club, searching for the lonely, the needy and the desperate among them. She settled on a girl sitting alone on a reclaimed church pew along the wall; her shoulders slumped as she tried to stifle the tears brimming in her heavily mascaraed eyes. Joyce crossed the club and sat down next to her without a word, leaning against her and offering a supportive shoulder. Seconds later, Joyce felt the girl's weight shift, and her head came to rest against the sleeve of her dress. She waited until the girl stopped crying, then handed her a cocktail and a black lace handkerchief.

"I'm sorry, I'm a real mess," she said with a sniffle, holding the handkerchief out to return it after gently blotting her tears. "I don't want to get my makeup all over it."

"It's already black," Joyce pointed out.

The girl laughed self-consciously and buried her face in the glass, feeling embarrassed both by her emotional state and by her apparent ditsyness. "What's your name, sweetie?"

The girl swallowed a gulp and answered. "Brielle."

"Well, Brielle, why don't you come with me and you can tell me all about what's troubling you." She took the girl by the hand and led her to where Charlie waited to unhook the rope to admit them back into their exclusive sanctuary. Chris glanced up as they approached; he had been busy both looking and feeling, incredibly bored. He was about to say something but the look he received from Joyce made him hesitate.

Suddenly, he heard her mental voice in his head: *Don't act like you're paying any attention to us*. He turned his gaze back to the dance floor and surveyed the crowd disinterestedly, keeping his attention firmly fixed on their conversation.

"So, what was all that about?" Joyce asked the girl.

"Just a stupid boy. What else," she said with exasperation and a hint of contempt, partially for him and all the stupid boys in the world, and partly for herself for caring so much.

"Did he do something to you?" she prompted, concern for her wellbeing coming through clearly in her voice.

"Yes. No. He doesn't even notice me," Brielle admitted. "That's the problem."

"Why would you think that?"

"Because it's true. He never looks at me, never seems to notice me looking at him, barely responds when I try to say hello. I mean, we go to the same school and everything... I know Auden's older but... he's just so beautiful."

Now it's your turn, Joyce sent to Chris as she leaned in close to Brielle. "Would you like him to notice you?"

"Of course I would!" she said, suddenly aware that Chris was standing over her, his hand extended in invitation. She looked at Joyce, who smiled and nodded encouragingly. She tentatively took Chris' hand in hers and he led her out on to the dance floor.

When they reached the center, the crowd seemed to melt away into the background, leaving them the sole focus of every eye as the DJ transitioned to a more melodic song. Chris began to lead her slowly, his graceful steps disguising her awkwardness. "Do you see how everyone is watching you, Brielle?" he asked in a deep voice that reverberated through her whole body.

"No," she said, looking only at Chris' chest. "I couldn't bear to look at them all staring at me."

"They're wondering who the beautiful, graceful young woman is, and asking themselves how they could have failed to notice her before." He felt her pulse quicken through her hands and see the color rise in her pale cheeks.

"No they're not," she protested meekly.

He took her by the chin and turned her face up towards him. She kept her eyes downcast for a moment, concealed behind her ratted out bangs, then slowly raised them to look into his. She was startled by the way they reflected the lights; seeming to sparkle with rainbows of color, like sunlight passing through a prism. "Join us, Brielle, and you will never have to worry what others think of you. You'll never be alone, never be lonely, never want for affection."

"Why would you want me?" she asked, her voice sounding as small as she felt looking up at him.

Chris looked deeply into her eyes, "You have much to offer, Brielle. Come with us and you will blossom into a Queen of the Night," he said quietly.

"Oh.... okay," she stammered.

Joyce was there beside them as soon as the word had passed the girl's lips. She linked arms with her and led her back towards the VIP lounge. Chris followed the women but paused for a moment when he passed a particularly stunned-looking boy. "You missed your chance," Chris said, giving him a conciliatory pat on the shoulder.

"You want her, you can have her," the boy said arrogantly, but his face betrayed his uncertainty and his eyes were glued to the two women.

Chris' grip tightened on the boy's shoulder and he looked him full in the face, his eyes blazing with intensity. "I do, and I will. And you will be amazed."

Lucifer, who had been hired as the floor manager, brought over a fresh round of drinks, including an extra Absinthe for the new addition. Chris leaned towards Joyce. "What is that around his neck?" he asked quietly.

Joyce looked up and saw the silver pendant hanging around Lucifer's neck. "The Crux Ansata. It's an ancient symbol from Egypt," she explained. "It means life."

"It looks cool. Maybe we should get some of those too," he suggested.

"That's an idea," she replied skeptically. Catherine Deneuve and David Bowie had worn them in the movie The Hunger only two years earlier and they had become de rigueur in the Goth scene ever since. "It's a little kitsch, but I suppose that's part of the point and they would easily identify our group as vampires."

After a moments consideration, she began to warm to the idea, "They would have to be extremely well done. We'll commission a set from a jeweler: Sterling with deep red garnets for the kids I think, Amethyst for me of course and for you..." She looked into his dark-rimmed eyes still sparkling with all the colors of the rainbow. "Black Fire Opal, definitely."

Chris followed the two women down the tunnel and up the stairs to the apartment. It had been a tedious few hours, spent meeting minor scene celebrities and members of various Goth and Black Metal bands, several of which had come to the city specifically to attend the opening. Joyce had been busy making and solidifying connections with the who's who, which had left Brielle in awe. However, after brief introductions and minor pleasantries, the small talk had left Chris in withdrawn boredom.

"Wow! This place is great!" Brielle exclaimed when they exited the stairwell and made their way into the bedroom. "You two live here alone?"

"Not anymore. At least, not if you choose to stay," Chris said.

"You want me you stay here with you? Like, live here... with you? Both of you?"

"I thought I had made that clear. We have invited you to become part of our family." His eyes shown with vivid colors as he exerted his influence on her. She discovered that what she had assumed were merely reflections of the multi-colored lights in the club, were actually the colors of his irises.

"Who are you anyway?" Brielle asked.

He stepped up to her, their faces mere inches apart, her black lips parted slightly due to her heightened need for oxygen. He took her by the hands and whispered, "My friends call me Christian. I would like you to be one of my friends, Brielle."

"Yeah," she said, swallowing hard. "I think I'd like that too." She didn't know if he was going to kiss her. It felt like he would kiss her, and part of her desperately hoped that he would. Her heart seemed to leap up into her throat and she quickly decided that it was actually a pretty big part. She closed her eyes and waited.

Her limited experience with the small number of boys from school who either wanted to get with the freak or were freaks themselves, had led her to expect to be mashed by a hungry mouth attempting to devour hers. But when it came, his touch was soft and tender. His gentleness felt warm and welcoming, and she thought she would melt into a puddle of goo and collect in the pointy toes of her bitch-boots. As she dissolved into the kiss, she felt hands on her back, tugging gently on the zipper of her dress. She sucked in a deep breath of surprise and excitement. She knew she should probably say no, just leave and go home, but that wasn't what she wanted.

She felt a shiver as her dress landed in a heap at her feet and suddenly wished she had worn nicer underwear. But who would have dreamed that she would end the night being seduced by two of the most beautiful Goths she had ever seen. The most she could have imagined would have been making out with some boy, messing up her lipstick and getting awkwardly felt up against a wall before taking a cab home, alone. The hooks of her bra were released and her hand jumped up involuntarily away from Christians hips to hold it in place.

Brielle laughed nervously. "Sorry. It's just that I've never done this before. I mean, I've done *it*, just not like this."

"There's no need to be shy. You are beautiful and no one here will do anything to hurt you," Chris said softly, making his voice as deep and resonate as he could. "Nothing will happen here without your consent."

"I'm not beautiful," she protested. "I'm fat, and my boobs are too small."

"You *are* beautiful and we will help you make everyone else sees it also," Joyce affirmed from behind her. "Every boy that was too blind to see you for who you are will be throwing themselves from the rooftops because that can't have you."

Brielle knew it wasn't true; they were just saying these things so that she would go along with them. She wanted to anyway, but it

165

was still nice to be flattered. She allowed herself to be maneuvered over to the bed by his kisses. Her panties slipped over her hips and down the length of her legs. She stepped backward out of the tangle of fabric, and the back of her legs bumped against the bed frame. Chris followed her back, his kisses perusing her until she was laying on the black satin sheets.

Chris followed her on to the bed, kneeling between the soft pale flesh of her thighs and gazing down at her. While she had been distracted, his clothes seemed to have also disappeared somehow.

Joyce lay on her side, propped up on her elbow, and ran the fingertips of her free hand along the puckered skin of the girl's breasts. Brielle turned her head to look at her and received a slow, smoldering kiss. When Joyce drew back, she allowed Brielle to catch a glimpse of her fangs. Her breath caught in her throat and she turned to look up at Chris, noticing the light reflecting off his elongated teeth. "I didn't know we were going to play vampire. Should I be scared?" She asked.

"No, you should not be afraid of us, but we are not playing." He looked at her from beneath shadowed lids and his eyes began to shine more brightly as his arousal grew. Brielle turned to look back at Joyce, whose eyes glowed a dark magenta in the warm candlelight.

"You mean, you're for real?"

"We are very real," she whispered.

"Oh, thank god. Will you make me like you?" she asked plaintively. "Please, I need this – I'll do whatever you want me to."

"Perhaps, in time."

"Thank you."

"We haven't said we would."

"I know. But you didn't say no. Are you going to feed from me now?"

"Yes, Brielle," Chris breathed against the pale expanse of her neck.

"Will it hurt?"

"No, dear, it won't hurt," Joyce assured her.

"Okay." Brielle stretched out her neck further, looking past Chris at a blank spot on the ceiling. "I'm ready."

Chris lowered himself down, supporting his weight with one hand pressed into the sheet near her head. He kissed the skin below her ear, breathing in the light floral scent of her perfume, and felt the pulse of her vertebral artery through his lip. He licked her delicate flesh, allowing the anesthetic quality of his saliva to numb the nerves. Brielle arched her back as he sank his teeth in, releasing the thick warm blood, causing it to flood into his mouth. She pressed her pelvis firmly against his, bringing him to a higher level of arousal.

"I want to," she breathed into his ear.

Chris spread his knees, coaxing her thighs further apart. She hooked her heels around the back of his calves, pulling as he pressed himself easily into her hot core and clamped her lips tightly together to prevent the sounds of her passion form becoming embarrassingly loud.

He glided slowly in and out, his cock advancing and retreating in time with the beat of her heart. His lips on her neck, sucking encouragingly at the flow blood that filled his mouth. When he had sated his lust for blood, he retracted his teeth from Brielle's ivory skin, which immediately began to heal, and licked away all remaining traces before leaning in and kissing her passionately.

Chris rose up onto his knees, holding on to Brielle's hips to support her as he continued his slow rhythm. She rested her feet on the back of his thighs and reached down between her legs to touch his muscular belly with her fingertips. She turned her head to where Joyce lay on her side, watching them.

"Are you gonna join in, or are you just the worst chaperone ever?" Brielle asked.

Joyce rolled away and stood next to the bed. Reaching behind her back, she pulled down the zipper of her dress and let it fall to the floor. She turned and sat on the corner of the mattress with her back to them and unlaced her shoes. Standing back up, she dropped her lingerie onto the pile and crawled slowly across the burgundy comforter, her sinuous movements reminiscent of a cat stalking its prey. She bent over Brielle, supporting herself on her elbow, and kissed her deeply.

The sight was almost more than Chris could take. He couldn't help but run his hand over the porcelain smooth mounds of

Joyce' upturned rear. She turned her head to look back at him over her shoulder, giving him a lustful smirk. She slid her hand over the girl's body, between her breasts, then down over the soft swell of her belly. Her fingers blazed a trail through the thicket of curls and her palm came to rest atop the rise of her mound. Her fingers stretched down between Brielle's thighs, feeling the heat rising off her.

Joyce squeezed her fingers together, applying pressure to the sides of Chris' cock as he continued his measured advance nearly bringing him to climax as he slipped between her slick knuckles into Brielle's hot center. Joyce buried herself in Brielle's neck, causing a quick intake of breath followed by a soft whimper as the sharp pain of her bite subsided to be replaced by the gentle pull of her lips.

Chris slid his hand down, following the inside curve of Joyce' ass to her inner thigh. She spread her legs wider and arched her back, raising her backside to him even further. Where he expected to find the soft folds of her flesh, he instead discovered passion-slicked fingers already nestled between her swollen ridges. Chris slid his hand over the other, feeling the fingers plunging in and out beneath him.

Joyce purred contentedly and began stoking Brielle's swollen clit with the pad of her thumb. Brielle gasped for air as the stimulation increased. "Oh fuck!" she exclaimed and suddenly clamped her hand over her mouth to prevent any sound from escaping. But her closed lips couldn't stifle the high pitched squeals as she rapidly approached her release. Brielle began to shake and buck beneath him as waves of orgasm ripped through her.

Joyce waited until Brielle's aftershocks had subsided, then swung her leg over, straddling her. She reached between them, took hold of Chris shaft, removed it from the exhausted girl and guided him upward until the tip pressed against her own wet opening. Chris positioned himself amid the tangle of legs. He placed his hands on Joyce' hips and guided her back as Brielle wrapped her calves around his thighs. Slowly he pressed forward, pushing past Brielle's fingers that were still nestled inside.

Gradually Chris' thrusts went from slow and steady to frenzied. Joyce pushed up onto her hands then walked them up the headboard, changing the angle of his thrusts, causing his tip to rub against the rough cluster of nerves on the front her vaginal wall.

Chris could feel the subtle influence of Joyce's mind in his, matching his state of arousal to hers. Brielle pulled him closer with her legs as they raced towards their simulations climax.

His hands encircled her, holding on to her hipbones like handles, pulling her back hard against him as he pushed forward into her. He bent forward, resting his forehead between her shoulder blades, his breath poured out in hot gusts down her spine as he released a torrent of seed into her.

Joyce let out a deep throaty laugh, pushed herself upright, reached back over her shoulder and began running her fingertips through the back of Chris' hair. Chris brushed her jet-black hair aside, nuzzled into the crook of her neck and gently kissed her shoulder. "Mmmmmm," she said in a throaty purr, "That was nice."

Chris slid his hands up her sides and over her ribs to cup the underside of her breast. His thumbs toyed with the small, metal rings that pierced her nipples. Joyce chuckled and pushed his hands down and away from her. Turning to the side, she gave Chris a quick peck on the lips, extracted herself from him and stepped over Brielle who was laying lethargically beneath them.

"You'd better take her to bed," Joyce suggested.

"Already done," Chris answered with a self-congratulating smirk.

Joyce punched him in the arm hard enough to make him lose his balance. "Don't be dense. I mean, take her next door and put her to bed."

Chris scooped up the semi-comatose girl and carried her from the room. He brought her to the dorm, deposited her on the bed nearest the door and gently pulled the sheet over her still form. When he returned to the bedroom, he found Joyce still naked. She lay back against the headboard, a stack of pillows propping her up. Her white skin stood out in stark contrast to the disheveled burgundy bedding. A brown kretek cigarette smoldered between her lips, sending tendrils of smoke wafting up to float in a heavy cloud around the wall sconce. She had one knee raised, her foot several inches to the side to allow Chris a clear view of all her bodily charms as he approached. He stood at the foot of the bed, feeling himself stir in response to the vision laid out before him.

Joyce raised one eyebrow quizzically. The tobacco crackled as she took a pull on her Djarum Special. She loved the scent of the burning clove and nutmeg, and the honey-sweet taste they left on her lips. Blowing out a plume of thickly perfumed smoke, she raised one closed hand, making a hammering motion. "Ding, ding," she said, announcing the start of round two.

Chapter 12

Ile de Biesse, 1440

On a gray and overcast October morning, the prisoners were rousted from their cells and led through the streets of the town. Crowds had been gathering in the chill air all morning, eager to watch the execution of the notorious child murderer and his two accomplices.

He had been stripped of what remained of his fine clothes and was dressed in a simple shirt smeared with sulfur to remind him of the hellish torments that awaited him in the hereafter. He stepped out onto the hard-packed dirt street and dutifully followed his armed escort. Rocks and rotten produce were hurled at them, as well as every manner of curse. They crossed over the Loire river to the Ile de Biesse, where the gibbet had been constructed close by the bridge of the Madeleine specifically for the day's events.

Three tall poles had been erected, and pyres had been prepared around their bases, composed of alternating layers of straw and wood, and rising nearly as tall as the height of a man. Care was taken to leave a ring of free space around the base of the stake for the condemned, along with an opening through which to lead him to it. This ring of fire would hasten the death of the victim and partially obscure the horror of their suffering from the view of the spectators.

He walked to the stake through the narrow opening in the pyre, climbed the ladder and mounted the gibbet's estrade. He reached up and placed the noose around his own neck, took a moment to gather himself, then lifted his head to face the crowd of prelates, executioners and the fetid tide of humanity that flowed in to witness his demise. "Good people who are here present to see what will be my end," he called out to quiet the throng.

"I remind you that, though I have sinned, I am still your Christian brother. Therefore, pray for me. I entreat the fathers and mothers of the children that I have killed to please forgive me and pray to God on behalf of my soul." He looked directly at the families of the victims. "When my soul leaves my body, may My Lord Saint Michael receive it and present it to God."

He turned to look at his weeping companions, who for years had aided him in his crimes. "My dear friends... Poitou, Henriet... I implore you. Take heart from my example and die bravely. Set your minds only on the salvation of your souls and you will find grace in the mercy of the Lord."

As the brush below him was set ablaze, he kicked the ladder over and dropped. The rope tightened around his neck and his feet kicked at the empty space below him as his lungs screamed for air. The heat of the flames intensified beneath him and began to lick hungrily at the soles of his feet. His body convulsed one final time, then hung still.

The executioners let his body hang above the flames until his legs were chard black before finally extinguishing the pyre to take him down. They delivered his body into the care of six veiled women dressed in white. They placed his body in a coffin and escorted him away to the Carmelite convent while his compatriots were roasted alive in his absence.

The coffin was carried down to the convent's cellar and the lid pried open. One of the women leaned in over him. "Wake up," she said. There was no movement, no sign of life at all. "Wake up," she repeated, pulling back her veil revealing kohl blackened eyes. A stray wisp of hair seemed to glow purple in the light of the setting sun shining through a small window high on the cellar wall. "Christian... *WAKE UP!*"

Chris woke with a start, he could still feel the heat of the flames consuming his legs and had to pull the sheet aside to make sure that he was still whole. "Are you okay?" Joyce asked sleepily.

"Yeah, I'm fine. Just a bad dream," he said.

Joyce stretched languidly beside him. "It was him..." she said definitively.

"Yeah. I know."

She propped herself up on her elbow and wiped the sleep from her eyes, smearing what was left of the previous night's makeup. Looking at him, she asked, "What are you going to do about it?" When he didn't respond, she continued, "You need to concentrate on keeping him out of your head. The closer you are tied, the more danger you are in, and the more danger you put the rest of us in."

"I'm trying, but how am I supposed to keep my guards up when I'm asleep?"

"You practice your visualizations," she said. "All the time. Practice layering your shields and randomly checking their strength. If you sense them faltering, then shore them up until they are impregnable."

Chris flopped back down and closed his eyes, imagining his body enclosed by a shell of steel, encasing a layer of stone and surrounded by a wall of blue fire. He concentrated on strengthening his shields until they seemed real enough to touch. When he was satisfied, he turned his attention to something that had been weighing on him. "About what happened last night..."

Joyce rolled over onto her side so she could look him in the face. "It's probably best not to make too much of it."

"I mean... am I like your boyfriend now?" he asked tentatively.

"Let's not make a big deal out of this by putting labels on it." She got up onto her knees and looked at him, letting the sheet slide down off her back. "We've been put here to do a job, but that doesn't mean we can't have a good time while we do it," she said, straddling him, her hands pressing him down into the bed. Chris felt the hard metal rings of her labia piercings against his skin and heard them clack faintly against each other as she began sliding back and forth, bringing him back to arousal.

"Okay," he said with an eager smile, running his hands up her legs to her hips. "I like having a good time."

When Brielle opened her eyes, she had no idea where she was. She looked around; there were steel shutters covering the window allowing only a thin sliver of light to penetrate the darkness of the room. There were rows of bunk beds lining the walls on both sides of the narrow room, which all seemed to be neat and empty.

She rolled to the side of the bed, intending to climb out of her bunk when she discovered that she was completely naked beneath the sheets. *What had happened last night?* she wondered. *And where are my clothes?*

As she thought about it, everything began coming back to her: The beautiful couple playing vampire. The blood games. The sex. Her cheeks blushed scarlet as she thought about the sex. She covered her face with her hands. She couldn't believe she had done that, any of that. She chuckled softly to herself, but what a story it would make if she ever had someone she could share it with.

She pulled the sheet off the bunk, wrapped it loosely around herself and quietly left the room through the only door. Her legs were still weak and wobbly as she made her way past rows of closets and out into a spacious living room. "Good morning," a voice called out cheerfully.

She nearly jumped out of her skin in surprise and turned to see Joyce sitting at the white marble kitchen counter. She looked disheveled in a black silk kimono adorned with embroidered purple Iris that did little to hide her figure. "I guess I should really say good afternoon. It's nearly three. Did you sleep okay?"

"Umm, yeah, I think so." She pulled the sheet tighter, keeping as much of the fabric bunched up in front of her as possible. "Where are my clothes?" she asked.

"They're still on the floor in our room... where you left them," said a masculine voice from behind her. She turned to see Christian approaching from the living room. "Come, I'll show you."

He was wearing nothing but a pair of silky black pajama pants and she couldn't help but gawk at him, remembering the way he looked and felt when he was inside her. She felt the blush crept back across her face. By the time she had followed him into the bedroom, a thin veneer of nervous sweat had coated her skin.

Chris smiled at her, bent down and scooped up the pile of discarded black garments. He stepped so close to her that she could

174

feel the heat radiating off his bare chest. "Is it hot in here or is it just you?" she joked.

Chris looked down at Brielle, gazing steadily into her eyes. She was so caught up the colors reflected in his eyes that she didn't notice him holding the bundle of clothing out to her. She wasn't quite sure how long they had been standing there like that, but she felt like a mouse mesmerized by a snake.

Eventually, she came to herself and reached out to accept the bundle. A sudden realization struck her when remembered that she had been holding the sheet around her, the sheet that was now covering nothing but her feet.

"I'm naked aren't I?" she asked, deliberately avoiding glancing down by looking directly into his eyes as awareness of her situation dawned on her.

"Yes, you are." He looked down and a smile pulled at the corners of his mouth. "Completely."

Brielle let out a deep sigh of resignation. "Okay then. Would you mind giving me a few minutes alone to try to get over my humiliation?"

"You have absolutely no reason to be nervous, you are lovely, but take whatever time you need. Please come and join us when you are ready."

After Chris had left the room, Brielle quickly threw on her clothing. Once dressed, she stood looking at the rumpled bed replaying every moment of the previous night in her mind until she felt a twinge of excitement start to take hold. She had to get out of that room but she would die of embarrassment if she had to face them again.

She glanced around the room looking for another way out, a back door, a window with a fire escape, a ventilation shaft, anything. She tiptoed down the hall back toward the kitchen intending to try to sneak out without being seen but stopped cold when she found Christian and Joyce drinking tall glasses of red liquid. "Sooo... how much of what happened last night was real?" She asked reaching up to touch her neck.

Joyce set her glass on the counter and swiveled on her stool to look at her. "What do you mean?"

"Well, I remember being bitten, by both of you, but there are no marks anywhere."

"That's true. Our bites will heal very quickly but that does not mean that what you remember didn't happen."

"So... you really are vampires?" she asked, her eyes wide in astonishment.

"Yes, Brielle, we are," Chris said seriously, allowing his fangs to elongate enough to be visible.

"I have to go," she said abruptly, pulling her coat around her and looking around the apartment in a near panic. "How do I get out of here?"

"Come, I'll walk you out," Chris offered.

She took a step back from him. "That's okay, just point me to the door and I'll find my own way."

Chris walked her to the door anyway, holding it open for her. She stopped on the other side of the thresh hold. "Can I come back?" she asked tentatively.

"You are welcome here, Brielle," he assured her.

"I wasn't sure if you were serious about that, or if it was just something you said to... you know." The red blush began to creep back into her cheeks.

"We are quite serious. You can take your pick of the beds in the dorm and there is plenty of closet space, but I wouldn't bring too much with you. I suspect that Joyce will be taking you out shopping." Brielle's face lit up at the prospect of a shopping spree and she looked past Chris for confirmation. Joyce crossed her legs, exposing a provocative expanse of upper thigh extending from beneath her robe, and gave an encouraging wink as she lifted her glass to her lips.

Chris closed the door behind the excited girl and waited for the sound of her footsteps to fade as she descended the stairs before returning to the kitchen. "How do you think that went?" he asked.

"I think... it was perfect." She gave him a big smile.

"So you think she'll come back?"

"Oh! I have no doubt. Not too bad for your first seduction."

"You don't think I poured it on too thick?"

"Welll, your eyes were smoldering so much I thought she might start to smoke," she said facetiously. When she saw the look of doubt that crossed his face, she quickly added, "No, you were perfect. It will get easier and I can always help make them more amenable."

"How is all this going to work out for her? I mean, she seems like a nice girl and I don't want her to..."

"Die?" Joyce asked, knowing where he was going. "You know I can't make any guarantees about that – for any of us. But, there is an opportunity here for her. We have a lot of resources at our disposal. We can influence her, guide her toward making good life choices. We can help with her self-confidence, we can help her complete her education, and we can help her financially."

The more he thought about it, the more excited Chris became about the potential benefits there were for their recruits. "So, what do we do now?" he asked.

"We find more."

Chris and Joyce spent the next few weeks looking for likely candidates. They drew from Chris' friends first; Mike and Mim were eager to join. Mike got so much emotional abuse at home that he crashed anywhere he could to avoid his parents, so the idea of staying at the loft sounded ideal. He even thought the whole vampire thing sounded fun, and Mim just had a huge crush on Chris and was eager for any excuse to be near him.

To find others, they started going to places where Punk and Goth kids gathered. They looked for those who were already attracted to dark things, the artists and poets, those who would gravitate to the idea of becoming a vampire, those who could be led, those who didn't have a deep seeded desire to dominate others.

They looked at the kids sitting against the fence outside Stuyvesant High School, hanging out in the park down the block or playing video games in the convenience store around the corner. They went to see the kids from LaGuardia High School sitting on edge of the fountain at Lincoln Center, hanging out at Momma's Pizza on Amsterdam Avenue, the boy reading alone at a back table in David's Bagels, the click at the rock on the verges of Sheep's

Meadow. They checked out the rich kids from Walden, Dalton, and Xavier. They went to The Fashion Institute of Technology, School of Visual Arts and Cooper Union.

In the end, they had eliminated all but two: Joselynne, an auburn-haired dance major from Ann Arbor studying at Juilliard, and Lucca, a particularly morbid FIT sophomore who was estranged from his family and roamed the streets in a vintage black leather motorcycle cap and matching full-length trench coat.

With Chris, Joyce and five people living in the dorm, the loft was starting to feel a bit crowded, but there was a sense of excitement in the atmosphere. Joyce kept them busy shopping for new clothes, which Lucca customized with unique touches in the makeshift tailor shop he set up in an unused bunk. In the afternoons, Joselynne took them down to the vacant second floor of the building for dance lessons, teaching them increasingly intricate routines.

At midnight, Chris and Joyce led their little coven down the back stairs and along the tunnel to the club. Once Charlie opened the ropes for them, they would fan out behind the pair in perfectly synchronized formation, like an elegant flock of black swans. They cut through the crowd, splitting the other patrons like a wedge. Chris and Joyce, as the royal couple, headed directly to the VIP lounge followed closely by Mim. Brielle and Joselynne typically peeled off to stay out on the floor to dance. Mike made a beeline for the bar and Lucca began searching the room for cute guys to flirt with.

A disturbance suddenly caught Chris' attention. Lucca was engaged in an argument with a guy at the bar. He seemed to fit Lucca's normal type: Tall, slim, short dark hair, just the sort that he would try to pick up. Chris usually didn't pay much attention to what their protégées did; he generally left that up to Joyce. However, something about the level of aggression of their interaction made him listen in.

"Don't deny it. I know all about you," the young man slurred angrily.

"I think you've had too much to drink. Why don't you go home and sleep it off?"

He poked Lucca in the chest belligerently. "I don't need to take advice from you. What are you supposed to be anyway, some sort of Fruit Bat? You vant to suuuck my Diiiik, Bla Bla," he said in a cheesy imitation of a Dracula movie.

"Listen, asshole, I've had about as much of your crap as I'm gonna take," Lucca began, when suddenly, the young man's eyes started to roll back in his head. He dropped bonelessly to the floor and began to shake violently.

The other patrons started to gather around him in a slowly shrinking circle as they pressed closer to get a better look. They all seemed to have a comment or suggestions: What should we do? We should put a belt in his mouth so he doesn't swallow his tongue! One without spikes. Someone should go call an ambulance. His skin feels clammy, do you think he's contagious?

Instantly, Chris was across the club. "Everyone back up and give him room. Stop looming over him." His eyes flared as he brought the force of his will to bear on the onlookers.

A second later, Joyce appeared at his side. "Lucca, get a Coke or juice from the bar. Something sweet." In just a few seconds, Lucca was back with a rocks glass full of pineapple juice. She began using the straw to drip the sugary liquid between the young man's partially open lips.

When the seizure subsided, Chris sat him up and leaned him against the bar. Soon, he was able to take some small sips on his own. "Are you feeling any better? Are you here with friends?"

"No," the man croaked out.

"What's your name?"

"Simeon."

"Is there someone we should call for you, Simeon?" He shook his head slightly in response. "Alright. Do you think you can walk?" Chris asked.

"Yeah, I think so," he said and started to climb to his feet, only to collapse back onto the floor, holding his head in pain.

"Charlie!" Joyce called without looking up to make sure the large black bouncer with the thick glasses was standing nearby. "Please help our guest up. I'm sure he'll be more comfortable away from this crowd."

Chris followed close behind as Charlie gently scooped Simeon up into his burly arms and carried him through the crowd of gawkers to the back stairs and up to the loft, leaving Joyce and

Lucca to disperse the onlookers and return the club to normal. He carried Simeon through the loft to the living room and deposited him on the sofa. "Thank you, Charlie," he said.

"Of course. Call down if you need anything," Charlie replied before heading back to the club to keep watch over the tunnel.

Chris went into the kitchen to find something to offer his guest. "Thank you for helping me," Simeon called out weakly from the couch. "I'd like to repay you if I can."

"There is no need, we were glad to do it."

After a few moments of silence, Simeon spoke again. "I know what you are. It's why I came here tonight. I wanted to offer myself to you, but I got nervous, so I started talking to that other guy instead. I haven't eaten for a few hours - trying to look thin and beautiful - and I guess I had a little too much to drink. I'm really embarrassed; I just wanted to make a good impression and now I've screwed it all up."

Chris came back, sat beside him and offered him a bagel. "Why would you want to give yourself to me?"

"Why would I? Who wouldn't? Look at you: You're beautiful, powerful, a fantastic dresser. I'm assuming you're rich," he said, holding out his arms to indicate their surroundings. "And you'll live forever... what's not to want?"

Chris studied Simeon closely, then said seriously, "You might find that this existence is not everything you dream it would be."

"I'm willing to take that chance."

"Why? What do you hope to gain?"

Simeon thought for a moment about how best to answer. "I have been sick ever since I was a kid. I can't remember a time when I wasn't. I have a lifetime of shots, probably with severe nerve pain, blindness, amputations, and death to look forward to. I figure, if I'm going to be a human pin-cushion anyway, I thought I could become one of you. At least that way I could end up healthy and living forever, right?"

"No one can say what the future will hold," Chris said as he moved to stand behind Simeon at the back of the couch. "You are certain that this is what you truly want?"

"Yes."

Chris placed his hand on Simeon's head and eased it to the side. He bent over the back of the couch and leaned in close enough to see the blood pulsing just beneath the freshly shaved skin. He could feel his mouth watering and his fangs beginning to lengthen. He lowered his mouth, breathing in the subtle mixture of Barbasol and Aquanet, then sank his teeth in. The warm liquid poured into his mouth. He started pulling it in, filling himself with its warmth, feeling new strength and vitality radiating throughout his body.

He was so enthralled with sensation that he didn't notice footsteps approaching. "How's our new friend?" Chris looked up to find Joyce standing in front of Simeon, her arms crossed under her breasts and a knowing smirk on her face.

"Very tasty, have some," Chris offered, wiping the corner of his mouth with his thumb.

"Hmmm, don't mind if I do." Slowly, she gathered her skirt up around her thighs, put one knee on the couch next to Simeon, swung her other leg across his lap and sat back on his knees. Her fingers ran through the stiff tangle of his hair and held his head to the side, giving her clear access to his neck. A smear of drying blood surrounded the small, rapidly closing puncture marks.

Joyce licked the skin around the wounds, her tongue tracing the bite marks like a figure skater making a figure eight, the tip gently probing the indentations. She allowed the taste to whet her appetite and waited for her saliva to numb the area further before her teeth poked more holes in his skin. Energy surged through her like lightning as she sucked in Simeon's lifeblood. She could taste the low level of blood sugar and, after the initial excitement had subsided, slowed her pace to avoid taking too much too quickly and push him over the edge into unconsciousness or collapse his artery.

Chris had been watching Joyce feed from Simeon when movement from the hallway drew his attention. He looked up to find Lucca leading the rest of the coven into the loft, a look of indignation clear on his face. "What's he doing here?" Lucca demanded.

Chris raised an eyebrow. "He is feeding your masters. He will serve at our pleasure as will you if you wish to remain here."

Joyce stood up and straightened out her skirt before turning to face the group. She looked at Lucca, her eyes taking on their usual lavender luminance as she let her power flair. "You are in no position to question your master. You are here to serve. Tonight, you will serve on your knees."

Immediately, Lucca dropped, his head low, his eyes to the floor. "Yes, mistress."

"You will stay there until the sun rises while you contemplate how much you truly wish to be here." She hooked her index finger into Simeon's shirt and pulled him to his feet. "You, come with me," she said. "Joselynne, would you be good enough to attend Christian?"

"Of course, mistress," she replied and crossed the room to take Chris' outstretched hand.

"The rest of you will find some way to entertain yourselves in our absence, I'm sure." Joyce pulled Simeon along behind her and headed to the master bedroom, followed close by Chris and Joselynne. When the door was closed behind them, she pushed Simeon back onto the bed, then turned to look over her shoulder at Chris. "Would you help me with this?" she asked, indicating the zipper at the center of her back.

Chris came up close behind her, his hands on her hips, pulling her against him. He leaned down and placed a gentle kiss on the top of her bare shoulder. He slid his hands up her ribs and across her back. She reached up to hold the dress up as Chris slowly pulled the tap down making a soft zipping sound as the teeth opened.

Joyce looked down at Simeon, "Well… what are you waiting for?" Simeon hurriedly kicked off his shoes and began shedding his clothing a quickly as he could, tossing them into a pile in the corner of the room.

Chris returned to Joselynne. Kneeling down, he reached his hands slowly up under her vintage black polka dot halterneck dress. Taking hold of her multi-layered black net and organza petticoat, he slipped it down her legs. She put her hand on his shoulder to steady herself as she stepped out of the tangle of ruffles and kicked the petticoat away. Chris helped her out of her shoes, then turned her around and slowly stood up, sliding his hands along the outside of her legs, hiking her skirt up to her hips.

One hand held her slim form hard against him, the folds of her skirt bunched up between them, while the other roamed across her firm belly. When his hand meandered lower, Chris was happy to discover that she had no underwear on. As his fingers continued their downward journey, Joselynne widened her stance, allowing him easier access, and lay her head back against his shoulder.

His fingers explored her, slipping further between her thighs and finding her slick with anticipation. She moaned softly as he gently stroked her eager opening, inhaling deeply and reaching to grip his wrist when his finger eased it's way inside.

Chris unzipped the back of her dress and spun her around to face him as it dropped to the floor. He wrapped her in his arms; one around her back while the other cradled and lifted the round orb of her ass. His fingers followed her curves, reaching down to pull her open further. He walked her backward, nuzzling and kissing her neck until the back of her legs bumped the edge of the bed. Chris held her tightly to keep her from falling backward as he eased her down onto the corner of the bed.

He knelt between her legs, hooking his arms beneath her knees and kissing her softly on the thigh. Slowly he kissed his way up, reaching around behind her, angling her legs higher until she was forced to lean back and brace herself with her hands. He kissed the tender flesh of her inner thigh, licking the smooth skin to numb it slightly before his teeth bit in.

Joselynne clamped her lower lip between her teeth and tossed her head back, her long auburn hair cascading over her shoulders as Chris began to draw the blood from her femoral artery. Her back arched with a mixture of pleasure and pain, thrusting her small breasts up proudly and she released a long, low moan.

Chris stood and wiped his mouth with the back of his hand. Looking past Joselynne, he saw that Joyce had positioned herself on top of Simeon and was rocking rhythmically along his shaft as she dotted his neck and chest with small, seeping puncture wounds.

Joselynne turned around and rolled over on the bed. Propping herself on her elbows, she opened the fly of Chris' slacks and reached inside. He felt himself swell as her blood coursed through his body. Her fingers wrapped around him, taking out his cock, she began slowly stroking the length of him with her tongue. Her lips parted and he slipped easily into the depths of her mouth.

Chapter 13

Simeon left the bedroom once Joyce had finished with him and walked tiredly back into the living room. He found Lucca still kneeling on the floor where they left him; the rest of the group were sitting at the kitchen island staring intently at a wine bottle as a small blue flame swirled around the lip.

"Hey, you're back," Mike called, drawing their attention to him.

"That didn't take long," Brielle commented before hopping down off her stool to escort him to the counter. "How are you feeling?"

"Tired. Weak," Simeon croaked.

"Not surprising. I'm amazed that they both fed from you... in your condition." She crossed to the refrigerator and started pulling things out. "You're going to have to eat to get your strength back. Spinach and liver are really good but roast beef will have to do for now." She set a handful of ingredients on the counter in front of him and went back to her seat.

"What are you guys doing?" he asked as he assembled his sandwich.

"We're trying to communicate with the spirits of the dead," Miriam informed him.

He watched the bottle for a moment in confusion until the flame went out. Mim picked up the bottle, swirled it around coating the inside of the glass with a clear liquid pooling at the bottom, then lit a kitchen match and dropped it in. Fire erupted from the mouth of the bottle with a whooshing sound, then settled into a dome of blue-tinted flame. The flame rolled around the lip of the bottle, occasionally dipping inside, making a moaning sound that seemed eerily human and grew louder the deeper inside the fire dropped.

"It's called The Spirit In The Bottle. Sometimes it sounds like the spirit is trying to talk to you."

"So, do you all live here?" Simeon asked.

"Of course we live together, we're family," Mike chimed in. "And we haven't been introduced. I'm Michael. This is Miriam and

Brielle, and of course, you've already met Joselynne and Lucca over there."

"Are you all vampires too?"

"We haven't received the Gift yet," Miriam admitted.

"So... you feed them and they do what for you exactly?" Simeon asked skeptically.

"We live here. All our needs are taken care of: Our food, clothing, and jewelry are all provided, and we all have bank accounts set up to cover things like college tuition, business investments or whatnot."

"And there are other benefits," added Joselynne, entering the room looking rather disheveled. Mike and Brielle gave her a small round of applause but she noticed that Miriam looked crestfallen. "I'm sorry, Mim. I know how disappointed you must be."

Her eyes began to water. "Is there something wrong with me?" she asked. "I know I'm not as pretty as you are, but I didn't think I was ugly."

"Oh no, sweetie. You're beautiful, and you've really blossomed since you've been here," Brielle said, wrapping her arm around the distraught girl's shoulder.

"Then, what is it? He only fed from me that one time, at my acceptance. Did I taste bad or something?" she asked, smearing her makeup as she wiped her eyes, remembering that first night when he had wrapped his strong arms around her and fed from her neck. It had been gentle and the pain had subsided very quickly, just as she had always heard it would when she lost her virginity. "Maybe I could change my diet."

"I'm sure that's not the case. You should ask Joyce?"

"What if it's something really bad and they decide to kick me out?"

"I'm sure it's nothing like that. Why don't you head back and get cleaned up? I'll come back in a few minutes, okay?"

Miriam nodded and headed obediently down the hall. When she was out of earshot, Simeon asked, "What's her deal?"

"She's had a crush on Christian since before he changed but he hasn't acknowledged it."

"I'm in the same boat, but you don't see me falling apart every night."

"God Mike, not everything is about you."

"Well, it's not all about her either," he protested.

Joselynne poured herself a tall glass of thick, green liquid from a pitcher in the fridge and started chugging it down.

"*Awwwwk*. That looks terrible. What's in it?" Simeon asked.

"Kale, prunes and raw eggs. Want some?" she asked, holding her nearly empty glass to him. Simeon shook his head vigorously and made a face like he was trying to keep himself from puking.

"Yeah, it's kinda disgusting, but it really helps replenish your blood after a feeding."

"So, wait... you said she knew Christian before he became a vampire? How? Isn't he like hundreds of years old?"

"No, Joyce maybe, but not him," Mike said. "Mim and I met him last summer and he was just a regular guy."

"You wouldn't know it to look at him."

"Yeah, he looks a lot different now. Acts different, too."

"You mean... he wasn't drinking people's blood before be became a vampire?" Simeon said with mock sarcasm.

"Yeah, one night we were out partying with Eric Arcane. You know, the singer for the Marianist Sisters?" he said smugly. "Then he just up and disappears for the summer. And when he comes back, he's like this sexy Lord of the Undead."

"Do you think Joyce turned him?" Simeon asked.

Mike thought about it for a second. "I don't know, maybe. She was already like she is now, just now she's got better clothes."

"I don't think she turned him," Brielle put in. "They always seem like partners, you know? Not like he's less than her or anything."

"Hey, so what should I do now?"

"What do you mean? You move in with us. That's what you wanted, right?"

"Yeah, I guess so. I hadn't really given it a lot of thought. I guess I just thought they would change me and I'd go off to be a Creature Of The Night."

"Yeah, okay, Frankenfurter. Well, it doesn't work like that. You have to be accepted, then you have to live the life to see if this is really what you want. And when and if they decide that you are ready, they will grant you eternity," stated Brielle.

"Okay. I'm gonna go check on Mim then get some sleep," Joselynne announced to the group. "You all might want to do the same." She looked over at Simeon. "I can show you an empty bunk if you want."

"Thanks, but I think I'd better be heading home."

"Pet," her master called as he descended the ladder that led down to their underground chamber of horrors.

"Yes, master," she replied instantly.

"Were you successful in your task?" the creature asked her, although it wasn't really a question. She knew full well what happened if she failed in even the most insignificant task.

"Yes, master. I think I found a place that will work." The Lowes Hollywood Theatre on Avenue A had been built in 1926 to seat 1,300 but had lain abandoned since it closed in 1959.

"Take me there," he commanded.

"Don't be scared," she whispered to Boy as she started getting to her feet. Pet knew her master could what she said as easily as he could hear the blood pumping through her veins, but whispering in the darkened room seemed to help Boy feel like they were in this terrible ordeal together. "I'll be back as soon as I can, okay?" Boy squeezed her hand before letting it slip through his small fingers as she moved obediently towards the ladder.

She led her master east on Houston Street, then turned north on Avenue A and headed uptown until they passed Sixth Street. In the center of the block, above the red and white awning of SOK's grocery, which now occupied the former orchestra level of the theater, stretched the forty-foot diamond-shaped diaper pattern brickwork facade.

They pushed up a graffiti-covered roll gate where the marquee had once protruded over the sidewalk and entered through the boarded-up door of a retail space that had been set up in the theater's lobby. She flicked on a lighter to help her pick her way through the aging cardboard boxes and debris left behind by the most recent occupant and entered the cavernous auditorium. The tiny orange flame barely penetrated the darkness but she could see the creature's eyes alight as he peered into the gloom.

Even in the dim light, he had no difficulty seeing. "Yes, this will do very well," he said. The once ornate interior was now a ruin; decades of neglect and a leaking roof had caused the paint to chip and baroque wallpaper to peel. The hand applied plaster ornamentation had crumbled and fallen to the floor in heaps and the once plush velvet seats had now rotted away.

"I will require you to bring me boys," he said.

She immediately thought of Boy sitting alone in the dark, waiting to see what new torments the creature would inflict upon him. "What kind of boys?" with growing trepidation she asked.

"I need young men, ones prone to violence, lacking discipline and direction. Bring them to me and I will judge their worth." He turned his back on her and walked to the center of the stage, facing the tiers of decaying seats. "I used to love the theater, the crowds, the pageantry. My productions of Le Mistère du Siège d'Orléans consisted of more than 20,000 lines of verse, with a cast of five-hundred and over one-hundred and forty speaking parts. It cost me several fortunes, but it was wondrous."

As the sun dropped below the rooftops on the opposite side of the Hudson River, the front door intercom began to buzz incessantly as someone jammed their finger relentlessly on the button. Mike was in the kitchen, making a cup of tea having just roused himself from his bed. He shuffled slowly over to the loft door and pressed the talk button on the plastic panel. "What the hell do you want? Do you have any idea what time it is?"

"Yeah, it's 8:30. I've been waiting out here for the sun to go down since six. Come on, let me in," said a crackling voice from the sidewalk out front.

"Who is it?" Mike asked.

"It's Simeon," the garbled voice said, sounding exasperated. "Come on, open up."

Mike held the door button for a few seconds, turned the knob unlocking the loft door and leaving it slightly ajar, went back to making his tea. When he heard the door close, he said, "We didn't think you were coming back."

Simeon set his duffel bag down with a heavy thud. "Sure I was. I just had to get my stuff and say goodbye to my sister."

"Will you keep it down? Some of us were out late last night," Brielle announced, coming out from the dorm, followed by Miriam and Lucca all in various states of undress. "What's going on out here anyway?"

"Simeon's back," Mike announced flatly while pulling the bag of Oolong from his cup, squeezing it against a spoon and tossing it in the trash.

"Hey, are Christian and Joyce here? I have some awesome news," Simeon asked excitedly.

"We are here!" Chris announced, coming silently into the living room in an open, black, silk robe, the ends of the belt dragging on the floor behind him, exposing the white skin of his muscular abdomen and his black silk boxer shorts.

"Okay, good. I wanted to come back sooner but I had some things I had to take care of first. Anyway, I wanted to come right over to thank you and let you know that the change has started," he said in a rush.

"What do you mean the change has started?" Lucca demanded as the others began casting curiously glances back and forth between them.

"So, I've been diagnosed with diabetes since I was a kid right, and over the past week all my prick tests have been normal."

"That's funny, 'cause he sure failed my prick test," Lucca quipped, earning him a quiet shushing from Miriam.

Simeon saw the blank looks on the faces around him and continued explaining. "That means that my insulin levels have been fine. I haven't needed a shot since I was bled."

"I've been dying to give him a shot ever since I met him, in the face," Lucca commented to Mim, pretending to whisper.

"Eww! You want to shoot on my face?" Simeon asked with a look of appalled shock.

"I thought you were trying to give him a shot in the sack and that's why you're so upset about it," Miriam replied, causing Lucca to stick his tongue out at her. "And I thought you didn't like girls..." Mim replied.

"Wait! You're a girl!?" he gasped in astonishment, then winced as she delivered a well-practiced jab to his shoulder.

"You're sure?" Joyce asked, stepping into the room. Interrupting their banter as she ran her fingers through her sleep-mussed hair. She wore a steel gray Chemise, spaghetti strap pajama top, with lilac embroidery on the bodice and matching tap shorts that accentuated her pale skin and stunning figure.

"Yeah, my diabetes is cured. My blood glucose levels are normal. The doctors say my pancreas is producing insulin at normal levels and they're not sure what to do with themselves. They want to study me but I didn't think that was such a good idea... what, with my transformation and everything."

"Probably a wise decision," Chris said, beginning to run through the potential ramifications of Simeon's news.

Joyce laid her hand gently on Chris' shoulder and addressed the group. "Why don't you get Simeon settled, then we would like to see everyone back here in a presentable state no later than ten." There were murmurs of "Yes, Mistress" as they left the room, leading their newest member to the dorm.

"What was that about?" Chris asked her.

"Not here," she whispered, taking him by the hand and leading him back to the master suite. She closed and locked the door behind them. "He's not changing," she assured him.

"How can you be sure? Have you ever heard of a Lesser Blessed's bite curing Diabetes?"

"No, I can't say that I have," she admitted, "but we do know that our saliva has curative properties. That must be what it is. Bites and minor lacerations, of course, even more grievous wounds can be treated with time. I've just never seen anything quite so dramatic before. This is a systemic disease we're talking about."

"I don't want to turn anyone into a vampire."

"Don't worry, you won't. We can't, but I think we should try to get word to Amym and see what he thinks. Maybe Promus…"

"Not yet," Chris said. "He'd have to tell The Chord and I'm still in my assessment period." He imagined what they might do with him, lock him away in some dark basement and send in an endless stream of decrepit and sickly people for him to feed on. Spit in this cup. Feed from this patient. Just one more vial of blood. Can he cure leukemia, heart disease, cancer? How long could something like that go on? A year? A decade? FOREVER? No, Chris decided, he needed to keep this to himself until he knew more about it.

Joyce put her hands on his cheeks and turned him to face her. "You can trust Amym, you know. He won't deliberately put you in any sort of danger."

Chris pulled away from her and started pacing the room. "What if he was ordered to? What if The Chord told him that he had to? What would he do then? How certain are you that you can trust him?"

"I always have, for as long as I've known him, and he's never let me down."

"Well, I don't trust the Chord. They could just as easily say I'm defective or something and have me killed."

Maybe there was something about it in that Vampire Bible Chris wondered. Something that talks about rare abilities among the Lesser Blessed. If there was a way to get a look at a complete copy, maybe he could decipher it. He might find something that would answer his questions, maybe give him some incites.

"He won't be back in New York for awhile, so why don't we think about it and see what we can come up with on our own until then? Then we can fill him in with what we've discovered when he gets back, okay?" Chris silently nodded his acquiescence. "Okay, now that that's settled, let's get dressed for the ceremony."

Chapter 14

When Chris and Joyce returned to the living room, they were pleased to find all six members of their retinue had reassembled, waiting and splendidly attired. "Thank you all for attending us this evening. You represent us in your conduct and your appearance. Therefore, in addition to everything that has already been provided for you, we have decided to give each of you a special gift. One that will clearly identify you as members of our enclave."

He held a dark wooden box out towards Joyce, who opened the lid to reveal a plush, red velvet lining. She reached in and took out a bright silver pendant dangling from a delicate chain. "This is the Ankh. It represents life, a new life that began for you when you made the choice to be part of this enclave... this family."

"Each of you will be called up and offered this symbol. If you accept, you will wear it continuously as long as you remain with us. If you decline, you may leave here as you were when you arrived, though we would hope somewhat richer for the experience," Chris announced.

"Brielle, please step forward." In the weeks that she had been living at the loft, Brielle had lost the weight that had been holding back her confidence and had begun to see in herself what Chris had seen on the first night. "As our first supplicant, please accept this token of our faith and acceptance of you as a member of our family."

Brielle nodded her head with a smile and Joyce hung the chain around her neck. "Thank you, Mistress," she said with a curtsy. Returning to her seat on the couch, she held the Ankh admiring the large, deep-red granite set into the junction of the ancient symbol.

The ceremony continued as Chris called up each initiate in the order in which they had been recruited. No one declined when Joyce offered them their pendants, though he was surprised to see the hesitation when Mim was summoned. Finally, Chris called Simeon up. Still in the clothing he had arrived in, he stepped forward and stood in front of the pair.

Joyce took a pendant from the box and held it out towards the young man. "Simeon, though you are new to us, we would like to extend to you the same invitation. Join us as the others have and benefit from all we have to offer. Now, and in the times to come. If you would like some time to think it over,"

"I don't need any time. Of course I will, thanks," he said, trying to sound casual, but a stern look from Chris and he immediately continued with "I mean, thank you, Mistress. It would be my honor."

Chris closed the lid and set the box on the white, marble, kitchen island. "Each of you has received a gift from us tonight. Now, each of you will present us with the gift of your blood, binding your lives with ours." Joyce looked at the faces arrayed around the room, some were eager, others resolved. Then, she refocused on the face before her. "Simeon, kneel," she commanded.

He slowly knelt on the floor and took her outstretched hand. Joyce guided it toward her and bent it back, exposing the chord of nerves and tendons that connected the hand to the arm. She felt his pulse begin to race and the blood throb in his radial artery. Lifting his hand high over his head, she brought it to her lips. He gasped as she sank her teeth into the sensitive skin, but the sudden pain was quickly alleviated by the anesthetic quality of her saliva.

Joyce let the blood flow into her, swallowing it down as quickly as his heart pumped it out, feeling it begin to fill her with its vitality, adding to her strength. When she had had enough, she offered the wrist to Chris, who moved instantly to her side to prevent any blood from falling to the floor. Chris sucked at the punctures, pulling the blood out forcefully, enjoying the flavor now that it was free of the taint of synthetic insulin.

When he was satisfied, Chris released Simeon, who sat tiredly back onto his heels before climbing to his feet and dropping into a vacant spot on the couch. Chris extended his hand, beckoning Mim to him. He wrapped her in his arms, pulling her into his close embrace. Her head fell back and a sigh escaped her parted lips as Chris brushed his own along her neck just below her ear. She closed her eyes, feeling her insides quiver with desire and anticipation.

One arm slid down to the base of her spine and the other wound around her back, pulling her slim body firmly against him.

His breath was hot on her skin, his hand slid slowly up her back to cradle the base of her skull, his fingertips tracing the contours of her neck. She bit down on her lip and whimpered softly as he sliced into her with his fingernail, catching the trickle of blood with his tongue.

Joyce moved up behind her, pressing herself against Mim's back, pushing her against Chris, squeezing her between them. Breathlessly, Chris took his mouth away from Mim's neck, making pace for Joyce to lean in from behind to take his place. Her knees went weak and her weight was instantly supported by the strength of Chris' arms.

They fed from each member of their retinue in turn, never taking much, just a symbolic submission to their positions as heads of the enclave and the alpha predators. When they had finished, Chris and Joyce went back to the master suite to freshen up before leading the group down to the Shambles. "You're going to have to do something about that girl," Joyce told him as she dabbed away the blood from the corner of her mouth, trying not to smear her lipstick.

"What do you mean?" Chris asked.

"Brielle and Joselynne are completely infatuated with you, aroused by you, but I'm not overly concerned with them. I'm quite certain they can handle themselves. Mim, on the other hand, is a different story. She's in love with you, at least as much as she knows how to be."

"I know, but what can I do about it?" he grumbled. "I've tried to distance myself, hoping she'd get over it."

"Take her to bed," Joyce suggested with more than a hint of exasperation. "It's ether deflower her or send her away."

"I know, it's just... Won't that make things worse?"

"Maybe, but I don't see that you have much choice if you want her to stay. Do you want me to help you? I could help make it easier for both of you," she offered.

"You mean... like the three of us?" he asked cocking his eyebrow suggestively.

"No! Don't be dense. That's not what she wants at all. I meant help you with your feelings, help you see someone you're more interested in," she said tapping her temple with her index finger.

"Oh," he said as understanding dawned on him. "No, that's not the problem. I do like her and I always thought she was kinda cute."

"Then you should do it, soon. She's already beginning to resent the others and it will start to affect the cohesion of the house if this goes on much longer."

"I know that everyone's eyes will be on you and that might make you feel nervous," Joyce told the group. She reached out with her mind, feeling the emotions swirling around her: self-consciousness, embarrassment, outright fear, and in Joselynne's case, impatience. That wasn't surprising since she was a classically trained dancer who had spent the past few weeks choreographing and rehearsing their entrance.

Joyce steadied her breathing and let a sense of peace and calm fill her and radiate out until it encompassed the group. "You all look beautiful and you've done wonderfully. You should be proud of yourselves. This is your moment to shine, so I want everyone to take a deep breath, shake out any jitters and wait for my signal." Joyce turned to Simeon who looked like he was about to be sick, "Just keep up with the others and I'll help you with the steps."

She reached out with her consciousness until she felt the mind of the DJ and implanted the queue to change the record. He faded out the music that had been softly playing in the background while the club filled up. Suddenly, the warbling Rockabilly sounds of Geordie Walker's golden 1953 Gibson ES295 began reverberating loudly off the brick walls. When Paul Ferguson's thundering drums shook the air, Joyce snapped her fingers to punctuate the beat like the crack of a whip, signaling the others to begin their entrance to their new official first song, Killing Joke's Eighties.

They entered in pairs, spreading out in a V formation from the tunnel entrance like a squadron of fighter jets, driving a wedge through the crowd.

Simeon moved out opposite Miriam, walking with the stiff and sullen gate of a boy forced to dance with an elderly great aunt at a wedding. No matter how Joyce tried, the best she could do was add a tiny sway to his hips and a slight bounce to his step. She joined hands with Chris and danced out into the club behind the others in the empty space left in their wake.

When the song faded out, Chris headed towards his throne in the VIP section while Joyce made her rounds of the club, checking on friends and special guests until she spotted an unexpected face at the bar. "Hello, Promus, what brings you to our humble establishment?"

"Just keeping an eye on our investment. You're looking magnificent as ever," he said giving her an air kiss on each cheek. "That was quite an entrance, I'm sure it will be the talk of the town for quite a while."

"I certainly hope so. It took a while to put together and I'm not sure how to top it."

"No doubt you'll think of something. I've been going over the books. It appears that you are well on your way to being in the black as it were. No small feat in this business. I didn't see a gambling den in the plans. Are you using the club as a drug front?"

She laughed musically. "Nothing so nefarious. We have the best DJs and a unique atmosphere; people like the speakeasy aspect, too. Everyone wants to be in the know about something secret and new."

"Well, we never really expected to turn a profit on this venture, but breaking even would be a pleasant change for once. And our boy? How is he progressing?"

She turned her head to look over her shoulder to where Chris held court in the VIP section. "He's performing well."

"That's good news, but we need you to be even more conspicuous. You can't just keep to your selves and still provide the level of distraction that we're looking for."

"Did you have something specific in mind? Some public feeding maybe?" she suggested.

"I don't think you need to do anything quite so drastic, although I wouldn't completely rule it out," he said, giving the idea some thought. "Yes, I can definitely see the potential, but why don't you just start off with some public appearances."

"I'm sure we'll think of something." Then, switching to another subject, she asked, "Have you had any news from Amym?"

He looked at her warily for a moment. "Nothing as of yet, although we do know some of the places he has been based on his credit card activity. But you know Amym, he's fiercely independent, though I'm sure he will report in when he has something that needs reporting."

"I'm sure you're right," Joyce said, an insincere smile of politeness on her face.

"On a side note, you may want to keep an eye on the fellow at the end of the bar." Joyce scanned the reflection in the mirror behind the bar, stopping when she came to the person Promus was obviously referring to. "He's rather distinct among this troupe."

Joyce agreed whole-heartedly. The man sat at the bar, wearing his signature tweed jacket and tan slacks, drinking a domestic light beer and casually watching the crowd. He was obviously out of his element, unless he had a fetish for Gothic women. *Or men*, she thought. One man in particular. "He's been here before, when we first opened. I assumed he was just curious but I'll definitely keep an eye on him."

"Hey!" Mim said cheerfully, plopping herself down in Chris' lap as he watched Joyce and Promus talking at the bar. "You look troubled. What's the matter?"

"Just concerned for a friend," he said.

"Is there anything I can do to help," she offered, gently tracing the lines of his palm with her fingertip.

Chris looked into Mim's almost cartoonishly large and innocent-looking hazel eyes and felt the tension he had been feeling begin to soften. "Would you care to dance with me, Miriam?"

"Of course, Master," she replied with a shy smile.

Chris scooped her into his arms as he stood up from the sofa, carrying her past the ropes that blocked off the VIP section, and set her easily on her feet in the center of the dance floor. The DJ started playing Desire by Gene Loves Jezebel and Chris led her through a complicated series of steps, staying attuned to her movements, slowing down when she had trouble keeping up, adjusting for any miss steps. It was nowhere near as graceful as it would have been if he had been dancing with Joyce or even Joselynne, but still, the crowd parted to make room for them and watch in admiration.

What are you waiting for? Take her upstairs, came Joyce's voice in his head. As they turned around the floor, Chris looked for her, eventually finding her near the DJ booth talking to Lucifer. His platinum blond hair hung loose around his shoulders like corn silk and he wore a tight black vest over his bare chest with wide, black leather wristbands to emphasize his overly muscled arms. Even knowing that there was no comparison between them as far as physical prowess, Chris still felt the pang of envy gnaw at him.

Joyce looked over at him. *Go now, and don't take your jealousy out on her. If you want to look like him, you know you could. Besides, I already told you that he's not my type at all,* she said telepathically, giving him a wink.

Chris took Mim by the hand and led her to the back of the club and up the stairway to the loft. He held her hand in his as they climbed. "I'm sorry if I haven't been giving you the time that you need," he said when they reached to door to the loft. "I would like to try to make up for it now."

He led her into the bedroom and started lighting the candles. "I'm sorry, would you excuse me for just a sec? I'm really sorry. I'll be right back, I promise." Miriam ducked into the master bath and closed the door. Moments later, Chris heard the water start running in the sink and the hushed murmur of her talking to herself. Chris smiled bemusedly, charmed by her nervousness, then remembered the night he had lost his virginity.

He didn't remember it well, due to the mescaline in a friends cup he had inadvertently swallowed, but afterword he clearly remembered waking up in Cara's room in Fetus Squat. It had been dim, lit only by the glow of the streetlights filtering up through the one window not sealed with scavenged plywood. He reached out tentative into the darkness. The sheets damp and cooling between them. His fingers brushed her arm and traveled up to the curve of her shoulder.

He took his time removing his boots and jewelry and returning them to his side of the closet, using the extra time to bring his emotions back under control. He lay down on his back, staring at the canopy over the bed and waited for Miriam to return from the bathroom. When he finally heard the water stop running, Chris propped himself up on his elbow and turned to face the door.

She stepped slowly out into the bedroom, naked except for the bundle of black clothing clutched to her breast that tumbled past her arm to hang just below her knees. As she stepped cautiously towards the bed, Chris sat up and swung his legs over the side. He stood up to face her, their bodies so close he could feel her tension through the narrow gap between them.

She stood before him, her eyes closed, swaying slightly as she fought to stay on her feet. He took her in his arms and kissed her deeply, catching her when her legs gave way beneath her. Her clothing fell forgotten to the floor as he gathered her in his arms and turned to lay her on the duvet. He crawled onto the bed and stretched out next to her, running his hand up her thigh, over her hip, and along her spine, sending a shiver through her.

"We can do as much or as little as you want. I don't want you to feel pressured in any way," he said, gently looking into her eyes.

"No, it's not that. I want to. I can't believe how much I want to. I'm just nervous," she admitted.

He pulled her closer to him, tucking her shoulder into his armpit so she could rest her head on his chest, winding his arm around her back. She pulled her knees up and flattened her shins along the hard plank of his stomach, curling as tight as she could. Chris encircled her with his other arm, his palm resting on the small curve of her ass, and gently pulled her in tighter, like a ball cradled against his body.

He shifted slightly toward her, rolling her over onto her back. He turned his head to the side, brushing her neck with his lips. Her arm, which had been wrapped protectively over the small mounds of her chest, was now reached out to encircle his back, her fingers buried in his long black hair. Chris let his teeth elongate, their sharp points grazing the smooth skin of Miriam's slender neck.

"Please," she whispered into the black cloth of his shirt that brushed agonizingly against her swollen nipples.

He plunged his teeth in then retracted them, freeing the blood to flow from within her to fill his mouth. Her fingers tightened their grip, pulling his head hard against her. He drank in her essence, her vitality coursing through his body, adding to his strength, feeling his cock stir with arousal in response.

Miriam could feel him stiffen against her hip, his cock straining beneath the surface of his pants, and reached down between them, caressing his shaft through the soft fabric. She fumbled with his belt but couldn't release the buckle with one hand. Chris broke off from feeding and got to his knees above her. He unhooked the buckle and pulled the belt free, tossing it to the floor with a heavy thud.

She scooted around on the bed so that he was kneeling between her upraised legs and reached between her spread thighs to open his fly. Once released, his cock sprang forward from its enclosure to throb with anticipation.

Even though she had never gone all the way with anyone, Mim had done some things before. She had always been able to put off guys who didn't want to take no for an answer with a little stroking while they dug around beneath her panties with their rough fingers. She had been called both a tease and a slut for not putting out, which she thought was funny in an odd sort of way, but now she felt that she was finally ready.

She reached out and took hold of Chris' cock with an underhand grip, gently pumping back and forth. Chris steadied himself by placing his hands on Mim's knees as she brought him to rigid attention. Her grip tightened and she pulled him forward, guiding him towards the inflamed lips nestled between her thighs. She rubbed it up and down along the folds of sensitive flesh, coating it with the essence of her arousal until the slick tip was nestled against the gate of her maidenhood.

Chris leaned forward onto his hands, his mouth drawn back to the red rivulets running down her neck. As his teeth once again pierced her skin, Miriam pulled him to her and thrust her hips upward to meet him, and a small squeak of both pleasure and pain escaped her lips.

Le Couvent Notre Dame de Lumière à Nantes, 1440

When he awoke, he found himself laying on a rough wooden table in a darkened cellar, the course grain scraped into his bare skin as a pair of nobly born women washed away the soot and burnt skin from his feet and legs. Underlying their ministrations, he could feel the tingle of his flesh being slowly regenerated. Weeks of deprivation had slowed his natural ability to heal himself, but that was nothing that couldn't be corrected with the use of a page, he thought.

He reached up and gently rubbed his throat, the flesh cut and torn from the bite of the rope. He turned his head to the side and found the young priest standing nearby. In a rasping voice, he said, "Do not mistake my temporary state of incapacity for weakness. If you hinder me or thwart my will, I shall never make you as I am: immortal."

"Have no fear, my Lord, I am here only to serve you," the priest said with a bowed head.

"You are here to serve yourself, but you must be willing to do what is necessary to achieve your ends." Achingly, he forced himself to sit up and swung his burnt legs to dangle over the edge of the table. "I will require something to wear. It would be rather conspicuous if I were to go about sans vêtements."

"Of course, my Lord." The priest signaled the attending women, who set two piles of neatly folded cloth on the table near him, then hurried from the room. "We will dress in the vestments of the Dominican order to avoid notice while we make our escape."

Once the women were gone, the priest stripped off his plain brown robes and began putting on a white woolen one-piece, shoe-top length gown with long sleeves and cuffs. He synched it with a black leather belt with a simple silver buckle. He hung a rosary from the cincture on his left side, then put his head through the white shoulder cape called a capuce and covered his head with the attached hood.

"Clothe me, O Lord, with the garments of salvation," the priest intoned as he dressed. "By your grace, may I keep them pure and spotless so that clothed in white, I may be worthy to walk with you in the kingdom of God"

"Leave off with your incantations; you sound like that infernal pack of fryers. You must know that if you follow me down the path to immortality, you will never look upon the face of God."

"Yes, my Lord. Old habits are hard to break."

He put on the cappa magna, a floor-length black cloak and covered his shoulders and head with a black capuce, then stood by as his new master slowly followed his example. Their disguises complete, the priest turned to him. "We must make haste if we are to be beyond Nantes before dawn."

"Yes," he replied dismissively, "but I must regain my strength if I am to be fit to travel. My preference would be to have a boy brought in, but that might draw unwelcome attention, so I will sate myself with you. Kneel here before me," he commanded, indicating a spot on the hay-strewn cobblestone floor.

The priest hesitantly knelt down and took a deep steadying breath to brace himself as his master stepped around behind him and removed the hoods from his head. Suddenly, an icy hand covered his mouth and his head was wrenched sharply to the side. Pointed teeth bit into his neck, rending his flesh. His throat constricted and he tried to scream in pain but little sound escaped his master's iron grip.

He could feel the slippery tip of his tongue probing the wound, nauseating him, but not inflicting any further torment. As the feeding continued, the priest noticed that the pain he had experienced had subsided and was instead becoming a nearly euphoric sensation. When his master finally finished feasting on his blood, he found that his entire body was enveloped by a pleasant, tingling feeling that seemed to emanate from the wound.

He looked down at his servant coldly as if he were gazing upon a tool rather than a person. Wiping his mouth clean with the hem of his black capuce, he said, "When you are sufficiently recovered, we should be going. Where had you intended for us to go?"

"Espagne," the priest whispered.

Chapter 15

When Chris woke up, Mim was gone and Joyce was asleep next to him, her breathing deep and steady. He climbed out of the bed, pulled his robe around his shoulders and headed into the kitchen. He certainly didn't need any more blood after the initiation ceremonies and his night with Mim, but he was feeling a little peckish. Something solid in his stomach seemed like a good idea.

As he combed through the refrigerator, looking for something appetizing, he kept thinking that there must be something that would help explain what was going on. Who the vampire was that had turned him? Did he do something different when he infected Chris that could cause his bite might to cure Lucca's diabetes, or cold he actually infect others? Was it possible for him to become human again? Did he want to?

His mind kept going back to the Gibborilium. Amym had insinuated that there might be a lot more to be learned if a complete copy could be found, but the only copies were in the possession of the True Born Vampires, and there weren't likely to give theirs up unless they were dead and that didn't seem like a viable option.

He had been standing in front of the open refrigerator door without actually looking at what was inside for several minutes. "Hey, you're letting all the cold out," said Simeon, coming in unnoticed from the dorm.

Chris was embarrassed by being caught daydreaming but he had to maintain his position as the unquestioned dominant force in the house. "We're running low on blood." He looked over his shoulder at Simeon, who had taken a seat at the island and was peeling a banana. "You may be required to give more sooner than expected," he said, trying to sound as ominous as possible.

Closing the fridge, Chris turned to face Simeon. "Where do you suspect would be the best place to search for a rare book?"

"When I'm looking for a book, I usually hit The Strand on 12th. I think they might have a rare book department upstairs. But I guess the best place to check first would be the library." Chris' mind was suddenly filled with an image of wide stairs flanked by two enormous stone lions leading to a white marble Beaux-Arts facade. He guessed that he was pulling the image from Simeon and probed deeper looking for its location. What he got was a vague memory of walking past the library on the way to Times Square. Not exactly an address, but enough for him to find it.

Chris thanked him and headed back to the master suite to get dressed. He would have to talk to Joyce about his vision but it would wait. After flipping through all the hangers in his wardrobe, he gave up on finding any combination of clothing that didn't say phantom cowboy and reluctantly decided that he really shouldn't break character anyway. After all, what if someone from the Chord saw him?

He finished getting dressed and left the loft with high hopes of having all his questions answered before evening, but several hours later, he hadn't learned a thing except that he should check Beinecke Rare Book Library at Yale University in New Haven. That didn't help him much as he only vaguely knew that New Haven was in Connecticut and that Connecticut was somewhere up past the Bronx.

When he returned, he found his entire retinue gathered around the kitchen island where Lucifer, wearing a white lab coat, was inserting something green and pink into Brielle's mouth. He walked up to where Joyce was standing at the outskirts of the group. "What's going on?"

"This is what I was arranging last night when you were getting pissy. Remember when Lou told us he was at NYU studying dental hygienics? Well... after Promus said we should be more flamboyant, I got to thinking that our little group should have fangs of their own and whala!" she said, indicating the scene playing out in their kitchen.

While Brielle sat at the counter with a piece of lime green plastic protruding from between her clenched teeth, Lucifer was busy mixing up another batch of powdered alginate in a waxed paper cup. He poured in a measure of water and stirred it with a tongue depressor until it looked like thick pink goop. Then, he spread the goopy substance onto another green plastic plate. "Who's next?" he asked the group.

Mike raised his hand immediately and Lucifer inserted it into his mouth to take an impression of his teeth. Once he had it in the right place, he turned back to Brielle and gently wiggled the plate until it came loose and he was able to remove it from her mouth without damaging the impression. He made some notes on an index card and laid it and the mold to the side, then started mixing up another batch.

"Where were you all day?" Joyce asked.

"On a wild goose chase," he said. "I went around the city looking for someone who knew about the Gibborilium or Angelic script, but I got nothing."

"Come with me," she said seriously and walked quickly to their bedroom, leaving Chris to trail in her wake.

When he entered the room, Joyce closed and locked the door. "That was incredibly stupid. No one outside of the True Vampires are even aware of the book's existence. If word gets back to the Chord that you are looking for one, what do you think they'll do?"

It was a rhetorical question because she didn't give Chris any time to respond. "I'll tell you what they'll do, they'll kill us all; you, me, Amym, all those kids out there. They'd tear us to pieces without batting an eye. Do you think anyone you talked to is likely to forget it? You don't exactly blend in, you know."

Chris felt his face heat up but he knew she was right, about everything. So, all he could do was admit it. "You're right. I'm sorry, I guess I didn't think it through very well."

"You didn't think at all!" She paced back and forth for a minute to cool down, then turned back to him. "Did you learn anything at least?"

"Nothing, but I did get another possible lead."

"Well, don't do anything without including me, okay? I can help you know."

"Yeah, I know. Sorry. Hey! That was a pretty good idea, getting everyone fangs," he admitted, though jealousy was still nagging at him. "Are you going to invite Lucifer to be part of our enclave?"

"I wouldn't invite someone into the group without running it past you first, and it certainly wouldn't be Lou," she scoffed.

"Why do you keep calling him that if you two aren't that close?" Chris asked defensively.

"Because I just can't bring myself to call him Lucifer, it's too ridiculous. I've seen evil and he ain't it. Besides, it gets under his skin. He was a small kid who got picked on a lot. That's why he's adopted his tough guy persona, taking steroids, working out, changing his name."

"You get that from your long meaningful talks?"

"I got it, if you need to know, by rummaging around in his repulsively, self-serving mind while he was staring at my tits."

"Oh, that reminds me. Earlier, when I was getting ready to go out, I got an image from Simeon's mind. It wasn't anything major, just a flash of memory, but nothing like that has happened to me except with my attacker."

"It's a form of Extra Sensory Perception. If you can open yourself up, you can receive what those around you are putting out, kind of like an antenna receives radio waves. You must not have had your defenses up while you were talking to him. " She explained. "Always keep your walls up. If you want to experiment, try opening a small hole, very small, like a peephole in the door of your defenses, then direct it towards the person you want to receive from."

"Okay, I'll give it a try," he said, thinking about what that would look like.

"Just make sure to keep the opening small. You don't want to leave yourself vulnerable. We'd better go back, I heard Simeon asking Lou for tusks," she joked, holding her index fingers up to her mouth barking like a Walrus.

She approached the flat, gray metal security door that faced 10th Street beneath the raised courtyard of P.S. 64. The five-story-tall, red brick Beaux Arts style school had been designed in 1904 to look like a French Renaissance Revival palace. Ornate cast-stone cornices and window detailing, extensive terra-cotta and limestone ornaments, moldings, keystones and pediments filled with fruit and foliage beneath a slate-covered mansard roof adorned the 'H' style floor plan that cut through the block to maximize light and air for classrooms amidst the city's narrow side streets.

Built to serve the booming immigrant population on the Lower East Side of Manhattan, the boys only school accommodated 2,500 pupils. Following the overall decline of Alphabet City, the city's Board of Education finally closed the school in 1977. The imposing structure was left to deteriorate until the city leased it to CHARAS-El Bohio, a Puerto Rican run community center and hub for homesteaders, squatters, community gardeners and other neighborhood activists.

Tonight, they were having a fundraising show in the schools ground-floor auditorium off the 10th Street entrance, where President Franklin Delano Roosevelt, Governor Al Smith, and Mayor Jimmy Walker had once held political rallies. This show promised to be much more energetic, even if the lineup of 2 Minutes Hate, Warmongers and Deadeye may not have been quite as illustrious.

She waited her turn and paid her three-dollar admission to a guy sitting behind a folding table. He clicked a chrome tally counter before stuffing the bills into a steel lock box and waved her into the auditorium. The walls and calling had gone through many different color schemes based on the layers of white, aqua and black revealed by the paint peeling from the walls and flaking off the ceiling due to leaks the courtyard above. The windows had been boarded up from the outside, blocking out the light, but leaving the painted-over glass exposed on the inside.

Pet worked her way through the shadowy figures towards the stage, searching the crowd for familiar faces. Judging by the sweat streaming off the kids in the pit, the first band had already been playing for a while, and everyone she squeezed past was slick with perspiration. The smell of unwashed bodies permeated the room with the rancid odor of feet, ass, and rotting onions. As unpleasant as it was, she was fairly confident that it would cover her own unique bouquet of purification and filth.

She shouldered her way to the front of the stage and watched the group of teenage boys in shiny, new, black leather jackets. She assumed that their parents had just bought them and wouldn't allow them to be decorated with band logos and stickers yet.

The crowd surged forward, pressed from behind by the movement of the pit as it traveled the room like a cyclone of angst and testosterone, pushing her against the edge of the stage that was nothing but an eighteen-inch tall plywood platform. She lost her balance and started to fall forward over the stage when she was steadied by a pair of hands that suddenly appeared on her hips.

Pet looked over her shoulder and saw a familiar face under a ridiculously short, bleached blond mohawk. "Hey girl!" he shouted over the music. "Haven't seen you in like forever. Where you been?"

She leaned back against his chest, tipping slightly to the side so she could look up at him, "I've been around, just getting into trouble," she yelled over the simple progression of power chords.

"I hear ya," he shouted back with a smile.

She turned back to face the stage but she wasn't thinking about the band anymore, she was thinking about Carlo. He kept his hands on her hips as they bounced up and down to the relentless hardcore beat, and when the crowd surged forward, she bent over at the waist, bracing herself with her hands on the rough plywood of the stage, and pressed her ass back against his crotch. When she stood back up she overcompensated, leaning hard against him. His hands moved from her hips to her waist to give her more support, and she took hold of his hands and pulled them tightly around her middle.

When the Warmongers finished their set, Pet spun around to face Carlo. She looked up at him, his hands on her waist, her arms draped loosely over his shoulders. "Hey, you wanna get out of here?" she asked. "There's a party going on pretty close to here. I was supposed to stop by... if you wanna come with."

Normally there would be no question, but Carlo dithered, saying, "I was really looking forward to seeing Deadeye."

"That's cool, but I'd be there to make sure you had a good time," she offered, running her fingertips up the back of his neck.

Carlo hesitated, glancing back towards the stage debating the pros and cons of staying for the rest of the show versus the possibility of getting laid. His indecision lasted for only an instant before he turned and dutifully followed her out of the makeshift punk club.

Out on the sidewalk, the air was cool, and even if it did smell faintly of piss from the people who had been relieving themselves between parked cars, it was still fresher than inside. Carlo followed as she crossed the street and headed west towards Avenue B. Once they rounded the corner, she stopped in the boarded-up front entrance of the Christodora and pulled the bottom corner of the plywood covering out revealing just enough of a gap to squeeze through.

"I thought we were going to a party?" Carlo asked, confused.

"We are. I told you it was close," she said. "Get in before someone sees us."

Carlo was reluctant to crawl through the opening but the promise of sex and beer outweighed the apprehension of any unknown dangers. Besides, if she didn't follow right behind, he would just turn around and crawl back out, but as soon as he was back on his feet she was pushing in past him. He brushed the years of dust off his acid washed Levi's and trailed after her across the rubble-strewn lobby, their shoes crunching softly on the shattered glass of the brass front doors.

Towering over the surrounding neighborhood, the seventeen-story, yellow brick building was a windowless hulk where the homeless took shelter and junkies could steal plumbing and wiring to sell to get their next fix. A far cry from its origins as a settlement community for the neighborhood's teeming, low-income immigrant population. The lower five floors, which were designated for public use, included a music school, a library, workshops, offices, a medical clinic, chapel, dining hall, and two kitchens.

A doorway at the end of the corridor led into the 22-foot high, ground floor gymnasium, where a splinter group of the Black Panthers once had their headquarters before they turned the fire hoses on the electrical system. The extensive damage caused the facility to be condemned by the city. Next to the gym, a dingy staircase gave the equally disagreeable options of either up or down.

She picked up a candle from the floor and lit it with the flick of a lighter, which she then stuffed into the front pocket of her jeans. Carlo followed her down, creeping as quietly as possible, every sound seemed to be amplified as it echoed up the cement stairwell. She led him down to the white subway-tiled cavern that held the basement pool and set the candle down on the dingy white deck tiles. The fifty-foot pool, which had been dormant since the 1969 closure, was unexpectedly full of water that glittered in the soft, flickering orange glow and the smell of opium smoke permeated the room.

"Where's the party?" the boy asked, confused.

She began to strip out of her Jeans. "You are the party," she said with an inviting smile.

Realization began to dawn on him and he quickly started to remove his own clothing, keeping his eyes glued to her as she kicked off her worn black Converses and slid her jeans down over her legs. She was thinner than he remembered, but that didn't bother him; he like all different girls. His philosophy was they all looked the same with the lights off. He sat down on the broken remains of a deck chair to battle his Docs off his feet as she pulled her shirt up over her head, slipped into the water and swam out into the darkness.

"Come on, what's taking you so long?" she called.

"How's the water?" he asked, tearing off his clothes and preparing to jump in.

"It's cold, but I bet you can warm me up," she teased.

Carlo didn't waste another second before leaping into the cold water. The splash sent a wave surging over the lip of the pool, extinguishing the candle and plunging the room into complete darkness. He started swimming, feeling for her in the water, sure that this intimate play would soon lead to him achieving his ultimate goal for the night. He'd always thought she was cute, and she had been one of the most sought-after scene queens before she dropped out a few months back, he thought, congratulating himself on this new conquest.

He reached out, groping in the darkness at the sound of lapping water, only to reach the opposite end of the pool without ever touching skin. He quickly concluded that he didn't appreciate being teased in this game of erotic Marco Polo after all. He pulled himself out of the pool, turning to sit on the lip with his feet dangling in the water. The smell of the heavy smoke was making him feel light headed and relaxed as he listened for the tell-tale sounds of her swimming somewhere in the distance.

Instead, he heard movement behind him and turned his head blindly towards it. "There you are." he said, "I was starting to think you ditched me." He paused, waiting for a reply but there was no answer. Suddenly, he heard splashing from the far end of the pool, as if someone were climbing out of the water. There was a rustling sound followed by the slapping of wet feet echoing throughout the chamber, as someone hurried across the tiled deck.

"HEY! WHAT THE FUCK! Where ya going?" he called after her as she rushed out of the room and up the stairs. As her footsteps faded, she whispered a silent I'm sorry into the darkness.

"She is gone, my young friend," said a male voice from the inky blackness behind him.

"Holy Shit. You scared the crap out of me dude. FUCK! Who the fuck are you anyway?" he said, thinking that he was dealing with one of the many homeless that lived in the park's shanty town of tents and the many abandoned buildings that surrounded it.

"If you agree to serve me, then I will be your Master. Perhaps then I will let you have a turn with my Pet as a reward, but for now, she has done her job and has gone to see to other business."

"Serve you? What the fuck do you mean by that? What are you, some kind of fucking CHUD?" he asked, referring to the subterranean homeless that were rumored to live beneath the city. The story was that these people lived in the forgotten subway tunnels and sewers deep underground where they subsisted on rats and each other, never seeing the light of day.

A hand wrapped around his neck, easily lifting him off the floor to swing in the air. He pulled and scratched at the fingers locked on his throat, his bare feet kicked out into the darkness. Nothing seemed to make any difference, he was completely at the mercy of his attacker. After dangling for a moment, he was tossed like a fish pulled from the water onto the diving board, which bounced slightly under his weight, the rough surface scraping his skin.

Carlo's hands were suddenly wrenched back and tied together beneath the diving board. His legs were similarly secured, leaving him trussed like a pig on a spit. Long moments passed as his captor let the terror build within him, then Carlo felt something sharp press against his sternum.

"What the fuck do you think you're doing?" He asked, a tremor of fear creeping into his voice. He had been trying to stay calm, relying on bravado to get him through, just like he did on the street, but this guy didn't seem impressed.

The knife slid down across his belly and beneath the elastic of his soaking wet, tiger-striped turquoise bikini briefs. In one quick motion, the fabric was cut, and the snug support fell away, leaving Carlo exposed to the cool air. He wasn't sure if he was going to be raped or killed – or both; but the night certainly wasn't shaping up the way he had hoped.

A tear scored a line across his cheek. "What are you going to do to me?" he asked.

"You shall be one of the blessed. You will no longer be mortal, but a god. You will have powers beyond your wildest imaginings, but you will obey me in all things and be one of my *glaives*." The blade bit into his skin, it's razor edge slicing through fat and muscle with ease as it was steadily pulled down, leaving a gaping hole from ribs to navel.

Carlo couldn't scream; he could hardly even breathe. His entire body burned with agony. His belly heaved with muscle spasms as he fought to inflate his lungs.

He was momentarily distracted by a splashing sound, as if someone was pissing into the pool beneath him, until the realization struck him that it was the sound of blood, his blood, pouring out if him. That was when the screaming started, but it quickly changed to an incoherent, whimpering gurgle. The splashing was interrupted momentarily, then started again as if the flow had been pinched off or something had passed through the stream.

He could feel himself getting weaker, becoming light headed. He was breathing rapidly, inhaling large amounts of the heady, floral-smelling smoke and started to drift into the inner reaches of his mind to escape the reality of his situation. "Now we will begin your rebirth as a member of the blessed," the voice told him.

Carlo felt something land heavily inside his wound, like thick drops of molten lead that felt like they would burn straight through him, and a final scream ripped from his throat.

Chapter 16

Andalucía, 1481

Seven-hundred and fifty Jewish conversos, those who had been forcibly converted to Christianity to avoid persecution under the Spanish crown, went in procession, bareheaded and unshod, howling loudly and weeping until they came to the cathedral. After a mass and sermon, each prisoner was made to publicly acknowledge their transgressions, and the sentences were read aloud to the crowd gathered there to witness the spectacle. Those few prisoners who were acquitted or whose sentences were suspended would fall on their knees in thanksgiving and praised the Lord loudly as they were led away.

The anonymous conversos were then condemned to go in procession to Seville's esplanade, their bodies disciplined with scourges of hemp cord under the authority of two Dominican inquisitors, with ecclesiastical and civil authorities in attendance. He watched with rapt attention, the black hood of his capuce pulled low to protect him from the burning sun, delighting in every lash inflicted upon the condemned.

In all, six relapsed Jews, called murranos, were condemned to baptism by fire and released to secular authorities for execution. To be burned alive for endangering the Catholic faith by continuing to practice Judaism after their conversion.

They were taken outside the city walls wearing tunics made of yellow sackcloth, decorated with elaborate visual symbols called Samarra, painted dragons, devils, and flames to distinguish those receiving different forms of punishment. Winding through the streets to the cheers and jeers of the spectators, they were driven to a site called the quemadero, or burning place, enduring the bombardment of rocks and rotten refuse hurled at them as they passed.

The condemned were stripped of their tunics and, wearing only their shifts, climbed the ladders to a small platform just wide enough for each of them to stand above a small pile of wood. Once there, they were bound to large wooden stakes. A prayer was offered and they were given a final opportunity to beseech the crowd and clergy to intercede with the Lord on behalf of their souls before the pyres were lit.

It was all very familiar and he relished the experience, now that he had the luxury of being on the other side of the pyre.

The flames quickly spread through the dry timber, licking the bottom of the platforms with searing heat. Soon, the condemned began crying out that the flames were too hot, pleading with their executioners to either pull away some of the wood to reduce the heat or throw wool on the fire so that they might become insensible from the smoke before being slowly devoured by the flames.

Instead, over the course of several minutes, he had the executioners add more wood to the fire, encouraging the flames to gradually lick higher and higher. He watched as their feet and legs charred black and began to disappear into the blaze. Their shifts burned off their bodies while their torsos were left relatively untouched.

He recalled Joan, the only woman who ever appealed to him, tied to a stake with faggots of wood piled high around her. Burned for wearing clothing unfitting to her gender. She had died quickly, succumbing to the smoke and hot gases from the pyre, but no such mercy would be shown for these wretches.

He listened as their screams of pain and pleas for clemency grew louder in a magnificent crescendo of suffering before trailing off and eventually fading until only the roar of the fire and the weeping of the spectators could be heard. He watched in fascination as their bodies were reduced to little more than blackened skeletons, with bright orange gouts of flame rolling within the gaping mouths and vacant eye sockets.

When Chris woke up, the house was quiet. He cautiously slipped from the bed, being careful not to disturb Joyce, and tiptoed from the room. His shoulders were sore from tension, but he swung his arms and stretched to try to loosen the stiff muscles. He soon decided that what would probably help the most was a nice hot shower. He didn't want to disturb Joyce, so he headed for the dorm showers instead of using the master bath. He would have to talk to Promus to see if a full bathroom could be built on the second floor where they had been holding their dance sessions.

He kept the lights off. With no windows, the room was completely dark, but Chris found it more soothing after a restless sleep than white tiles and bright bulbs would have been. He hung his kimono on a hook and settled himself in the center stall, then turned on the tap.

The water felt like needles of ice piercing into his skin, but gradually it warmed until it was almost uncomfortably hot.

He couldn't stop thinking about his dream; the suffering of those poor people being burned alive was horrific, and he knew he should have tried to block it or at least manipulate it, but he thought that he might be able to gain some sort of insight into his tormentor if he allowed it to play out. He couldn't be sure how much was a memory and how much was fantasy. Either way, it was like nothing he had ever imagined.

He braced himself against the wall with his hands and let the scaldingly hot water run through his hair and down his back, melting away the tension on its way to the drain.

The faint patter of bare feet padding across the bathroom floor caught his attention. He wished he had thought to close the stall door when he came in, but it would look like he was embarrassed if he shut it now. Besides just about everyone in the house had seen him in more compromising positions than this so what did it really matter, he thought.

"Is everything okay?" a voice asked hesitantly.

"I'm fine, Michael."

"I heard the water and when I didn't see the lights, I got worried that someone was in trouble," Mike explained.

"I just needed to relax a little and the lights weren't helping," Chris replied.

There was a slight hesitation before Mike asked, "Would a blow job help?"

At first, Chris was shocked by the proposition, but he made sure to keep his expression neutral to avoid showing any reaction.

He had been there when Joyce fed and made use of both the boys and girls in the house. She didn't appear to have any favorites, so it didn't make him feel too jealous, though he had never made use of the boys in that way. He had never given any thought to being with another man, even when Joyce was having her way with one a few inches away. However, the more he thought about it, he couldn't see any difference between getting head from a man or a woman. After a moment's consideration he slowly, deliberately, nodded his head. "It might," he finally admitted.

Mike stepped into the shower and turned off the water. He reached down and took hold of Chris' cock and started stroking it, kissing his way down Chris' chest until it grew thick and hard in his hand. He knelt on the wet tiles and took the tip between his lips, running his tongue over the engorged head.

The situation didn't seem natural. It felt forced, as if neither participant was really interested in what was happening and were just going through the motions for the other's benefit. "Is this something you wanted to do or are you just trying to please me?" Chris asked, trying to address the awkwardness he felt.

Mike stopped what he was doing and looked up. "Well yeah, I guess," he hedged. "I mean... sure I've always sort of wanted to but... I don't know. I've just been kind of lonely since I've been here."

"You're not getting along with the others? I'm sorry, I hadn't picked up on that."

"No, it's nothing like that. We all get along okay, even Lucca and Simeon are starting to get over their differences. I'd just like to have something special, you know. Something with someone that was just... for me." Chris could see tears beginning to well up in the corners of Mike's eyes and put his hands on his upper arms, coaxed him to his feet and hugged him tightly with one arm, pinning his arms to his side while guiding Mike's head towards his shoulder with the other.

Chris held him close, letting him cry onto his shoulder, mixing hot tears with the water still beading on his skin until he felt like he was all cried out. Eventually, Mike stood up straight, wiped his eyes with his palms and smiled up at Chris. "You don't have to tell anyone about this do you?" he asked falteringly.

"Of course not. This is between us and will remain between us, but I would like it if you would come to me if you ever need to talk."

"Could we go out sometime?" Mike asked. "I mean, not just to the club, but actually go out?"

"What did you have in mind? Just you and me?"

"Well... Skinny Puppy is playing at the Pyramid soon. I mean, it's not the Marianist Sisters, but it should be a good time. Maybe we could all go."

"That should be possible. I know Joyce was looking for some sort of outing for the house. She wants to make a bigger impression on the scene and this might be just the thing. Why don't you try to get some sleep and I'll talk to her about it, okay?"

Their heels echoed loudly on the polished stone floor in the nearly silent library as they strode toward a very perplexed-looking graduate student at the information desk. They had taken the 8:30 train from Penn Station to the Metro-North station in New Haven, where they Joyce had drawn open-mouthed stares from the straight-laced, Ivy League college students on their way across the campus. As agreed, Chris let her take the lead in trying to gain information from the Research Services Librarian.

"The central stacks contain one-hundred and eighty thousand volumes," the student explained, referring to the six-story, temperature and humidity-controlled structure behind him that made up the central core of the building. It was surrounded by a windowless shell of translucent marble panels, which emitted a defused luminance from the outside that made the stacks glow like amber, while also providing protection from direct sunlight. "And below us are more than six-hundred thousand more. Could you be a little more specific about what it is you're looking for?"

"It's really not that complicated, Stephen," she said, using the name on his nametag. Her eyes shown with a pale purple glow, a clear sign that she was using her psychic abilities on him, as she placed her hand over his to create a feeling of intimacy. "We are looking for any and all works written in or containing Angelic Script. That shouldn't be too hard to find, should it?"

"No, of course not," Stephen readily agreed. "I'll just go see what I can find for you. You can wait up in the main lobby and I'll come to get you as soon as I have something." They turned to climb the wide stairs as the librarian disappeared into the stacks.

Joyce sat on one of the couches while they waited, closed her eyes and either dozed off or began meditating, Chris couldn't tell which. He didn't want to disturb her so he walked over and busied himself by inspecting the objects in glass cases scattered throughout the lobby. An original Gutenberg Bible in a square display lay open to a page intricately decorated with color illustration of intertwined flowers and birds filling the margins around the text.

The wait was interminable but eventually, Stephen came back and led them to a reading room where a cardboard file box sat on the plastic laminated table. "This is all I could find for now. It's a research file on Heinrich Cornelius Agrippa. He wrote the 1533 De Occulta Philosophia libri which translates to 'Of Occult Philosophy'"

Joyce held up her hand to cut him off. "We know what it means, why are we interested in him?"

"He wrote these books near the end of his life. They deal with Elemental, Celestial and Intellectual magic, and its relationship with religion. In book three, he describes a celestial alphabet used to communicate with the angels and gives examples on page 440 and 441... here." He turned to pages that showed symbols that, while not identical to those Amym had show him, were similar enough that Chris had no doubt the author had based his on something older. "I'm sorry but I'll have to ask you to put on gloves before you touch the manuscripts. Library policy."

Joyce slipped her black liquored fingers into a pair of white cotton gloves. "You said he believed these letters could be used to communicate with angels?" She asked leaning over the ancient book.

"He seems to have outlined an intricate hierarchy: Seraphim, Cherubim, Thrones, Dominations, Powers, Vertues, Principalities, Archangels, and Angels. He also outlined methods the Hebrew Mecubals used to obtain their sacred names and communicate with them via these esoteric symbols."

220

"You said he wrote this near the end of his life... do you know what happened to him?" Chris interjected.

"There isn't much written about his death except that, it was believed at the time, that his dog was possessed by a demon."

"Why was that?"

"Because, around the time of his death, it ran off and jumped into the Rhone River and died."

"Maybe he was just hot," suggested Chris dryly.

"If this is the sort of thing you are looking for, I can see if there is anything else in the LSF." When he saw that they didn't understand, Stephen clarified. "Library Shelving Facility. It's off-site storage. Requires thirty-six-hour advance request to have something pulled, but they have literally tons and tons of material there. I can check the catalog and talk to the Early Books & Manuscripts Curator to see if I can find anything else if you'd like me to?"

Joyce stepped around the table to his side, sat on the corner and looked directly into his eyes. "I want you to make locating this information your primary goal in life, your obsession. You will make up some excuse as to why you are looking into this, a new area of study for your thesis or something, and you will never mention having met the two of us. One day we will come back and ask you about your research, and you will be delighted to share everything you've uncovered."

"Sure thing," he said, smiling up at her amicably. "Can't wait to get started."

Chapter 17

"Do you want to go back to the loft?" Chris asked as they walked arm-in-arm across the marble floor of Grand Central Terminal's main concourse. The four-faced brass Henry Edward Bedford clock on top of the information booth in the center of the concourse read 7:53.

"Not necessarily. What did you have in mind?"

"I have no idea. I'm just not interested in going back just yet."

"Do you want to get someone to eat? You feel like a little Indian?" she asked and waited expectantly for him to catch the joke. "They are easier to catch when they're small," she explained, laughing lightly.

They strode silently for several steps. Chris absently watched the commuters passing by while Joyce gazed up at the painted ceiling, obscured by decades of cigarette smoke, diesel exhaust and the oils from human sweat that had accumulated since the mural had been repainted on asbestoses boards in 1944, covering the original water damaged mural.

"Interesting thing about this ceiling," she said. "The design is actually backward, west is east and east is west."

"Really?" Chris asked, looking up at the darkened gold constellations 125 feet above. "How can you tell?"

"Well, Cancer should be in the east and Aquarius in the west." When it was clear that Chris had no idea what she was talking about, she continued. "You don't know anything about astrology, do you? Okay, take Rigel, for example. That's the big star in Orion's right ankle. The name comes from an Arabic word meaning 'left leg,' so clearly it should be on the other side."

"How did that happen?"

"No idea. They probably just reversed the drawing when they painted it. Hey, instead of Indian, how about we go for Thai?"

They walked down the stairs to the IRT Lexington line, dropped tokens into the brass slots and with a loud ratcheting sound, pushed through the turnstiles into the subway station. The still air was hot and humid, and smelled like the creosote used to preserve the track ties. Soon, a warm breeze from the tunnel began blowing the litter along the track in advance of the arrival of the number 6 train. They stepped aboard and Joyce held on to the vertical stainless steel pole near the door. Chris waited for the double chime that signaled the closing doors, then leaned back against them facing her, with one hand on a pole attached to the neighboring bench seat.

Graffiti writers would fill 4oz shoe polish bottles with paint to make graffiti mops which they used to tag up the trains. The dim amber utility lights strung along the tunnel flashed through the dripping, oily lettering streaked across the windows as they rolled past the abandoned 18th Street stop.

The 23rd Street station had been extended in 1948 to accommodate ten-car trains, which the shorter platform of the neighboring station was unable to handle. Now, its intricate, mosaic tiled walls were covered with layers of spray paint. Fat and bloated lettering identified the writers by their tags as if they were made of chalky white bubbles.

The breaks squealed loudly as the train came to a stop. The doors opened and the couple stepped off onto the platform at the Astor Place station. Named for John Jacob Astor, the station was completed in 1904 as one of the original twenty-eight New York subway stations. As they walked along the grimy cement platform covered with black polka dots of long discarded chewing gum towards the exit, Chris was struck by the large colorful Arts and Crafts style ceramic reliefs of beavers installed high on the otherwise white tiled walls. The plaques, produced by the Grueby Faience Company, were an homage to Astor, who made his fortune trading beaver pelts and were used to help the city's non-English speaking immigrant population navigate the 840 miles long subway system.

Their destination was Holy Basil, a second-floor Thai restaurant on Second Avenue just off St. Marks Place, in the hub of the East Village, the Punk Mecca of New York. So many things had happened on that street that Chris found himself lost in reminiscing; from shopping for his new Punk look at Trash and Vaudeville with his first friends Justin, Alex and Javier when he arrived in the city

223

from his isolated home in east Texas, to hanging out at the pizza place next to Gem Spa on the corner the night Cara was killed.

He was caught completely by surprise when Joyce leaned in, indicated a figure on the opposite side of the street, and asked, "Isn't that your friend over there?"

It didn't seem like that much time had passed, but the girl sitting on the wide marble steps outside Sounds record store panhandling for change was nearly unrecognizable. Chris let go of Joyce's arm and, in a supernatural flash of speed, maneuvered between the densely packed cars and pedestrians that choked the street, materializing on the step beside her.

"Hey, Jen," he said casually.

She looked up at him with unseeing eyes, then her face brightened as recognition slowly dawned on her. "Chris!" she said slowly as if she was submerged in mental molasses. "How've you been?"

"I'm fine, Jen, how are you doing?" he asked with concern.

"Oh, you know. I'm getting by," she said, sniffling from the winter chill and scratching the inside of her elbow through the sleeve of her black wool Peacoat. "You got any money?"

"The last I heard you were crashing with Adam."

"Yeah, well I'm not now, am I?" she said absently. She was scanning the faces of the people on the street intensely as if looking for someone.

"What happened?"

She turned her attention back to Chris as if he had just arrived. "Hey! Well, we were up partying one night and we started throwing two-liter soda bottles off his balcony. Okay, well I was throwing them off, but it wasn't like he was telling me to stop. They take off like a torpedo and do a shit-ton of damage when they fall from twenty-two stories up. Anyway, his parents heard about it and came back, so I had to split."

"Where have you been staying since then?" he asked, although judging by the smell, he could make a pretty safe guess.

"Well... McDonald's was having this twenty-cent cheeseburger deal, so I hooked up with a bunch of Gutter Punks and we bought like eight dollars worth. We snuck up onto the roof of that building over there." She indicated a red brick apartment building with an arched glass doorway at 7 St Marks. "We stayed up there for a few days until the food ran out. It was warm on the top landing and no one bothered us so long as we kept quiet, but that didn't last very long. Some people just don't know how to keep it down, you know? I stayed with some people in the park for a while after that, but it's pretty sketchy, especially for a girl. Besides, it's too fucking cold. Now I've got a place in a squat on 13th over near B. It's nothing special, but it beats sleeping on a bench in Tompkins."

Chris remembered his first night in New York: he had slept on a bench in Washington Square Park. He had been warned off by an old homeless man and ended up alternating back and forth between the park and a squat for a while before Amym found him. "You can come stay with us," he offered.

"Are you sure? I wouldn't want to intrude," Jen said, giving Joyce a sidelong glance.

"Don't worry, we have plenty of space," Joyce assured her.

"Okay, maybe just for a few days. So, do you have any money? I need to make a stop first."

When they arrived back at the loft they found the house in turmoil. The whole court seemed to be in a panic. "What's happening?" Chris asked Joselynne.

"Lucca was doing that stupid bottle thing again, trying to contact the spirits. Anyway, the bottle got way hot and shattered, and he got a piece of hot glass in his eye. I think it might have popped his eyeball because there was some blood and fluid discharge."

"You've got to turn him now!" Mike insisted, running in from the dorm and grabbing a hold of Chris' arm.

"Okay, let's all try to calm down," Joyce interjected. "Where is he?"

"We put him on his bed and have a damp cloth over his eye. I don't know if it will help, but we didn't know what else to do. It was so disgusting that none of us wanted to see it," Joselynne almost whispered. "Did we do the right thing? Should we have called an ambulance?"

"You did fine. Would you please see that our guest gets something to eat and drink and we will take care of Lucca from here.

EVERYONE OUT NOW!" Joyce ordered, closing the dorm door firmly once the room had cleared. She walked over to Lucca's bunk and sat on the edge. "Hey, Lucca," she said in a soothing tone. "I'm just going to take a look and see what's going on under there, okay?"

"It doesn't hurt, really. I just don't want to lose my eye," he said tearfully.

With Chris looking over her shoulder, Joyce cautiously lifted the washcloth away and looked at the damage. Lucca's eyelid was plastered shut with red, tinged discharge and lacked the roundness that would indicate an intact ocular globe. She laid the cloth back over the ruined eye, patted him on the chest and stood up, motioning Chris to follow her.

She led him into the dorm bathroom where they could talk without being easily overheard by all the interested ears in the house. "His eye is gone," she told him flatly.

"Is there anything we can do?" Chris asked with deep concern.

"Of course there is, we're vampires." She pulled a Dixie cup from the wall-mounted dispenser put it to her lips and dribbled saliva in as quietly and daintily as possible then handed it over to Chris. "Spit," she ordered.

He added his bodily fluid to hers and gave the cup back. "What's that for?" he asked.

"You'll see." She took the cup and headed back to the dorm, returning to her spot next to Lucca. "Okay, I'm going to treat your eye now. This will probably burn a little at first but it should begin to numb quickly."

"Okay," he agreed.

Joyce stuck her finger into the cup, swirled it around and spread a thin coat across the edge of Lucca's eyelid. "How does that feel?"

"Okay, I can defiantly feel it tingling but it's not bad."

"Good," she said and applied more, watching as it seemed to seep in, between his pinched lids.

Lucca closed his other eye and Joyce used that opportunity to apply about half the remaining saliva to the wound. She covered it once again with the cloth and stood up. "You try to get some rest and we'll be back to check on you soon."

"I'll be here," he said, trying to sound cheerful.

Chris closed the dorm door behind them with a soft click and led the way out to the kitchen where Mim and Mike were trying to scrub the scorch marks off the white countertop while the rest of the court waited nervously. When the pair entered the room, all attention turned towards them expectantly. "Lucca will be alright," Chris announced. "His eye was badly damaged but it will heal. For now please let him rest and recover." There was a collective sigh of relief from the group.

"I take it you have all met Jennifer?" he asked, holding his hand out to where she sat on the sofa. There was some agreement and a few tentative hellos from around the room. "She will be staying with us for a while. Please help make her feel at home."

He crossed the room and took a seat next to her. "I'm sorry about all the drama, but it's really not that unusual. This is a highly emotional group."

"Why didn't you tell me you were a vampire?" she asked. "That's so cool."

Chris gave a disapproving look at the group for sharing their secret so freely. "It's not something that comes up easily in casual conversation. 'So how was your summer? Well, I went to the beach to work on my tan and I became a vampire.' Not something you just throw out there."

"And Joyce... is she your girlfriend? Did she turn you?"

"She is my consort and partner, and the rest of the people here are our retinue, like an extended family," he explained.

"Mike said there aren't any exclusive relationships here and that you and Joyce feed from all of them. Is that true?"

"Mostly," he admitted. "Though the term exclusive relationship could be a little misleading. Joyce and I are on a different level and the bounds of our relationship are both looser and more secure at the same time. As for the other, yes, we do feed from our retinue. That is their purpose here, but they do benefit from it also."

"It doesn't seem to be hurting them," she said, looking around at the group of well-dressed young people going about their business. "And they don't mind being bitten?"

"They are all here because they choose to be. Have you eaten?" he asked her.

She absently wiped a bead of sweat from her eyebrow. "I'm not really very hungry," she said, but it seemed to Chris that she was starting to need a fix and the symptoms would only get worse as time went on. Before long, she would be sneaking out to cop some dope, then she might bring it back to the loft. *Who knows, soon this could turn into just another shooting gallery*, Chris thought.

While Chris sat thinking over the possible ramifications of bringing Jen into the house, a commotion developed that pulled his attention away. The house members were gathered around the entrance to the dorm as Lucca came walking out. Chris jumped to his feet and hurried over to find out what he was doing out of bed, but as he came closer, he saw that his injured eye was now open with a round, milky white globe swiveling back and forth along with his good eye.

Joyce pushed through the throng to examine him. "You're making excellent progress, but you really shouldn't be out of bed yet."

"I feel fine though, really. This popped out then everything started to heal up." He held up a small piece of green glass between his thumb and forefinger. "I think I'll keep this as a souvenir, but I still can't see very much."

Joyce pulled Chris aside. "That should have taken hours," she said. "Maybe even days. Not minutes."

"Is that a bad thing?" He asked.

"No, but it is unusual, very unusual really. Like curing Simeon's Diabetes. There must be something else going on here."

She walked past the wrought iron fence and climbed the wide front steps. Bouncers stood on either side of the double doors that led into the venerated nightclub.

For the past few years, The Ritz occupied had occupied what had previously been Webster Hall on East 11th Street. The red brick, Queen Ann style building was constructed in 1886 as a hall-for-hire and served the local immigrant community, hosting everything from weddings to labor rallies. During prohibition, it was rumored that Al Capone had purchased it and the hall served as a venue for decadent mob functions. RCA bought it and used it as a recording studio during the 1950s and 60s, recording such notable artists as Julie Andrews, Harry Belafonte, Tony Bennett, Ray Charles, Perry Como, Frank Sinatra and Elvis Presley who recorded Hound Dog there in 1956.

Now the Dead Kennedy's were set to take the stage at eleven, but she wanted to get in and check out the crowd before the show started. She worked her way through the punks and Skinheads milling around in groups on the main floor but didn't see any familiar faces. It was the same story at both the bar behind the sound booth and the one through the doors to the right of the stage.

Running her hand along the wrought iron railing and pressing against it when people squeezed past on their way down, she headed up the stairs to the red and gold scalloped balcony. The balcony was horseshoe-shaped, providing views of the stage from various vantage points, though the left side was roped off for VIPs and the view from the center was partially blocked by the massive mirrored chandelier where Marcel Duchamp once swung.

Along the back wall, near where the stairs ended, she finally saw someone she recognized. Sitting against the red velvet patterned wallpaper was Curtis. His cronies were arranged in a circle around him as if he were the most important thing in the world, and as far as scene status was concerned, they weren't too far wrong.

She walked up and stood behind the bald head of one of his fawning sycophants, jutting her hip out in what she hoped was still a provocative way. "Hey, Curtis. What's going on?" she asked, interrupting whatever pearl of wisdom he was in the process of butchering before his captivated audience.

He looked up to see who had the gall to break his flow of unenlightened consciousness. "Well look who's here. I haven't seen you a while. How've you been?" he asked, looking her up and down.

"Not too bad I guess," she said.

"You kinda dropped off the face of the earth for a while. Why don't you come have a seat by me?" he suggested.

She walked around the outside of the circle and had to fight the urge to start slapping them on their freshly saved scalps in a game of skinhead Duck Duck Goose. When she got to the spot Curtis had indicated, she stood frowning with her hands on her hip until the dimwit who was sitting there moved over to make room for her. She leaned back on one arm with one knee raised and her other leg tucked beneath it. The position caused her jeans to bunch tightly, forcing the pale skin of her inner thigh to bubble out through a hole in the frayed denim. She listened absently to what he was saying about the benefits of living life, according to the teachings of Krishna, while playing with the ragged strands that surrounded the hole.

Her plan seemed to be working as his eyes intently followed the movements of her fingers until he lost his train of thought and had to bring his monologue to a halt. He leaned over towards her. "Why don't we go somewhere more private where we can talk?" he suggested.

She lowered her head, looking up at him through her eyelashes and smiled. "Okay, sounds good."

He stood over her and reached down to take her hand to help her up. As cool as he thought he was, she knew he didn't have the pull to get into the VIP area or backstage so when she was on her feet, he held on to her hand and led her back towards the stairway. That could only mean that he was taking her down to the restrooms in the basement.

The loud clomping sound of boots on the stairs behind her made her glance over her shoulder to find his entire entourage following close behind. They reached the restrooms just as she had predicted and Curtis propelled her into the woman's room with a hand at the small of her back. His posse spread out to block the door so no one would come in to disturb them.

He leaned back, with his ass resting against the counter, his feet slightly apart. She stepped up to him, slipping her worn Chucks between his gleaming black Doc Martens, leaned forward with her hands on the hips of his meticulously pressed 501s, and brought her lips slowly towards his.

"Is this what you had in mind?" she whispered. She was glad that she had chewed a piece of Cherry Cola Bubblicious on the way over to mask the stench of decay with the artificially fruity smell of a gum-popping teenage girl.

He grabbed her by the hips, his fingers digging uncomfortably into her skin, and pulled her to him, mashing his mouth painfully against hers. She pulled her head back but he clamped her bottom lip between his teeth for a second before letting her pull away. "Mmmmmmm, sweet. I'm glad you came back around," he said.

With a knowing smirk, she said, "I bet you are."

Raised voices from beyond the door let her know that his group of skins had prevented some girl from coming in to use the toilet. It probably wouldn't be long before security arrived to find out what the commotion was all about. She knew that Cutis was interested, but wanting a quick bathroom fuck was different from being willing to leave the show and follow her to where she needed him to go. She reached between them and started running her hand up and down the front of his jeans, feeling him swell and stiffen beneath the tight fabric.

He pulled her hips toward him, causing her to lean against him, trapping her hand between them so that the motions meant to arouse him were, in fact, stroking them both. As her fingers traced the outline of his stiffening cock, the back of her hand was being pressed against her groin. She could feel the heat begin to build and she started feeling flushed from the sudden flow of blood to her face. She braced herself with a hand on the counter behind him, rested her forehead against his shoulder, her breath coming rapid and hot against his neck.

She pulled back in surprise as the restroom door opened and another boy came in wearing a Strength Through Oi! t-shirt featuring a tough looking skinhead putting his boot into the camera lens. She wondered if he knew that the guy was actually a gay model who had to have his Nazi tattoos airbrushed out of the picture before it could appear on the record cover.

Curtis kept her pressed against him with an arm quickly thrown around her waist. "What's going on?" she asked, beginning to become concerned for her ability to stay in control of the situation that was unfolding.

"You don't mind if we share, do you?" Curtis asked, although it wasn't really a question.

She swallowed her panic. "Ummm... three's company I guess," she said to buy herself some time to think through what to do.

Smiling at her, Curtis said, "I didn't think you were gonna be any trouble. You're a good girl, right?"

The second boy who she didn't recognize approached her from behind and inserted his boots between her feet, stepping to the side to push her legs further apart. Curtis shifted his feet to make room and his friend stepped in closer, pressing his groin against the seat of her jeans.

He reached around her, his hands slipping easily under her loose t-shirt to cup her breasts, pulling her backward, forcing her back to arch toward him. His fingers found her swelling nipples through the coarse fabric of her worn-out bra and he pinched them roughly between his thumb and forefinger, causing her to gasp from the sudden pain. His grip loosened and he rolled her nipples gently between his fingers to sooth the tender flesh until it was a throbbing ache that tugged at her like ropes of nerves connected deep within her groin.

Curtis was grinning to himself as he fumbled with the buttons of her fly. Time was running out but she wasn't entirely sure she really wanted them to stop anymore. These weren't nice boys and she was utterly convinced that they weren't above hurting her to get what they wanted, but at least they were human.

Having warm hands caressing her, warm lips kissing her skin, hard cocks throbbing with living blood felt like something real after months of nothing but torment with her master. She was tempted to just give in to the sensation and let the situation take her wherever it would, simply so she could feel alive again.

Someone started pounding, "They're starting, we're heading upstairs," they called through the cracked door.

"Shiiiit!" Curtis exclaimed. "Sorry, babe, this'll have to wait."

"Whoooo!" she exclaimed with a big exhalation of breath as he pushed her back away from him. "And it was just starting to get hot. Why don't you two find me after the show, I have a place we can go."

"Bet," the other boy said, adjusting himself within the tight confines of his jeans as he hurried from the room to the opening chords of Nazi Punks Fuck Off began reverberating through the ceiling.

"I didn't realize you were down for this sort of thing," Curtis said, repositioning his hard cock into a more comfortable position as he followed his friend from the room.

"A girl can have her fun too," she called after him. Someone was definitely going to get a beatdown in the pit by those two before the show was over she thought.

Chapter 18

Lucca crossed the dance floor to the VIP lounge, his eye almost completely healed except for an overall pink tinge and a bright red spot where the glass shard had punctured the Sclera.

"Oh my god! Take those ridiculous things out of your mouth!" Brielle exclaimed, coughing as she choked down a swallow of her drink.

"Why? What's wrong with them?" Lucca asked with a heavy lisp.

"You can't even close your mouth. You'll be drooling all over your shirt," she continued.

Simeon leaned over. "We could get you a bib that says 'I only suck as hard as I bite.'"

"Are they really that bad?" Lucca asked, beginning to sound crestfallen.

"Even the loneliest sea lion would take one look at you and say 'No, sorry. No fuggos!'" Brielle teased.

"I think it's walruses that have the tusks, not sea lions," Simeon added.

"Are you sure?"

"Pretty sure," Simeon said sarcastically. "Where did you get them anyway?"

"Lucifer made them for me," Lucca protested.

"Was he messing with you?" Simeon laughed. "What did you tell him you wanted?"

Feeling embarrassed, Lucca admitted, "I said I wanted them to be big. You know, the bigger the fangs the more powerful the vampire."

"Do you really believe that?" Joyce asked with one eyebrow arched, having come unnoticed upon the cluster of minions, her Cheshire smile revealing the petite white faces of her canines peeking out demurely from behind the veil of her darkly painted lips.

"It's as true as most of the rumors circulating around here," Lucca grumbled.

Brielle put her hand gently on the boy's shoulder. "Don't worry about it, I'm sure Lucifer'll make you another set in a few days."

"I think I'll try these for a while first. You don't mind if I go find some guy to nibble on?"

"As long as you don't do any damage that we have to clean up, have at it," Chris said, joining the group.

"If he doesn't die laughing at you," added Simeon.

"I'd be more worried about impaling him." Brielle teased.

Lucca ignored their taunts and leaned over to speak into Chris' ear over Peter Schilling's Major Tom. "Your friend Jen's in a bad way." He nodded towards the bar where she was flirting with a patron while trying to slip the tip he had just left the bartender into the cuff of her sleeve without being noticed.

Joyce took Chris by the hand and dance-walked to the center of the room, her pelvis swiveling from side to side like a pendulum whose arks were punctuated by a provocative jut of her hips. With a look of grim determination, Chris continued heading towards Jen. The man she had been talking to was already walking away when he reached the bar. "Hey, Chris. Having a good night?" she asked brightly.

"Please give Jeremy back his tip. He works hard and deserves what he earns." She opened her mouth to protest but ended up sitting heavily on a stool in defeat. She lay the bills on the bar, covering them with her hand to make it less obvious. The club was warm and humid with the body heat of a few hundred people dancing and socializing in the subterranean nightclub, but it wasn't hot enough to account for the sheen of sweat that covered her skin. "How are you doing?"

"I'm fine," she snapped irritably, taking a cigarette out and flicking the flint of her red Bic lighter repeatedly, trying to strike a flame.

Chris took it from her trembling hand, lit it for her, then gently laid it on the bar. "You look fine," he agreed.

"It's nothing a few bucks won't fix," she replied while scanning the room like a hunter searching the underbrush for signs of prey.

"Interesting that you use that word. Is that what you need... a fix?" She rounded on him angrily, ready to protest against the accusation, but he caught her eyes with his, and her denial stuck in her throat. "Why don't I take you back upstairs so you can rest?"

"Yeah, okay. Maybe that would be a good idea. I'm not feeling all that well after all."

Chris took her hand and helped her stand up, leading her towards the back of the club with a supportive hand under her elbow. He glanced over to where Joyce was dancing with Joselynne and she nodded knowingly at him. Charlie opened the ropes when he saw them coming his way and hurried ahead of them to open the door to the back stairs. "Do you need any help?" he offered.

"Thank you, Charlie, but I think we'll be alright."

"Yes, sir. Call down if you need anything," he said and closed the heavy door behind them.

Jen found climbing the steps exhausting and stopped to rest on one of the landings only to double over. With a single, violent heave, she vomited up the meager contents of her stomach all over Chris' shoes. "Oh wow, I'm really sorry," she said, spitting the bile from her mouth onto the floor.

He shook his foot to dislodge the white chunks and pinkish goo that clung stubbornly to the black leather. "Don't worry about that," he said and scooped her into his arms to carry her the rest of the way back to the loft.

When he laid her on the couch, the tremors had worsened noticeably. Chris covered her with a throw and sent a silent request for Joyce to join him. By the time he had gone to the kitchen to pour a glass of water and returned to the couch, Joyce had arrived. "Jen's not doing well."

"She's dope sick," She said, but Chris just looked at her in confusion. "It means she's going through withdrawal. It will get a lot worse before it gets better: cramping, muscle and bone pain. That's on top of what's already going on: shakes, sweats, and I saw what happened on the stairs."

"Can we do anything?"

"Well, normally I'd say she just has to wait it out, but it might be worth seeing if you have the ability to help her with her detox."

"What would I have to do?"

"Feed from her. Your saliva has worked remarkably well for Simeon and Lucca, who's to say it wouldn't have a similar effect on her."

"But won't she just go back and start shooting up again?"

"I can help with that," she said with a purple twinkle in her eye.

Chris went back and sat on the edge of the couch where Jen was laying. She scooted over slightly to make more room for him. "Joyce and I have discussed it and we believe we can help you. I can help you through your withdrawal and she can help ensure that the craving doesn't return. I wouldn't make that kind of choice for you, but if that is something you would like us to do, we'd be happy to help."

"You're going to bite me?"

"Yes. I would feed from you and hope that my ability to heal would be enough to get you over your symptoms."

She took a breath, releasing it in a sigh of resignation, and said, "Okay, let's do it."

"You're not going to ask if it will hurt?"

"I guess I just assumed it'll hurt, but I have been sticking needles in my arms, armpits even between my toes for the past few months. How much worse could it be, right? So go on, nosh away."

He helped her sit upright and scooted in behind her so that she could lay back across his lap. He took her in his arms, turning her face into his chest, and bent down to her neck. The hot blood hit the back of his throat like a mini explosion of pure pleasure and a rush of intense euphoria spread throughout his entire body. A feeling of post-orgasmic contentment came over him as if his body was wrapped in a warm blanket.

"Christian?" Joyce asked, rushing to his side. "Christian, can you hear me?"

The concern in her voice didn't register with him; he floated in blissfulness, his nerve endings afire with sensation. He smiled broadly at her with a feeling of pure joy at simply being, of having a body that was experiencing such incredible sensations. He imagined delicious fingers running along his skin, massaging every inch of his mind and body. "You are so beautiful," he told her, his eyes a prism of color. Looking down at Jen laying in his lap he said: "You all are."

"You're high," she stated with a smile. "But I appreciate the compliment." He closed his eyes and began to nod off. "Come on, let's get you into bed where you won't cause any trouble."

"Are you both coming?" he asked suggestively.

"You wouldn't be any use to either of us right now, let alone both," she teased.

"Maybe not," he admitted. "But it would feel so nice."

"Okay. Nighty-night, lover boy," Joyce said maternally as his eyes closed.

Mar Caribe, 1502

The smell of the sea was heavy in the hot, stale air of the sealed room. Thin strips of light penetrated the gaps in the wooden shutters that blocked out the sun and kept the room in a perpetually dim gloom. The cabin pitched and swayed as the ship rode over the swells on its way to Hispaniola as part of the largest fleet that had ever been dispatched to the New World.

The occupant, an elderly man known to those aboard as Friar Bartolomé de las Casas of Seville, a Dominican monk assigned to be the representative of the order to the island, lay near death on one of two small bunks that filled the tiny space. Over two thousand colonists and crew crowded aboard the thirty ships headed to Santo Domingo on the east bank of the Ozama River under the command of the newly appointed royal governor and Captain-General of the West Indies, Fray Nicolás de Ovando y Cáceres. Under those crowded conditions, having a private cabin set aside for the delegation's use was a luxury to be envied.

Sitting on the edge of the bunk, his assistant waited for him to wake. His eyes began to flutter open and he looked up without recognition at the younger man sitting over him, then his eyes seemed to brighten with awareness. "There you are, old friend. I was worried that you had slipped away without me knowing," he said with a toothy smile meant to be reassuring.

"I... am... here still," the old man croaked.

"Though not for much longer I think. I am sorry you will not live to see the New World as we planned."

"I could if you would keep your bargain," he said, his voice finding strength with the accusation. "I have served you well these last sixty years and I deserve the reward you promised."

"You have served faithfully and loyally, no master could have wished for more, yet I have no desire to produce progeny. Therefore, that is one blessing you shall not receive, and I dare say it is less than likely that there will be any awaiting you in heaven either. Though I suppose you could still petition the Almighty for his grace."

The ship rocked hard to port and the wooden beams creaked and groaned under the pressure of the sea. On the deck above them, sailors shouted to one another as they worked in the rigging beneath the bright sun. "Bear in mind that it is my power that has kept you as strong and vigorous as you have been all these many years. There is yet one more service that I require of you, my old companion."

He pulled the collar of the old man's shift roughly, tearing the thin fabric down the front, exposing a bony chest shrouded in thin pale skin and fine wisps of silver hair. He removed a long dagger from within the voluminous sleeves of his robe and raised it in the air above his intended victim. Skeletal arms wavered feebly to ward off the coming blow but he took the old man's wrists in his hand and wrenched his arms over his head.

The brittle bones snapped with an audible sound but it made no difference; any pain he felt would soon be submerged beneath a flood of agony. Slowly he drew the blade down the center the man's chest, parting the parchment-like flesh and muscle to reveal the bony plate below.

As an inquisitor, he had worked under the precept that no blood be spilled, and though he hadn't been entirely sure what to expect with someone so old, there was surprisingly little bleeding. He greatly preferred young boys to old men, their small bodies tended to bleed copiously and if there had been another option at hand beside this shriveled husk of a man, he would have gladly availed himself of it.

He put his hand over the man's mouth to stifle his cries of anguish, being careful not to smother him and bring his torment to a premature end. He cut through the ribs on each side with extreme caution so as not to puncture the lungs beneath and gently lifted the bony plate away in one piece. He placed it on his black cappa like a bowl and laid his knife in it.

He watched the air rush in and out as the lungs struggled to fill and empty. The heart pulsed feebly as it continued to pump blood through tired veins. The end, though painful, would likely be a welcomed relief, even if it wasn't the gift he had hoped for over the past decades. He bent low over the open chest cavity, took the heart between his teeth, and bit down. Thin, watery blood flooded into his mouth, and he drank it down as fast as it was delivered.

Gradually the lungs faltered, the heart failed and stopped beating and the pulse faded beneath his lips. He sat up, removed his hand from his servant's mouth and wiped the blood from his face with the torn edge of his shift. Quickly, he arranged the scene, placing the section of ribs back over the open chest, wrapped the shift around the body tightly to prevent leaking and dressed it formally as befit a senior brother of the Dominican order. Satisfied that everything appeared as it should, he called for a sailor to attend him.

"Friar Bartolomé has died," he announced solemnly.

"I am sorry, Padre. I know you both have been stricken with seasickness, perhaps with his age, this voyage was ill-advised," the sailor lamented.

"Perhaps, but that was not for us to decide."

"Land has been spotted and we will make port tomorrow. We can move him until he can receive a proper burial," the man suggested.

"That will not be necessary. I have performed his last rights and his soul had gone to God. This is now merely an empty vessel and does not require any special treatment. Toss it over the side and be done with it."

After the body had been removed from the cabin, the sailor stopped on his way back to his duty. "You must be eager to go ashore and begin your holy work with the native children, eh, Padre?"

"Yes, my son, and maybe in some way, Friar Bartolomé's death will help bring salvation to the Taíno savages."

The audience was exhausted and soaked in sweat when the set finally came to its conclusion with California Über Alles. The frenzy of stage diving had petered out when Jello went into a free jazz political rant, but the temporary interlude ended when the band came back for the final rousing chorus. When the song ended and the band had cleared the stage, the house lights came up and Tears For Fears Shout started playing through the P.A. to let the crowd know it was time to go.

She waited until most of those who packed the balcony had filed down the narrow stairs, closed her eyes and said a secret prayer that Curtis and his friend wouldn't be there before heading down herself. Though, she knew that wasn't likely.

She didn't see them on the main floor or in the lobby, but when she walked out the front doors of the club, there they were leaning against a parked car with a group of six other Skins. "Hey, baby. I was worried that you'd already split," Curtis said, pushing himself up off the car and strutting towards her.

"Not a chance," she said, accepting the weight of his arm around her shoulder. "I couldn't miss seeing Jello again."

"You ready to split?" he asked, already walking her towards the corner followed closely by his friend. "Where are we going anyway?"

"I got a place on A," she offered.

They crossed Third Avenue and continued on the quiet, tree-lined 11th Street. The boys entertained themselves by kicking over trashcans, causing them to bang loudly on the pavement, and singing Too Drunk To Fuck at the top of their lungs. Suddenly, Curtis' partner came around in front of her, blocking her way. He bent down, wrapped his arms around the back of her knees, lifted her up, tossed her over his shoulder and started running off down the block.

Screaming with surprise, she pressed her palms into the small of his back to keep from bouncing as the Air Cushion soles of his boots beat against the sidewalk. He stopped, panting for breath when he reached the corner but didn't put her down. When Curtis caught up to them, he jumped up and brought his hand down, slapping her hard across her upturned ass. She let out a high-pitched squeal of shock and pain that made the boys break up laughing.

She stood on the corner, rubbing at the seat of her pants to lessen the sting when Curtis took her face in both hands and pulled her towards him, kissing her forcefully. He took one step towards her, pushing her off balance, forcing her to take a step back in order to stay on her feet, then another and another until she bumped into someone. She tried to turn her head to see who it was but Curtis kept her face pressed to his. Hands took hold of her shoulders and pulled her backward.

She leaned back into the embrace of the person behind her, resting her weight against his chest. Curtis took another step forward, wedging himself between her legs, pressing his crotch against hers. He released her jaw and dropped his hands to her hips, grinding himself against her until she could feel his excitement building with the swell in his pants. She lay her head back on the shoulder of the boy behind her, breathing hard from her own mounting arousal.

Looking into Curtis' eyes, she asked, "What's your friend's name? If I'm supposed to fuck him too, I should at least know what to call him."

"I'm Walt," said the boy into the back of her head as he fumbled with her right breast."

A passerby gave them a look that made her feel dirty and cheap, as if she should be ashamed for what they were doing. And she was ashamed, for more reasons than she could easily identify, but it all led back to her master. She hated the things he made her do, but if she didn't obey he would hurt her, or Boy, or he'd just withhold his power to keep her animated and let her deteriorate. "Are we going to stand here on the street all night or are we going to go do this thing?" she asked to get them all moving again.

"Oh yeah, we're gonna do this, but I sorta like the idea of doing it right here in the open. Maybe I want people to watch." For a moment, her heart caught in her throat. Would they really do that, she wondered. She imagined them getting arrested for public lewdness, her master probably wouldn't even know how to bail her out, but even if he did, he would probably let her literally rot away in the tombs instead of wasting his time and money on her.

"Oh, come on, man, let's just go. I can't wait to dip my wick in you," Walt whispered and gave her a playful bite on the ear.

She led them past the white brick Boy's Club and St. Nicholas of Myra Russian Orthodox Church, past 7A and the Pyramid Club to the theater's entrance. She pulled up the security gate and pushed the glass door open to let them in, then closed them again, locking them from the inside. They followed a string of bare bulbs covered with yellow plastic cages stolen from a construction site through the dusty lobby and up the stairs into the dimly lit auditorium.

"Cool place you got here," Walt said. "You stay here by yourself?"

"Not quite," Carlo said, grabbing him from behind and pinning his arms to his sides.

Out of the shadows, a figure approached the group from across the stage. Pet dropped to her knees and bowed her head. "I have done what you wanted, master."

"Yes, you have, my Pet." His steps were silent and left the dust on the stage undisturbed as he moved to face Curtis.

"What the hell are you?" Curtis asked.

"Your new master."

"Fuck that noise," Curtis said. "You can take your fagot S&M bull shit and stuff it up your ass."

His right shoulder pulled back, and his arm bent in preparation for throwing a punch. Suddenly, his intended target was no longer standing in front of him, seeming to vanish into thin air only to reappear at the same instant behind him.

Before his arm had started its forward motion, a hand reached around in front of him and razor-sharp talons ripped into his throat, pulling away a handful of flesh and flinging it to the wooden floor with a sickeningly wet plop.

Curtis dropped onto his knees clutching at his neck, his fingers slick and red with the blood that bubbled out of the wound, trying vainly to hold the edges together and staunch the flow. His breath made a gurgling sound as it bubbled out through the space between his fingers. Within moments, he fell forward, lying twisted like a broken puppet in the pool that spread quickly around him.

The master put a foot on him and kicked him over onto his back and with a flick of his thumbnail, cut a thin slice into the palm of his hand. Holding it over the twitching form, he let three drops of his tainted blood fall into the gaping hole, then clamped his fist shut and turned. Licking the blood from his fingers, the convulsing body on the floor all but forgotten, he moved towards the second boy.

Walt stood motionless, held immobile by Carlo's grip and the horror of watching his friend die right in front of him until the master stepped into his line of sight. The man took hold of the neck of his t-shirt and with a sudden downward yank, ripped the front down to his waist.

He felt a sudden weight press against his chest and looked down to see the man's wrist pressed against his stomach. For a moment, it didn't quite register. Maybe he had tried to punch him with an amputated stump, but he thought the man had a hand, but it wasn't there now. Suddenly, he felt fingers start to root around inside his chest and blood began to seep out around the hand that was embedded in him to the wrist.

"Why?" he asked weakly as his head drooped with the loss of consciousness.

The master removed his hand and speared a small amount of his blood onto the wound. "Lay them in the corner until they are recovered enough to hunt," he ordered Carlo. He crossed back to where Pet knelt, took her chin in a bloody hand and lifted her to her feet. "Your work is not finished yet." He locked eyes with her momentarily to make sure she understood and turned to leave.

"Please, you haven't fed from me, master," she begged. She had to stay alive to make sure Boy would be alright.

"You can offer yourself to them when they recover. Their power won't be as strong as mine, but they should be enough to sustain you for a while. Come!" he called to the child who cowered on his mattress in the darkest corner of the theater. Immediately the boy scurried to him, walking by his side with the master's hand resting dominantly on top of his head.

Chapter 19

The car arrived at its destination and the passengers stepped out onto the sidewalk. Flanked by a four-man security team, the stoic group made their way through the white marble and steel lined lobby to the elevators. The man in charge of the black-suited escort turned a key and punched in a combination on the elevator buttons and the car began its gentle descent.

They exited into a clean but sparsely furnished lobby and were led towards a door to the right of the receptionist's desk, a subtle click let them know that the impassive women had released the lock allowing the point man to pull the door open for them. The door opened onto a hallway lined with offices, men and women went about their business glancing up occasionally but otherwise giving no indication that the groups passing was in any way unusual.

They were directed to a small glass-walled conference room. "Please have a seat." Their guard said, indicating the chairs that surrounded the six-foot rectangular table. "Someone will be with you shortly."

He turned and left the room, closing the door behind him. "What do you think..." Chris started to ask but stopped short when Joyce frowned and glanced up at the smoke detector in center of the ceiling. They sat in silence after that and Chris used the time to erect and reinforce his mental barriers with his visualization exercises.

Eventually, a harried-looking Promus opened the door and stepped in. Chris occupied the chair at the near end of the table so he made his way around to take the seat opposite him. He set down a mug that, based on the smell that now permeated the room, contained warm blood with a splash of whiskey and opened a manila folder.

"I apologize for bringing you here under such mysterious circumstances but there have been some recent developments, disturbing developments that require immediate attention," he said spreading the contents of the folder out on the table in front of him.

He slid stacks of 8x10 photographs across the table to each of them. They looked like police crime scene photographs. Bodies lay in heaps, ripped open and partially dismembered, but being in black and white seemed to mitigate the horror they depicted. What was surely a slick of gore spilling across the pavement, appeared as nothing more sinister than a dropped cup of coffee.

"These were taken last night at Hamilton Fish Park on Pitt Street." In the background, Chris could make out the landmark red brick, and limestone Beaux Arts pavilion that had been the central feature of the park since it's opening in 1900. "These were just vagrants but the way they were killed and left in the open is a clear indication that someone is attempting to get our attention."

"You think it was one of the Brethren?" Joyce asked, pushing the photos back towards him.

"It doesn't seem likely. All indications seem to point to an unauthorized group of newly turned Lessers."

"So what does this have to do with us? Our group are just playacting, none of them have the desire or ability to do anything like this," Chris said, becoming defensive at the perceived accusation.

"I am not trying to impugn the reputations of your precious little flowers, and it has little to nothing to do with them as far as we can see," Promus assured him.

"What is it then? Why are we here?" Joyce asked in order to keep Chris from saying something less diplomatic.

He gave them the look of a parent whose patience was failing. "The purpose of your visit tonight is that you have been assigned to deal with this problem before it reaches the public's attention."

"Deal with it how?" She asked.

"And why us?" Demanded Chris.

"How is simple, find them and eliminate them as quickly and quietly as possible. As to why you, normally this would be assigned to Amym, but as he is otherwise occupied at the moment and you are his protégé, you are to be given his responsibilities while he's away. I presume you are up to the task."

"That's not..." Chris started to say fair, but Joyce reached over and put her hand on his to stop him.

"What do we know about them?" She asked not wanting to be sidetracked with whys and what-ifs and just get down to the business at hand.

Promus closed the folder and slid it across the table to her. "They started showing up a few weeks ago, killing addicts and the indigent, people who didn't matter and wouldn't be missed, at least not much. They are cavalier about leaving their victims where they fall so it is unlikely that they have received any sort of training or direction. Likely they will be faster and stronger than they were as humans but they should pose little additional danger. With the training you received at Haven, they shouldn't give you very much trouble."

"Have you seen any pattern to their feeding?" asked Joyce.

"Aside from the fact that they are increasing in frequency and brutality, they have all centered around the Lower East Side. If I were a gambling man, I would bet their lair is somewhere in that area," Promus surmised.

The Lower East Side, or L.E.S., ran from Houston to Canal, from the Bowery to the East River covering what had once been Manhattan's seventh, tenth and thirteenth wards. It also unofficially included Alphabet City, formerly ward eleven, to the north. That was a lot of territory for the two of them to cover if they didn't want to send the rest of the house into danger.

Promus stood up and collected his cup, he lifted it to his lips and looked at each of them over the brim as he drank. "We still need you to make a public showing, there have been no rumors or reports of vampire activity circulating besides what you have in that folder. That needs to change."

"We've been waiting for the right opportunity," Joyce explained.

"There's a show at the Pyramid tomorrow night, I already told Mike we would all go," added Chris.

"There is no right opportunity and I'm past caring what you do, bleed someone out in the middle of Time's Square for all I care, just make sure they walk away with a smile on their face afterward."

Ma' ya'ab, 1517

Stone steps lead down from the temple into a canote, a hole in the earth resulting from the collapse of the limestone bedrock exposing a massive system of underground rivers of fresh groundwater. At a landing, at the water's edge, a canoe was tied. A single temple priest stood guard over a captive native waiting bound and naked for his arrival.

He had learned much in his months among the jungle people. He had learned their languages very quickly and understood the basics of their bloody religion, it was that which brought him to this dark cavern. He had threatened the temple priests with an excruciating death if they did not give him the secret to entering their sacred underworld. Many had accepted their fate with stoic silence, but eventually, he had found one who valued living more than they feared the wrath of their gods.

The crystal clear water, lit by small beams of bright sunlight that filtered through the jungle canopy high above, seemed to glow with a turquoise blue light in the scattered places where the ceiling had collapsed. He took his seat at the back of the canoe so he could keep his eyes on the blue painted prisoner and began rowing out of the light into the darkness of the cave. The river network connected population centers and temples across the Yucatan and it was to one of these temples that he was now conducting his captive.

The air was cooler underground, and he decided to remove the black hood he wore to protect himself from the tropical sun that scorched the world above. There were definite benefits to utilizing this tunnel network he thought as the canoe skirted around the edges of the pools of mottled sunlight that illuminated the darkness.

Vines stretched down towards the water from the edges of small jungle canotes, their tendrils like long skeletal fingers grasping blindly into the darkness, and the sounds of brilliantly colored tropical birds echoed off the cavern walls. In the world above, this trip would have taken days of hard trekking through the dense jungle's relentless humidity, but down below it was a pleasant and leisurely trip of only a few hours, though he found it difficult to measure the passing of time in the gloom of perpetual twilight.

The passage narrowed suddenly and they were forced to duck beneath the jagged teeth of low hanging stalactites. He paddled the canoe into a wide chamber with a low ceiling that gradually rose to a soaring height as they crossed the quiet water, still as glass except for the ripples created by their passing. When they arrived at the far side, he stepped over the gunwale and pulled the canoe up onto a muddy subterranean shore.

The beach was empty except for a large rock that had been placed in the center and a wooden ladder intertwined with vines lead up into the vast darkness above. He looked around with his enhanced vision and saw a figure squatting down against the wall of the cavern.

"Have you come to dislodge me from my position?" The figure asked speaking Maya.

"Of course not," he replied in the same language. "I have merely come to bring you a gift and to ask that you accept me as an initiate."

"Why should I wish to be the teacher of my replacement?"

"If you agree to teach me your ways, I swear I will make no attempt to take your place or act against you. I will go north into the Tepetzallantli Mexihco, the Land Between the Waters, and find a new place."

"Bring your offering and I will decide." The Aahau c'an mai priest said. He stood, removed his feathered cloak and walked across the muddy ground to stand behind the large stone.

He grabbed the rope tied around the prisoner's neck and lead him to stand before the altar, as it was now clear that that is what the stone was. The small priest looked up at the captured warrior and his eyes began to glow with a green light that brightened noticeably as the two locked eyes. The captive seemed to slowly wilt under the priest's gaze, he was turned around and guided backward until he was laying with his back bent over the stone.

The convex shape of the rock stretched him and pushed his chest upward. The Priest watched intently as the Aahau c'an mai pulled a flint knife from the waste of his loincloth and cut into the ribs just below the captive's left breast. He reached his hand into the cavity and with one firm jerk, removed the still-beating heart. He held it to his lips and sucked the oxygen-rich blood from the quivering knot of muscle, squeezing it above his head until he had swallowed the last drop.

After stripping off his loincloth, the Aahau c'an mai quickly cut the body around the wrists and ankles then along the length of the arms and legs. With a deftness born of uncounted years of practice, he skinned the body except for the hands and feet, rinsed the hide in the water and draped it around his own body. Dressed in his skin suit, the priest began performing his ritual sacrificial dance on the shore of the underground river.

Exhaust billowing in the chill air caught the distant glow of a streetlight as the limousine idled on the cobblestone street awaiting the arrival of its passengers. The driver leaned back in his seat, eyes closed, his black suit illuminated by the blue light of the dashboard radio. A sudden rap on the window jolted him into action and he hurried out of the warm car to open the rear door. Once everyone had settled themselves into the plush black leather seats he pulled away and began navigating the narrow West Village streets heading for their destination on the other side of the island.

It wasn't much of a trip, Manhattan was less than a mile wide at that point and they came to a stop in front of the club in a matter of minutes. He put the car in park and held the door as his passengers climbed out, offering a hand of support to the beautifully dressed ladies. He stood by until they had all filed between the parked cars that lined the avenue and stepped up onto the sidewalk outside the club before driving off to look for a nearby place to park until they needed him again.

The Doorman and bouncer held open the black double doors with a golden pyramid painted below the two small triangular shaped windows that allowed access to the rundown Polish bar turned drag dance club where not long before the Red Hot Chili Peppers had played their first New York show. Bystanders stopped to see who the glamorous young men and women were and they were happy to flash a fanged smile in response to an admiring onlooker. As they entered the club to attend the performance of the Toronto based Skinny Puppy, something caught Chris' attention.

The scent of fresh blood was strong on the still air and Chris turned his head trying to identify its source. Looking diagonally across the avenue, beyond the sometime Hardcore hangout A7 on the corner, it's façade recently decorated with an Egyptian motif, loomed the dark expanse of Tompkins Square Park.

He had avoided the park since the night Amym discovered him cowering in the bushes, naked and covered in blood. He had fled there after waking to discover his first girlfriend, Cara, lying dead next to him following their first night together. Now it seemed he would have to enter the shantytown of makeshift tents and shopping cart hovels to investigate the origin of the scent.

Having once been a parade ground for the Seventh Regiment of New York, the city redesigned the 10-acre site as a public park in 1878. Now it had become a haven for the more adventurous Punks, Puerto Rican gangs and the destitute. But no longer were the homeless just drunks on the Bowery, leaning idly out the windows of the Palace Hotel above CBGBs. The wholesale release of patients from state-run mental health facilities and the upward trend in substance abuse, including the influx of vast quantities of cheap heroin, and the more recent emergence of a new form of cocaine had put a large population of desperate, unstable and dangerous people on the city streets of the city.

Funded by U.S. government payments, Nicaraguan Contras had smuggled so much cocaine into America that a new method of storing and trafficking it had been needed. The hypocrisy of a drug epidemic facilitated by the very government that was at the same time proclaiming "Crack Is Wack" and "Just Say No" would only become apparent years later.

Property owners in depressed neighborhoods abandoned buildings or forced residents out of rent-controlled units and let them sit vacant until the realestate market picked up and higher rents could be demanded. Builders and developers concentrated solely on the luxury housing market, creating a shortage of affordable housing adding many younger people and families to the growing ranks that called the park home.

Joyce looked at Chris, fully understanding what was going through his mind. "I'll get them settled inside, don't go before I get back." She made it a statement but there was a plea in her eyes that held him firmly in place.

When she returned moments later, they began walking side by side to the park entrance on the corner. Chris reached under his black Duster and adjusted the Khukuri nestled at the small of his back, took a steadying breath and stepped past the five-foot-tall cement caped brick pedestals that flanked the entrance. The pathway led diagonally into the center of the park, past primitive structures built onto the remains of park benches where wary eyes watched with keen interest from the shadows. They took the first right and headed in the direction of the band shell.

Constructed in 1966, the band shell had played host to countless concerts and rallies throughout the social upheaval of the sixties and seventies, including a free concert by The Grateful Dead in 1967. Now, except for the occasional summertime concert, it had devolved into a shelter where homeless men and women huddled together for warmth and security. But on this night, it hadn't worked out very well for them.

When Chris and Joyce reached the structure, the smell of blood and viscera was overpowering. "Up on the stage," Joyce whispered, indicating the heaps of rags that littered raised platform.

They split up and approached from opposite sides, Chris with his Khukuri held at the ready and Joyce with small double-edged push daggers gripped firmly in her fists. They nudged the piles with the toe of their boots, turning over the detritus of a precarious existence. Amid the torn clothing and shredded bedding, they discovered human body parts strewn haphazardly.

"These bodies are fresh, their core temperature hasn't dropped more than a few degrees. I'd guess they couldn't have been killed more than ten minutes ago," Joyce said softly.

"That means the killers are probably still close."

"Close your eyes and concentrate on feeling the warmth in the bodies" she instructed.

Chris closed his eyes and concentrated. "Okay, I think I've got it," he said after a few moments.

"Now, reach out with your senses until you can feel the heat radiating from me." He nodded to indicate success. "Good, now open your eyes," she said.

Slowly Chris raised his eyelids. The world around him looked vastly different than it had only minutes earlier, the trees, the band shell, even the tenement buildings beyond the park had all taken on a bluish hue. Joyce, on the other hand, glowed a brighter blue, fading to green. The cooling blood on the stage around his own glowing feet was a dim red that reminded him of the taillights of a car fading off into the distance.

"Our bodies run cooler than normal people, they'll look brighter green than our surroundings," she informed him.

"I've never been able to do this before."

"You have, you just haven't had a need to or someone to guide you. Now that you know what to look for, let's go hunting."

They leapt off the stage and slipped soundlessly across the cobblestone open area and stalked down separate pathways into the deepest part of the park. Chris stopped when he heard a quiet 'Pssst' coming from a section of bench that was surrounded by shopping carts and heaps of rags.

"You better come sit here by me," said a voice that sounded like its owner had been gargling with broken glass. "There's a lot of strange things going on these days. A lot of strange folks lurking about. The bad sort." Chris went to sit down next to a large pile of dirty laundry while he scanned the area for his quarry.

He was fairly certain the mound concealed a person based on the dim orange glow being emitted, like the embers in a dwindling fire, but he was by means sure. "I don't hold with those type of people, I find it's better to keep to my self, except for God of course."

"Of course," Chris agreed.

"You may think I'm just some crazy old man, but I know that God will kick your butt. God and I are one you know, and what I don't like, God doesn't like and vice versa. You may have never been this close to God before. I'm telling you all this because the spirit is on me and I don't know why. Maybe it's something between you and God, I don't know."

"You see, what we, God and I, are trying to do is… When I say we I'm not talking about you and me, I'm talking about God and me. And he wants the best for me and for himself. God and I have one aim. That's how close I am to God. It's a big responsibility. It's a lot of pressure I'm under."

"I'm sure it is," Chris said absently as he concentrated on listening to the darkness for any unusual sound that might indicate the presence of his quarry.

"You gotta put God in the driver's seat. Just let go and let God as they say. Do you like car racing?" He asked, but Chris didn't make any response. There was something happening further into the park.

Undeterred, the man continued unabated. "You do. You may not even know you do, but you do. You may not love it the way God and I love it, it's like family to us, but you like it. You see, today is the 15th, my daddy was killed on the 15th and I got my dog on the 15th. Ricky Rudd's driving number 15 now and that's why I named my dog Ricky. That's not a coincidence, that's a fact."

Chris hadn't been aware that there was a dog, but be now noticed the cold dark nose of a sleeping Pit Bull mix, buried deep in the folds of the filthy tattered scraps. He wanted to caution the man to keep quiet, but he thought that if he continued on, it might accomplish the same thing. He began to stand but the man reached out and grabbed onto his arm. "You can get the CIA to investigate it, get the Russians on it too. You'll see."

He extracted himself and stepped away from the bench and followed the path as it wound around. Through purple lines of the trees, Chris could see a fire blazing in the darkness. As the path opened, he came across a figure in a dirty white suit with pink pinstripes, warming his hands over the flames of a trash fire in an expanded steel trashcan near the Cogswell Temperance Fountain. His long dark hair hung in greasy curls down to his shoulders and his pointed toed shoes were beginning to split where the white leather upper joined the soles.

The fountain, which had not functioned for more years than anyone could remember, had been a gift to the city by a wealthy San Francisco dentist and temperance crusader in 1888. It was the belief of the Moderation Society that if the public had ready access to cool, fresh drinking water, they would abstain from drinking beer and spirits. It was therefore ironic that the fountain was now the centerpiece of a park overrun with dealers, winos, and addicts.

Out of the darkness opposite him stepped two figures, the bright glow of their body heat hidden behind the fire until they stepped clear of its glow. "Hey dudes," the man cheerily greeted the newcomers. "You guys holding?" He asked.

"Great, another junkie," one said, nearly toppling the trash can as he leapt awkwardly over the fire. He collided with the junkie and sent him sprawling on the pavement. The assailant was a Skinhead, the fire reflecting off the smooth white dome of his freshly shaved scalp, dark smears streaked across his bare chest and a pair of uselessly thin red suspenders dangled at the sides of his bloodstained acid washed Levi's. He stood above his intended victim, placing one polished Oxblood steel-toed boot on either side of the man's body, bent over and started tearing pieces of his clothing away until he came up with the man's wallet.

"Hey man gimme that back," the man pleaded, but the boy tossed it over his shoulder to his partner.

"Why? You won't be needing it," he casually informed the man.

Chris stepped out of the shadows and edged slowly towards the unfolding scene. His eyes blazed beneath the brim of his black cavalry hat and he flexed his fingers around the handle of his Khukuri to secure his grip. "Who the fuck are you?" The boy demanded.

"Get out of here," Chris told the junkie.

"But they have my wallet," the man protested.

Without taking his eyes from the Skinheads in front of him, Chris replied: "It's not worth your life."

The Skin stepped away from the man, giving him a parting kick in the ribs as he scurried away into the darkness and faced off against Chris. "You're interfering with our fun dipshit. That's gonna cost you big time."

"I'm looking for your master," Chris said flatly, ignoring the threat.

"Yeah, well you'll have to deal with us first."

"I intend to."

The boy charged, his fist ratcheted back poised to deliver a blow that would probably cave in the skull of a normal person, but Chris was far from normal and to him, this boy seemed to him to be moving in slow motion. Chris easily ducked under the clumsily thrown punch and turned smoothly on the balls of his feet. He extended his arm in a sweeping motion, his coat spun out behind him surrounding him in its blackness. Small pieces of dirt and rock ground into the pavement beneath the leather soles of his boots. As he stood to face his second opponent, a dull thud followed by a howling scream of pain erupted behind him shattering the silence of the park.

Chris took a determined step towards the other boy who casually dropped the junkie's wallet into the flames as he circled around the fire. He laced his fingers together and cracked his knuckles in what Chris assumed was meant to be an intimidating gesture but just made Chris wonder if he was suffering from some sort of early onset arthritis. He pondered the idea in his mind as he advanced on the boy, wondering why the change wouldn't have corrected that, if that was in fact what was going on. Suddenly, Joyce rushed up behind the boy from out of the darkness. She slammed both fists into the sides of his neck and pulled back.

The blades of her knives cut easily through the muscles and tendons, shattering the C7 vertebrae between them when they came together at the back of his neck. He stopped his forward motion and his buzz cut head drooped slightly then tipped forward. His chin came to rest against his chest, his head connected to his trunk only by the trachea.

His legs buckled and he collapsed to the ground, his body landing hard on his knees and toppled over to the side, landing with the back of his hand twisted awkwardly against the side of the hot trashcan, his skin smoking as his flesh started to grill on the hot metal.

"You mother fuckers!" Screamed the first boy.

Chris turned back towards him, his leg was laying in a small pool of blood a few feet away from where the rest of his body writhed. "I'll fucking kill you."

"You'll have to be able to stand up first and it looks like that may be an issue for you for a while. I'd offer to help you up but I don't really appreciate being attacked."

"What are you going to do, hop after us? 'It's only a flesh wound?'" Joyce teased. Then becoming serious again, she squatted down next to him and asked, "Where is your lair? Tell us or this will become very unpleasant for you."

"This sucks fucking balls!" The boy exclaimed. "I'm gonna be a fucking gimp for the rest of time thanks to you assholes!"

"We can take care of that, if you tell us what we want to know," she promised.

The boy thought it over for a minute. "He keeps us cooped up in that old abandoned theatre over there," he said pointing in the direction of the lair less than two blocks away. "Only lets us out to hunt. Says he's waiting for something but he never says what."

"That's right across the street from the club," Chris said in astonishment.

Joyce leapt to her feet. "I'll go round up the kids."

"What about my leg?" The dismembered Skinhead demanded.

"Okay, let me help you sit up," she said stepping behind him and propping his back against her legs. Suddenly she bent forward over him and punched the blade of her knife through his sternum into his heart. He looked up at her with a momentary expression of surprise and betrayal before his features went slack and he seemed to crumple inwardly. She let his still body fall back to the ground, "That's two down."

"Why did you do that? I thought we were going to reattach his leg," Chris protested in shock.

"Once a Lesser has commited these types of atrosities, they can't be rehabilitated, and we're not here to save them. Our job is simply to illuminate them."

"Well, it doesn't feel right, lying to him like that."

"We needed information and I didn't get the feeling he was going to cooperate with us without getting something in return. So I offered him hope when he had none. It may seem wrong to lie to him but the alternative was torture, so you tell me, which would really have been worse?" She asked seriously.

He was quiet for a while, pondering the morality of their options. "That wasn't nearly as difficult as I thought it would be," he finally admitted.

"They were weak and slow, probably from not getting enough blood when they were turned. And they were stupid. Don't start feeling cocky, it won't always be that easy. Let's stash them somewhere then we can call it in for cleanup."

"Maybe you should take the kids back to the loft and keep them there. I'll stay and keep an eye on the theatre, see what I can find out." She nodded and raced off down the darkened path towards the club.

Chris stood in the glow of the fire appraising the scene. He wasn't looking forward to moving the bodies, there was a real chance of becoming covered in blood. That wasn't likely to be overlooked, even in Alphabet City, and he didn't want to be any more conspicuous than he already was.

He picked up the first body by the waist of its jeans and tossed it over the benches into an unoccupied patch of dirt. The second was a little more problematic as blood had completely soaked both the front and back of its shirt. He rolled it over with his boot, grabbed it by the seat of the pants and threw it over to join its friend, happy that the dangling head hadn't come loose in the process. Chasing the severed head around the park like a soccer ball wasn't something he ever wanted to have to experience.

Last into the heap was the leg. It had been cleanly severed just below the knee. He walked over and retrieved it from its resting place beneath the bench. Before tossing it onto the pile Chris stopped to admire the shine on the boot. The guy certainly did take pride in his footwear, Chris thought.

Chapter 20

When Chris finally reached the edge of the park and stepped into the pool of tangerine light from the high-pressure sodium street lamp on the corner, he saw that the limousine was just pulling away from the curb. He crossed to the west side of the street and headed south past the Pyramid, stopping in the doorway of a Laundromat opposite the newly opened SideWalk Cafe. Stepping back into the entry, he positioned himself as far off the pavement as possible to watch for anyone coming or going from the sealed off theatre entrance. He pulled his hat down low over his eyes and wrapped his coat closed around him, not to block out the chill, he could handle that by simply putting it out of his mind. He wanted to make himself as unobtrusive as possible to avoid being noticed.

People came and went along the avenue, and eventually, the show let out. For a few minutes, the street was filled with young Goths in search of cabs to ferry them away to better neighborhoods. Soon the drag queens began to arrive in their street attire. They hurried inside to change into their alternate personalities before the late crowd showed up to dance. But eventually, as late night turned to early morning, even they filled back out again. The club was locked up and a new subset of urban denizens passed Chris' doorway, either weary and bedraggled, making their way home to their beds after the bars let out, or half drunk and eager, looking for after-hours clubs.

As the sun began to rise Chris finally notice some activity across the street, the plywood covering the theatre doors began to bulge outward and a shaggy mop of hair started to emerge through the gap. His interest perked up when the person stood up and he noticed that it was skinny girl in a dirty white t-shirt, worn out jeans and black converse sneakers. She turned and began walking south and Chris got his first glimpse of her face. Instantly, his blood turned to ice.

He dashed across the street and started walking behind her trying to decide what to do. When she had reached the middle of the next block he moved up behind her as quietly as possible, working up his courage. He was so close to her that he could almost feel her hair against his cheek when he leaned in next to her ear and spoke her name, "Cara."

She came to a sudden stop in front of the red brick Con Ed power substation, its entrance cinder-blocked and covered with a thick layer of posters and handbills. Slowly she turned around and looked at the tall, dark-haired man standing in front of her.

Her face didn't show even the slightest hint of recognition as she looked up at him, but gradually her lips parted slightly as realization dawned on her. Then the expression of surprise turned to one of rage as she launched herself at him, pummeling him with her fists.

"YOU SON OF A BITCH!" She shouted. "Why are you here? Have you finally come to finish me off?"

"What, NO! I can't believe you're alive," he said, his open palms out in front of him to indicate that he wasn't being aggressive towards her.

"Yeah! Still here, no thanks to you, MURDERER!" she screamed, reaching behind, under her shirt. She pulled the stolen pistol from the waistband of her jeans, pointed at the center of Chris' chest and squeezed.

The roaring crack of the bullet echoed deafeningly off the brick facades of the tenements across the street. The impact forced Chris backward, doubling him over around the wound that was already rapidly closing beneath his clothing. He righted himself and instantly stepped forward, wrapping his hand around the gun, shielding it from anyone who might look down from surrounding windows. He was prepared for her to try to fire a second shot but he was not ready for Cara's left fist slamming into the side of his head.

"You killed me and left me to rot in that squat," she said and landed one blow after another on his unprotected face and chest. He retreated a step but made no move to defend himself as she advanced on him.

"Hold on a sec," he said, still holding her wrist firmly. Dodging away from a few of the better-placed punches, he caught hold of her other hand and said, "Stop hitting me, okay. And put the gun away before someone sees it."

He continued to restrain her until she stopped struggling, then cautiously let her go. She dropped the gun to the pavement and punched him in the face as hard as she could. She had heard the cartilage in his nose break but hissed in pain raising her hand protectively to her chest. It felt like she had sprained her wrist. A small price to pay she thought, and her master could repair it later.

"Are you finished? Can we talk now?" Chris asked.

She stepped back away from him, cradling her injured hand. Chris pinched his nose causing his eyes to water but he could already feel the damage beginning to mend as he bent down to retrieve the weapon.

"You look... different. Are those hair extensions or are you wearing a wig?"

"A lot has happened," he admitted. "You've changed too."

"Yeah, no shit Sherlock. While you've been off getting all Gothed up, I've been a zombie slave." Her angry glare looked him up and down. "You do look good though. You seem taller than I remember."

"Wait! What do you mean, a zombie?" He asked confused.

"What don't you understand? I'M A FUCKING ZOMBIE YOU ASSHOLE!"

She saw that he had no idea what she was talking about. "You know, the living dead. A walking corpse."

"I've heard of zombies, but obviously I didn't kill you if you're standing there."

She released an exasperated sigh, "The only thing keeping me moving is the power of my master, and without him, I'd just decompose," she explained.

Chris couldn't help it, he tried not to let it show, clamped his lips tightly together, but the corners of his mouth started to turn up and a single choked bark escaped. It was more of a cough than a real laugh but that did nothing to lessen its impact.

"Is that what the collar is all about?" he asked, indicating the black leather choker with PET spelled out in chrome letters around her neck.

"Fuck you," Cara muttered and started to walk away.

"Hey wait. I'm sorry," he said reaching out to catch her elbow.

261

She yanked her arm out of his grasp and turned to glare at him over her shoulder. "I didn't mean to laugh, it's just... you're not a zombie. You're a living, breathing, heart beating, warm-blooded person."

"How would you know?" she asked folding her arms angrily across her chest. She winced in pain, uncrossed her arms, placing one hand defiantly on her hip and letting the other dangle uselessly at her side.

He lowered his head, extended his fangs and flared his eyes, "Because I'm a vampire," he said dramatically.

"Well, no shit!" She replied without even a hint of surprise. "That's why you did it, I was just food to you."

"No! I didn't even know I'd been turned then," he explained. "Joyce thinks it was a combination of hormones, the mescaline in my drink and the influence of the Vampire who turned me. I would never have hurt you, I loved you."

She looked doubtful. "And now what? You love this Joyce person?" She asked. "Lucky girl." Her tone was meant to be sarcastic but it seemed to mask an underlying sadness.

Chris paused for a moment, he hadn't really considered that he might have serious feelings for Joyce. Everything had just seemed to happen so fast, sure she was beautiful and they had been intimate, though not exclusively, and he had been dreaming about her for months. They got along great and she seemed to like him too. They made good partners, but love? "Maybe, I don't know. But look, come with me. We can protect you, you could stay at the loft or we could get you out of the city if we need to."

"I can't leave," she whispered.

Chris' level of concern was growing by the moment. "I told you, you're not a zombie, he's not keeping you alive he's using you for his own purposes," he said emphatically.

"I know, and I'd love to kill him, but I can't leave. Not now anyway."

"Why not?" Chris asked.

A melancholy seemed to come over her. "There's someone who's depending on me," she said. "Let's just leave it at that, okay."

"How many vampires does he have in there?" Chris asked.

"There's him and the six he turned. He tried to make a few others but they didn't all live through the process." She felt the guilt of their deaths just like she did for the boys he had successfully turned. Their lives were over because of her, but what choice had she had? If Chris was right, she'd actually had plenty. She had thought she'd needed him to but it looked like he needed her more and anger was quickly overtaking her guilt.

With a twinge of remorse, he said, "We just took out two who were killing people in the park, so now he's down to four I guess."

"Who were they?" She asked.

"I didn't stop to ask their names. They were Skins, one was freshly shaved with red braces and oxblood Docs. His buddy had about a number three crop," he said, describing the corpses that had recently been removed from the park by the cleanup crew Joyce had ordered.

"Yeah, that's Curtis and Walt," she informed him.

Tentatively he asked, "Were they friends of yours?"

She looked at him with disbelief. "Not a fucking chance in hell. You couldn't have killed a more deserving pair of man-sized shit stains.

Relief washed over Chris. He knew they had to be taken out, not just because the Chord demanded it, but they were obviously terrible people even before they were turned or they wouldn't have enjoyed randomly killing people. "I can't tell you how glad I am to hear you say that."

"You're welcome to kill the whole lot of them for all I care, but I want the master. And can I have my gun back?"

"Not if you're just going to shoot me again. I may heal quickly, but it still hurts."

She held her hand out in silent insistence until he pressed the cool metal into her palm and placed his gently on her shoulder, intending it as a reassuring gesture. "You wouldn't be able to kill him. He's way too powerful."

She shrugged his hand off and returned the pistol to her waist. "There's a way. Crosses… holy water?"

"Don't work," he told her softly.

"Sunlight?" She asked.

"It might do it. I've seen him in direct sunlight and it definitely hurt him. Maybe if he were exposed longer..."

She thought about that for a few seconds. "That must have been the day he came back smoking."

Shocked Chris asked, "You've been with him that long?"

"I've been with him since the night you attacked me and left me for dead. Where did you think I would be? Jerk!"

"Oh god, I'm so sorry."

"Well, you didn't know right?" She said begrudgingly and without conviction.

"If you need me we have a club, The Shambles on Washington. Come find me there, okay?"

"Sure. Fine."

As she walked away down Avenue A, she heard him call after her, "I really am sorry Cara." A lot of good that did her, she thought as she rubbed away a tear that wouldn't quite come.

When Chris returned to the loft he found Chord guards standing outside, they held the door for him and closed it firmly shut after he crossed the threshold. He climbed the stairs and discovered another pair standing guard inside the apartment. As he entered the living room, he found Joyce sitting on the couch opposite Promus. She stood and crossed the room, wrapping him in her arms.

"Christian, please join us," Promus called indicating the vacated sofa.

"Hey. What's going on? Where is everyone?" Chris asked her.

"The kids are okay, they're down in the club. When I called for the cleanup, Promus thought we should talk." She took his hand and he followed her back to her seat.

"How did your surveillance go? Did you uncover anything useful?"

"I think so," Chris said lowering himself onto the couch next to Joyce. "This group is being run by the same vampire who turned me. His lair is in an abandoned theatre on Avenue A and he has, had, six Lesser Blessed, minus the two we took out earlier. From what I understand, they are all teenage boys from the hardcore scene."

Promus stood and walked to the kitchen. "That is very interesting," he said opening the refrigerator and pouring a glass of blood spiked juice. He returned to the sitting area, leaned over the coffee table and handed the glass to Chris. "And how did you come by this information?"

"He has a girl working for him and she told me." He leaned closer to Joyce and whispered "Cara" under his breath.

"Ah, yes. The girl you killed. Only now it appears that perhaps you merely thought you had killed her." He waved away their questioning looks. "Amym filed a full incident report on the matter with the Chord, though I seem to recall that there was a badly burnt body of a young woman discovered at the scene. So either you killed another girl, or someone planted the body there for us to find." Promus was quiet for a moment and just sat there looking at Chris until the silence began to feel awkward. "Curious," he continued. "It almost seems personal."

"Yeah, I think it's very personal," Chris muttered under his breath.

"I do too," Joyce added. "Chris has been under low-level psychic attack for as long as I have known him."

"Yes. We believed that your maker had bestowed the Blessing on you by accident and was trying to rectify the situation by eliminating you. Though his attitude seems to have changed somewhat if he is making other Lessers."

"So where does that leave us?" Joyce asked.

"Nothing has changed. You will continue to eliminate his support and when Amym returns he will deal with this unknown Vampire. Might I suggest that you begin training your minions in self-defense? Against one of the Brethren their efforts would be futile, but against a Lesser, they might stand a chance, especially if they can take them by surprise."

"Why would the Chord care?" Chris asked. "I mean, I get that they want to keep a low profile and these killings could bring unwanted scrutiny, but why would you want to take out another Vampire?"

"There are rules to any society, a code of conduct that all must abide by for the benefit and security of the whole. When an outlier flaunts those laws, they put everyone in danger. In this case, by risking discovery with the creation of unsanctioned Lessers. The blood is life. It is a gift from God and must not be diluted or watered down."

He stood up and straightened his suit. "You have done well so far, keep up the good work." He patted Chris on the shoulder and leaned in to give Joyce a kiss on the cheek. "I'll be in touch soon," he said and left the loft taking his guards with him.

When they were alone, Chris asked: "What do we do now?"

"I guess it's time to let the kids know what's going on," she offered.

They descended the back stairs into the club and found their six subordinates draped unconscious across the couches and chairs in the VIP lounge. "Okay everyone, wake up," Chris said loudly, and gradually, heavy eyelids began to flutter open and bodies shifted into more upright positions. "We have some things we need to discuss."

Ten minutes later, they were all wide-awake. "Are we supposed to go to and kill vampires?" Joselynne asked.

"No, I wouldn't ask that of you, but it never hurts to be prepared," Chris said. "We will use the dance space on the second floor and hold training sessions in the afternoons to get everyone as proficient as possible, as quickly as possible. I don't expect any of you to be Shaolin masters, but you still need to be able to take care of yourselves."

Chapter 21

Cara couldn't believe it. She had wondered what would happen if she ever came face to face with Chris again. She thought she would just kill him, take her revenge on the psycho who ripped out her throat after screwing her. She had given some thought as to how she would do it, a stake through the heart was her favorite. She had imagined him writhing on the ground at her feet as he slowly liquefied and became just another puddle of goo for the sanitation department to clean up.

Instead, he had told her that her entire existence over the past several months had been based on a lie. Chris hadn't killed her as she'd been led to believe, so her dead body hadn't been kept animated by the power of the master vampire she'd been serving. She thought about all the humiliating and disgusting things he'd made her do and it filled her with a rage and self-loathing that only one of his death could possibly diminish.

He would be sleeping now that the sun was up, at his most vulnerable. If she could get him out into the sunlight maybe he would just burn up and blow away, she thought. No muss, no fuss. She got a toasted bagel with cream cheese, coffee and a pint of milk at the corner bodega and headed back to the theatre, the beginnings of a plan percolating in her head.

She crept across the stage as quietly as possible. She could hear the sounds of the boys settling in for the day after hunting all night and she really didn't want them to hear her come in. Now that the master had others to do his bidding, she wasn't as indispensable as she had been and he sometimes loaned her out as a reward to whoever his current favorite was. Usually, she could fend them off by just letting them feed a little, but sometimes they wanted a lot more. Those times took a while to recover from and she didn't want to have to deal with that now that she had something important to do.

The creaking sound of the wood flexing beneath her weight brought her to a sudden stop in the center of the stage where the movie screen had once hung. She stood frozen, waiting to make sure that no one had noticed. She had never paid too much attention to the theatre since they had moved from the abandoned subway utility room, but now she took a good look around. The dim lighting wouldn't let her clearly see the peeling gold paint and water damaged plaster details of the ceiling high in the gloom high above her, but she could make out the terraces that still held the remains of the wooden seats and the black openings of the private boxes on each side of the stage where the boys slept.

She looked around for something she could use as a weapon. She still had the revolver she had taken from the dead cop tucked into the back of her jeans, it hadn't seemed to do more than faze Chris, so she couldn't hope that it would do more than slow the master down a little, if it did anything at all.

There weren't any windows that she could see, though there was probably some sort of access hatch to the roof above the curved ceiling, but that wouldn't do her any good she thought. She needed a way to flood the whole place with light, to make it bright enough that the master couldn't find anywhere to escape to.

There were pieces of the broken seats and a few ancient looking mop handles that could serve as stakes in a pinch she thought, but if it got to that point she was probably already a goner. She needed something much more effective, but the only other things around were a pile of old cardboard boxes filled with supplies left over from an aborted rehabilitation decades earlier. She had looked through the contents when they first moved in and knew there weren't any weapons. She tried to remember what was in them and suddenly an idea came to her.

She walked softly, her feet making a subtle scraping sound on the dusty floor, to the backstage storage room that the master used as a bedroom. He was laying as still as death on an old futon mattress she had been forced to roll up and pull through the opening in the doors. Then she had to drag it up the stairs for him, by herself. It wasn't luxury by any stretch, but it sure beat the pile of discarded clothes that she and Boy slept in.

Creeping over to her bed she gently put her hand on Boy's arm. He jumped, startled awake by the touch, but didn't make a sound. She didn't have to warn him to be quiet, he hadn't said a word since the master brought him, she just pressed the brown paper bag with the bagel and milk into his hand and motioned for him to follow her. They picked their way through the debris back to the stage where Cara pulled a rusty metal can of turpentine out of a box.

"Wait by the stairs, I'll be right back," she whispered into his ear and went to the aisle farthest from the exit.

The cap was fused on with a layer of rust and something that looked like amber, but she eventually got it off with a loud screech from the protesting metal lid. After a long pause to make sure she hadn't roused anyone, she brought the can to her face and took a sniff. The fumes burned her nose and eyes but that was a lot better than being surprised when it turned out to be full of plain old ordinary water. Cautiously she dribbled the fluid on the steps as she made her way to the back of the house, across the last row of seats, then back down to where Boy stood eating his bagel, a white smear of cream cheese gleaming on his cheek in the dim light.

"We have to be ready to run when this goes up, okay?" she asked, and the child solemnly nodded his head. "I just need something to set it off."

She was looking with growing desperation, around hoping that something would jump out at her when she felt Boy tug on the hem of her t-shirt. She looked down to see what he wanted and her heart caught in her throat, he was pointing up in the direction of the private box on the far side of the theatre. She whipped her head around reaching behind her for the gun but the box was empty. She squatted down to be at eye level with him, "What is it?"

The boy held up his hands and made blinking motions with his fingers then pointed again. Cara felt really stupid when she finally realized what he was trying to tell her, maybe the light bulbs could be used to ignite the turpentine.

She tiptoed over and retrieved a paint bucket to use as a step stool and as quietly as she could, took down the string of utility lights. She laid them gently along the floor, thankful that the yellow plastic cages kept the bulbs from making noise on the cement. Then, sending Boy down the stairs to the lobby, she held the can of turpentine a few inches off the floor and started pouring out the remainder of the liquid.

"What are you doing Pet?" Came her master's voice reverberating throughout the theatre.

269

"We're leaving," she announced trying to put more resolve into her voice than she actually felt as she looked around for the source. "You lied to me. All this time you let me think that I needed you to live when it was you who needed me. You were just using me. Then what was going to happen? Would you just drain me, or pass me off to your minions and let them do it for you?"

Behind the master, she could see his boys begin to stand up from their beds and look out from their boxes to see what was going on. She knew that there was at least one more looking down from the box directly above her head.

"I can honestly say that I have been amazed at your consistent inability to see what was right in front of you. Though I have learned over the centuries that humans will choose to see what they wish to see, and not what is. Therefore I must assume you wished to believe that you were dependent upon my grace to live, rather than be complicit in your own servitude," he said taking a step closer.

His words stung because they had the ring of truth. It was possible that she had subconsciously turned over responsibility for her predicament to this monster rather than take charge of her life herself. Even if that were true, she thought, it all ends now. "Well, we're leaving."

Her hands trembled on the wire causing the yellow plastic safety cages to rattle against the damp floor as two of the skinheaded vamps dropped easily to the stage behind their master to await his instructions.

"I can't allow that Pet," he said calmly. Across the room, she saw the deep red light begin to flair in his eyes. She had to act before he sapped away her resolve. If she couldn't manage to kill him now it was certain that he would kill her and Boy both and she did not want to imagine what form that death would take.

Suddenly, she thrashed her arm up and down as fast and hard as she could, cracking the string of utility lights against the floor like a whip. The yellow covers began popping open and clattered across the stage. The hollow pop of bulbs shattering and the tinkle of glass shards skittering over the cement floor momentarily filled the silence.

270

There was a whoosh as the turpentine fumes exploding into flame and Cara took a step backward, pushed by the rush of heat, towards the stairs. She hesitated just long enough to see the fire race around the parameter of the theatre and begin climbing up the walls before she turned and ran down the steps to where Boy anxiously waited.

She took him by the shoulders and turned him towards the door, pushing him out and following him as fast as she could onto the sidewalk. She set a brisk pace as she fled and Boy had to skip to keep up. Taking his hand, they dodged through the morning traffic on Avenue A. Pulling him along beside her, she turned down a tree-lined footpath beside a small gated parking lot opposite 5th Street, into the Village View housing project.

They had just made it past the first two twenty-one story, tan brick tenement buildings when a hand hit Cara in the center of her back sending her stumbling forward. She skidded to a stop, scraping her hands and knees as she sprawled on the asphalt. Rolled over onto her back, she saw Boy standing defiantly between her and her attacker, his small fists clenched at his sides. It was one of the master's boys, but she couldn't tell who because the fire had charred his skin to a blackened crisp. His clothing had been partially burnt away and the remnants still smoked, filling the air with the acrid stench of flesh and cotton.

"The Master says I can kill you now. I only wish we had time to make it more fun," he said in a rasping voice and took a step forward. Instantly, Boy launched himself at him, his tiny fists beating harmlessly against Skinhead's stomach.

The burnt vampire backhanded Boy across the face and sent him flying into the short, black steel fence that guarded the grass against trespassers. His legs kicked as if he were trying to get back up then fell back to the pavement and lay still.

Cara reached behind her and pulled out the pistol and fired a shot at where she thought his heart ought to be, but it didn't seem to have any effect. A stuttering hiss escaped the lipless mouth, which she assumed was a laugh. Her second shot was better aimed and entered his skull just below his right eye and removed a large section of his skull on its way out the back. He paused, and if he still had more of his face, he might have looked surprised. As it was, he lurched drunkenly to the side, his arm reaching out as if searching for something to steady him. His hand grasped at the empty air before his corpse collapsed to the pavement.

Cara rushed to where Boy lay and rolled his still form onto his back. The morning sun streamed through the canopy of leaves above, and the mottled light played over his dark skin as she pressed her fingers against the side of his neck looking for a pulse. When she couldn't feel the surge of blood beneath his skin, she lay her ear against his chest, there was no rise and fall of air filling his lungs and no sound of his heart beating.

Cara bent down and kissed Boy's forehead and wiped the smudge of cream cheese from his cheek with her thumb. "You didn't have to do that you know. We were so close to getting away, all you had to do was just kept running and let me handle him."

She settled back on her heels, cradling his lifeless body in her arms and waited for the tears to come but her eyes remained dry. After all the months they had been together, all the suffering they had endured, had she become so desensitized to pain and death that she couldn't even manage to shed a single tear for this little boy who gave his life trying to protect her? What did that say about her, she wondered.

She knew she couldn't stay there. The gunshots were sure to draw unwelcome attention and she didn't want to be hanging around when the police came to investigate. With two dead bodies and a gun belonging to a murdered cop, there would be a lot of difficult questions to answer.

"I'm sorry. I wish I had found out your name so I could tell..." She was about to say his family, but she knew the master had killed them. "someone."

She felt physically and emotionally drained as she gently laid the body back onto the walk and climbed to her feet. He looked peaceful, as if he were merely taking a nap, but the appearance of serenity was a lie disguising the brutality of his violent death. She couldn't bear to keep looking at him like that so she tucked the gun back into her pants and started walking away towards the First Avenue side of the project. She had the urge to start running and had to will herself not to. Not yet she said to herself. Don't look around, keep your eyes on the pavement in front of you. Don't look suspicious.

She walked two more blocks before she started running, but once she started she couldn't, wouldn't stop. She ran as fast as she could, changing directions when she hit a red light with too much traffic to weave through. She was heading west, she didn't know exactly where The Shambles was but she knew she'd find it.

Hector's Cafe & Diner was a squat little red brick building at the corner of Little West Twelfth Street and Washington, nestled among the cobblestone streets and brick warehouses of the Gansevoort Market. Since 1949, Hector's had hunkered down under an elevated spur of the New York Central Railroad that had sat unused since 1980.

With a gritty exterior and a cheerful bright yellow sign above the door, the diner stayed open from 2 am to 10 pm in order to cater to meatpackers, truckers, and trannies that worked the area day and night. While the men in bloodstained aprons and baseball caps, who once produced one-third of the nation's meats, loaded dripping carcasses onto the waiting trucks, Hector's was busy serving breakfast sandwiches and burgers.

Cara pushed open the glass door and entered the surprisingly spacious, black-and-white tiled neighborhood mainstay. She walked over and sat down on the cushioned seat of the shiny stainless steel stool closest to the window where she could kind of keep an eye on the comings and goings on Washington street. She knew that eventually someone would come to push up the roll gate and open the club, and she wanted to be ready. The server came and lay a menu on the spotlessly clean Formica counter in front of her.

She looked it over, eggs and omelets, muffins and rolls, they even offered fresh fruit, though she wondered how many of the early morning customers actually ordered any. "You want some coffee?" The man asked as she flipped the menu over to the lunch side.

"Yeah, thanks," she replied. "And cream if you've got it."

"Sure," he said as he poured the steaming black liquid into a heavy ceramic cup, its off-white glaze laced with a spider web of cracks.

The cup clattered and rocked on the saucer as he set in on the counter. "It's cash only," he informed her, just to set the right expectation. Not that she looked like she'd be using a credit card, but you never could tell.

"No Problem," she said pouring a quarter cup of sugar into her coffee.

"You decide what you want, or do you need another minute?"

"Yeah..." Turning her attention back to the menu, "I'll take the cheeseburger special," she said, hoping it wasn't too early to order lunch.

"Right," he replied absently and turned back to start getting her order ready.

"And could you make them chili cheese fries instead of plain?" She asked hopefully.

"Sure thing," he said over his shoulder. He laid a patty of locally sourced, freshly ground meat on the grill with a loud hiss and set a foil-wrapped iron on top to hold it flat while it cooked.

Cara stared blankly through the haze of light coming through the window, absently stirring the sludge of sugar at the bottom of her coffee cup, waiting for the hot liquid to dissolve the granules before pouring in the cream from the stainless steel dispenser.

Her food arrived quickly and she was surprised at how hungry she was. It had been a long time since she had eaten a full meal like a regular person and before she knew it she had scarfed down the whole burger.

"You were really hungry huh?" the man asked, topping off her coffee.

"Yeah, I guess so."

"You want something else?"

She was feeling a little nauseous and her stomach felt uncomfortably bloated and stretched, but the oblong plate of French fries dripping cheese and chili was calling out to her. "No, I think I'll stick with these."

She picked at the fires slowly, letting the chili cool and the cheese congeal into firm yellow blobs that she scraped off the plate with her finger and popped into her mouth. The waiter kept her coffee cup filled and replaced the cream with an amused smile when it ran dry.

Other customers came and went as the morning blended into the lunch rush. The diner filled up but her server kept the coffee flowing and her place was still vacant when she had to use the restroom so she never got the impression that he wanted her to give up the stool.

When it quieted down again, he came back with the coffee pot but she waved him off. "No, thanks. I think I've had all I can take."

"You want something else to eat?" He asked.

"No, I'm just waiting for someone to open up the club across the street."

"Stay as long as you like. And let me know if you need anything, okay?" He offered as he set the pot back onto the coffee maker to stay warm. He walked down to the far end of the counter, collecting a discarded copy of the Post on the way and sat down to read while he had the chance.

She watched the men in blood-spattered white shirts and aprons hose the sidewalk clean in preparation for closing up shop for the day. Meatpacking was an early morning business and the majority of shops locked up in the midafternoon. She hadn't been paying close attention, her mind was replaying every moment that surrounded Boy's death, but a movement under the corrugated steel awning across the street drew her immediately out of her gloom.

A large man in a black coat bent down to unlock the security gate, he rolled it up over his head and secured the lock through the track to keep it in place. His hair, when he stood up, was the pale blond of corn silk and she didn't need to see his face to know who it was. She dropped a handful of crumpled bills on the counter and ran out the door. She hoped it would be enough to cover the check that had been tucked under her saucer for the past few hours and leave some sort of tip for the guy who'd taken care of her, but she couldn't risk taking the time to figure it out.

"Lucifer!" She called as she dodged a large white panel van and dashed across the cobblestone street. He hadn't heard her and jumped when she grabbed his arm as he was unlocking the black metal door that led to the club below.

A look of vague recognition crossed his face but he couldn't quite place the dirty squatter girl that stood with her hand on his bicep. Cara could see that he clearly had no idea who she was. "Hey Lucifer, I guess you don't remember me. I used to hang out at Pos," she explained, referring to Positively 8th Street Pizza, which was a popular hangout for people going to see Rocky Horror on Friday and Saturday nights.

"Okay, right. I haven't seen you around for a while. Sorry, I don't remember your name," he said apologetically while blocking the entrance with his body.

"That's okay, I'm Cara. Chris told me to come here if I needed to find him." She hedged for a few seconds, "Is he around?"

Lou took a short pause to think about that. "Come on in, I'll call up for you," he finally said.

She stepped inside the door and waited while he reached inside the coat check room to switch on the stairway lights then followed him down the stairs. "Wait here," he told her when they reached the bottom and took a small flashlight from his coat pocket and headed into the darkness.

She watched the circle of light bounce and weave as it receded into the undetermined vastness of the space, then it blinked out and she was plunged into near total darkness. Flashbacks to her days spent in the lair beneath the boiler room raced through her head and she trembled with fear imagining the master there in the dark about to take hold and rip her to pieces.

The house lights seemed blinding after the inky blackness of the subterranean chamber, but now that she could see where she was, Cara shook off her fear and admitted that it was a pretty cool place. The fourteen-foot tall brick walls reached up to vaulted arch ceilings supported by buttresses that gave the large space the impression of being divided into separate chambers yet still had an openness that kept it from seeming too confining. Gothic and medieval replicas and architectural remnants added to the atmosphere and made it look like the basement of an old castle.

"What was this place originally?" she asked as she walked toward the bar where Lou waited.

"From what I was told, it used to be the holding pens for cattle before they went to the slaughterhouses. I don't know how true that is, but it sounds good. Hang on a sec and I'll call the loft for you." He picked up the handset of a phone from behind the bar, its spiraled chord slapped lightly against the edge of the wooden bar top as he punched a series of numbers on the keypad.

He held the speaker to his ear and after a short wait he moved the microphone closer to his mouth, "It's Lucifer, get Christian for me. I don't care," he snapped. "Just get him." Some things never changed, she thought, he was still a bully.

She was expecting Chris to come and collect her and take her somewhere else. Instead, he walked in from a tunnel in the back of the club trailing a large group of beautiful and exotic looking Goths, all dressed to make an impression, which they certainly did. The majority of the group took seats at the bar but two hurried up to her. "Oh my god, Cara! I'm so glad you're here," said a girl with short curly hair excitedly giving her a big hug. It took a second for her brain to catch up but she realized that she knew these two from before, "Wow, Mim. Look at you. And Mike." He squeezed in and made it a group hug. "You guys look great."

"Things have been going pretty good around here. But are you okay?" Mim asked.

"What did Chris say?" She asked with trepidation.

"He hasn't said a word, just told us that we needed to have a meeting after Lou called, so we all came down, but you look like you've been through a tough time." Mike could see the tears beginning to form in her eyes and squeezed her tighter. "It's okay now, you'll see. Christian and Joyce will take care of whatever it is," he said with the utmost confidence.

"Yeah," she said with a sniffle, not believing for a second that they could do much to help but desperate enough to give it a try.

Chris walked up and placed his hands on Mim and Mike's shoulders. "Why don't you two have a seat while we go talk in the office," he said and guided Cara away. "Everyone, please hang out here. We'll be back in a few minutes." He took her hand and led her through a door next to the bar into a small cluttered office. There was a desk littered with liquor orders, bills and staff schedules. A high back office chair was pushed back from the last person to sit at the desk and one uncomfortable looking chair faced it. She turned to close the door behind her but there was someone in the way.

Chris had moved around the desk to the office chair and Joyce followed them into the cramped space, throwing Cara off balance and leaving her nowhere to go except to fall back heavily into the other seat. She scooted her chair around to an angle so that she had a better view of the room. Joyce closed the door behind her and sat on the corner of the desk making Cara feel as if she were about to be interrogated.

"Cara, this is my partner Joyce. Joyce, Cara." He said and tried to give Cara a look that conveyed both warning and pleading. The two women smiled politely at each other and said subdued greetings. "I've filled her in on what you told me earlier, but why don't you go over it yourself."

"That's not really important now," she started to say but Joyce cut her off.

"It's very important, both to you and to us. We need to understand what has been happening, what you've been through, if we're going to be effective in helping you," she explained patiently.

"I get that, but now's not the time. I set the theatre on fire and shot one of them in the head. I'm pretty sure I killed him but I can't say for sure. I mean, I took out a big chunk of his skull but I don't know if that will kill you guys or not," she said looking back and forth between them. "I mean, I'm assuming you're a vampire too," she added looking at Joyce.

"That would be an accurate assumption, and yes, provided that there was significant damage to the brain stem, that would kill a Lesser Blessed." Cara looked at her blankly. "A turned vampire rather than a born vampire."

"Okay, so with the two you guys took out, there would only be three of them left plus the master."

"You said there was someone else..." Chris began.

"Not anymore," Cara said with a sad finality.

The sounds of raised voices began to penetrate from beyond the office door, Joyce unconsciously cocked her head to listen then jumped to her feet. "Chris!" she said and left the room in a blur of black.

"Wait here," he told Cara and rushed to follow.

The club was in turmoil. Lou lay sprawled on the floor his arms wrapped tightly around his ribs, the rest of the house was spread out facing off against four charred and blackened figures, one sporting a recent gunshot exit wound to the back of his head that was just beginning to heal. Chris drew his Khurkuri and shouted, "EVERYONE BACK!" Joyce pulled out her push daggers and took a position at his left flank.

Chris and Joyce assumed their fighting stances, their weapons at the ready and cautiously stepped forward as the rest of the group retreated backward past them. "You were stupid to come here," Joyce said.

"You're the stupid ones," said one boy with a snarl that cracked his blackened skin revealing the raw flesh beneath. "Hey Chris, We're going to kill you and take turns fucking your new girl, just like we did Cara. Then we'll bleed everyone here."

"You'll all be dead long before you could get your little roasted weenies out of your pants." taunted Joyce.

Chris had a sense of recognition but with the blackened and missing skin and a voice seared into a hissing rasp, it was difficult to be sure. "Carlo? Well, it's nice to know that being turned hasn't changed you at all, you've always been an asshole."

The boy with the missing skull released a guttural sound that was probably meant to be a scream of rage and leapt at Chris hoping to take him by surprise. Instead, Chris took one graceful step to the side and out or his path. The boy lost his footing as he passed and floundered forward, his arms swatting at the air in front of him as if he were doing some sort of vaudeville performance until he landed face down on the dance floor.

Chris set one boot down between his shoulder blades and with a downward swing, severed the back of his neck. There was no movement, no sound, nothing to indicate that a life had just been snuffed out, he simply stopped and lay still.

He checked on Joyce, but she was busy rapidly punching holes in her opponent so he turned his attention to the remaining two. Carlo was coming at him, unwrapping a section of heavy chain from around his waist and his friend had leapt onto the bar and was skirting around the outside of the fray to attack from the rear. The chain smashed into Chris' left arm with enough force to easily shatter the Humerus of a normal person and it was still very painful, but his body immediately went to work repairing the damage.

Carlo used the chain like a whip, slashing it through the air at Chris' head then aiming for his knees, forcing him to duck and dodge to avoid being struck and preventing him from getting close enough to use his knife. The sound of a heavy footstep alerted him to the boy rushing towards his back. He hesitated just long enough for the chain to whistle past his face then leapt backward and did a mid-air walk over, landing behind his attacker.

The boy's arms closed on the empty space where Chris had been a moment before and a look of astonishment seemed to appear on the ruin of his face as the blade of Chris' Khukuri emerged from the center of his chest. His hands closed around the blade. His weakened fingers fumbling to find purchase but the blood-slicked steel slipped from his grasp. Chris placed his palm against the boys back and pulled the long knife, turning it upwards as he extracted it to ensure that it severed his heart.

Chris let the corpse drop to the floor and looked for Carlo but in the few moments it had taken Chris to eliminate one boy, the other had slipped past him and was menacing the group of black-clad kids that had fortified themselves behind the bar. The bottles of liquor they swung like clubs made for a poor defense against a Lesser, but Joyce was already moving quickly to their rescue.

Carlo swatted away a bottle of tequila that had been aimed at his face. Glass shards rained down like glittering confetti as he lashed out with his right hand, catching Lucca's throat with his nails. Blood gushed forth, coating the bar and Lucca's eyes opened wide in fright as he took a faltering step backward. His heel snagged in the rubber floor matt but Mim and Joselynne caught him before he could fall and helped him sit down with his back against the storage cupboards. Thinking quickly, Mim grabbed a clean bar towel from a stack next to the sink and pressed it to Lucca's neck to staunch the bleeding.

Chris and Joyce came at Carlo from opposite sides, trapping him against the bar. He wrapped his chain around his fists like a pair of interconnected brass knuckles to defend himself against the onslaught of flashing blades. "I've got this," Joyce said. "Go take care of Lucca."

Chris leapt over the bar and knelt on the black rubber matt where the boy sat with his head leaning back against the wooden cupboard doors. Joseylynn moved aside to let him get closer while Mim continued to apply pressure with the blood-soaked towel. "He's really bad," she said, her voice shaking with worry.

Lucca's eyes locked beseechingly onto Chris as he struggled to draw breath. "It's going to be okay. I'm going to take a look and we'll get you patched up," Chris promised. Lucca tried to give a slight nod but released a sputtering cough that splattered blood onto Chris' face.

As gently as possible, Chris lifted the sodden towel away to get a look. Three distinct channels had been cut into the pale skin, two of which had ripped through both his Carotid Artery and his External Jugular Vein. Blood still seeped from the wound but not in the volume that he expected. He spit into his hand and quickly applied it to the gashes, clamping his fingers over them.

No blood dribbled out between his fingers as he waited for the healing to begin. Seconds ticked by and Chris could see consciousness fading from Lucca's eyes. "Come on Lucca, hang in there. Just a few more seconds," he urged, but there was no response.

He pressed his thumb against the opposite side of Lucca's neck to look for his pulse but could find nothing. He bent down, laying his ear against Lucca's chest, but even with his enhanced hearing, he could not detect a heartbeat.

Chris hung his head and confirmed their fears with a subtle shake. The panic that had fueled the girl's actions turned immediately to grief. Their tears began to flow when Chris removed his hand from Lucca's neck and wiped the traces of blood and saliva off onto his pants.

A look of anger and resolution washed over Mike's face. He jumped to his feet and pulled a bottle of Bacardi 151 from the second shelf, opened the cap and poured the contents over Carlo's head. Carlo squinted as the alcohol washed over his face. He struggled to keep his eyes open and continue fighting without using his hands to wipe them clear. His battle with Joyce was difficult enough and he couldn't afford to be distracted.

Chris leapt over the bar to rejoin the fight, pressing the attack from Carlo's flank as he whipped his chain to keep Joyce at enough of a distance that her knives were ineffective.

Chris sliced his heavy blade across Carlos back, opening the blackened skin to reveal the bloody pink meat beneath. Carlo spun around to face the new threat, wrapping the loose end of the chain around his hand and stretching it to catch Chris' blade as he came in for another slash.

He turned around, tangling the knife in the twisting chain. Pulling Chris off balance, he forced him into the path of Joyce's attack, using his body as a shield against the onslaught of her daggers.

On the other side of the bar, Mike grabbed a book of matches from an ashtray, lit it and let it fly. Chris watched it sail through the air, the flair of potassium chlorate igniting as the small flame lit the rest of the pack.

The matchbook slapped against the back of Carlo's head and immediately, the alcohol covering the vampire burst into flames, immolating him in a column of blue fire. He dropped to his knees, frantically beating at the flames with his hands, all thoughts of gleaming knife blades lost to his panic.

Joyce paused, catching her breath while the burning vampire looked up at her in desperation. Silently he beseeched her to intervene on his behalf and save him from burning a second time in one day. Chris stepped around the spectacle to stand next to where she stood motionless, watching, unmoved by his plight as his struggles gradually lessened. As the moments stretched, the remaining members of the house began coming around from behind the bar to join them.

Carlo rocked back onto his heels, slowly slumping over to one side. No longer able to move, the weight of his body was supported by one blackened arm as he waited for the fire to reduce him to ash.

Once the sounds of combat had subsided, Cara left the office and moved to the edge of the group. Carlo's eyes had disappeared and his mouth hung open in silent agony except for the occasional crackle and hiss of his blood boiling within his charred body.

"This could go on for a long time," Joyce announced into the silence. "Does anyone want to put him out of his misery?" She looked into the faces that surrounded her but no one made a move to respond.

Cara edged her way towards the front. "As happy as I am to watch him suffer after everything he's done..." She paused, unsure if she really wanted to say out loud what she was feeling. "I want to be the one to kill him."

No one made any immediate move, no one shifted their positions, no one lifted their heads to look at her, but a collective sense of acquiescence seemed to ripple through the group. She felt something bump up against her arm and looked down to see the handle of Chris' Khukuri. She hesitated just a moment then steeled herself with a deep breath. She took a tentative grip on the wooden handle, surprised by the sudden weight when Chris released the blade. The others all took a step backward giving her room to move into striking distance.

The body that sat in front of her burning a hole into the wooden floor, looked more like chunks of black volcanic rock with rivulets of glowing orange lava running beneath. Even the subtle movements that occasionally took place couldn't easily be perceived as signs of life and more closely resembled the settling of coals in a campfire. "Is he really still in there?" She asked of no one in particular.

"He's still there," Joyce said coming up behind her. "Not all of him, but some. And enough that he would probably recover if the fire was put out. Eventually."

"Can he hear me?"

"I don't know," she said. "There's no way to tell how much of his brain is left at this point. Really you'd be doing him a kindness."

Cara bent down and put her face as close to Carlo's ear as she could stomach. He smelled like the pieces of hamburger that fall through the grill and slowly sizzle down to blackened lumps of charcoal, mixed with an undertone of kerosene.

"I'm sorry for what he did to you," she whispered. "I wish none of this had happened. He never gave me a choice, but you chose to be a monster. If you really are in there, I hope you rot in hell."

She pulled her arm back, aimed and swung the heavy knife as hard as she could. The others hopped out of the path of the glowing embers as what remained of Carlo's head thudded to the floor.

Chapter 22

They sat on their stools with their heads hung low like a group of career alcoholics while behind the bar, Joyce stood pouring them fresh drinks. Lou rested in a nearby high back chair, nursing several broken ribs with a bottle of cheap domestic beer as the others tried to process the events of the last few minutes.

Lucca's body had been placed on the couch in the VIP lounge and what remained of Carlo's body still smoldered in the middle of the floor. "What happens now?" Brielle asked despondently.

"We figure it out," Chris said.

"We'll call it in and the Chord will collect the bodies, notify Lucca's family and get a crew here to work on the damage," Joyce told them in a matter of fact tone.

Simeon looked at the puddle of water coated with flecks of black flotsam that spread out across the dancefloor from the steaming heap. "There's no way the club will open tonight."

"I should say not," announced a voice from the stairs.

Everyone turned to look at the man who had silently entered the club. His expensive looking clothes were dark with soot and his skin shown through where the material had been completely burned away. One side of his face was a mass of red welts and oozing blisters, and the majority of his hair had been singed off. The most striking thing about him, however, were his gleaming white fangs and eyes that blazed with a deep red light as if the fire that had scorched him still raged within his skull.

He scanned the shocked faces the people sitting at the bar until he lighted on the ones he was looking for. "There is my firstborn, and my sweet little Pet. I have missed you both, but my aim is improving." He chuckled to himself and took several steps closer.

He paused to study the charred corpse, his brow furrowed, "Who is that?" He glanced briefly at the pile of dead skinheads along the wall, "Ahhh, Carlo," he sighed. "Well you seem to have taken out my entire coterie, you even enticed my faithful Pet from my side."

Everyone's head swiveled to follow him as he strolled around the club, idly examining the fixtures and decor. "It is your betrayal that I find the most disturbing, Pet."

As the creature moved closer to the bar, Chris wrinkled his nose at the awful smell coming off him. "What is that smell?" He asked. "Have you been crawling through shit?"

"Well, when your house is on fire and you can't go out into the sun, you are left with few options." He admitted stepping behind Cara and running his fingernails from the top of her head down the back of her neck, coming to rest on the edge of her black leather collar sending a shudder of fear through her.

"Take your hand off her or I will," Chris said moving to confront the creature who had turned him, enslaved his former girlfriend and killed who knows how many of his friends. His lip curled up and his eyes shimmered to match the opal ankh that hung around his neck beside his mother's medallion.

He's much faster and stronger than you are, but he doesn't have the training you do. Keep moving and attack from where he doesn't expect. Remember what Sensei Hisao taught you and keep your walls up. Cautioned Joyce's voice in his head.

Chris took a deep breath, placed his hand over the string of black tourmaline around his wrist and erected the psychic barrier around his mind. He thought back on all the lessons he had learned. His teacher had used so many esoteric sayings that he could have written fortune cookies. Pretend to be weak, so that your enemy may grow arrogant. Let your plans be dark and impenetrable as night, and when you move, fall like a thunderbolt.

As he tried to formulate a plan of attack that had any chance of success, a gunshot ripped through the silence, echoing loudly off the brick walls. Chris turned to see Cara pointing her pistol at the side of her former master's head, a wisp of smoke rising from the barrel, her rage-filled face spattered with blood.

Gilles staggered to the side from the impact but righted himself almost instantly and responded with a backhanded blow that sent Cara crashing into the bar. Her head bounced off the wood with a loud crack and she lay motionless on the floor between two bar stools like a discarded piece of crumpled paper. The members of the house shifted nervously on their seats but Chris noticed that Joselynne extended her leg protectively to serve as a barrier in front of Cara.

Chris took another step forward. He held his hands out to his sides with his palms up and his head bowed in supplication. "Please don't hurt anyone else, just tell me what you want."

Gilles rubbed his temple where the bullet had entered, and came away with a deformed slug dripping blood and bits of tissue pinched between his fingertips. "What do I want? It was simple at first, I only wanted your heart," he said, remembering the clerk who interrupted his feeding in the bus station restroom. His interference had saved Chris' life but had caused him to be accidentally turned. "But that didn't work out as planned"

"I never wanted to spawn any progeny and your existence became a continual annoyance, invading my dreams and spying on my thoughts. Then I just wanted you dead." He paused surveying bodies around the room. "And now you have taken my coterie. So not only will you die, I will also take possession of your little group and turn them to serve me."

Chris tried to think of what he could do to steer the situation in a better direction than what Gilles had just outlined. An idea suddenly came to him. He had become painfully familiar with Gilles' predilections from the endless streams of disturbing and perverse visions that had bombarded his psyche. Maybe there was a way to use that, he thought.

"Your servants have killed my favorite," he said, indicating Lucca's body lying peacefully on the red velvet couch. "But of the rest, perhaps you would enjoy Michael?"

A strangled squeak escaped Mike's gaping mouth at Chris' betrayal, and his eyes opened up so wide the irises looked like islands in a vast sea of white. Gilles turned his attention towards the shaking boy and looked him over critically. "Are you hoping to bribe me into letting you live?"

"Not at all. I know full well you will take my life when it suits you, I simply thought that you might appreciate the gesture and allow me to die painlessly. After all, it was never my intent to interfere with your ascent to power."

He hoped he wasn't laying it on too thick but Gilles had once referred to himself as a god, so Chris wasn't sure that was even possible. "You can use him to help you recover after your ordeal. His blood has a very pleasant, earthy flavor, which I'm sure you'll enjoy."

Mike couldn't believe what Chris was doing. He had never minded it when he and Joyce had fed from him, they were always gentle and the euphoric feeling afterward was worth a little pain. And he was a little bit in love with Chris anyway. But he couldn't believe Chris was about to sacrifice him to avoid a painful death. Then again, maybe he could.

Gilles walked over to Mike, took hold of a fist full of hair and pulled firmly turning his head from side to side. "He is an acceptable looking young man, a bit old for my taste, and I don't care for all the makeup, but acceptable."

While Gilles back was turned, Lou slowly rose from his seat and began making his way around the perimeter of the room looking to escape down the cattle tunnel. "Have your large blond friend join the rest of his companions," Gilles said without turning around.

Chris nodded to him and Lou slunk guiltily over to the bar like a child caught misbehaving, sure he would soon be severely punished. He took the stool at the far end of the bar, closest to the tunnel just in case an opportunity to make a break for it arose. "Perhaps I will keep him while I turn the rest, to entertain me," he said. He let go of Mike's hair and turned his attention back to Christian. "Still, sacrifices must be made."

He grabbed Chris by the front of his shirt, lifted him easily into the air and slammed him down onto the bar top. With a hop, Gilles landed above him, his feet firmly planted on the wooden counter on either side. He dropped down into a crouch, pinning Chris' arms to the bar with his knees. The Khukuri bit painfully into Chris' back, but he didn't dare move. Appear weak when you are strong, and strong when you are weak, he heard his teacher's voice say in his head.

Gilles pulled a long dagger from his belt. Light gleamed along its fourteen-inch silver serpentine blade, one edge cut into wicked serrations like the top fin of a sailfish. The house stood in open mouth horror as he stretched his back and raised his arms, holding the knife in a reversed two-handed grip and prepared for the downward thrust that would end Chris' life.

Suddenly, a searing pain erupted in his side. Gilles lashed out with his knife but just missed the dark-haired Lesser with the purple rhinestones glittering brightly along her dramatically arched eyebrows. Joyce leaned sharply backward to avoid the blade which cut the air an inch above her face.

Dark blood seeped from a wound several inches long and deep enough to have cut into Gilles' kidney. Normally it would only take a few minutes to mend but he had not fed since before the fire so healing would take longer. It would make movement uncomfortable in the meantime and that might just give them a slight edge. He climbed down off the bar wincing as the wound opened and closed with every shift.

Holding his knife at the ready, Gilles advanced on Joyce, stalking her like the alpha predator he was, forcing her further backward with every step. Chris removed his Khukuri from the black leather sheath concealed at his back and slid silently off the bar.

Behind him, Chris cautiously mirrored every step Gilles took, watching every movement for any indication of an intended attack on Joyce. When it came, however, it was not aimed at Joyce.

He attacked in a sweeping backhand designed to take Chris' head off at the neck. Chris' instincts immediately took over and he was able to keep his head attached by quickly bending as far to his left as possible. As the blade sliced through the air next to his ear, Chris spun on the ball of his foot and delivered a powerful roundhouse kick to the side of Gilles' blistered head, sending him staggering backward directly into Joyce's waiting knives.

She came in low and drove the points into his back then pushed upward with enough force that it lifted him off the ground. The blades cut channels through the muscle and organs until they reached the hard edge of his ribs. After only a moment's hesitation, the bones too gave way and he dropped back to the floor with a series of jolts as the blades sliced through the bones.

Gilles howled with pain and rage, lurching forward to escape the punishment, pulling himself off the razor-sharp blades, and stumbled right into Chris.

Chris heard Joyce's voice in his head urging him to bite. *Feed from him while you have the chance,* she said. *Add his strength to yours.*

He didn't hesitate. Chris closed his eyes and latched on to Gilles, pushing his teeth through skin that felt like iron in his mouth.

The foul blood flooded his mouth like hot sludge but he choked it down as fast as he could, taking as much of his makers strength and speed into himself while he had the opportunity.

Gilles hissed with a primal rage. He reached back, grabbing Chris by the hair and pulled him over his shoulder.

Turning in the air, Chris rotated his body to land on his feet in front of his opponent. His eyes flooded the room with a kaleidoscope of color, painting the walls like the light of God flooding in through the transept rose of a church. Only this was no cathedral, more a temple of pop bacchanalia suddenly turned into an arena of death. Chris' reflexes and training were in overdrive and he couldn't afford to squander his advantage.

Gilles looked up in time to see the bent blade of the Khukuri dropping rapidly towards his neck. He threw up his arm, sacrificing the ring finger and pinky of his left hand to ward off the blow.

His lips curled back displaying his fangs, and he snarled like a feral animal. Chris and Joyce circled just outside the range of his reach, feigning and testing his reactions. Avoid what is strong, and strike at what is weak, Chris' inner voice told him.

Gilles staggered forward lashing out at Chris with his mangled hand, spattering him with tiny droplets of blood and Joyce took a step forward to keep the distance between them as close as possible in order to maintain the harassment. He swung around in a blur of speed and jabbed his knife at Joyce and she responded with a skillful flick of the wrist that barely missed taking out his eyes. Chris moved in from behind while Gilles' back was turned and slashed the back of his knee, severing the hamstring tendon. His leg gave way beneath him and he crashed to the floor.

Chris was just stepping forward to deliver a killing blow when Joyce stumbled backward, lost her footing and sat heavily on the floor. He dashed around to take a defensive position between her and Gilles but as he drew near, he saw what the problem was.

Buried in the floral embroidery of her corset, was the handle of Gilles' knife.

He reached to pull it out but didn't want her to lose any more blood than what was already staining the purple satin. Frantically he looked around for some sign of what to do but Mike and Brielle were already on the move. They took hold of her arms and dragged her as quickly as they could to the relative safety behind the bar.

Chris knew there was nothing he could do to help her until the threat was eliminated so he turned his attention back to Gilles only to discover that the fiend was back on his feet and moving to attack. With one hand little more than a cluster of bloody stumps and his knife still embedded in Joyce' stomach, his offensive options were limited to his remaining hand and his teeth. Chris watched Gilles' movements, readying himself to counter whatever he did.

Gilles lashed out towards Chris but he was ready. He swung the heavy knife with enough force to easily separate the arm from the rest of his body. The blade arched through the air but just as it would have sliced through Gilles' forearm, he spun. The deadly steel passed harmlessly behind his butchered back and he completed his turn, locking his good hand around Chris' throat.

He lifted Chris off the ground looking into his multi-colored eyes, "I would have turned your friends, given them everlasting life. Now they will all die in screaming agony. All except for my pet. Her I will turn just so I can make her pain last indefinitely. How long would be an appropriate punishment for her betrayal, do you think? One hundred years? Two hundred maybe? There is no limit to how long I can make her torment last."

He squeezed harder and Chris began seeing stars flash in front of his eyes as his blood slowed and finally stopped reaching his brain. "You, on the other hand... I believe I'm finally finished with you."

The light was fading from his vision and the room was going black. As he lost his grip on consciousness, Chris wondered; if there really was a god in heaven, how could an all-powerful, loving God, allow something as evil as this monster to exist, to bring pain and death on innocents for centuries.

Somewhere in the muddled recesses of his mind, he thought he heard knocking. Someone wanted to come in, but it was dark and he couldn't remember where the door was.

"Creature, unhand that boy!" Boomed a heavily accented voice.

It held an air of command, even though it seemed to be coming from a far distance and was in danger of being drowned out by the blood pounding in his ears.

Suddenly the pressure on his neck disappeared and he dropped to the floor. His lungs screamed but his throat hurt terribly and the air couldn't seem to get through. The knocking came again only it seemed closer than before and his eyes fluttered open to see what it was.

Standing at the far end of the club where the stairs emerged from the daylight world above, stood a woman. She was old but not elderly and wore a tightly buttoned off-white cashmere coat over matching slacks and shoes. She carried a red wood cane with a golden knob handle held tightly in her hand and she was slamming it repeatedly into the floor.

Gilles turned to face the newcomer, "And who might you be?" He asked.

"Filia autem a sanguine," she said, walking slowly and deliberately closer, her cane booming heavily against the planks of the floor with each step. "Mia kóri tis grammís. Una hija de la línea de sangre. Une fille de la lignée."

"Is that supposed to mean something to me woman?"

"It means that, at long last, your doom has arrived. You may flee, and I will pursue you, or you may face me at your peril," she said taking another step closer.

While Gilles was distracted, Lou slipped off his stool and ran in a low crouch to the cattle tunnel, waving his hands to encourage the others to follow. Mike, Mim, and Simeon quickly joined him and disappeared into the darkened corridor. Brielle and Joselynne hesitated, not wanting to abandon Cara's unconscious body but Joyce nodded weakly for them to follow the others.

Gilles was cautious in approaching this old woman who had the nerve to confront him. She didn't seem to be much of a threat but appearances were sometimes deceiving. When he was nearly within striking range, he started circling around, trying to get between her and the exit to cut her off from escape but she took a backward step rather than turn to keep him in sight and he was forced to reconsider his approach, deciding instead to overwhelm her with speed.

In less than the time it takes to blink, Gilles crossed the space separating them and dug his clawed fingertips into her upper arm. She stumbled back in surprise at his sudden appearance, lost her footing and began to stumble. He released his hold on her arm, allowing her to fall to the floor and stood over her. "You do not seem nearly as formidable as you led me to believe."

A loud metallic click echoed through the hall and a six-inch long blade sprung into view from the end of her cane. With a quick thrust, the woman buried the blade in his chest. Driving him backward she climbed to her feet. Pressing her advantage, she propelled him backward until he stumbled over Carlo's remains and fell to the floor. Taking hold of the golden knob, she leaned all her weight on the cane, pushing it through his heart and embedding the tip in the wooden planks.

A thin wisp of white smoke began to rise from the wound. "This is the blade of La Pucelle d'Orléans, sanctified by God, consecrated in battle and removed from the Basilique Cathédrale Sainte-Croix d'Orléans before the Revolution. It is right and good that this blade should be what sends you back to the pit."

The smoke was billowing up around the shaft of the cane making it difficult to breathe and a yellow light began to glow from within his chest. Chris came closer to watch the demise of his maker, but when he came into view, Gilles lurched upward, sliding the wooden shaft of the cane through his chest. He lashed out his with hand but grasped the amulets hanging from Chris' neck instead. Pulling at the chains with his faltering strength, he drew their faces closer.

He looked into Chris' eyes, a sneer of contempt on his face and let out a howl of rage and pain. Chris became aware of a growing heat and looked down expecting to see flames shooting up from Gilles' chest, instead he saw that the fist that had grabbed hold of him was glowing around the edges, as if it held a bright light within the curled fingers. Sparks began to pop and crackle sending orange embers rising into the air.

Gilles opened his fist, looking with astonishment at his illuminated hand. The flesh cracked and fell away in large pieces as he watched in open-mouthed fascination. The glow spread along the length of his arm while jagged chunks broke off to join the pile of smoking blobs that were slowly turning a darker orange as they cooled.

A soft moan cut through the silence and Chris saw that Cara was beginning to regain consciousness. He rushed over to help her sit up and when she saw what was unfolding behind him, she wrapped her arms around him and pressed her face to his chest.

Having removed her cane from the amber termite mound that had been Gilles, the woman called out to Chris, "Come, child. It's time we were leaving."

She stepped over to where he knelt comforting Cara. "I have come to take you home, mon chéri," she said kindly.

Chris looked confused, "Home? You mean back to Texas?"

"No, my boy, your real home. Come we have much to discuss, you and I."

"But my friends?"

"They have nearly all gone," she said holding her arms wide and looking from side to side, taking in the empty club.

"Joyce and Cara are injured."

"They will soon recover."

"I won't just leave them here," he stated firmly.

"The car is waiting outside," she said. Turning her back on him, she walked to the stairs and climbed out of sight.

He helped Cara haul herself onto a stool. She rested her head on one hand, her arm propped up on the bar. "Will you be okay here for a minute?" he asked. She nodded weakly, it would have to be good enough he thought and rounded the end of the bar. Joyce lay on the floor matt, covered in blood and for a moment he was sure she had been killed but she smiled at him and reached for his hand, "My hero," she said with a fragile smile.

Her fingers were red and slick with blood, clutching the handle of Gilles' knife still embedded in her abdomen. She put her arm around his shoulder as he lifted her to her feet. "Can you walk?" he asked.

"Walk? You just watch me," she replied with a wink.

With her free hand, she lifted a blood-soaked bar rag to her mouth. At first, Chris assumed she was just using it to blot a cut lip but when he heard her sucking he realized what was she was doing. It was the towel used to staunch Lucca's wounds before he died and she was sucking his blood out of the worn terrycloth. It seemed inappropriate somehow, but if Lucca were still living he would have been the first to volunteer to help her recover, and besides, that was far less traumatic under the circumstances than feeding from one of their followers.

She held on tightly and leaned her weight on him as they came out from behind the bar. "What do you think?" He asked. "Should we go with her?"

Joyce took a moment before answering, "I didn't get a sense of any evil intent, at least not towards you. If anything it felt like something akin to fondness. I got next to nothing when you mentioned Cara, but she didn't seem too thrilled that you included me in this."

"Sooooo.... he prompted looking for her to make the decision for him.

"So. I don't know if the Chord will be happy about the way things went down here or not. We don't know who this woman is or what her motives are, but she pulled our assess out of the fire. I say we take a chance and see what this is all about."

They collected Cara and with arms linked, the three awkwardly climbed the stairs, passing from the twilight world of the club into the mid-afternoon sun.

Waiting at the curb was a black town car. The woman sat patiently in the front passenger seat next to a uniformed driver while Chris opened the back door, helped Cara in then slid in beside her. The blood from the towel had done a lot to help restore Joyce and she managed to climb into the back seat with a minimum of discomfort.

Once the door was closed, the driver pulled away. He maneuvered through traffic and followed the line of cars into the Midtown Tunnel. "Where are we going?" Chris asked, his apprehension increasing by the moment. He had never driven through the tunnel and wasn't sure exactly where it went.

"We're going to MacArthur airport," she told them. "There is a plane waiting for us."

"You're taking us on a plane?" Cara asked feeling as if she had jumped from the frying pan into the fire.

"We can let you out somewhere on the way if you'd prefer," the woman replied testily.

She didn't know what she would do if she was put back on the street. Without the master and his gang of thugs maybe she could go home she thought. She had no idea what would be waiting for her, if anything, when she got back to Ocean Parkway in Brooklyn where she had lived with her cokehead ex-model mother and her random boyfriends in a one bedroom apartment.

After everything that had happened, she decided that it was probably better for her to stay with Chris, even if he was a murderous, blood-sucking fiend. Besides, he had just helped kill her master, that had to count for something.

The driver got off the Long Island Expressway at the Ronkonkoma exit after two hours of near silent traveling and made several turns along residential suburban streets. They pulled through a gate in a ten-foot high chain link fence behind the flight academy hanger and followed the access road around on to Schaefer Drive. The car pulled into an unmarked white corrugated steel hanger and came to a stop several yards from a gleaming Citation S/II s550.

The driver climbed out of the car and hurried around the front to open the passenger's door for the woman who wasted no time climbing the steps to the hatch of the small private jet. Chris looked from Joyce to Cara and back, but Joyce just shrugged and followed the woman on to the plane without a word.

"Are you okay with this?" He asked Cara. "I mean, she did help kill Gilles but if you don't want to go, maybe we could go back to the loft or something."

She looked up at him steadily, "There's nothing left for me here but bad memories, so I don't have any reason to stay. Do you?" He thought about it for a moment and decided that he really didn't. "Besides, it can't be any worse than what I've been through already, right?" Chris had a sense of what had happened to her, and as bad as it must have been, he could always imagine something worse.

Chris followed close behind as she climbed aboard the plane, the steps shifted and bounced under their combined weight and he had to duck down to avoid hitting his head on the top of the hatch. He leaned to the side to see past Cara and get a look at the inside of the plane. He halfway expected to see Amym sitting in one of his expensive dark suits, drinking a glass of Hennessey.

The plane was richly appointed, with highly polished exotic wood and creamy leather upholstery. As Chris was stepping into the aisle, the copilot stepped out behind him suddenly, pulled up the stairs closing the hatch.

Joyce had taken the first seat and Cara moved to sit in the second row right behind her, squeezing into the curve of the cabin to make room for Chris to pass along the narrow gangway. Beyond her stood a figure Christian had never thought to see again.

"Mrs. Brooks?" Chris asked in astonishment of the woman who had driven his mother into town once a month to buy supplies.

"Oh Christian, I am so glad to see you boy!" She exclaimed in her thick Texas sing-song way, holding out her arms to embrace him.

He hesitantly stepped into the hug, and just for a moment, he remembered what it felt like to be the lost and lonely boy he once was. "How did you find me? Is mother here too?"

"Oh, bless your heart, no. She's not. I'm so sorry, we told her but she decided not to come," she said, squeezing him tighter for another moment before letting him go.

"It's okay I guess. But what are you doing here? Are you involved with the Chord?"

"Heaven forbid. No, I work for your grandmother, always have," she said and stepped back out of the way so he could see the woman occupying the lounge seat in the center of the fuselage. She had removed her cream-colored coat and her cane was propped against the arm of her seat next to a middle-aged man with a bad haircut and a tweed blazer.

"Sit down Christian, I wouldn't want you to fall when we start moving." Almost on cue, the plane jolted into a slow rolling taxi out of the hanger.

"Grandmother?" He said with trepidation as he searched his memory for any recollection of her.

She had not been involved in his life since he was a very small child but he remembered the day his mother had taken him from Louisiana and boarded a westbound bus, only stopping in East Texas when her money ran out. It was strange that he had never been able to remember that before, he thought. The plane rocked as it turned onto the runway and Chris stumbled into the vacant seat across from her.

She had been arguing with his mother about him. He hadn't understood it at the time, but thinking back on it with his enhanced memory he was able to recall the basics. The fight had been about succession in an unbroken line of first-born daughters, as a boy, he had inadvertently disrupted that pattern leading to a rift in the family. The medallion he wore had come from his great-grandmother and been meant for the daughter he was supposed to have been.

"Where are we going?" He asked.

"Home."

"To Texas?" Chris asked as feelings of both excitement and trepidation warred at the thought of facing his mother after everything he had been through.

"We will fly to Marseille then drive to a villa outside Arles, the ancestral home of our family."

"That's in France?" He asked dumbly.

"Yes."

"And this is your plane?"

"I have the use of it when need be," she said as she smoothed imaginary wrinkles from her suit with her hands.

"And this villa, it's where our family comes from originally? Do you live there, because I thought you lived in Louisiana."

"It is the seat of our family, and yes, as head of the family I will live out the rest of my days there. It, like our mother Mariamne, has been known by many names over the centuries. The Romans once called it Ra when they occupied Gaul. Later it was known as Saintes Marie de la Mer, Notre Dame de Ratis and Sara la Kali for Saint Sarah, the daughter of Mary. It is her likeness that you wear on the amulet around your neck and her power that defeated the creature earlier."

"I thought it was the silver in my ankh," he admitted. "But at least he's finally dead."

"I wouldn't be too sure of that," she cautioned. "These creatures are notoriously difficult to kill."

PLAYLIST

Killing Joke - Eighties
Fields Of The Nephilim - Psychonaut
The Sisters of Mercy - Lucretia My Reflection
Echo and the Bunnymen - The Killing Moon
The Southern Death Cult - Moya
Flesh For Lulu - I Go Crazy
Gene Loves Jezebel - Desire(Come And Get It)
Echo and the Bunnymen - Lips Like Sugar
Joy Division - Love Will Tear Us Apart
Depeche Mode - Strangelove
The Sisters Of Mercy - Dominion
Peter Murphy - Cuts You Up
The Cult - She Sells Sanctuary
Soft Cell - Tainted Love - Where Did Our Love Go
The Psychedelic Furs - Heartbreak Beat
The Call - The Walls Came Down
The Cure - Killing An Arab
Bauhaus – Dark Entries
The Lords of the New Church - Dreams and Desires
Depeche Mode - Never Let Me Down Again
Modern English - I Melt With You
The Church - Under The Milky Way
The Cure - Fascination Street
Echo And The Bunnymen - The Cutter
Tones On Tail - Go!
The Psychedelic Furs - The Ghost in You
Fields Of The Nephilim - Preacher Man
The Marionettes - Ave Dementia
The Sisters of Mercy - Temple of Love
Bauhaus - Bela Lugosi's Dead
Alien Sex Fiend - Now I'm Feeling Zombified
Ministry - I Wanted to Tell Her
A Flock Of Seagulls – Wishing
The Lords of the New Church - S.F. & T.
Strawberry Switchblade -- Since Yesterday
Gang of Four - Damaged Goods

The Icicle Works - Birds Fly (Whisper To A Scream)
The Psychedelic Furs - Love My Way
The Alarm - The Stand
Sisters of Mercy - This Corrosion
Killing Joke - Love Like Blood
Echo and the Bunnymen - Bring on The Dancing Horses
Strawberry Switchblade - Trees and Flowers
The Sisters of Mercy - First and Last and Always
The Damned - Smash It Up (Part 1 & 2)
The Cure - A Forest
Siouxsie and the Banshees - Lullaby
The Damned - I Just Can´t Be Happy Today
Velvet Underground - Venus in Furs
Ministry - Revenge
Sigue Sigue Sputnik - Love Missile F1 11
The Cure - Lovesong
Peter Murphy - Indigo Eyes
The Damned - Jet Boy Jet Girl
The Cure - Boys Don't Cry
Siouxsie and the Banshees - Happy House
The Church - Reptile
Public Image Ltd - This Is Not A Love Song
The Lords of the New Church - Opening Nightmares
A Flock Of Seagulls - Space Age Love Song
The Lords of the New Church - I never believed
The Mission – Wasteland
Tones On Tail – Burning Skies
London After Midnight - kiss
London After Midnight - Psycho Magnet
Siouxsie And The Banshees - Cities In Dust
Red Lorry Yellow Lorry - Talk About The Weather
Bauhaus - Telegram Sam
The Smiths - How Soon Is Now?
Peter Schilling - Major Tom Völlig Losgelöst
Bauhaus - Stigmata Martyr
Siouxsie And The Banshees – Spellbound

Listen to the NYV: GOTH soundtrack on YouTube

NYV: GOTH

A NOTE FROM THE AUTHOR

Thank you for reading. I hope you have enjoyed this installment of the New York Vampire series. I would love to hear your impressions and thoughts so please leave an honest review on Goodreads, Amazon, Barnes & Nobel or wherever you buy your books. I am working on the next book in this series but I also have some other very interesting projects in the works so I hope you will keep watching. Here is a sneak peek at NYV: RAVE.

-KD

NYV: GOTH

NYV: RAVE, SNEAK PEEK

The wind off the sea did nothing to lessen the stifling heat, it served only to increase the already oppressive humidity as it drew the moisture inland off the ocean. The white Land Rover Defender 110 sped along the rocky path that passed as a road, finally reaching the dig site. The driver brought the vehicle to a stop and the lone passenger climbed out of the back. He stretched muscles that had gone stiff from hours of sitting still but it was much better than it would have been on horseback.

He wore a long white cotton thobe with a high collar like a priest, under a richly embroidered black redan robe that stretched down to his ankles. The traditional Bedouin dress was belted closed with a curved khanja knife secured at his waist. His head was covered with a white kufeya held in place with an igal cord of camel wool wound in gold thread.

As his welcoming comity made their way towards him, he retrieved his sword from the back seat and settled it in its place at his waist.

"You must be the representative from the Chord," the man said, his English thickly accented with German. "I'm so glad you were able to come," he enthusiastically greeted his guest while holding out his thick, calloused hand in welcome. "I'm Dr. Sternberg, of the German Archeology Institute. I am leading this excavation. Please, come inside. The sun is brutal this time of day."

He followed the man inside and sat on a cushion on the floor of a large camp tent at the base of a desert mountain outside Al-Madam, Shajah, on what had once been known as the Pirate Coast of Oman. After the British treaty relationships had ended in December of 1971, the seven Trucial Sheikhdoms had united for mutual security against their larger neighbors and became the recently independent United Arab Emirates. In his hands, he cradled a small glass of Arabic Qahwa coffee made from lightly roasted Arabica beans spiced with crushed Cardamom. His portly host passed him a bowl of dates and laboriously lowered himself onto a cushion opposite him.

"We are very close to making a major discovery that I am sure will please our mutual employers," the man assured him.

He didn't know how someone could make such a claim about a discovery that had yet to be made, but he had to give the man credit for his salesmanship. "I'm sure that will come as a great relief, Dr. Sternberg. This excavation represents a small portion of a very large investment for our organization, we are all very concerned about its success," he said flatly.

"We have uncovered several beautiful cylinder seals belonging to the early Akkadian Empire, possibly even the period of King Sargon Sharru-kin of Akkad, circa 2334 BCE," he said excitedly. "I would be happy to show them to you if you like."

"That won't be necessary. I'm certain they are quite impressive but what we are looking for is much older, as you are well aware."

The Archeologist looked crestfallen for just a moment but quickly recovered his zeal. "We have made significant progress on that front as well. We have discovered evidence of a Paleolithic settlement from about 100,000 to 125,000 years ago, of course, we won't know for certain until the carbon dating results are back from the laboratory," he said, pronouncing it with a long o. "Burial tombs containing some very unusual remains."

Amym sat up straighter and took a measured sip of his coffee, this could well be the news he was hoping to receive. "Unusual how?" He asked calmly.

The man paused for a moment before answering. "Well... They are remarkable really. They appear to be Homo Sapien but they are exceptionally tall, with abnormally thick bones."

Amym set his coffee cup down on the wooden footlocker that served as their table and adjusted his sword as he rose to his feet. "Show me," he demanded.

Pulling the end of his kufeya across his face, he followed the man out of the tent into the blistering heat. They walked across the camp, towards a dig site further along the slope, arriving at a circle of stacked stones that made up the outer wall of an ancient structure,

It looked as if it had been buried in the sand for eons. The walls were a foot and a half thick and had been excavated to an equal depth. A façade of flat stones still covered portions of the exterior surface. Looking over the wall, Amym saw that the central chamber was divided into sections by equally thick interior walls, which created a series of oddly shaped rooms.

Amym stepped around his guide and hurried to peer deeper inside. What he saw took his breath away. Standing just over six feet tall, he had never considered himself a small man, but looking down at the massive skeleton that lay curled at the bottom of the chamber, he could easily imagine how David must have felt trying to stare down Goliath.

"Each burial chamber we have excavated has contained similar remains, and - as you can see - we have merely scratched the surface. There could be as much as fifteen feet or more of the structure still waiting to be unearthed."

"Have you found any artifacts?" Amym asked.

"No, and that is very strange for a burial site, especially one as sophisticated at this. Normally we would expect to find tools, some broken pieces of jewelry, pottery or other burial goods. Things that set the remains in the context of their society. But here we have nothing. Perhaps we will find something once we have excavated further."

"Perhaps you will, however, this is evidence enough that the region was inhabited by the sort we are interested in."

Amym walked slowly around the circumference until the pattern of the walls suddenly became clear, it was a three-dimensional representation of one of the many undecipherable symbols that filled the pages of the Gibborilium. He assumed it had been designed to be seen from above so there should be other similar structures nearby.

"I would suggest, Doctor, that you widen your search along this axis," he said, pointing first in one direction then pivoting around to point the opposite way.

The archeologist seemed puzzled. "Why in that direction, if I may ask? It's neither East/West or North/South."

"I'm sure there is some astrological explanation that can be ascribed to the direction, but the reason for this insight is that this shape is actually a letter, or more accurately perhaps, a form of hieroglyph. If you dig, you should be able to locate the rest of the sacred inscription written out in similar tombs."

"This is all quite fascinating, and I'm sure the Chord will want to be kept abreast of all future discoveries, but it is not the reason for this excavation. Somewhere in the Makkan region, there should be a sealed subterranean crypt. If you locate it, you are not to open it. If you do the consequences would be severe. Do you understand?" He asked, his eyes blazing with orange light like the coals of a roaring fire.

"Yes! Of course. I understand completely," he sputtered. "No one will touch it, if we locate such a tomb."

"The site would date from approximately eight to eleven thousand years ago," Amym explained. "This would place it in the time before the existence of the Persian Gulf."

Around that time, a period of heavy rains and earthquakes had partially destroyed the natural dam that kept out the waters of the Indian Ocean, plunging the once fertile Edinu valley beneath the waters of the Arabian Sea. Where once the abundance of fresh water supplied by the Tigris, Euphrates, Karun, and Wadi Baton Rivers, as well as by upwellings of underground springs had made the valley an agrarian paradise, water had also been the cause of its destruction.

"Then might it be under water?" Dr. Sternberg asked, hoping that would mitigate the consequences of failure.

"Yes, it could be, but that is unlikely based on the documentation we have."

"Would it be possible to see this documentation? It may be useful in determining where to search," the archeologist asked hopefully.

"I wish that were possible Doctor, but even I have only been given the barest understanding of what they contain." He looked down at the skeleton. Have that crated and loaded on the truck along with any related artifacts and photographs. I will take them back for analyses personally."

"Of course, right away," The archeologist said and waived workers to quickly see to crating up the remains and prepare them for transport. He presumed they would go to England or possibly America, but everything about this excavation was being kept so close to the vest that he often wondered if it was even legal. Not that it mattered very much, with what he was being paid. At these rates he had to assume a certain amount of risk and digging around in the desert sands came with a wide variety of hazards.

ACKNOWLEDGMENTS

First and foremost, a huge thank you to my family who help make this writing adventure possible, I love you very much. Thank you so much to my beta readers, your opinions and suggestions have been invaluable along the way. And finally a special thanks to you, writers are nothing without readers.

Library of Congress Cataloging-in-Publication Data is available.
http://www.loc.gov/publish/cip/
FIRST EDITION
Ebook Edition © October 2018
ISBN-13: 978-0-578-43422-3
10 9 8 7 6 5 4 3 2 1